I love to lose myself in a thriller—
especially the rare one that
moves along like an out-of-
control freight train.

The thriller that actually got
me started writing was *The Day
of the Jackal.*

With BLACK FRIDAY, I wanted
to concoct a shamelessly manipulative story that the reader
couldn't wait to finish, but didn't
want to end.

Now get on this freight train!

—JAMES PATTERSON

"A WILD RIDE . . . ALEX CROSS IS TO THE '90s WHAT MIKE HAMMER WAS TO THE '50s."

—*Denver Post* on *Kiss the Girls*

"A FIRST-RATE THRILLER–FASTEN YOUR SEAT BELTS AND KEEP THE LIGHTS ON!"

—Sidney Sheldon on *Along Came a Spider*

"HAS TO BE ONE OF THE BEST THRILLERS OF THE YEAR."

—Clive Cussler on *Along Came a Spider*

"TERROR AND SUSPENSE THAT GRAB THE READER AND WON'T LET GO. JUST TRY RUNNING AWAY FROM THIS ONE."

—Ed McBain on *Along Came a Spider*

BLACK
FRIDAY

Novels by James Patterson

JAMES PATTERSON

BLACK FRIDAY

WARNER
VISION
BOOKS

A Time Warner Company

WARNER BOOKS EDITION

Copyright © 1986, 1994, 2000 by James Patterson.
All rights reserved. No part of this book may be reproduced in any form or by any electronic or mechanical means, including information storage and retrieval systems, without permission in writing from the publisher, except by a reviewer who may quote brief passages in a review.

The author gratefully acknowledges Al Gallico Music Corporation for permission to reprint the lyrics from "What's Made Milwaukee Famous Has Made a Loser Out of Me" by Glenn Sutton. © 1968 Al Gallico Music Corporation. Used with permission.

Another version of this book was previously published as BLACK MARKET.

Warner Vision is a registered trademark of Warner Books.

Cover illustration by Gabriel Molano

Warner Books, Inc.
1271 Avenue of the Americas
New York, NY 10020

Visit our Web site at
www.twbookmark.com

 A Time Warner Company

Printed in the United States of America

First Paperback Printing: April 2000

10 9 8 7 6 5 4 3 2 1

For Janie, who is Nora.
For Mary Katherine, who is a saint.

*For anyone who's ever dreamed about
some small and delicious revenge
against the money changers on
Wall Street and around the world.*

ACKNOWLEDGMENTS

Although *Black Friday* is written as fiction, all of what follows could happen, especially the Wall Street financial parts. I would like to thank the people who helped so much in making the background information interesting and authentic.

Sidney Ruthberg—financial editor, Fairchild Publications
James Dowd—Wall Street attorney, formerly of the United States Army
Stephen Bowen—former captain, United States Marines Corps
Katherine McMahon—New York and Paris backgrounds
Joan Ennis—Irish Tourist Board
Thomas Altman—Sedona, Arizona
Barbara Maddalena—New York, Wall Street area
Mindy Zepp—New York
M. Blackstone—Soho

BLACK FRIDAY

PART ONE

Green Band

The pure products of America go crazy.
—William Carlos Williams

Chapter 1

COLONEL DAVID HUDSON leaned his tall, athletic body against the squat, battered trunk of one of New York's Checker-style taxis.

Raising one hand to his eye, Hudson loosely curled his fingers to fashion a "telescope." He began to watch morning's earliest light fall on the Wall Street scene.

He carefully studied 40 Wall Street where Manufacturers Hanover Trust had offices. Then, No. 23 Wall, which housed executive suites for Morgan Guaranty. The New York Stock Exchange Building. Trinity Church. Chase Manhattan Plaza.

Once he had it all vividly in sight, Colonel Hudson squeezed his fingers tightly together. *"Boom,"* he whispered quietly.

The financial capital of the world completely disappeared behind his clenched right fist.

Boom.

Seconds before 5:30 on that same morning, Sergeant Harry Stemkowsky, the man designated as Vets 24, sped down the steep, icicle-slick Metropolitan Avenue Hill in the Greenpoint section of Brooklyn.

He was riding in a nine-year-old Everest and Jennings wheelchair, from the Queens VA. Right now, he was pretending the chair was a Datsun 280-Z, silver metallic, with a shining T-roof.

"Aahh-eee-ahh!" He let out a banshee screech that pierced the deserted, solemnly quiet morning streets.

His long thin face was buried in the oily collar of a khaki Army fatigue parka replete with peeling sergeant's stripes, and his frizzy blond ponytail blew behind him like ribboning bike streamers. Periodically, he closed his eyes which were tearing badly in the burning cold wind. His tightly pinched face was getting as red as the gleaming Berry Street stoplight he was racing through with absolute abandon.

His forehead was burning, but he *loved* the sensation of unexpected freedom.

He thought he could actually feel streams of blood surge through both his wasted legs again.

Harry Stemkowsky's rattling wheelchair finally came to a halt in front of the all-night Walgreen's Drugstore.

Under the fatigue jacket and the two bulky sweaters he wore, his heart was hammering wildly. He was so goddamn excited—his whole life was beginning all over again.

Today, Harry Stemkowsky felt he could do just about *anything*.

The drugstore's glass door, which he nudged open, was covered with a montage of cigarette posters. Almost immediately, he was blessed with a draft of welcoming warm air, filled with the smells of greasy bacon and fresh-perked coffee.

He smiled and rubbed his hands together in a gesture that was almost gleeful. For the first time in years he was no longer a cripple.

And for the first time in more than a dozen hard years Harry Stemkowsky had a purpose.

He *had* to smile. When he wrapped his mind around the whole deal, the full, unbelievable implications of Green Band, *he just had to smile*.

Right at this moment, Sergeant Harry Stemkowsky, the official messenger for Green Band, was safely at his firebase inside New York City. Now everything could begin.

Chapter 2

INSIDE THE FORTRESS that was New York FBI headquarters in Federal Plaza, a tall, silver-haired man, Walter Trentkamp, repeatedly tapped the eraser of his pencil against a faded desk blotter.

Scrawled on the soiled blotter was a single phone number *202-456-1414*. It was a private number for the White House, a direct line to the President of the United States.

Trentkamp's telephone rang at 6:00 exactly.

"All right everybody, please start up audio surveillance now." It was early in the morning, and his voice was harsh. "I'll hold them as long as I possibly can. Is audio surveillance ready? Well, let's go then."

The FBI Eastern Bureau Chief cleared his throat self-consciously. Then he picked up the telephone. The words *Green Band* echoed perilously inside his brain. He'd never known anything like this in his Bureau experience, which was long and varied and not without bizarre encounters.

Gathered in a grim, tight circle around the FBI head were some of the more powerfully connected men and women in New York. Not a person in the group had ever experienced anything like this emergency situation either.

In silence, they listened to Trentkamp answer the expected phone call. "This is the Federal Bureau. . . . Hello?"

There was no answer over the outside line.

The tension inside the room was as sharp as the cutting edge of a surgical blade. Even Trentkamp, whose calm in critical police situations was well known, appeared nervous and uncertain.

"I said hello. Is anyone there on the line? *Is anyone out there? . . .* Who is on this line?"

Walter Trentkamp's tentative, frustrated voice was being electronically monitored in a battered mahogany phone booth at the rear of the Walgreen's Drugstore in Greenpoint, Brooklyn.

Inside the booth, Sergeant Harry Stemkowsky finger-combed his hair as he listened.

His heart had gone beyond mere pounding; now it was threatening to detonate inside his chest. There were new and unusual pulses beating all through his body, opening and closing with the sharpness of mechanical claws.

This was the long overdue time of truth. *There would be no more war game rehearsals for the twenty-eight members of Green Band.*

"Hello? This is Trentkamp. New York FBI." The plain black phone receiver cradled between Stemkowsky's shoulder and his jaw seemed to tremble and vibrate on each phrase.

After another interminable minute, Harry Stemkowsky firmly depressed the play button on a Sony 114 portable recorder. He then carefully held the pocket recorder flush against the pay phone's receiver.

Stemkowsky had cued the recorder to the first word of the message—"Good." The "good" stretched to "goood" as the recorder hitched once, then rolled forward with a soft whir.

"Good morning. This is Green Band speaking. Today is December fourth. A Friday. A history-making Friday, we believe."

Over a squawk box the eerie, high-pitched voice brought the unprecedented message the men and women sequestered inside the Manhattan FBI office had been waiting for.

Green Band was beginning.

Ryan Klauk from FBI Surveillance made a quick judgment that the prerecorded track had been purposely speeded-up and echoed, to sound even more eerie than the circumstance made it; to be virtually unrecognizable, probably untraceable.

"As we promised, there are vitally important reasons for our past phone calls this week, for all the elaborate preparations we've made, and had you make to date . . .

"Is everyone listening? I can only assume you have company, Mr. Trentkamp. No one in corporate America seems to make a decision alone these days. . . . Listen closely then. Everybody please listen . . .

"The Wall Street financial district, from the East River to Broadway, is scheduled to be firebombed today. A large number of randomly selected targets will be completely destroyed late this afternoon.

"I will repeat. Selected targets in the Wall Street financial district will be destroyed today. Our decision is irrevocable. Our decision is nonnegotiable.

"The firebombing of Wall Street will take place at five

minutes past five tonight. It might be an attack by air; it might be a ground attack. Whichever—it will occur at five minutes past five precisely."

"Wait a minute. You can't—" Walter Trentkamp vehemently began to object, then he stopped just as suddenly. He remembered he was attempting to talk back to a recorded message.

"All of Manhattan, everything below Fourteenth Street, must be evacuated," the voice track continued methodically.

"The Target Area Nuclear Survival Plan for New York should be activated right now. Are you listening Mayor Ostrow? Susan Hamilton from the Office of Civil Preparedness?

"The Nuclear Target Plan can save thousands of lives. Please employ it now . . .

"In case any of you require further concrete convincing, this will be provided as well. Such requests have been anticipated.

"Our seriousness, our utter commitment to this mission, must not be underestimated. Not at any time during this or any future talk we might decide to have.

"Begin the evacuation of the Wall Street financial district now. Green Band cannot possibly be stopped or deterred. Nothing I've said is negotiable. Our decision is irrevocable."

Harry Stemkowsky abruptly pushed down the stop button. He quickly replaced the telephone receiver. He then rewound the Sony recorder, and stuffed it in the drooping pocket of his Army fatigue jacket.

Done.

He took a deep breath that seemed to grab into the very

pit of his stomach. He shivered uncontrollably. Christ, he'd done it. He'd actually goddamn done it!

He'd delivered Green Band's message and he felt terrific. He wanted to scream out inside the drugstore. More than that, he wished he could leap two feet in the air and punch the sky.

No formal demands had been made.

Not a single clue had been offered as to why Green Band was happening.

Harry Stemkowsky's heart was still beating loudly as he numbly maneuvered his wheelchair along an aisle lined with colorful deodorants and toiletries, up toward the gleaming soda fountain counter.

The short order cook, Wally Lipsky, a cheerfully mountainous three-hundred-and-ten-pound man, turned from scraping the grill as Stemkowsky and his wheelchair approached. Lipsky's pink-cheeked face immediately brightened. The semblance of a third or fourth chin appeared out of rolling mounds of neck fat.

"Well, look what Sylvester the Cat musta dragged in offa the street! It's my man Pennsylvania. Whereyabeen keepin' yourself, champ? Long time no see."

Henry Stemkowsky had to smile at the irresistible fat cook, who had a well-deserved reputation as the Greenpoint neighborhood clown. Hell, he was in the mood to smile at almost anything this morning.

"Oh he-he-here and there, Wally." Harry Stemkowsky burst into a nervous stutter. "Muh-Manhattan the mo-most part. I been wuh-working up in Manhattan a lot these days."

Stemkowsky tapped his index finger against the tattered cloth tag sewn into the shoulder of his jacket. The patch said VETS CABS AND MESSENGERS. Harry Stemkowsky was one of seven licensed wheelchair cabbies in New York; three of them worked for Vets in Manhattan.

"Gah-gotta good job. *Real* job now, Wah-Wally. . . . Why don't you make us some breakfast?"

"You got it, Pennsylvania. Cabdriver special comin' up. You got it my man, anything you want."

Chapter 3

AS EARLY AS 6:15 that morning, an endless stream of sullen-looking men and women carrying bulging, black briefcases had begun to rise out of the steam-blooming subway station at Broadway and Wall Street.

These were the appointed drones of New York's financial district; the straight salary employees who understood abstract accounting principles and fine legal points, but perceived little else about the Street and its black magic.

By 7:30, gum-popping secretaries were slouching off the Red and Tan Line buses arriving from Staten Island and Brooklyn. Aside from their habitual gum-chewing, several of the secretaries looked impressively chic, almost elegant that Friday morning.

As the ornate, golden arms on the Trinity Church clock solemnly reached for eight o'clock, every main and side street of the financial district was choked with thick, hypertense pedestrian traffic as well as with buses and honking cabs.

Over nine hundred and fifty thousand people were being melted into less than half a square mile of outrageously expensive real estate; seven solid stone blocks where *billions* were bought and sold every workday: *still the unsurpassed financial capital of the world.*

The New York police hadn't known whether or not to try and stop the morning's regular migration. Then it was simply too late—the slim possibility had disintegrated in a frantic series of telephone calls between the Commissioner's office and various powerful precinct chiefs. It had petered out into a nightmare of impossible logistics and mounting panic.

At that moment, a wraithlike black man, Abdul Calvin Mohammud, was very calmly entering the bobbing parade of heads and winter hats on Broad Street, just south of Wall.

As he walked within the spirited crowd, Calvin Mohammud found himself noticing corporate flags waving colorfully from the massive stone buildings.

The flags signaled BBH and Company, the National Bank of North America, Manufacturers Hanover, the Seaman's Bank. The flags were like crisp sails driven by strong East River winds.

Calvin Mohammud continued up the steep hill toward Wall Street. He was hardly noticed. But then the messenger caste usually wasn't. They were invisible men.

Today, like every other workday, Calvin Mohammud wore a thigh-length, pale gray clerk's tunic with a frayed armband that said VETS MESSENGERS. On either side of the capitalized words were fierce Eighty-second Airborne fighting eagles.

But none of that was noticed either.

Calvin Mohammud didn't look like it now, but in Vietnam and Cambodia, he'd been a Kit Carson Army scout. He'd won a Distinguished Service Cross, then the Medal of Honor for conspicuous gallantry at the risk of his life. After returning to the U.S. in 1971, Mohammud had been rewarded by a grateful society with jobs as a porter at Penn Station, a delivery boy for Chick-Teri, a baggage carrier at LaGuardia Airport.

Calvin Mohammud, Vets 11, unslung his heavy messenger's shoulder bag as he reached the graffiti-covered newsstand at the corner of Broadway and Wall.

He tapped out a Kool and lit up behind a plume of yellow flame.

Slouched in a nearby doorway, Vets 11 then casually reached into his shoulder bag and slid out a standard U.S. Army field telephone. Still concealed in the deep cloth bag was a sixteen-inch machine gun pistol, along with half a dozen 40-millimeter antipersonnel grenades.

"Contact." He moved back into the cold building shadows, then whispered into the field telephone. "This is Vets Eleven at the Stock Exchange. I'm at the northeast entrance, off Wall. . . . Everything's very nice and peaceful at position three. . . . No police in sight. No armed resistance anywhere. Almost looks too easy. Over."

Vets 11 took another short drag on his dwindling cigarette. He calmly peered around at the noisy hustle and bustle that was so characteristic of Wall Street on a weekday.

Broad daylight.

What an amazing, completely unbelievable scene, just to imagine the apocalyptic firefight that would be coming down here at five o'clock.

At 0830, Calvin Mohammud carefully wound a tattered strip of cloth around a polished brass door handle at the back entrance of the all-powerful New York Stock Exchange—*a proud, beautiful green band.*

Chapter 4

GREEN BAND STARTED savagely and suddenly, as if meteors had hurtled themselves with malevolent intensity against New York City.

It blew out two-story-tall windows, and shattered asphalt roofs, and shook whole streets in the vicinity of Pier 33–34 on Twelfth Avenue between 12th and 15th streets. It all came in an enormous white flash of painful blinding light.

At approximately 9:20 that morning, Pier 33–34—which had once hosted such regal ships as the *Queen Elizabeth* and the *QE II*—was a sudden fiery cauldron, a crucible of flame that raked the air and spread with such rapid intensity that even the Hudson River seemed to be spurting colossal columns of flames, some at least four hundred feet high.

Dense hydrocarbon clouds of smoke bloomed over Twelfth Avenue like huge black umbrellas being thrown open. Six-foot-long shards of glass, unguided missiles of molten steel, were flying upward, launching themselves in eerie, tumbling slow motion. And as the river winds suddenly shifted there were otherworldly glimpses of the glowing, red hot metal skeleton that was the pier itself.

The blistering fireball had erupted and spread in less than sixty seconds' time.

It was precisely as the Green Band warning had said it would be: an unspeakable sound and light show, a ghostly demonstration of promised horrors and terrors to come . . .

The dock for the *Mauretania,* for the *Aquitania,* the *Ile de France,* had been effectively vaporized by the powerful explosions, by the sudden, graphic flash fires.

This time, one of the thousands of routinely horrifying threats to New York was absolutely real. Radio listeners and TV viewers all over New York would soon hear the unprecedented message:

"This is *not a test* of the Emergency Broadcast System."

At 10:35 on the morning of December 4, more than seven thousand dedicated capitalists—DOT system clerks, youthful pages with their jaunty epaulets and floppy Connecticut Yankee haircuts, grimly determined stockbrokers, bond analysts, bright-green-jacketed supervisors—were busily, if somewhat nonchalantly, promenading through the three jam-packed main rooms of the New York Stock Exchange.

The twelve elevated ticker-tape TV monitors in the busy room were spewing stock symbols and trades comprehensible only to the trained eyes of Exchange professionals.

The day's volume, if it was only an average Friday, would easily exceed a hundred fifty million shares.

The original forebears, the first Bears and Bulls, had been ferocious negotiators and boardroom masters. Their descendants, however, their mostly thin-blooded *heirs,* were not particularly adroit at moneychanging.

At 10:57 on Friday morning, "the Bell"—which had

once actually been a brass fire bell struck by a rubber mallet, and which still signaled the official beginning of trading at 10:00 sharp, the end of trading at 4:00—went off inside the New York Stock Exchange. "The Bell" sounded with all the shock value of a firework popping in a cathedral.

Absolute silence followed.

Shocked silence.

Then came uncontrollable buzzing; frantic rumor-trading. Almost three minutes of unprecedented confusion and chaos on the Stock Exchange floor.

Finally, there was the deep and resonant voice of the Stock Exchange Manager blaring over the antiquated p.a. system.

"Gentlemen ... ladies ... the New York Stock Exchange is officially closed. .... *Please leave the Stock Exchange floor. Please leave the trading floor immediately.* This is not a bomb scare. This is an actual emergency! This is a serious police emergency!"

Chapter 5

OUTSIDE THE HEAVY stone and steel entranceway to the Mobil Building on East 42nd Street, a series of personal stretch limousines—Mercedes, Lincolns, Rolls-Royces—were arriving and departing with dramatic haste.

Important-looking men, and a few women, most of them in dark overcoats, hurriedly disembarked from the limousines and entered the building's familiar Deco lobby.

Upstairs on the forty-second floor, other CEOs and presidents of the major Wall Street banks and brokerage houses were already gathered inside the exclusive Pinnacle Club.

The emergency meeting had commandeered the luxurious main dining room of the private club, which was glowing with crisp white linen, shining silver and crystal set up and never used for lunch.

Several of the dark-suited executives stood dazed and disoriented before floor-to-ceiling nonglare windows, which faced downtown. None of them had ever experienced anything remotely like this, nor had they ever expected to.

The view was a spectacular, if chilling one, down uneven canyons to lower Manhattan, all the way to the pencil pocket of skyscrapers which was the financial center itself.

About halfway, at 14th Street, there were massive police barricades. Police department buses, EMS ambulances, and a paradelike crowd could be seen waiting, watching Wall Street as if they were studying some puzzling work of art in a Midtown museum.

None of this was possible; it was sheer madness.

Every rational mind in the executive dining room had already reached this conclusion privately.

"They haven't even bothered to reestablish contact with us. Not since six this morning," said the Secretary of the Treasury, Walter O'Brien. "What the hell are they up to?"

Standing stiffly among four or five prominent Wall Street executives, George Firth, the Attorney General of the United States, was quietly relighting his pipe. He appeared surprisingly casual and controlled, except that he'd given up smoking more than three years before.

"They certainly were *damned* clear when it came to stating their deadline. Five minutes past five. Five minutes past or *what?* What do the bastards want from us?" The Attorney General's pipe went out in his hand and he relit it with a look of exasperation.

Madness.

What they'd experienced for a decade in terrorist-plagued Europe. But never before in the United States.

A somber businessman named Jerrold Gottlieb from Lehman Brothers held up his wristwatch. "Well, gentlemen, it's one minute past five . . ." He looked as if he were about to add something, but whatever it was, he left it unsaid.

But that was the unlikely place they had all entered now.

An unfamiliar territory where things couldn't be properly articulated: the uncharted territory of the unspeakable.

"They've been extremely punctual up to now. Almost obsessive about getting details and schedules perfect. They'll call. I wouldn't worry, they'll call."

The speaker was the Vice-president of the United States, who'd been rushed from the U.N. to the nearby Mobil Building. Thomas More Elliot was a stern man with the look of an Ivy League scholar. He was a Brahmin who was out of touch with the complexities of contemporary America, his harshest critics carped.

For the next hundred and eighty seconds, there was almost uninterrupted silence in the Pinnacle Club dining room.

This tingling silence was all the more frightening because there were so many highly articulate men crowded into the room—the senior American business executives, used to having their own way, used to being listened to, and obeyed, almost without question. Now their voices were stilled, virtually powerless.

Their power, normally awesome, had distilled itself into a sequence of small, distinct, noises:

The scratchy rasp of a throat being cleared.

Ice cracking in a glass with an almost glacial effect.

The tapping of fingers on the bowl of a dead pipe.

Madness. The thought seemed to echo in the room.

The most fearsome urban terrorism had finally struck deep inside the United States, stabbing right to the heart of America's economic power.

There were anxious, repeated glances at the glinting faces of Rolex, Cartier, and Piaget wristwatches.

What did Green Band want?

Where were the final demands? What was the no-doubt outrageous ransom for Wall Street to be?

Edward Palin, the seventy-seven-year-old Chief Executive of one of the largest investment firms, had to slowly back away from the darkly reflective picture windows. A few of the others embarrassedly watched as he sat down in a Harvard chair pulled up beside one of the dining tables and, in a gesture that was almost poignant, put his head between his gray pinstriped knees.

There were less than twenty seconds left to the expiration of the Green Band deadline.

"Please call. Call, you bastards," the Vice-president muttered.

What seemed like thousands of emergency sirens were screaming, a peculiar high-low wail, all over New York. It was the first time the emergency warning system had been seriously in use since 1963 and the nuclear war scares.

Finally, it was five minutes past five.

The sudden, terrifying realization struck every person in the Pinnacle Club's dining room—they weren't going to call again!

They weren't going to negotiate.

Without any further warning, Green Band was going to strike.

"A fast recap for you," said Lisa Pelham, who was the President's Chief of Staff, an efficient, well-organized woman who spoke in the clipped manner of one whose mind was used to making succinct outlines from mountains of information.

"By twelve noon, all trading had been halted on the New York and all regional exchanges in the U.S. There is no trading in London, Paris, Geneva, Bonn. The key New York business people are meeting right now at the Pinnacle Club inside the Mobil Building.

"All the important securities and commodities exchanges have ceased trading around the world. The unanswered question is the same everywhere. What's the nature of the demands we are *secretly negotiating?*" Lisa Pelham paused and stroked a strand of hair away from her oval face. "Everyone believes we're negotiating with somebody, sir."

"And we are definitely not?" President Justin Kearney's expression was one of extreme doubt and suspicion. He had discovered the awkward fact during his term of office that one branch of government all too frequently didn't know what another was doing.

"Which we are not, Mr. President. Both the CIA and FBI have assured us of that. Sir, Green Band has still made *no* demands."

President Justin Kearney had been rushed, under intensified Secret Service guard, to a windowless, lead-shielded room buried deep inside the White House. There, in the White House Communications Center, several of the most important political leaders in the United States were standing around the President in a manner that suggested they intended to protect him.

From the White House Communications Center, the President had been put into audio and visual contact with the Pinnacle Club in New York City.

The FBI Chief, Walter Trentkamp, stepped forward to appear on the monitor screen from New York. Trentkamp had short, silver-gray hair; time and his job had also added a tough, weathered policeman's look and a harassed attitude to match.

"There's been no further contact from Green Band, other than the firebombing of Pier 33–34, which is the demonstration they promised us, Mr. President. It's the kind of guerrilla warfare we've seen in Belfast, Beirut, Tel Aviv. *Never* before in the United States . . .

"We're all waiting, Mr. President," Trentkamp went on. "It's five zero six and about forty seconds. We're clearly *past* their stated deadline."

"Have any of the terrorist groups come forward and claimed responsibility?"

"They have. We're checking into them. So far none has shown any knowledge of the content of the warning phone call this morning."

5:06 became 5:07. The time was leaden.

5:07 became 5:08. A minute had never seemed so long.

It was 5:09 . . . 5:10 and slowly, slowly counting.

The Director of the CIA moved before the lights and cameras in the White House emergency room. Philip Berger was a small, irascible man, highly unpopular in Washington, chiefly skilled at keeping the major American intelligence agencies competitive among themselves. "Is there *any* activity you can make out on Wall Street? Any people down there? Any moving vehicles? Small plane activity?"

"Nothing, Phil. Apart from the police, the fire department vehicles on the periphery of the area, it could be a peaceful Sunday morning."

"They're goddamn bluffing," someone said in Washington.

"Or," President Kearney said, "they're playing an enormous game of fucking nerves."

No one agreed, or disagreed, with the President.

No one said anything now.

Speech had been replaced by the terrifying anxiety and uncertainty of waiting.

Just waiting.

5:15 . . .

5:18 . . .

5:20 . . .

5:24 . . .

5:30 . . .

Waiting for what, though?

Chapter 6

AT 6:20 P.M., Colonel David Hudson was doing the single thing that still mattered—*that mattered more than anything else in his life.*

David Hudson was on patrol. He was back in combat; he was leading a quality-at-every-position platoon into the field again—only the field was now an American city.

Hudson was one of those men who looked vaguely familiar to people, only they couldn't say precisely why. His blond hair was cut in a short crew, which was suddenly back in vogue again. He was handsome; his looks were very American.

He had the kind of strong, almost noble face that photographs extremely well, and a seemingly unconscious air of self-confidence, a consistently reassuring look that emphatically said, *"Yes, I can do that—whatever it is."*

There was only one thing wrong, which a lot of people didn't notice right away—David Hudson had lost his left arm in the Viet Nam War.

His Checker cab marked VETS CABS AND MESSENGERS rolled cautiously forward, reconnoitering past the bright green pumps at the Hess gas station on Eleventh Avenue and 45th Street. This was one of those times when David Hudson could *see himself,* as if in an eerie dream, when he could objectively watch himself from somewhere outside the scene. He knew this uncomfortable, distorted feeling extremely well from combat duty.

Now he felt it again, this time in the sharp wintry wind blowing through the snowy gray streets of New York City.

Colonel David Hudson was purposely allowing the Green Band mission to wind out just a little longer; one important notch tighter.

Every second had been rigidly accounted for. More than anything else, David Hudson's mind appreciated the subtleties of precision; Hudson appreciated detail and the fine-tuning involved in getting everything absolutely right.

He was back in combat again.

This strange, strange passion was alive again inside David Hudson.

He finally released the hand microphone from the PRC transmitter built into the Vets cab's dash.

"Contact. Come in Vets Five." Colonel David Hudson spoke in the firm, charismatic tones which had characterized his commands through the latter war years in Southeast Asia. It was a voice that had always elicited loyalty and obedience in the men whose lives he controlled.

"This is Vets One. . . . Come in Vets Five. Over."

A reply immediately crackled back through heavy static over the PRC transmitter-receiver. "This is Vets Five. Over."

"Vets Five. Green Band is affirmative. I repeat—Green Band is affirmative. . . . *Blow it all up . . .*"

Chapter 7

"YOUGOTAQUARTER, SIR? PLEASE! It's real cold out here, sir. You got two bits? . . . Awhh, thank you. Thanks a lot, sir. You just about saved my life."

Around 7:30 that evening, on Brooklyn's Atlantic Avenue, a familiar bag man called Crusader Rabbit was expertly soliciting loose change and cigarettes.

The bag man begged while he sat huddled like trash against the crumbling red brick facade of the Atlantic House Yemen and Middle East Restaurant. The money came to him as if he were a magnet made of soiled rags.

After a successful hit, forty-eight cents from a trendy-looking Brooklyn Heights teacher-type and his date, the street bum allowed himself a short pull on a dwindling half pint of Four Roses.

Drinking while begging change was counterproductive, he knew, but sometimes necessary against the raw cold wintertime. Besides, *it was his image . . .*

The deep, slack cough that followed the sip of whiskey sounded convincingly tubercular. The man's lips were bloated. They were corpse white and cracked, and they looked as if they'd bled recently.

For this year's winter wardrobe, he'd selected a sleeveless navy parka over several layers of assorted, colored lumberman's shirts. He'd picked out open-toed high top black sneakers, basketball player snow bird socks, and painter's pants that were now thickly caked with mud, vomit and spit.

The tourists, at least, seemed to love him.

Sometimes, they snapped his picture to bring home as an example of New York City's famed squalor and heartlessness.

He enjoyed posing: asking them for a buck or whatever the traffic would bear. He'd hold his two puffy shopping bags, and smile extra pathetically for the camera. *Pay the cashier, sport.*

Now, through gummy, half-closed eyes, Crusader Rabbit stealthily watched the usual early evening promenade along Atlantic Avenue's Middle Eastern restaurant row.

It was a constant, day-in day-out noisy bazaar here: transplanted Arabs, college assholes, Brooklyn professionals who came to eat ethnic.

In the distance, there was always the *clickety-clack* of the El.

A troupe of McDonalds counter kids was passing by Crusader Rabbit, walking home from work. Two chunky black girls; a skinny mulatto boy around eighteen, nineteen.

"Hey, McDonalds. Whopper beat the Big Mac. Real tough break. Gotta quarter? Something for some Mccoffee?" Crusader coughed and wheezed at the passing trio of teens.

The McDonalds kids looked offended; then they all laughed together in a high-pitched chorus. "Who asked you, Aqualung? You old geek sheet-head. Kick your ass."

The kids continued merrily on. Rude little bastards when Ronald McDonald wasn't watching over their act.

If any of the various passersby had looked closer, they might have noticed certain visual inconsistencies about the bag man called Crusader Rabbit.

For one thing, he had impressive muscle tone for a sedentary street bum. His shoulders were unusually broad.

Even more unusual were his eyes, which were almost always intently focused. They scanned the avenue over and over again, watching all the street action.

There was also the small matter of the quality of the dirt and dust thickly caked on his ankles, on his exposed toes. It was a little too perfect. Almost as if it might be black Kiwi shoe polish—*shoe polish carefully applied to look like dirt.*

The conclusion was obvious after a careful look at the street bum. Crusader Rabbit was some kind of undercover New York cop. He had to be some kind of cop on a stake-out . . .

His real name was Arch Carroll and he *was* on a stake-out, a five-week one, with no end in sight.

Meanwhile, across the busy Brooklyn street, inside the Sinbad Star Restaurant, two Iraqi men in their early thirties were sampling what they believed to be the finest Middle Eastern cooking available in New York City. They were the objects of Carroll's long and painful stakeout.

The Iraqi men had chosen a rear alcove of the small,

cozy restaurant, where they noisily slurped thick carob bean soup.

They gobbled up mint-flecked tabbouli, and cream-colored humus. They eagerly munched greasy mixtures of raisins, pine nuts, lamb, Moroccan olives, their favorite things to eat in the world. Life was good.

Chapter 8

BACK OUT ON Atlantic Avenue, Arch Carroll shivered unhappily in the probing icy-cold fingers of the rising night wind.

At times like these, Carroll sometimes wondered why it was that a reasonably intelligent thirty-five-year-old man, someone with decent enough prospects, someone with a law degree, could regularly be working sixty- to seventy-hour weeks, invariably eating stone-cold pizza and Pepsi-Cola for dinner, was sitting outside a Middle Eastern restaurant on a Friday night stakeout?

Why was that?

Was it perhaps because his father and two uncles had been pavement-pounding city cops?

Was it because his grandfather had been a rough and tumble example of New York's finest?

Or did it have to do with things he'd seen a decade and a half ago in Viet Nam?

Maybe he just wasn't a reasonable, intelligent man, as he'd somehow always presumed? Maybe, if you got right down to it, there was some kind of obvious short-circuit in the wires of the old brain, some form of synaptic fuck-up.

As Arch Carroll pondered the tangible mistakes of his life, he noticed that his attention had begun to wander.

For several minutes at a clip, he'd stare at his sadly wiggling toes, at the equally fascinating burning ember of his cigarette, at almost anything mildly distracting.

Five-week-long stakeouts weren't exactly recommended for their entertainment value. That was exactly how long he'd been watching Anton and Wadih Rashid.

Now Carroll's attention had suddenly snapped back . . .

"What the . . ." he mumbled out loud as he stared down the congested street. *Is that who it looks like? . . . Can't be . . . I think it is . . . but it can't be.*

Carroll had suddenly noticed a skinny, frazzle-haired man coming directly his way from the Frente Unido Bar and Data Indonesia. The man was scurrying up Atlantic Avenue, periodically looking back over his right shoulder.

At a distance, he looked like a baggy coat walking on a stick.

Carroll slowly pushed himself up out of his half-frozen lounging position against the restaurant wall.

He squinted his eyes tight for a better look at the figure approaching from down the street.

He couldn't believe it!

He *stared* down the street, his eyes smarting from the bite of the wind. He had to make sure.

Jesus. *He was sure.*

The fast-walking man had a huge puffy burr of bushy, very wiry black hair. The greasy hair was combed straight back; it hung like a limp sack over the collar of his black cloth jacket.

Carroll knew the man by two names: one was Hussein Moussa; the other was the *Lebanese Butcher.* A decade before, Moussa had been recruited by the Russians; he'd been trained at their famed Third World school in Tripoli.

Since then Moussa had been busily free-lancing terror and sophisticated murder techniques all over the world: in Paris, Rome, Zaire, New York, in Lebanon for Colonel Qadaffi. Recently, he'd worked for François Monserrat, who had taken over not only Juan Carlos's European terrorist cell, but South America, and now the United States as well.

Hussein Moussa halted in front of the Sinbad Star restaurant. Like a very careful driver at a tricky intersection, he looked both ways.

Twice more he looked up and down Atlantic Avenue. He even noticed the bag man camped out across the traffic-busy street.

He finally disappeared behind the gaudy red door of the Sinbad Star.

Arch Carroll sat up rigidly straight against the crumbling brick wall of the Syrian restaurant.

He groped inside his jacket and produced a stubby third of a Camel cigarette. He lit up and inhaled the gruff, North Carolina dirt farm tobacco.

What an unexpected little Christmas present. What a just reward for endless winter nights trailing the Rashids. *The Lebanese Butcher on a silver platter.*

His bosses in State had said not to touch the Rashids without extremely strong physical evidence. But they'd issued no such orders for the Lebanese Butcher.

What was Hussein Moussa doing in New York, anyway? Carroll's mind was reeling. Why was Moussa here with the Rashids?

The firebombing of Pier 33–34 went through his mind

quickly. He had picked up strands of information from gossip he'd heard all day long on the street—somebody had taken it into his head to blow a dock and the surrounding West Side area, it seemed, and for a moment Carroll pondered a connection between Hussein Moussa and the events on the Hudson River.

Arch Carroll had been ramrodding the Anti-Terrorist Division of the DIA for almost four years now. In that span of time only a few of the mass murderers he'd learned about had gotten to him emotionally and caused him to lose his usual policeman's objectivity.

Hussein Moussa was one of those few.

The Lebanese Butcher liked to torture. The Butcher apparently liked to kill. The Butcher enjoyed maiming innocent civilians . . .

So Carroll didn't particularly want Moussa dead, as he studied the Sinbad Star Restaurant. Carroll wanted the Butcher locked away for the rest of his natural life. Give the animal *lots* of time to *think* about what he'd done, *if he did think.*

From underneath newspapers and rags inside one of his shopping bags, Carroll began to slide out a heavy black metal object. He checked the firing chamber of a Browning automatic. He quickly fed in an autoloader.

A stooped, ancient Hasid was passing by on the sidewalk. He stared incredulously at the street bum loading up a Browning handgun. His watery gray eyes almost fell out of his sagging face. The old man kept slowly walking away, looking back constantly as he moved. Then he cantered a little faster. *New York street bums with guns now!* The city was beyond all prayers, all possible hope.

*   *   *

Carroll finally began to weave forward through the thick, fuzzy night traffic. He only half heard the bleating car horns and angry curses directed at him.

He was drifting in and out of reality now; there was a little nausea involved here, too.

A middle-aged couple was leaving the Sinbad, the fat wife pulling her red overcoat tight around bursting hips.

She stared at Crusader Rabbit and the look said, *You don't belong inside there, Mister. You know you don't belong in there.*

Carroll pulled open the ornate red door the departing couple had let slam in his face.

Hot, garlicky air escaped as he started inside. A muffled *snick* of the Browning under his coat. A deep silent breath. *Okay, hotshot.*

The tiny restaurant was infinitely more crowded than it had looked from the outside. Arch Carroll cursed and felt his stomach drop. Every dining table was filled to overflowing.

Six or seven more people, a group of boisterously laughing friends, were waiting in the front to be seated. Carroll pushed past them.

Carroll's eyes slowly drifted along the back of the crowded dining room. Only his eyes moved. His head was absolutely still.

Hussein Moussa had already seen him.

Even in the packed, bustling restaurant, the terrorist had noticed his entrance. The Butcher had been instinctively watching every person who came in from Atlantic Avenue.

So had the restaurant's owner. An enormous, two-hundred-and-fifty-pound man, he charged forward now, an enraged bull guarding his herd at mealtime.

"Get out of here! You get out, bum! Go now!" the owner screamed.

Carroll tried to look desperately lost, dizzily confused, as surprised as everyone else that he was inside the small neighborhood restaurant.

He stumbled over his own flopping black sneakers.

He weaved sideways toward the left, before moving suddenly toward the right rear corner of the dining room.

He hoped to God he looked cockeyed drunk and absolutely helpless. Maybe even a little funny right now. Everybody should start laughing.

Carroll groped down his body with both hands, graphically scratching between his legs. A middle-aged woman turned away with obvious disgust.

"Bayt-room?" Carroll convincingly slobbered, rolled his eyes back into his forehead. "Gotta go to the bayt-room!"

A young bearded man and his girlfriend started laughing at a front table. Bathroom humor got the youth crowd every time.

Hussein Moussa had stopped eating. His teeth finally showed—a serrated blade of shining yellow. It was the smile of an animal, a brutal scavenger. He apparently thought this scene was funny, too.

"Gotta go to the bayt-room!" Carroll continued a little louder, sounding like a drunken Jerry Lewis. Jesus, you had to be a decent actor in this line of work.

"Mohamud! Tarek! Get bum out! Get bum out now!" The owner was screeching at his waiters.

Suddenly, fluidly, Arch Carroll wheeled hard to his extreme left.

The Browning automatic flew out of the ratty and cumbersome parka.

It was completely out of place in the family restaurant: a gun as ugly and menacing as unexpected death. Women and children began screaming.

"*Freeze!* Don't move! *Freeze God damn you!*"

At the same time, one of the Lebanese waiters hit Carroll hard from his blind side, spinning him in a fast half circle to the right.

He had ruined the drop Carroll had on the three terrorists; he had turned everything into a complete, instantaneous disaster.

Moussa and the Rashids were already scattering, rolling sideways off the red vinyl dining chairs. Anton Rashid yanked out a silver automatic from under his brown leather car coat.

Movies sometimes show particularly violent scenes in flowing slow motion. It wasn't like that, Carroll knew. It was a jumpy collage of loud, shocking still photos.

The disconnected photos clicked at him now in random order. They stopped. They started. They stopped. They started again.

"*Everybody hit the floor!*" Carroll screamed. At the same instant, he fired the Browning.

He didn't watch the results. The first bullet brutally uncorked the right side of Anton Rashid's throat, spilling his blood like wine from a broken jug.

Hussein Moussa's gun flashed; it roared as Carroll dove across the backs of a couple already lying on the floor.

Seconds later, Carroll peered back over the table. His eyes and forehead were exposed for an instant. He fired off three more quick shots.

Two of the bullets drove stocky Wadih Rashid hard against a hollow partition wall, decorated with black skillets.

Twin holes opened in the terrorist's chest. The heavy skillets clattered noisily to the tile floor.

"Moussa! Hussein Moussa! You can't get out! You can't get past me." Carroll began to scream, to negotiate with the man.

There was no answer.

Somewhere in the front of the restaurant, an old woman was wailing like an Arab imam. Several people were crying loudly.

"Give up now, and you live. . . . Otherwise, I'll kill you."

Carroll had to chance another fast look. He was gasping for a breath. *One, two, three.* He raised his head.

He saw nothing of the Butcher this time. Moussa was down under the tables as well, hiding and crawling, looking for some advantage.

He was moving either toward the front door or the kitchen. Which one was it?

Carroll guessed it would be the kitchen.

He began to scramble toward the kitchen.

"I have antipersonnel grenades!" The Butcher suddenly let out a piercing, high scream. "Everybody dies in here! *Everybody dies* in this restaurant! Everybody dies with me! Women, children, I don't care."

Carroll stopped moving suddenly; he almost didn't breathe.

Straight ahead, he stared at a badly shaking, very frightened woman curled like a snail on the floor. She looked about thirty years old.

Carroll peeked above the dining tables again. A gunshot rang out to his immediate left. A salt shaker disintegrated in his eyes.

Moussa was in the far right corner!

The question was whether he did have grenades. It could be a bluff, but the worst was always possible with somebody like the Butcher.

The people sprawled on the floor were inching toward panic; they were close to rising en masse and bolting for the door. This would be perfect for Hussein Moussa. In the confusion, Carroll wouldn't run the risk of shooting.

Food was spattered everywhere on the dining room floor. Carroll finally reached for a platter holding the relics of an unfinished meal of pungent lamb and rice. With a sudden wrist snap, he hurled the dripping plate hard against the kitchen door.

At the same time he shifted upright into a professional shooting crouch—a two-handed pistol grip with both arms rigid.

Moussa came up again, shooting. The Butcher fired twice at the slapping noise against the kitchen door. *Moussa had a grenade in his left hand! Son of a bitch!*

Arch Carroll squeezed the trigger.

Moussa looked incredibly surprised.

The far right of Hussein Moussa's forehead gushed blood. He slid down against a table still covered with mounds of food and tableware. His back dragged the cloth, plates, wine and water glasses. He spit out a throaty curse across the room.

Then the terrorist's gun rose again.

Carroll shot Hussein Moussa a second time, the bullet exploding his right cheek. The Lebanese Butcher fell heavily forward onto the back of a fat diner lying on the floor.

Carroll shot Moussa again, as the man trapped underneath wriggled like a beached fish and screamed.

There was an eerie, terrible silence inside the Sinbad Star. A second or two passed like that. Then loud crying started. There were angry shouts and relieved hugging all over the restaurant.

His gun thrust stiffly forward, Arch Carroll moved awkwardly across the chaotic room. He was still in a police school crouch. It was as if he were locked into that position.

He carefully examined the Rashid brothers. Wadih and Anton were still alive. He looked at Moussa. The Butcher was dead, and the world was instantly a better place in which to live.

"Please call me an ambulance," Carroll spoke softly to the astonished restaurant owner. "I'm sorry. I'm very sorry this had to happen in your establishment. These men are terrorists. Professional killers."

The Sinbad Star restaurant owner continued to stare with disbelief at Carroll. His black eyes were small, shiny beads stuck in his broad forehead and they pierced to the rear of Arch Carroll's skull.

"And what are you? What are *you*, please tell me, mister?"

Chapter 9

GREEN BAND HAD struck like an invisible army.

Two nervous New York City TAC patrolmen, Alry Simmons and Robert Havens, were carefully threading a path through the smoldering ruins of the Federal Reserve Bank located on Maiden Lane. The two men were attached at their belts to five-hundred-yard-long safety lines snaking back toward the street.

The patrolmen were deep inside what had once been the Fed's massive and richly ornamented public lobby. Indeed, the gray and blue limestone, the sandstone bricks of the Federal Reserve had always impressed visitors with a sense of their durability and authority. The fortlike appearance, the stout iron bars on every window, had reinforced the image of self-importance and impregnability. The image had obviously been a sham.

The destruction which officers Simmons and Havens found downstairs in the Coin Section was difficult to comprehend and even more difficult to assess.

Mountainous coin-weighing machines had been blown apart like a child's toys. Fifty-pound coin bags were strewn open everywhere.

The marble floor was easily three feet deep in quarters, dimes, nickels. Building support columns had been knocked down everywhere on the basement floor. The entire structure seemed to be trembling.

In the deepest basement of the Federal Reserve Bank was the largest single accumulation of gold stored anywhere in the world. It all belonged to foreign governments. The Fed both guarded the gold and kept track of who owned what. In an ordinary change of ownership, the Fed merely moved gold from one country's bin into another's. The gold was transported on ordinary metal carts, like books in a library. The security system in the deep basement was so highly elaborate that even the Reserve Bank's president had to be accompanied when he ventured into the gold storage area.

Now patrolmen Havens and Simmons were alone in the cavernous basement.

Suddenly gold was everywhere around them. Rivers of shining gold ran through the dust and rubble. Gold bars, more than they could possibly count, surrounded them. There was well over *a hundred billion dollars* at the day's market price of $386 an ounce, all within their reach.

Patrolman Robert Havens was hyperventilating, taking enormously deep breaths that were almost yawns. His broad, flat face held almost no expression and hadn't since he and Simmons had entered the Fed building.

Both emergency policemen stopped inching forward suddenly. Robert Havens unconsciously let out a sharp gasp.

"Christ Jesus! What the hell is *this?*"

An armed Security Guard was sitting in a caned wooden

chair directly blocking their path from the gold section into the Fed's main garage. The cane chair still smoldered.

The guard was staring directly into Robert Havens' eyes. Neither man spoke.

The Federal Reserve Bank guard couldn't; he was beyond words. The man was horribly burned, charred a blistering charcoal black. The sight was so upsetting that the two policemen missed the most important clue at first . . .

Wrapped around the bank guard's right arm was a shiny bright green band.

Chapter 10

AS ARCHER CARROLL maneuvered his battered station wagon along the Major Deegan Expressway, the words of the Atlantic Avenue restaurant owner came back to him with the persistence of an unanswerable philosophical question . . . *And what are you? . . . What are you, please tell me, mister?*

He glanced at his tired face in the rearview mirror. *Yeah, what are you, Arch? The Rashids and Hussein Moussa are bad people, but you're some kind of national hero, right?*

He was drained, completely numb from the night's carnage. He wanted everything to be quiet and still inside his throbbing head now.

And what are you, mister?

He turned on the car radio, looking for a diversion from his mood.

Almost immediately he heard the news about Wall Street, delivered by a voice edged in the hushed hysteria so favored by newscasters when they describe events of national importance. Carroll increased the volume and stared at the tiny light emitted by the radio.

He concentrated on the newscaster's tensely delivered

reportage. Then there were man-on-the-street interviews recorded against a brassy background of screaming sirens. It was impossible to mistake the shocked tones of the people who spoke.

Carroll tightened both of his hands on the car steering wheel. His mind was crowded with images of urban guerrilla destruction. He understood that Wall Street was a perfect target for any determined terrorist group—but he couldn't make the necessary jump from his thoughts to the horrible reality of what had happened.

He didn't want to think about it. He was almost home and he didn't need to drag the world inside the last sanctuary left to him. Not tonight, anyway.

Chapter 11

MOMENTS LATER, CARROLL swung his stiff, aching body inside the familiar, musty front hallway of his house in the Riverdale section of the Bronx. Automatically, he hung his coat up on the hook under an ancient totem—the snoopy-eyed Sacred Heart of Jesus.

Turn out the night light. Home from the wars at last, he thought.

As he slumped into the living room, Carroll sighed out loud.

"Oh *poor* Arch. It's almost eleven-thirty."

"Sorry. Didn't see you there, Mary K."

Mary Katherine Carroll was sitting neatly curled up on one corner of the couch. The room was only dimly illuminated by an amber light from the dining parlor.

"You look like a scuzzy Bowery bag man. Is that *blood* on your sleeve? *Are you all right?*" She stood up suddenly.

Carroll looked down at his torn, dingy shirt sleeve. He turned it into the dining parlor light. It was blood all right.

"I'm fine. The blood isn't mine."

Mary Katherine frowned deeply as she came forward to examine her brother's arm. "The bad guys get banged up too?"

Carroll finally smiled at his twenty-four-year-old "baby" sister. Mary Katherine, who was the keeper of his house, the substitute mother for his four children, the uncomplaining cook and chief bottle washer, all for a two-hundred-dollar-a-month stipend, *"a scholarship."* It was all he could possibly afford to pay her right now.

"I had to kill one of them. . . . The kids all asleep?"

The kids, in order of arrival, were Mary III, Clancy, Mickey Kevin and Elizabeth.

All four of them were too Irish-American cute for their own good: tow-headed and blue-eyed, with infectious smiles and quick, almost adult wits. Mary Katherine had been their house mother for nearly three years now.

Ever since Arch's wife Nora had died on *December 14, 1982.*

After Nora's funeral, after just one desolate night at their old New York apartment, the six of them had moved into the Carroll family homestead in Riverdale. The old house had been closed and boarded-up since the deaths of Carroll's mother and father back in '80 and '81.

Mary Katherine had immediately redecorated. She even set up a huge, light-filled painting studio for herself in the attic. The kids were out of New York City proper, at least. They suddenly had acres of fresh air and space in which to ramble around. There were definite advantages to being up in Riverdale.

Carroll had held on to their old rent-controlled apartment on Riverside Drive. Sometimes he even stayed there when he had to work weekends in New York. It wasn't ideal, but it could have been a lot worse. Especially without Mary K.

"I have several *important* messages for you," Mary Katherine announced brightly.

"Mickey says, if I might paraphrase, that you work too hard and don't make enough skoots. Clancy says, if you don't play catch with him this weekend (and not video game baseball), you're a dead man. That's a *direct* quote. Let's see . . . oh, yes, I almost forgot. Lizzie has decided to become a prima ballerina. Lessons for the spring semester at the Joliere school start at three hundred per, Dad."

"That all?"

"Mairzy Doats left you a humongous kiss, and a hug of equal magnitude and intensity."

"Uncomplicated young woman. Shame she can't stay six years old forever."

"Arch?" Mary Katherine suddenly looked concerned. "You heard about this Wall Street thing? The bombing?"

Carroll nodded wearily. He wanted to box Wall Street off in a dark, private corner until he was ready to deal with it.

Carroll finally bent and loosened his flopping high-top sneaks. He peeled off a discolored, satin Tollantine High School jacket. His fatigue had yielded to a kind of peaceful, ethereal, waking slumber.

In the large bathroom on the second floor, he turned on the tub full blast. Curling hot steam rose toward the ceiling from the chipped and scratched white porcelain. He took off the rest of his squalid street bum ensemble. Finally, he rolled a fluffy bath towel around his waist.

Quick mirror check. Okay. He was still around six-two, solid, durable and sturdy. Pleasant face, even if it was a little pug ordinary, like some friendly mutt people generally take in out of the rain.

While the hot water ran, Carroll stiffly padded back downstairs to the kitchen and popped the top of a cold Schlitz. Mary Katherine had bought the Schlitz as a "change of pace." Actually, she was trying to stop him from drinking so much.

Carroll took three chilled cans and headed back to the pleasantly steamed bathroom. Stripping off the soft bath towel, he slowly, luxuriously entered the hot tub.

As he sipped the cold beer, he began to relax. Carroll used a bath the way some people use psychiatric therapy—to get back in touch, to sort it all out. Among other things, hot water and soap was the only therapy he could afford.

Carroll began to think about Nora almost immediately. *Damn.* Always at night when he got home from work. . . . Their time. The emptiness he felt right then was unbearable. It beat against him with the consistency of a pulse. He was filled with a terrible, hollow longing.

He let his eyes gently close and he could *see* her face. *Oh, Nora, sweet Nora. How could you leave me like this? How could you leave me alone, with all these kids, fighting against this crazy, crazy world out there?*

She had been the best person Carroll had ever met. It was as simple, and no more profound, than that. The two of them had made a perfect fit. Nora had been warm, and thoughtful and funny. That they had found each other convinced Carroll such a thing as fate might indeed exist. It wasn't all randomness and whim and unseeing chance.

Strange, the ways of life and death.

Growing up, all through high school in New York, at College (South Bend, Notre Dame), Carroll had been secretly afraid he'd never find anybody to love him. It was a curious fear, and sometimes he'd imagine that just as some people were born with a talent for art or music, he'd been given a gift of solitude.

Then Nora found him and that was absolute magic.

She'd discovered Carroll the second day of law school at Michigan State. Right away, from their very first date, Carroll simply *knew* he could never love anybody else; that he would never need to. He'd never been more comfortable around another person in his life.

Only now Nora was gone. Nearly three years back in the cancer ward of New York Hospital. *Merry Christmas, Carroll family. Your friend, God . . .*

"I'm just a kid, Arch," Nora had whispered to him once, after she found out she was dying for certain. She'd been thirty-one then, a year younger than he.

Carroll slowly sipped his can of watery beer. An old country song played through his head . . . *"the beer that made Milwaukee famous, made a loser out of me."* Ever since she'd died, he understood he'd been trying to commit slow, sure suicide. He'd been drinking too much; eating most of the wrong things; taking stupid chances on the job . . .

It wasn't as if he didn't understand the problem, because he did. He just couldn't seem to do a damn thing to stop his steep downhill slide. He was like some daredevil skier determined to destroy himself on the most treacherous, glacial slopes. He didn't seem to care enough anymore . . .

Arch Carroll, supposed tough-guy, well-quoted cynic around town—there he sat in the tub with one of his kids' rubber toys floating next to him. All four of the kids delighted and astonished Carroll. So why was he screwing up so badly lately?

He was tempted to wake them up now. Maybe go sledding at midnight on the back lawn. Play catch with Mickey Kevin. Teach Lizzie how to do a plié and become a hot-shit little ballerina.

Arch Carroll's ears suddenly tuned in sharply. . . . *Something odd. . . . What was it?*

In another part of the house, he heard voices.

Then, a door slammed.

There were steps in the hallway. The floorboards creaked loudly.

The kids were up! Exactly what he needed, Carroll thought, and he began to smile broadly.

There was a light tap on the bathroom door.

That had to be Lizzie or Mickey trying to be cute. Soon to be followed by Dolby stereo kid screams and uncontrollable belly laughs.

"*Entrez.* Come right in you little assholes," he called.

The bathroom door opened slowly, and Carroll cupped his hands, ready to splash a tidal wave of water.

He managed to control his impulse just in time.

The man framed in the bathroom door was wearing a black London Fog raincoat, wire-rimmed eyeglasses, a white button down shirt and striped rep tie. Carroll had never seen him before. "Er. Excuse me, sir," the man said.

"Uh? Can I help you with anything?" Carroll asked.

The intruder looked like a banker, maybe an account executive at a brokerage firm. Carroll started to turn bright red. The blush immediately swept up to his forehead. He couldn't think of anything smart or funny to say, especially when he was still holding a rubber duck in his hand.

The man in the doorway spoke with Ivy League formality, not seeming to notice the duck at all. Nothing even close to a smile crossed his pale, thin lips.

"Sorry to bother you, to trouble you like this at home. I need you to get dressed and come with me, Mr. Carroll. The President wants to see you *tonight.*"

Chapter 12

AS EARLY AS the hot and steamy summer of 1961, John Kennedy had confided to close advisers that the stressful work of the presidency had already aged him ten years.

As he hurried down the plush, half-darkened corridors on the second floor of the White House, Justin Kearney, the forty-first President of the United States, was realizing the same inescapable truth that Kennedy had put into words. He had begun recently to question the motives that had driven him to gain his present residence at 1600 Pennsylvania Avenue.

Kearney was only forty-two years of age; by one month, he was the youngest American President ever elected and the first Viet Nam War veteran to reach the White House.

At 1:50 on Saturday morning, President Kearney took what he hoped would be a calming breath, then he entered the National Security Council conference room. Those already gathered there rose respectfully, Archer Carroll among them.

Carroll watched the President of the United States take his customary place at the head of the heavy oak conference table. He'd never seen Kearney so nervous, so clearly uncomfortable during any of his three previous visits to the White House.

"First of all, I thank all of you for getting here on such very short notice." The President sloughed off his wrinkled navy blue suit coat.

"I think everyone knows everyone else. One, maybe two exceptions . . . down there, sitting between Bill Whittier and Morton Atwater, is Caitlin Dillon. Caitlin is the Chief Enforcement Officer for the SEC.

"Down at the far *right* corner, gentleman in the tan corduroy sport coat, is Arch Carroll. Mr. Carroll is the head of the DIA's antiterrorist division. This is the group that was created following Munich and Lod." The President licked his lips nervously, then he gazed around the assembly.

Commissioner Michael Kane from the New York Police Department was asked to report first.

"Right now, we have men down inside the rubble of all the buildings that were hit. We have explosive-arson squads underground. They've already reported that Number 30 Wall as well as the Fed are badly damaged and extremely dangerous. Either building could collapse tonight."

Claude Williams of the Army Engineers was called to speak next. "There's a disturbing attention to detail in every area—that's what is particularly frightening about this. The river pier, the initial setup with the FBI, the elaborate study of Wall Street itself. I've never seen anything like this, and I'll tell you, I'm not standing here exaggerating for effect. It's as if a well-organized Army hit Wall Street. It's as if a war's been started down there."

Walter Trentkamp from the FBI was asked to go next. Trentkamp had been an old friend of Arch Carroll's father.

He'd even helped talk the younger Carroll into his first police job. Carroll leaned forward to listen to Walter's report.

"I agree with Mike Kane," Trentkamp said in a gravelly, imposing voice. "Everything has the veneer of an expert paramilitary operation. The explosives on Wall Street were placed for maximum damage. Our ordnance boys actually seem to admire the bastards. The whole operation was very thoughtfully devised.

"The plan must have taken months, *maybe years* to develop and execute with this high a level of success. PLO? IRA? Red Brigade? I assume we'll know more on that score before too long. They *have* to contact us eventually. They must want something. Nobody goes to this extreme without having some kind of demand in mind."

Each of those present was called upon to give a report, from the Secretary of Defense to the SEC Representative Caitlin Dillon. They all spoke briefly. Although Caitlin Dillon didn't have a great deal to add, she spoke with the kind of fluency where you could *see* the semicolons in her speech. Carroll found it challenging to take his eyes away from her face.

"Arch? Are you with us?"

Carroll gave the room a smile of vague embarrassment as he rose to address the group. All the important, mostly recognizable faces now swung his way.

Carroll was characteristically rumpled. His long brown hair and street clothes brought to mind underground witnesses and policemen called in drug-related grand jury trials. He'd thought about wearing his one good Barney's Warehouse sale suit, but then he had changed his mind.

Several of the principals attending the emergency session knew Carroll by reputation. As a modern-day policeman, Carroll was thought to be appropriately unorthodox, and effective. The team he supervised was credited with helping to make terrorists think twice about their raiding forays into the United States.

Carroll had also occasionally been characterized as a troublemaker; too much of a perfectionist for the Washington politicians to handle, too Off-Broadway theatrical at times. Moreover, he was increasingly becoming known as an Irish drunk.

"I'll try to be brief," Carroll began softly. "For starters, I don't think we can make the assumption yet that this *is* an established or known terrorist group.

"*If it is,* then it probably means one of two groups. . . . The Soviets, through the GRU—which could include François Monserrat. Or a second possibility—a *free-lance* group, probably sent out of the Middle East. Financed there, anyway.

"I don't believe anyone else has the organization and discipline, the technical know-how or money to manage something this complex." Carroll's intense brown eyes roamed the room. Why did his own remarks sound so hollow? "You can cross out just about everyone else as suspects." Carroll sat down.

Walter Trentkamp raised an index finger and spoke again. "For everyone's general information, we've set up an investigative unit down on Wall Street. The unit is inside the Stock Exchange Building, which suffered limited damage during the raid. Somebody from the New York P.D. already released Number 13 Wall to the press. So that's what we'll call headquarters.

"There's no such address, actually. The Stock Exchange is on Wall, but the actual address is Broad Street. *That* may be significant. See, we've made our first mistake, and we haven't even started the investigation."

Most everyone laughed inside the White House conference room, but the irony was lost on none of them. There would be more mistakes; a lot more mistakes before anything was resolved. No. 13 was surely an omen of things to come.

President Justin Kearney stood once again at his end of the massive conference table. His face registered the day's stress.

Justin Kearney said, "I need to clear the air about something else. Something that must never go beyond this room." The President paused, looked up and down the rows of his closest advisers. Then he went on.

"For several weeks now, the White House, Vice-president Elliot and I, have been receiving intelligence leaks, steady information about a dramatic counterinsurgent plot. Possibly a scenario involving the elusive François Monserrat."

The President paused again, deliberately pacing himself. Arch Carroll turned the name Monserrat over in his mind. "Elusive" didn't quite do Monserrat justice. There were times, indeed, when Carroll had seriously doubted the man's existence, times when he considered Monserrat as the *nom de guerre* of *several* different individuals acting in collaboration. He was in France one day, Libya the next. He might be reported in Mexico even as somebody else claimed to have seen him stepping aboard an unmarked plane in Prague.

Kearney continued. "Our intelligence people have learned that Middle Eastern and South American oil-producing countries have been considering a run on the New York Stock Market.

"This action was to be 'just' retribution for what they considered broken promises, even *outright fraud* practiced by U.S. banks and the New York brokerage houses.

"At the very least, the oil cartel hoped to initiate a short-term panic, which they alone would be in a position to take advantage of. *Is this rumored scenario related to tonight?* At this moment, I don't know . . .

"I have fears, though, that we're at the beginning of a grave international economic crisis. Gentlemen, it would not be an exaggeration to postulate, to prepare ourselves for the possibility, that the Western economy could effectively collapse on Monday, when the Market will reopen."

President Kearney's intensely blue eyes continued to make contact around the crisis table.

"We must find out *who* initiated the attack on Wall Street last night. We have to find out how they did it. We have to find out *why*. . . ."

Chapter 13

ARCH CARROLL'S HEAD was buzzing and his eyes stinging as he filed out of the White House conference room at 2:55 A.M. The other participants were mostly subdued and silent; they looked either somberly reflective, exhausted, or both.

Carroll had already started down a flight of creaking, thickly carpeted south White House stairs, when a hand rested on his shoulder, startling him.

Carroll twisted around to see Walter Trentkamp, impressive as ever at three in the morning.

"Trying to run out on me?" Trentkamp shook his head in the manner of a father about to chastise his son in the friendliest terms possible. "How have you been? I haven't seen you in a while. Have a minute to talk?"

"Hello, Walter. Sure we can talk. How about going outside? It might clear our heads a little."

Moments later, Carroll and Trentkamp walked side by side through the early morning mist shrouding Pennsylvania Avenue. The sky was a heavy gray slab covering the capital city. In the distance, the Washington Monument looked like the sword in the stone.

"I haven't seen enough of your homely face lately. Probably not since you and the kids moved back to the old homestead."

"It was kind of odd, going back there at first. Now it's good, the right choice. The kids call it their 'country house.' They think they live on a Nebraska farm. Riverdale, right?" Carroll grinned in spite of the hour.

"Wonderful kids. Your sister Mary Katherine's a gem, too." Trentkamp hesitated a moment. "How are *you* doing? *You're* the one who concerns me."

"Holding up pretty well. I'm all right. I'm doing fine." Carroll shrugged.

Walter Trentkamp shook his silver-gray head. His eyes held a knowing look, and Carroll felt tense. The cop part of Walter had a knack of wheedling his way inside you, so that you were left feeling transparent and obvious.

"I don't think so, Archer."

"No? Well I'm sorry. I *thought* I was all right." Carroll felt his lower back clutch and stiffen.

"You're not so fine. You're not even in the general ballpark of being fine. The late-night drinking bouts have become legend. Risks you're taking with your life. Other cops talk too much about you."

It was the wrong hour for this kind of talk. Carroll bristled. "That all, Father Confessor? That all you wanted to see me about?"

Trentkamp abruptly stopped walking. He laid a hand on Carroll's shoulder and squeezed it. "I *wanted* to talk to the son of an old friend of mine. I wanted to help if I could."

Arch Carroll turned his bleary eyes away from those of the FBI director. His face began to redden. "I'm sorry; I guess it *has* been a long day."

"It's been a long day. Been a long couple of years for you since Nora. You're close to being broken out of your unit in the DIA. They like the results, but not your working style. There's talk about replacing you. Matty Reardon's one name I've heard."

Arch Carroll felt his stomach suddenly dropping. He'd known this—somewhere in the back of his mind *he'd known this was coming.*

"Reardon'd be a good choice. He's a good company man. Good man, period."

"Arch, please cut the crap. You're playing games with someone who's known you thirty-five years."

Carroll frowned, and he began to cough in the manner of Crusader Rabbit. He felt like a real shit. "Awhh, hell, I'm sorry Walter. I know what you're trying to do."

"People *understand* what you've been through. I understand; please believe that, Archer. Everybody wants to help . . . I *asked* for you on this one. *I had to ask."*

Carroll shrugged his shoulders, but inside he was hurt. He hadn't known his reputation had slipped so badly, maybe even in Trentkamp's eyes.

"I don't know what to say. Not even a typical Bronx Irish wisecrack. Nothing."

"Talk to me on this one. Just talk to me, okay? . . . Don't go it alone. Will you promise me that?" Trentkamp finally spoke again, a voice of reason and understanding.

"Promise." Carroll nodded slowly.

Walter Trentkamp turned up the collar of his overcoat

against the early morning mist. Both he and Carroll were over six feet tall. They looked like father and son that morning in Washington.

"Good," Trentkamp finally said. "We'll need you on this nasty son of a bitch. We'll need you at your best, Archer."

Chapter 14

AT SIX O'CLOCK Saturday morning, December 5, a bleak Lexington Avenue subway train, its surface covered with scars of graffiti, lackadaisically rocked and rattled north toward the Pelham Bay station.

Colonel David Hudson sat in an inconspicuous huddle on an uncomfortable plastic train seat. He was wearing clothes no one would look at twice. Uninteresting clothes that created a street camouflage of drab gray and lifeless, boring brown. He realized it wasn't an altogether successful disguise because people had looked at him anyway. Their probing eyes invariably discovered the missing arm, the empty flap of his coat.

A series of hot and cold flashes coursed through his body as the train hurled itself north. He was drifting in and out of the present, remembering, trying to accurately replicate long hours spent at a Viet Nam firebase perimeter listening post. . . .

Every one of his senses had been at its sharpest back then. *Head cocked:* listening, watching, trusting no one but himself. . . . He needed exactly the same kind of clarity right now, the same kind of self-reliance.

From 14th Street, where he'd boarded the subway train, up past 33rd, 42nd, 59th Street, Hudson objectively contemplated the first days of his capture in Viet Nam.

He was vividly remembering the La Hoc Noh prison now . . .

La Hoc Noh Prison; July, 1971

Captain David Hudson's nervous system was a mass of fire. He felt each bruising, jarring bump, even the smallest stones underfoot, as four prison guards half carried, half dragged him toward the central hut at the La Hoc Noh compound.

Through the white glare of the Asian sun, he squinted at the pathetic hootch, with its tattered North Vietnamese flag and sagging bamboo walls.

The command post.

What an incredible joke this all was. What a cruel joke all of life had become.

Well-muscled once, clean-cut and always so perfectly erect, so proper, the U.S. Army officer was pitiful to behold now. His skin was uniformly wrinkled and sallow, almost yellow; his hair looked like it had been pulled out in great, diseased clumps.

He accepted the fact that he was dying. He weighed less than a hundred and fifteen pounds; he'd had the yellow shits literally for months without end. He'd gone beyond mere exhaustion; he lived in a shifting, hallucinatory world where he doubted his own sensations and ordinary perceptions.

All Captain Hudson possessed now was his dignity. He refused to give that up, too.

He would die with at least some essential part of himself

intact; that secret place deep inside that nobody could torture out of him.

The SNR officer, the one they had called Lizard Man, was waiting for him inside the command hootch. The North Vietnamese leader sat in silence, crouched behind a low, lopsided table.

He seemed to be posing for a photo beneath a twirling bamboo fan that barely stirred the hundred-and-five-degree air.

North Vietnamese cooking smells—green chili, garlic, lichee and durians, spoiled river prawns—made David Hudson suddenly gag. He clutched violently to his mouth. He felt himself begin to faint.

But he wouldn't allow that. No! Honor and dignity! That was everything. Honor and dignity kept him alive.

He stopped on his own mental command, drawing on the scant resources, the spirit that remained inside of him.

A guard punched David Hudson's jaw with a hard bare fist. Hot blood filled his mouth. He gagged on the metallic taste.

Honor and dignity. Somehow.

"You Cap-tan, ah Hud-sun!" the senior officer suddenly screeched.

He peered down onto the wrinkled note pad he always carried. His fingers struck hard into the page to emphasize certain words.

"Ho-Ho. Twen-six yea-ah old. Veet Nam, Lah-ose since nineteen-six-nine. Yow spy six yeah. Ho-Ho. You 'ssain! 'ssassin! Convic to *die,* Cap-tan."

The prison camp guards let Captain David Hudson fall toward the dirt floor, which was littered with gaping fish heads and rice.

Hudson's mind was reeling, crashing, exploding with sharp-pointed lights. His own private light show, his own palace of pain, he thought.

He'd understood only a few of the Lizard Man's fractured English words. *"Viet Nam ... spy ... assassin ... convicted to die."*

On the table sagging between him and the North Vietnamese officer, there was a teakwood game board.

Captain Hudson's eyes absently ran over the board surface. Games? *Why did they all love games?*

The Lizard Man snorted. A distorted smile appeared suddenly across his lower face. His jaw moved slowly, seemingly unattached to the rest of his skull.

"Yow play game? *Yow* play game me, *Hud-sun?"*

David Hudson's eyes were riveted to the low-slung game table, trying to gain focus.

Play a game with Lizard Man?

The board appeared to be real teak. It was precious wood, exotic and beautiful, incongruous in this sodden armpit of a place.

Even more striking were the hundreds of polished black and white stones, exquisite game playing pieces. They were circular in shape, convex on each side.

For a nearly lucid moment, David Hudson remembered a marble collection. Something magical and forgotten from his youth in Kansas. Father's farm. Collecting solids and cat's-eyes. Had he actually been a boy in this same lifetime? He couldn't seem to remember. *Die with dignity! Dignity!*

"Play game for your life? Ho?" the Lizard Man asked.

The game board was divided into vertical and horizontal lines, creating hundreds of intersections. There were 180 white stones, 181 black.

Beside the pile of black stones, the Lizard Man's hand rested on a bulky Moison-Nazant military revolver. One of his long yellowed fingers relentlessly tapped the table.

"Yow play. Play game me! Loser die!"

Captain Hudson continued to stare hard at the game board, at the beautifully gleaming teak table. *Focus, he thought. Concentrate. Die with dignity.*

He only vaguely understood what was happening. What did this man want from him now? It was some kind of joke, Hudson knew. One more way the Lizard Man had of torturing him.

The black and white stones seemed to be moving by themselves. Spinning, crawling like insects in his badly blurred, tunneling vision.

Finally, Hudson spoke up. His voice was surprisingly strong, angry, even defiant when he finally found it.

"I have never lost at the game of Go," Captain Hudson said. "You play, asshole!" *Dignity!*

Chapter 15

THE NEW YORK SUBWAY noisily braked at a Midtown station stop. The platform was bathed in eerie blue.

A few passengers on the early morning train were absently staring at David Hudson.

Hudson stared back at the passengers. He peered into their eyes, until most glanced away. The majority of American people were devoid of any basic integrity, any sense of themselves. Civilians tended to disappoint David Hudson again and again.

More listless passengers struggled onto the subway train at the West 86th Street stop. There were mostly older whites, time-bent men and women, small merchants, ciphers who managed or owned the rip-off clothing stores, the rip-off food markets, in Harlem and Upper Manhattan.

One of the men boarding at 86th, however, was completely different.

He appeared to be in his mid-thirties. His black hair was brushed straight back. He wore a tan cashmere overcoat with a paisley scarf, pressed navy dress slacks, super-Wasp duck boots. The impression he gave was of someone boarding a subway for the first time in his life and finding something amusing in the phenomenon of a slum on wheels.

He sat beside Hudson and immediately snapped open Saturday's *New York Times,* idly coughing into his fist. As the subway rumbled forward, he crisply folded the newspaper into quarters.

"You made the front page. Congratulations." Laurence Hadford finally offered a guarded, casual whisper.

His voice was controlled and as smooth as his expensive silk scarf. "I watched the intriguing spectacle on the six o'clock, the seven o'clock, the ten and eleven o'clock news shows. You've succeeded in baffling them."

"We've done reasonably well so far," Hudson nodded in agreement. "The difficult steps are still ahead, though. The true tests of the plan's legs, Lieutenant."

"You brought me a present, I hope? Christmas present?" As Laurence Hadford slid closer to Hudson on the plastic subway bench, Hudson could smell the man's citric cologne.

"Yes. Exactly as we agreed the last time."

David Hudson turned his head sideways for the first time. He stared into the blue eyes and persistently mocking half smile of Laurence Hadford. He didn't like what he saw. Never had. Not now and not back in Viet Nam either, when Hadford had been a smug young officer.

Laurence Hadford was impassively cool. He showed nothing of his emotions. The well-shaved face might have been a door closed on private rooms.

Reaching inside his coat, Hudson handed over a thick, overstuffed manila business envelope. The package bore no external marking, nothing to identify it in case there was any problem.

The envelope disappeared inside the rich softness of cashmere.

"There's one small hitch. A tiny problem has come up. The amount here isn't enough." Hadford smiled easily. "Not considering what's happened. What you've gone and done now. You've made this a very dangerous business arrangement for me. If you'd told me what you actually planned to do—"

"You wouldn't have helped us. You would have had too many doubts. You would have been scared shitless."

"My friend, I *am* scared shitless."

The subway train buckled slightly, but only seemed to slow minimally as it charged into the 110th Street station.

"We *agreed* on a figure before you did any work for us on Wall Street. Your fee, half a million dollars, has now been paid in full." Hudson felt a familiar alarm sounding inside him. "Any information you've supplied us, any personal risks you took, were infinitesimal considering your financial gain."

Hadford's perfectly capped white teeth gritted slightly. "*Please.* Don't tell me how well I've been paid. I know what you're all about now. You've got so much money, you couldn't *possibly* know what to do with it. Another half million is meaningless. What's another million for that matter? Don't be so uptight."

Colonel David Hudson managed to smile. "You know, perhaps you're right. Under the circumstances—what *is* another half million? . . . Especially if you're willing to do a little more investigation for us."

"I suppose for the right price I could be convinced, Colonel."

The next station David Hudson noted was 157th Street.

Between 110th and there, he and Laurence Hadford talked of the next steps to be taken on Wall Street; the kinds of information needed.

Stenciled numbers announced the train stop on mottled, blue standposts. A sullen black face slowly slipped past the spray-painted train windows. The brakes screeched, then let out a loud, gaseous *whump*.

The last few passengers besides Hadford and Hudson exited at the 157th Street stop. The subway doors slammed tightly shut. They were completely alone.

David Hudson felt himself tense. The blood coursed rapidly through his veins. All his senses were suddenly alert, and his perceptions had an astonishing clarity. Everything around him stood out as if illuminated by a harsh arc light.

"I'm sorry, Hadford."

As the train rumbled out of the station, the flashing knife appeared. What made David Hudson's parlor trick so unexpected was that the blade was so long—six inches at least, the handle another four.

The sharp blade jabbed hard and disappeared into Hadford's underbelly, just below the wall of his rib cage.

It shredded the cashmere coat, tearing fibrous material and parting soft flesh and clenched muscle with no effort. Almost instantly, the long blade reappeared.

As Laurence Hadford was sliding face up off the subway bench, Hudson relieved him of the weighty envelope. Hadford's eyes were staring sightlessly at the ceiling.

Colonel Hudson quietly slipped off at the next stop. He was shaking. His mind was filled with tiny white explosions. It was the first time he had ever harmed a fellow officer.

Once he was out on Broadway, David Hudson struggled onto a city bus headed south. The Lizard Man screeched at him like a jungle monkey as the bus lurched forward. The Lizard Man screamed so loudly, Hudson had to grit his teeth. The Lizard Man laughed and laughed as David Hudson escaped into the awakening daytime city.

Dignity!
Revenge!

Chapter 16

A LITTLE MORE than an hour later, Hudson reached the Washington-Jefferson Hotel. He had a room at the far end of a depressingly drab second floor hallway. He'd had this room for almost five weeks, and that was pushing his luck perhaps.

But the northern Times Square district was perfectly anonymous, and so convenient for the work he still had to do.

Hudson sat on the edge of his hotel room bed for a moment. His thoughts turned idly back to Laurence Hadford, but he knew he couldn't allow himself to dwell on the man.

He picked up the telephone, and dialed a local number in Manhattan.

"Hello, this is Vintage."

"Yes. This is David. . . . My number is 323." Hudson spoke in his usual soft but firm voice. "I can tell you exactly the kind of escort I'm looking for. She's between five foot six and five foot ten. She's between the ages of nineteen and twenty-six. I'll be paying cash."

Hudson waited, then he received a time, and a name for his "date." "In thirty minutes at 343 West Fifty-first. Thank you. I'll be expecting . . . Billie."

*   *   *

As she walked down the dimly lit second floor hallway Billie shut off her Vintage beeper. It would be tacky to get an electronic message while she was in the middle of a session.

The Washington-Jefferson, though? She shivered involuntarily.

Billie tapped on the hotel room door. The door swung open almost immediately—and she found herself surprised. He was good-looking, actually. His smile was open and pleasant. He was tall, slender, and . . . *uh-oh.*

She saw the catch! The left sleeve of his mufti shirt flopped open . . .

Billie couldn't feel *too sorry* for the man in the hotel doorway, though. There was nothing about him that inspired pity. He was certainly attractive, and his disability didn't seem to trouble him because he was not at all self-conscious.

"Hi. I'm Billie." She smiled courteously. "You're David?"

Colonel Hudson stared at her for a few seconds before answering. Her hair was rich, ash blond with thick bouncy curls. She was long-legged and thin. Her breasts were firm under a silk blouse. She wore a flattering straight skirt, dark stockings, and polished high heels.

"I'm sorry," he finally managed a smile. "I was staring, wasn't I? Come in. I didn't expect so beautiful a girl."

Billie smiled—as if she'd never heard any of this before. The hint of a blush rose along her cheekbones. The color sloped down her neck to the hollow of her throat.

"I'm sorry. I wasn't paying attention. It was Billie what? Your last name?"

"Just Billie," she smiled again.

Hudson gestured around his Spartan hotel room. "I know, it isn't exactly the Plaza."

For some reason, Billie found herself slowly relaxing with this one. He was easy to be with, and he sounded halfway intelligent.

Billie sat down on the edge of the bed.

Very nonchalantly, she unfastened the top button of her blouse, then the next.

"Sit down by me?"

Hudson did, and she lightly kissed his cheek. Her perfume drifted luxuriously up into his face.

"You said I was beautiful. I'd like to repay the compliment—you're very handsome."

Billie lightly slid her hands inside his shirt. She unbuttoned the middle two buttons.

Her touch was light and warm. Suddenly something extraordinary happened. Something unusual: Hudson began to feel.

A warning went off deep inside. He ignored it. But *something was wrong.*

She was so natural, so relaxed with him.

The lightest touch of fingers.

She was massaging him as she undressed.

The silk blouse delicately *shushed* off. Then the straight black skirt.

She stood over him—sheer dark stockings, garters, high heels.

There was a glistening droplet on her golden patch of hair.

He felt as if he were sinking through the mattress.

The inner warning sounded again. He ignored it.

He stopped and watched her breathe—so unexpectedly beautiful—and she smiled when she realized what he was doing.

"You *are* beautiful."

Her breasts were swelling. Hudson gently touched them, exploring their roundness, exploring each pink aureole.

She slid on top of him, and her blond hair glowed in the light from the overhead lamp. She rocked back and forth on top, a peaceful, swaying motion. Everything seemed so natural. The warning signals quieted, like a siren fading in the distance.

He was breathing faster and faster.

Her eyes shut, then opened, shut again.

Faster and faster, faster and faster.

He played with her as she gently rocked on top of him like a cresting sea wave. He manipulated her with his hand as she moved to her own rhythm.

Then her body stiffened and she began to fall forward against his chest. She arched dramatically backward, and jerked forward again. It was as if currents of electricity were passing through her body.

He was almost certain . . .

She was coming, her body shuddering.

This expensive escort from Vintage.

This beautiful prostitute was having an orgasm with him.

Billie. Just Billie.

Warning signals were going off like police sirens in his head. David Hudson listened this time. He didn't come. He never did.

Chapter 17

ARCH CARROLL WAS flying on People Express to Miami that morning. It wasn't the most enjoyable experience he'd ever had.

The airline service crew was young and inexperienced. They giggled during the seat belt and air bag pep talk. They sold cellophane-wrapped danishes in the aisle for a dollar.

The first possible break in the Green Band mystery had come quickly. Almost too quickly, Carroll thought cautiously. He'd spotted the clue himself the night before. Immediately, he was on the first flight to Florida to check it out.

He opened his eyes and stared the length of the aisle at two stewardesses talking in conspiratorial whispers. Then, about halfway through the two-hour-and-forty-minute flight, he got up wearily and trudged to the bathroom.

Everyone on the early bird flight looked thoroughly depressed and groggy, as if they'd risen way too early and their constitutions hadn't had time to quite catch up. Several business people had early edition newspapers with stark Wall Street bombing headlines.

Inside the bathroom, he cupped water in his hands and splashed it over his eyes. He took a tiny red plastic case out of his pants pocket.

When Nora had been sick, she'd used this container to hold her day's supply of Valium and Dilantin, and a few other prescriptions to help control seizures. Carroll slugged down a small yellow pill, a light upper to keep him alive.

He would have preferred a drink. An eye-opener Irish whiskey. Double Bloody Mary. But he'd promised Walter Trentkamp.

Carroll continued to stare at himself in the clouded airplane mirror. He thought about Green Band, as he examined the puffed, purplish bruises sagging under each eye. When it came to terrorists and their various specialties, Carroll had a long, reliable memory. During his first year with the DIA, all he'd done was to catalogue terrorist activities. He'd learned his early lessons well.

The hard evidence so far suggested . . . what? Maybe Soviet-inspired GRU activity? *Why*, though? Qadaffi? A very long shot there. The Wall Street plan showed too much patience for the usual Third World types.

Cubans? No. Provos? Not likely. Crazed American revolutionaries? Doubtful.

Who then? Most of all—*why?*

And how did the latest sketchy report from the Palm Beach Police Department fit? . . . *A South Florida drug dealer had been talking about the Wall Street attack the day before it happened?* The local hood had even dropped the unannounced code name—*Green Band!*

How would a South Florida drug dealer know anything about Green Band? What possible connection could there be?

Like everything so far, it didn't make much sense yet. It didn't seem to lead anywhere Arch Carroll particularly wanted to go. Certainly, he didn't want to be in southern Florida at this hour of the morning.

He rubbed his eyes, splashed more cold water on his face and looked back at his reflection. *Death warmed over,* he thought. It was like one of the photographs on wanted posters inside Post Office buildings, the kind that seem always to have been taken in dim lighting.

Carroll turned away from the mirror. It would soon be time to come down in the fantasy land of orange juice, Disney World, multimillionaire dope dealers, and hopefully Green Band.

Chapter 18

THE LOCAL FBI CHIEF, Clark Sommers, accompanied by an assistant, was there to meet Carroll at the arrival gate. As usual, Miami International Airport was experiencing an electrical brownout.

"Mr. Carroll, I'm Clark Sommers of the Bureau. This is my associate, Mr. Lewis Sitts."

Carroll nodded. His head ached from the flight and the effects of the upper he'd swallowed, which was just kicking in now, buzzing through his bloodstream.

"Walk and talk?" Sommers suggested. "We've got an awful lot of ground to cover this morning."

"Yeah, sure. Tell me something, though. Every time I come through this airport the lights are half out. Am I just imagining that?"

"I know what you mean. It can seem that way. Dope dealers claim the bright lights hurt their eyes." Clark Sommers flashed a very low key, cynical smile. He was *definitely* FBI all the way.

Sommers' assistant, Mr. Sitts, was wearing a lightweight blue sweater, tan golfing slacks and a matching Banlon shirt. The only thing missing were some espadrilles. Probably getting a promotional fee from Jantzen, Carroll thought. He tried to picture himself as a successful Florida police officer, but he couldn't make the right visual or emotional connection.

As they walked down the corridor, Carroll glanced at the cheery posters depicting surf and sun. They seemed to assault him personally. The sea was a shade too blue, the sun a touch too garish, the people having fun in the photographs a little too all-American beautiful for Carroll's taste. He yearned for New York, where at least there was a sense of reality to the gray, wintry half-tones of the familiar streets.

Sommers, fidgeting with a pair of sunglasses, spoke in a quietly assured voice.

"Mr. Carroll, one thing you probably should understand about this territory down here. For reasons of morale, in order to keep my men fully efficient and organized, this bust has to be mine. I have to make the calls. These are my men. You can understand that, I hope?"

Carroll didn't break stride. His face showed nothing. Almost all policemen were fiercely, irrationally territorial—something he knew from personal experience.

"Sure thing," he nodded. "This is your bust. All I want to do is talk to our drug dealer friend afterward. Ask him how he likes the nice Florida weather."

Chapter 19

THE SOUTH OCEAN BOULEVARD neighborhood was pretty much 1930s Spanish and Mediterranean in style: it was a six-block cluster of pastel blue and pink million-dollar estates. Carroll had the impression of everyone and everything lying dormant around him. People still sleeping peacefully at twenty past eight, flagstone patios sleeping, red clay courts sleeping at the Bath and Tennis Club, putting-green lawns and candy-striped cabanas and swimming pools—all sleeping, as if everything had been placed under a pleasant narcoleptic spell.

Clark Sommers spoke in a steady drone as they rode alongside the glittering, bluish-green ocean. "Real estate dealings on South Ocean here aren't exactly handled by Century Twenty-One. Most sales are actually arranged by Sotheby's, the big antiques outfit. Owners in Palm Beach, they think of their homes as valuable works of art."

"Reminds me of my neighborhood in New York," Carroll said.

Agent Sitts suddenly spoke up from the back seat. His long, well-tanned arm pointed between Carroll and Sommers. "That's our people up ahead there, Clark."

Gathered together at one of the quiet, perfect palm tree and sea grape intersections were six nondescript blue and green sedans.

The cars were parked in clear sight. Several of the FBI men were checking pump-action shotguns and Magnums out on the street.

"There goes the neighborhood," Carroll muttered. "I hope Sotheby's not showing any houses real early this morning."

The seven-vehicle caravan began to drift slowly up South Ocean Boulevard. Carroll glanced out at the peaceful neighborhood. Every house was set back from the street, isolated by closely cropped, bright green lawns that looked as if they'd been spray-painted on by meticulous gardeners.

A Miami *Herald* paperboy rode by in the opposite direction, mounted on a chugging mo-ped the same impossible blue color as the sky. He braked to a stop, scratched his crewcut and stared.

One of the FBI men signaled for him to keep going.

"That's it. Number 640," Sommers finally spoke up again. "That's where our friend Diego Alvarez lives."

Carroll tucked the loaded Magnum back into his shoulder holster. His stomach was rocking and rolling and the speed was lighting fires throughout his nervous system.

The FBI cars turned single file down an impressive side street off South Palm. They parked one after the other in front of two adjacent Spanish-style estates.

Car doors clicked open and shut very quietly.

Carroll slipped into step with a dozen or so gray-suited FBI agents. They trotted back toward the Alvarez place.

"Remember what I said back at the airport, Mr. Carroll. I give all the orders. I hope the capture of this guy's going to help you get what you want, but don't forget who's running the show, okay?"

"I remember."

Handguns and shotguns caught the hard, bright glint of the early morning Florida sun. Carroll listened to bolt-action apparatus slamming into ready. The FBI agents looked like young professional athletes, as they fanned out in the manner of a dance team.

Combat was *full* of visual paradox.

Carroll could see peaceful gulls rising from the sea, lazily sliding west to check the early morning sunrise party at the Alvarez house. Being a seagull seemed like a pretty good idea right now, but he had never been much for vocational planning.

The ocean wind was pleasantly warm. It carried a curious scent of salty fish and orange blossoms. The sun was already intense, too blinding to look at without a hand shade.

"Elegant house Diego has for himself. Run about three, three point five million with Sotheby's. When I give the signal we're going to put men in every wing of the villa."

Carroll remained silent. These were Sommers' men. This was Sommers' little planet where he reigned supreme. Carroll looked at the FBI man for a moment then finally took his handgun out again. He pointed the massive black barrel upward, a safety precaution where people were concerned, though not seagulls.

Just then, as Carroll knelt in a sniper-shooter's crouch, the heavy wood door of the Alvarez house came flying, crashing open. The door banged hard against the pink stucco front wall.

"What the fuck?" Clark Sommers whispered out loud.

Chapter 20

FIRST A BLOWZY white-haired woman in a tattered Maranca shirt stumbled outside. Then came a dark, well-built man bare chested in white trousers. All across the front lawn automatics and revolvers clicked off their safeties.

Then Diego Alvarez suddenly began to scream at the FBI men. "You motherfuckers! I shoot this old lady, man. She jus' innocent old lady. My cook, man. Put down all those motherfucker guns!"

Sommers was suddenly quiet. His beach-hero tan seemed to be fading.

Carroll glared in the direction of the drug dealer. The dark eyes of the man were frantic, desperate. There were flecks of saliva at the corners of his mouth. Then he turned to Sommers and said, "We have to take him. No matter what, we have to take him."

Sommers continued to be deadly quiet. He didn't even look over at Carroll.

"We *have* to take Alvarez. There are no other options."

Sommers barely glanced at Carroll. His look still said, *You're a New York City cop, this is my backyard, we do things my way down here.* Carroll had a vision of Alvarez escaping, and it was an exasperating vision. That was a possibility he had to prevent. Sommers didn't know what was involved here.

Diego Alvarez was awkwardly pulling the fat cook toward a red Cadillac parked outside the garage. The drug dealer had on white flare-bottom trousers. He was almost black in skin tone, as well-muscled as a pro fighter. The cook's eyes were as wide and round as coffee saucers.

Carroll tried to sort through the chaotic confusion of the moment. If he controlled his breathing, he could usually concentrate better, which was something he'd learned during his combat days.

He had an idea—one solution that came to mind.

Carroll waited for Alvarez to eye-check the FBI agents on the far left. As he did so, Carroll smoothly slid behind a flower-decked wall which concealed him from the drug dealer.

He waited a few seconds to see if he was missed, then continued hustling down behind the flowered wall, back through the side yard between Alvarez's and the house next door. Sparkling clean garbage cans stood in a neat silver row.

A green watering hose snaked up the walkway to a swimming pool with a floating rubber horse which looked ludicrous to Carroll as he started to run. He stopped when he was back out on the street where the FBI team had parked their cars.

A very disturbing thought entered his mind as he climbed into Sommers's Grand Prix.

He never would have done this if Nora was still

alive. . . . Never in a thousand years would he have tried this stunt.

Even as he had the thought, which cut deeply, Arch Carroll eased the FBI sedan to the corner, where he made a sweeping right turn, then a quick left onto South Ocean.

A block ahead, he saw Diego Alvarez backing into the Cadillac. He was still holding the white-haired cook against his bare chest. He was screaming wildly at the FBI men, his words lost now in the sea breeze.

Carroll kicked down hard on the accelerator. The sedan's engine twitched from first into third gear.

The car licked forward with a screech from the expensive radial tires put on for precisely this kind of breakneck situation.

Suddenly, Carroll's back arched, and his lungs sucked in a deep burst of air.

Don't think about this. Get it over with now.

His gun lay on the car seat right beside him.

The speedometer read *thirty, forty, fifty.*

Then the front wheels struck the concrete curb loudly with a jolting crunch. The car's front end leaped at least three feet in the air.

All four wheels were off the ground, and the vehicle moved in slow motion because *slow* is the speed at which a car flies.

Carroll double-pumped the sedan's brakes at the last possible moment.

"What the hell—" An FBI man yelled and dove to one side of the lawn.

"Holy shit!" He heard another high-pitched policeman's shout.

Diego Alvarez fired three wildly aimed shots at the

careening Pontiac and at Carroll himself inside the car. The sedan's windshield shattered, spitting glass fragments into Carroll's face.

The car was back on all four wheels again, bouncing over the lawn, and over a red tiled walkway. Suddenly it was skidding helplessly on the turf.

Carroll's foot stomped down full force against the gas pedal again. At the last possible instant before contact, he tucked his head down.

He held the steering wheel in a vise grip, held on as tight as his arms and hands possibly could.

The bounding FBI car crashed broadside into Diego Alvarez's cherry-red Cadillac. The convertible crumpled. It slid sideways like a hockey puck floating on ice and smashed into the side of the garage.

Half a dozen FBI officers were instantly sprinting across the front lawn.

They got there before the two interlocking cars had actually stopped moving.

Revolvers, riot shotguns, M-16 rifles were thrust inside the Cadillac's open front windows.

"Don't move, Alvarez. Don't move an inch," an FBI man screamed. "I said *don't move!*"

Carroll grunted, then he pushed himself painfully out of the wrecked Pontiac. He roared out Diego Alvarez's name at the top of his voice, surprised by his own intensity.

He was still yelling when he grabbed the shirtless drug dealer out of the hands of the FBI agents.

"Arch Carroll, State Department Special Terrorist Force! You have *no rights!* You hear me? . . . *How did you know about Green Band?* Who talked to you? You look at me!"

Diego Alvarez said, "Fuck you!" He spat into Carroll's face.

Carroll shuffled a little to his left, then hit the drug dealer with a sharp-looking right hand delivered to the mouth. Alvarez fell to the ground, already out cold.

"Yeah, fuck you, too!" said the former Bronx street-kid still lurking somewhere inside Carroll. He wiped the dope dealer's saliva from his cheek.

Clark Sommers' mouth fell open, creating a surprised *O* at the center of his face. A few other Florida FBI studs just shook their heads.

At the FBI office on Collins Avenue in Miami, Diego Alvarez was taken inside a small interrogation room where he told Carroll everything he knew.

"I don't know *who* they are, honest, man. Somebody jus' want you down here to Florida," he said with almost believable sincerity. Because he had been busted with three hundred and fifty thousand dollars' worth of cocaine, and because his prospects of freedom looked grim, he didn't have much to gain by lying. Carroll studied the man as he spoke.

"I swear it. I don't know nothin' more, man. But I got a feelin' somebody playin' some kind of games with you. They set me up, my big mouth. But somebody playin' wit' *you*. . . . Somebody jus' want you come here 'stead of someplace else. They playin' wit' *you,* man. They playin' wit' you real good."

Carroll suddenly wanted to put his head down on the interrogation table in front of him. He'd been used, and he had no idea why. All he knew was that whoever was doing it was smart. They were telling him: *See, we can manipulate you—any which way we like.*

Carroll eventually wandered outside the Miami FBI building and leaned against the warm-baked white stucco wall.

He tried to let the Florida sun soothe his weary brain. He thought that Miami might be a better climate for playing Crusader Rabbit than New York.

He was relatively certain about a couple of disturbing things. . . . The Green Band group, whoever they were, *knew* who he was, and that he would be assigned to the investigation. *How* did they know? What should that tell him about who they might be? . . . They seemed to want him to know how superior, how well organized they were. They wanted him to be a little in awe—and frankly, right now anyway, *he was*.

On the plane home, Eastern—the wings of man—Arch Carroll had two beers, then two Irish whiskeys. He could have gone for another two Irish, but he'd promised his rabbi Walter Trentkamp—promised Uncle Walter *something* he couldn't quite remember. Finally, he slept the rest of the way home to New York.

He had a real nice dream on the flight, too. Carroll dreamed that he quit his job with the DIA's antiterrorist division. He and the kids and Nora went to live on the nicest, sugar-white beach in Florida.

Chapter 21

BEFORE THE BREAK of dawn on Sunday morning, Caitlin Dillon waded through a river of ice and slush that rose four inches above her ankles.

Once she successfully emerged on Fifth Avenue, the Director of Enforcement for the SEC's Division of Trading and Exchange hailed a cab which reluctantly ferried her down to the 14th Street Police and National Guard Barricades.

From 14th Street, Caitlin was transferred by a snazzy police blue and white down into the smoldering chaos and confusion of the financial district itself.

The thirty-block ride went by amazingly fast. There were no working traffic lights below 14th Street. There was almost no other traffic on any of the downtown streets.

The sergeant driving the police car was as good looking as an actor in a Hollywood cop show. He had long blue-black hair curling over his uniform collar. His name was Signarelli.

"Never seen *everything* this bad." The police sergeant revealed a nasal Brooklyn accent when he spoke.

"Can't even call in to your normal communications

desk. Nerve center they set up is always busy, too. Nobody knows what the Army's doing. What the FBI guys are doing either. It's completely nuts!"

"How would you handle it?" There was nothing patronizing in the question. Caitlin was always curious about the rank and file. That was one reason she made a good boss at the SEC. A second reason was that she was smart, so knowledgeable about Wall Street and the workings of business that most of her associates held her in awe. "If this was your show, what would you do, Sergeant?"

"Well . . . I'd hit every terrorist hangout we know about in the city. We know about a hell of a lot of them, too. I'd blow into their little maggot nests. Arrest everybody in sight. That way, we'd sure as hell get some information."

"Sergeant, I believe that's what teams of detectives have been doing all night. Over sixty separate squads of NYPD detectives. But the maggots are just not cooperating on this one."

Caitlin arched her eyebrow, then smiled gently at the cop.

Predictably, he asked her for a date next, and just as predictably Caitlin turned him down.

With police and Army helicopters whirring overhead, Caitlin stood still and numb on the northwest corner of Broadway and Wall.

She allowed her eyes to roam across the most chillingly surreal scene she hoped to view in her lifetime.

What appeared to be billions of tons of granite block, of gray stone, shattered glass, concrete and mortar had crashed down onto Wall Street and Broad Street and Pell, and all the narrow, interconnecting alleyways. According to the latest Army Intelligence estimate, as many as sixty separate *plastique* bombs had detonated at 6:34 Friday evening. The police theory was that the bombs had been exploded by sophisticated radio signals. The signals could have been transmitted from as far away as ten to twelve miles.

Caitlin craned her neck to gaze up at nearby No. 6 Wall Street.

She winced as she observed the sheared, swinging clumps of wiring: thick elevator cables dangling between the highest floors of the office building. Here and there, patches of sky shone through great yawning holes in the building's walls. The overall effect reminded her of a doll house disemboweled, utterly destroyed by a child in a temper tantrum.

She stood all alone, shivering and cold on the stone portal of the New York Stock Exchange. She couldn't stop herself from impassively staring at the abysmal destruction, the incomprehensible damage on Wall Street. More than anything, she wanted to be sick.

She saw an oil painting, a Yankee sailing clipper hanging absurdly in a district office with two of the room's walls blown away.

In the foyer of an adjacent building, an overturned copier had apparently collapsed through several floors before striking the unyielding marble in the lobby. She could see the shattered screens of computer terminals and the melted remains of keyboards that reminded her of some nightmare art form. All over the littered, desolate street, police and hospital emergency vehicles were flashing bright red and blue distress signals.

Caitlin Dillon could feel a cold, deadweight pushing

down on her. Her body was numb. Her ears buzzed softly, as if there had been a sudden drop in air pressure.

She couldn't stop a disturbing feeling of nausea, of sudden weakness in both her legs.

She understood what many of the others still didn't— *that an entire way of life had quite possibly been destroyed, here, on Friday night.*

Inside No. 13, Caitlin was confronted immediately by noisy squads of secretaries typing frantically in the marble and stone entryway corridors. Stock Exchange clerks milled around with a kind of busy uselessness, carrying clipboards with a hollow show of self-importance, carting files from one office to another.

Caitlin took in the command post scene and then, as she stepped nimbly around broken glass and debris that had been shaken loose from the ceiling, she was surrounded by heavily armed policemen who demanded to see her identification.

She smiled to herself as she showed her ID. *No one knew who she was;* not a single one of them recognized her here in the Stock Exchange foyer.

How very typical that was. Damn it, how typical.

For the past three years, the SEC's Director of Enforcement had been a most unlikely Wall Street figure: Caitlin Dillon was clearly a force, yet a person of mystery to almost everybody around her.

Women in general had only been permitted on the floor of the Stock Exchange since 1967. Nevertheless, the idea hadn't particularly caught on. A prominent sign in the visitor's gallery of the Exchange still read:

WOMEN MAKE POOR SPECULATORS. WHEN THROWN UPON THEIR OWN RESOURCES, THEY ARE COMPARATIVELY HELPLESS. EXCELLING IN CERTAIN LINES, THEY ARE

FORCED TO TAKE BACKSEATS IN SPECULATION. WITHOUT
THE ASSISTANCE OF A MAN, A WOMAN ON WALL STREET
IS LIKE A SHIP WITHOUT A RUDDER.

Caitlin Dillon had actually inherited her job because of
her predecessor's bad luck in the shape of a fatal coronary.
Caitlin knew that insiders had predicted she wouldn't last
two months. They compared the fateful situation with a
politician's wife taking over for an unexpectedly invalid
husband. Caitlin was called by some "the interim enforcer."

For that reason, and some strong personal ones from her
past, she had decided that—for however long she might
last in the job—she was going to become the sternest,
hardest SEC Enforcement Officer since Professor James
Landis had been doing the hiring himself. What did she
have to lose?

She was, therefore, stubbornly serious. Some said
Caitlin Dillon was unnecessarily obsessed with white-
collar criminal investigations, with skillfully prosecuting
malfeasance by senior officers of major American Corporations.

"I'll tell you something off the record," Caitlin had once
said to a dear friend, Meg O'Brian, the financial editor of
Newsweek. "The ten most wanted men in America are all
working on Wall Street."

As the "interim" Enforcement Officer at the SEC,
Caitlin Dillon made a lot of news very fast. The mystery of
Caitlin Dillon—how she had surfaced virtually from
nowhere—grew each week she held on to the job. The
powerbrokers on the Street still wanted to replace her, but
suddenly they found they couldn't do so very easily.
Caitlin was too good at what she did. She'd become too

visible. She was almost instantly a symbol for the disen-franchised in America's financial system.

At 7:45 that morning, Caitlin finally reached her office inside No. 13 Wall. It was respectably large.

She removed her coat and, as she started to sit down, took a deep breath.

On her desk lay a damage report prepared for her the previous night. As her eyes quickly scanned the page, she felt a deepening despair at the sheer amount of destruction done.

The Federal Reserve Bank.
Salomon Brothers.
Bankers Trust.
Affiliated Fund.
Merrill-Lynch.
U.S. Trust Corporation.
The Depository Trust Company.

The list went on to detail fourteen downtown New York buildings that had been partially or completely destroyed.

She closed her eyes, placing the palm of her hand flat against the surface of the report. *Fourteen different build-ings in the Wall Street financial district—the whole thing was beyond her, out of control by any measure.*

She opened her eyes.

It was the start of the second day of the formal investi-gation of Green Band, and she knew no more than she'd known before. This disturbing state of ignorance settled in-side her head like a spreading black cloud.

It was going to be a long, long Sunday.

Chapter 22

CARROLL STRODE BRISKLY from a State Department limousine toward the ominous gray stone entranceway to No. 13 Wall.

At least Green Band had left this building mostly intact—a fact that caused him to wonder. If a terrorist cell was going to strike out at U.S. capitalism, why wouldn't they destroy the Stock Exchange?

Carroll had on a knee-length, black leather topcoat which Nora had given him the Christmas before her death. At the time she'd joked that it made him look like a tough guy hero. The coat was now one of his few personal treasures; that it was a little too tight under the arms didn't matter. There was no way he'd have it altered. He wanted it exactly as it was when Nora had given it to him.

Carroll was smoking a crumpled cigarette. Sometimes on the weekends he wore the coat and smoked crumpled cigarettes when he took Mickey Kevin and Clancy to New York Knick or Ranger games.

It made both kids laugh hysterically. They told him he was trying to look like Mel Gibson in the movies. He wasn't, he knew. Gibson was trying to look like him: like some nihilistic, tough-guy city cop.

Hurrying down the long, echoing corridors, Carroll pulled his way out of the leather coat. For a few long strides, he left it cape-like over his shoulders.

Then he folded it over one arm, in the hope that he'd look a little more civilized. There were a lot of very straight business people in the hallowed halls of No. 13 Wall Street.

Carroll pushed open leather-covered doors into a formal meeting room thick with perspiration and stale tobacco smoke. The room where the New York Stock Exchange professional staff usually met was the size of a large theater.

The scheduled meeting was already in progress. He was late. He was also weary from his flight, and his nerves—kept moderately alert by an infusion of amphetamine—were beginning to complain.

He glanced at his watch. There was another long day ahead of him.

Carroll quickly glanced around the shadowy room. It was filled with New York City police, and U.S. Army personnel, with corporate lawyers and investigators from the major banks and brokerage houses on Wall Street. The only seats left were way in front.

Groaning under his breath, Carroll crouched low and made his move toward the front row. He clumsily climbed over gray and blue pinstriped legs, and over someone's abundant lap. It felt like everybody in the room was staring at him—which was probably true enough.

The speaker was saying, "Let me tell you how to make a hell of a lot of money on Wall Street. All you have to do is steal a little from the rich, steal a little from the middle rich, steal a lot from the lower rich . . ."

Nervous laughter cascaded around the vast meeting room. It was a muted, mirthless outbreak that sounded more like a release of fears than anything else.

The speaker went on, "The Wall Street security system simply *doesn't* work. As you all know, the computer setup here is one of the most antiquated in all of the business world. That's why this disaster *could* happen."

Carroll finally sat down, sliding lower and lower until only his head peeked above the theater's gray velvet seat back. His knees were actually pressed against the wooden stage in front.

"The computer system on Wall Street is a complete disgrace . . ."

Carroll's eyes finally rose and took in the meeting's speaker. *Jesus.* He was taken aback by the sight of Caitlin Dillon on the podium. Her hair was bobbed at the shoulders, a sleek chestnut-brown. Long legs, slender waist. Tall—maybe five foot ten.

She was staring down at the first row. Her brown eyes were very calm, measuring everything they saw. Yes, she was staring directly down at Carroll.

"Are you expecting trouble during my briefing, Mr. Carroll?" Her eyes had fastened onto his Magnum, his beat-up leather shoulder holster. He was embarrassed by her question and the way his name had sounded through her microphone. Those pale red lips seemed to be mocking him.

Carroll didn't know what to say. He shrugged and tried to sink a little deeper into his seat. Why didn't he have one of his usual wisecracks to throw back at her?

Caitlin Dillon smoothly switched her attention back to

the audience of senior police officers and Wall Street businessmen. She resumed her briefing at exactly the point where she had interrupted herself.

"In the past decade," she said, and her next chart efficiently appeared on the screen at her back, "foreign investment in the United States has skyrocketed. Billions of francs, yen, pesos, deutschemarks have flowed into our economy to the sum of eighty-five billion dollars. . . ."

He watched attentively. Nothing could have drawn his eyes away from her, short of a second Wall Street bombing raid . . .

There was a twinkle in her eyes, an unexpected hint of sweetness in her smile. Was it really *sweetness* though? How could she hold down the job she had if she was sweet? Sweet was not in the Wall Street lexicon.

She was chic—even in a conservative, salt and pepper tweed business suit.

Most of all, though, she looked *untouchable.*

That was the single word that seemed to sum up Caitlin Dillon best.

Untouchable.

His attention drifted back to her speech, which was a succinct description of the Green Band emergency, of the current state of Wall Street's insufficient computer records, and the stoppage of all international transfers of funds.

She had some sobering and scary material up there on the podium.

"Surprisingly, there's still been no further contact by the terrorist group. *Whatever* kind of group they are. . . . As you may know, *no* actual *demands* were made. No ultimatums. Absolutely no reason has been given so far for what happened on Friday.

"There'll be another meeting after this, for my people and for the analysts. We have to get something going with the computers before the Market opens on Monday. If not. . . . I would expect major unpleasantness."

The meeting room was suddenly still. The scraping of feet, all paper shuffling stopped.

"Are we talking about a Stock Market panic? Some kind of crash? What sort of *major unpleasantness?*" someone called out.

Caitlin paused before she spoke again. It was obvious to Carroll that she was choosing her next words with extreme care and diplomacy.

"I think we all have to recognize . . . that there *is a possibility,* even a likelihood of some form of Market panic on Monday morning."

"What constitutes a panic in your mind? Give us a for-instance." A senior Wall Street man spoke.

"The Market *could* lose several hundred points very quickly. In a matter of hours. That's *if* they decide to open on Monday. In Tokyo, London, Geneva, the subject's still under discussion."

"Are we talking about a potential Black Friday situation? Are you saying there could actually be a Stock Market crash?" A voice rose from the back of the auditorium.

Caitlin frowned. She recognized the speaker, a stiff, stuffy bean counter from one of the larger Midtown New York banks.

"I'm not saying anything yet. As I suggested before, if we had a more modern system of computers down here, if Wall Street had joined the rest of the twentieth century—we'd know a lot more. Tomorrow is Monday. We'll all see what happens then. We should be *prepared*. That's what I'm suggesting—preparedness. *For a change.*"

With that, Caitlin Dillon abruptly stepped down off the auditorium stage. As Carroll watched her walk alone to the back doors of the room, he became conscious of another figure approaching him from the side.

He turned in his seat and saw Captain Francis Nicolo from the New York City Bomb Squad, a cop who liked to think he was something of a dandy in his three-piece pin-striped suits and sleek, waxed moustache.

"A moment, Arch," Nicolo said, and gestured for Carroll to follow.

They hurried out of the room and along various dimly lit Stock Exchange corridors, Carroll trailing behind.

Nicolo opened the door to a small inner office tucked directly behind the Trading Floor. He closed it with a secretive gesture when Carroll was inside.

"What's happening?" Carroll asked, both curious and slightly amused. "Talk to me, Francis."

"Check this," Nicolo said. He pointed to a plain cardboard box propped on the desk. "Open it. Go ahead."

"What is it?" Carroll hesitantly stepped toward the desk. He laid the tips of his fingers lightly against the box lid.

"Open it. Won't bite your widgit off."

Carroll removed the lid. "Where the hell did this come from?" he asked. "Christ, Frank."

"Janitor found it behind a cistern in one of the men's rooms," Nicolo answered.

Carroll stared at the device, at the length of shiny green ribbon that was wound elaborately around it. *Green Band.*

"It's harmless," Nicolo said. "It was never meant to go off, Arch."

Arch Carroll continued to stare at the makings of a professional terrorist's bomb. *It was never meant to go off, he thought. Another warning?*

"They could have totaled this place," Carroll said with a sick feeling.

Nicolo made a clucking sound with his tongue and the roof of his mouth. "Easily," he said. "Plastique, like all the others. Whoever did it knew what the hell he was up to, Arch."

Carroll wandered over to the office window and peered down into the street, where he saw New York cops standing all over the place, where he saw the incomprehensible war zone.

Chapter 23

USING A SINGLE TINE of his fork, Sergeant Harry Stemkowsky surgically punctured each of the three sunny-side-up eggs staring up from his breakfast platter.

He lathered on a thick wave of ketchup, then buttered and spread strawberry preserves on a row of four, hot-toasted bialy halves. He was ready to rock and roll.

The superb, greasy spoon meal was his usual, corn beef hash, eggs and bialy breakfast. The place was the Dream Doughnut and Coffee on 23rd Street and Tenth Avenue. The meal arrived at the table approximately three hours into his dayshift driving for Vets. Stemkowsky had been looking forward to the food all through his first dreary hours on the road.

Harry Stemkowsky almost always went through the same exact thought process while he was devouring breakfast at the Dream . . .

It was so unbelievably good to be out of that piss and shitting hole Erie VA Hospital. It was just so goddamn tremendous to be alive again.

He had a valid reason to keep going now, to get really psyched about his life . . .

And it was all thanks to Colonel David Hudson. Who happened to be the best soldier, the best friend, one of the best men Stemkowsky had ever met. Colonel Hudson had given all the Vets another chance. He'd given them the Green Band Mission to get even.

Later that same morning, as he slalomed through the deep slush of Jane Street in the West Village, Colonel David Hudson thought he might be seeing apparitions. He finally leaned his head out of the half-rolled Vets taxi window. His green eyes sparkled intensely against the street's murky gray.

He shouted ahead into the cold driving rain, the dripping winds ripping and grabbing at his face. "You're going to *rust* out there, Sergeant. Get your pitiful ass inside."

Harry Stemkowsky was solidly perched outside in his familiar, battered aluminum wheelchair. He was huddled zombielike against the drowning rain, right in front of the Vets garage entrance.

It was an incredibly moving sight, probably more sad than weird, Hudson thought. A true retrospective on what was ultimately accomplished in Viet Nam.

There was Harry Stemkowsky, as poignant as any journalist's picture taken of the wounded in the Southeast Asia combat zone. Hudson could feel a tightening of his jaw muscles, and the beginnings of an old rage. He fought against it. This wasn't the time to allow himself the luxury of personal feelings. This wasn't the time to wallow in old, pointless anger.

Stemkowsky was grinning broadly by the time David Hudson finally jogged to the weathered door of the Vets garage.

"You're section eight for life, Sergeant. You're out of your mind," Hudson said firmly. "No explanations accepted."

Actually though, Hudson was beginning to smile. He knew why Stemkowsky was waiting outside, knew all of the Vets' Sad Sack stories by heart now. He was betting everything on knowing the Vets at least as well as he knew their military histories.

"I-I wha-wanted to be ri-right he-here. When, when you got in. That-that-that's all it was, Cah-Cah-Colonel."

Hudson's voice softened. "Yeah, I know, I know. It's real good to see you again, Sergeant. You're still an asshole, though."

With an audible sigh, Colonel Hudson suddenly bent low. He then easily scooped up the hundred-and-thirty-seven-pound bundle of Harry Stemkowsky with his powerful good arm.

Since the spring offensive of 1971, Stemkowsky had been a helpless cripple. Harry Stemkowsky had also been a violent, totally incurable stutterer ever since he'd been splattered with seventeen rounds from a Soviet SKS automatic rifle. A pitiful wreck, right up until a few months ago, anyway.

As he pushed his way to the top of the cramped, mildewed stairway inside Vets, Hudson decided not to think about Viet Nam anymore. This was supposed to be an R&R party. Green Band was a rousing operational success so far.

George Thorogood's "Bad to the Bone" blared loudly from the room above. Good tune. Good choice.

"It's the Colonel himself!"

As he stalked inside a large, drab yellow room on the

second floor, Hudson heard shrill hollers and shouts all around him. For a moment he was embarrassed by the clamor. Then he thought about the fact that he'd given these twenty-six veterans another lease on their lives, a purpose that transcended the bitterness they had brought back from Viet Nam.

"The Colonel's here! Colonel Hudson's here."

"Well, shit. Hide the good Johnny Walker booze. . . . Just kidding, sir."

"How the hell are you, Bonanno? Hale? Skully?"

"Sir . . . we goddamn did it, didn't we!"

"Yes, we did. So far, anyway."

"Sir! It's great to see you. Went just like you said it would."

"Yeah. The *easy* part went great."

Chapter 24

THE TWENTY-SIX VETS continued to cheer. Hudson shielded his eyes as he stared around at the dingy room where they'd been plotting together for almost a year and a half.

He scanned the rows of familiar faces, the scraggly, homecut beards, the unfashionably long hairstyles, the drab green khaki jackets of the Vets. He was home. He was home and he was obviously welcome.

He could feel the vibrations of unadulterated warmth that these men felt toward him. And for one brief moment Colonel David Hudson almost lost control.

Hudson finally offered a wry conspiratorial smile. "It's good to see you all again. Carry on with your party. That's *an order.*"

Hudson ambled on, gripping hands, greeting the rest of the Vets group: Jimmy Cassio, Harold Freedman, Mahoney, Keresty, McMahon, Martinez—men who hadn't been able to fit back into American society after the war, men he'd recruited for Green Band.

As he walked, Hudson thought about his men; his final combat command; the final mission.

The Vets were antisocial, chronically unemployable; they were dramatic losers by the standard American measurements of success and accomplishments. At least half of them still suffered some form of PTSD, the Post Traumatic Stress Syndrome so common among war veterans.

The men packed into the cabdrivers' locker room had performed spectacularly. Every one of them had served under Hudson at one time or another. Each was a highly trained technical specialist; each had a totally unique skill, which no one other than Hudson seemed to want or need in civilian society.

Steve "the Horse" Glickman and Pauly "Mr. Blue" Melindez were the finest rifleman-sniper team Hudson had ever commanded.

Michael Doud and Joe Barreiro were experts at ordnance, at assembling and creating complex plastique explosives.

Manning Rubin could have been making a thousand a week for either Ford or GM. *If* his skill at fixing automobiles had been matched by patience, just a little ability to handle bullshit . . .

Davey Hale had an encyclopedic knowledge of just about everything, including the Stock Market.

Campbell, Bowen, Kamerer and Generalli were high-caliber professional soldiers and mercenaries.

"All right gentlemen. We have to do some homework now," Hudson finally spoke. "This is the last time we'll have the chance to review these details and any of our operating schedules. If this sounds like a formal military briefing, that's because *it damn well is*."

Hudson paused and looked around at the circle of assembled faces. Each was turned toward him with intense concentration.

"Personal anecdote, gentlemen. . . . At the highly thought of JFK School at Fort Bragg, they repeatedly told us that 'genius is in the details.' When the truth of that finally sunk in, it held like nothing I've ever learned before or since . . .

"So I want to go over the final details one last time. Maybe two last times with all of you. Details, gentlemen . . ."

Vets One had purposely modeled his presentation after the concise and technical Special Forces field briefings. He wanted the men to vividly remember Viet Nam now. He wanted them to remember how they'd acted: with daring and courage, with dedication to the United States.

Hudson could feel his body pulsing and tingling lightly. He spoke to the men without using written notes.

For nearly two and a half hours, Hudson painstakingly reviewed every scenario, every likely and even unlikely change that might occur up to and including the end of the Green Band mission. He used memory aids: reconnaissance topographical maps, mnemonics for memorizing; Army-style organization charts.

A gravelled voice finally sounded from the shadowy rear of the Vets locker room.

One of the combat mercenaries, a Southern black named Clint Hurdle, had taken the floor. "Why you so sure there won't be no attacks of conscience? This going to heat up now, Colonel. Who says nobody going to fuck up and run?"

There was a hush around the room.

Hudson considered the question carefully before an-

swering. He had posed almost the same question hundreds
of times in his own head.

"*Nobody*, not a single one of you men, broke during
combat. . . . Not even in a war none of you wanted or believed in. . . . *Nobody broke in POW camps!* . . . None of
you will break now, either. I'm prepared to bet everything
on that."

There was an uncomfortable silence after the question
and emotional answer. David Hudson's intense eyes
slowly surveyed the Vets dressing room one more time.

He wanted them to feel that he was sure about everything he'd just said. Even though it might not look it, every
man in the room had been handpicked from hundreds of
possible vets. Every soldier in the room was special.

"If any one of you wants to leave, this is the time. . . .
Right now, gentlemen. This afternoon. . . . Anybody? . . ."

One Vet slowly started to clap. Then the rest of them.

Finally, all twenty-six men were solemnly clapping their
hands. Whatever was going to happen, they were together.

Chapter 25

COLONEL HUDSON NODDED: the military commander once again took control.

"I've saved the foreign travel assignments until last.

"I'm not going to entertain any discussion, any disagreement over these assignments. The operational environment is already confused. We will not be confused. That's another reason we're going to win *this war.*"

Colonel Hudson walked to a long wooden table. He began to pass out thick, official-looking portfolios. Each one had a white tag pasted onto the front.

Inside the envelopes were counterfeit U.S. passports and visas, first-class airplane tickets, generous expense monies; copies of elaborate topographical maps from the briefing. *The genius was in the details.*

"Cassio will go to Zurich," Hudson announced.

"Stemkowsky and Cohen have Israel and Iran . . .

"Skully will go to Paris. Harold Freedman to London, then on to Toronto. Jimmy Holm to Tokyo. Vic Fahey to Belfast. The rest of us stay put right in New York."

A schoolboy's groan went up. Hudson silenced it with a short, chopping hand motion.

"Gentlemen. I'll say this one time only, so you have to remember it. . . . While you're in Europe, in Asia, in South America, it is absolutely *essential* that you act, that you groom and dress yourselves in the *particular style* we've laid out for you.

"All your air travel arrangements are first class. All your clothing and restaurant expense money is meant to be *spent*. Spend that money. Throw it around. Be more extravagant than you've ever been in your lives. Have fun, if you *can* under the circumstances. That's an order!"

Hudson eased up. "For the next few days, you have to be self-assured, successful American business types. You have to be like the people we've been studying on Wall Street for the past year. *Think* like a Wall Street man, *look* like one, *act* like a high-powered Wall Street executive.

"At 0430, you'll be given corporate haircuts, shaves, and—believe it or not—manicures.

"Your wardrobes have been carefully selected for you, too. They're Brooks Brothers and Paul Stuart—your favorite shops, gentlemen. Your shirts and ties are Turnbull and Asser. Your billfolds are from Dunhill. They contain credit cards and plenty of cash in the appropriate denominations you'll need in your respective countries."

Colonel Hudson paused. His eyes slowly roamed across the room.

"I think that's all I have to say. . . . Except one important thing . . . I wish you all the very best luck possible. I wish you the best, in the future after this mission. . . . *I believe in you. Believe in yourselves.*"

Chapter 26

IT WAS THREE O'CLOCK on Sunday afternoon when Carroll kicked both weathered Timberland work boots up on his desk inside No. 13. He yawned until his jaw cracked.

He'd finished four draining and futile interrogations. He'd been lied to by the very best—the most dangerous *provocateurs* and terrorists from all around New York.

Carroll had purposely chosen a cramped office for himself, tucked away at the back of the Wall Street building. His small but hardy DIA group, a half-dozen unorthodox police renegades, two efficient and extremely resilient secretaries, surrounded the uninspiring office in a satellite of Wall Street–style cubicles.

Paint peeled from the walls of Carroll's office like diseased skin; the windowpane had been shattered courtesy of Green Band. He'd tacked a square of brown paper to the hole but rain soaked through anyway.

The first four suspects Carroll had interviewed were known terrorists who lived in the New York City area: two FALN, a PLO, an IRA fund-raiser. Unfortunately, the four were no more knowledgeable about the Wall Street mystery than Carroll was himself. There was *nothing circulat-*

ing on the street. Each of them convincingly swore to that after exhaustively long sessions.

Carroll wondered how it could be possible.

Somebody had to know something about Green Band. You couldn't calmly blow away half of Wall Street and keep it a state secret for over forty hours.

The scarred and rusted wooden door into his office opened again. Carroll watched the door over the smoking cardboard lid of his coffee container.

Mike Caruso, who worked for Carroll at the DIA, finally peeked inside. Caruso was a small, skinny, ex-office cop, with a black fifties pompadour pushed up high over his forehead. He habitually wore wretched Hawaiian shirts outside his baggy pants, attempting to create a splash of colorful identity in the usually drab police world. Carroll liked him immensely for his dedicated lack of style.

"We got Isabella Marqueza up next. She's already screaming for her fancy Park Avenue lawyer. I mean the lady is fucking *screaming* out there."

"That sounds promising. Somebody's upset at least. Why don't you bring her in?"

Chapter 27

MOMENTS LATER THE Brazilian woman appeared like a sudden tropical windstorm inside the office.

"You can't do this to me! I'm a citizen of Brazil!"

"Excuse me. You must be mistaking me for somebody who gives a shit. Why don't you sit down." Carroll spoke without getting up from his cluttered work desk.

"Why? Who do you think you are?"

"I said, sit down. I ask the questions, not you."

Carroll leaned back in his chair and studied Isabella Marqueza. The Brazilian woman had shoulder-length, gleaming black hair. Her lips were full and painted very red. There was an arrogant tilt to her chin.

Her hair, her clothes, even her skin seemed expensive and cosmopolitan. She had on tight gray velvet riding pants, a silk shirt, cowboy boots, a half-length fur jacket. *Terrorist chic,* Carroll thought.

"You dress like a very wealthy Che Guevara." Carroll finally smiled.

"I don't appreciate your attempt of humor, senhor."

"No, well, join the crowd." Carroll's smile now broadened. "I don't appreciate your attempts at mass murder."

Carroll already knew this woman by reputation. Isabella Marqueza was an internationally renowned journalist and news-magazine photographer. She was the daughter of a wealthy man who owned tire factories in São Paulo, Brazil. Though it apparently couldn't be proved, Isabella Marqueza had sanctioned at least four American deaths.

She was responsible, Carroll knew, for the disappearance, then the cold-blooded, heartless murders of a Shell Oil executive and his family. The American businessman, his wife, their two small girls had vanished that past June in Rio. Their pitiful, mutilated bodies had been found in a sewer ditch inside the *favelos*.

Marqueza reportedly worked for the GRU through François Monserrat. According to rumors, Isabella had also been Monserrat's lover.

She tossed Carroll the coldest, most indignant look he could imagine. Her dark, sullen eyes smoldered as she stared him down.

Arch Carroll wearily shook his head. He set aside the steaming coffee container. The impression he got from Isabella was that of a tempest about to unleash its force. He watched as she leaned forward and thumped her hands on the desk: the fiery light, the gleam in her dark eyes was something.

"*I want to see my lawyer!* Right now! I want my lawyer! You get my lawyer. Now, senhor!"

"Nobody even knows you're here." Carroll spoke in a purposely soft, polite voice. Whatever she did, however she acted—he would do the exact opposite, he'd decided.

Carroll knew that two of his agents had intercepted Isabella Marqueza as she walked down East 70th Street after leaving her apartment that morning. She'd screamed out, struggled and fought as they grabbed her off the streets. "Somebody please help me!"

Half a dozen East Side New Yorkers, with the anesthetized look of people observing a distant event which interests but doesn't particularly involve them, had watched the scene. One of them had finally yelled as Isabella Marqueza was dragged, fighting and sobbing, into a waiting station wagon. The rest did nothing at all.

"You people kidnap me off the streets," Isabella Marqueza complained. Her red mouth pouted.

"Let me confess to you. Let me be honest, and kind of frank," Carroll said, still going gently. "In the last few years, I've had to kidnap a few people like yourself. Call it the new justice. Call it anything you like. Kidnapping's lost most of its glitter for me."

The louder Isabella Marqueza got, the softer Carroll's speaking voice became. "I kind of like the idea of being a kidnapper. I kidnap terrorists. It's got a nice ring to it, you know. Don't you think?"

"I demand to see my lawyer! Goddam you! My lawyer is Daniel Curzon. You know that name?"

Arch Carroll nodded and shrugged. He knew Daniel Curzon.

"Daniel Curzon's a piece of sorry shit. I don't want to hear Curzon's name again. I'm serious about that."

Carroll's eyes now fell to a manila package, a plain-looking folder wrapped in brown string on his desk. Inside was his moral justification to do whatever he needed to do right now.

Inside the tan envelope were a dozen or so black-and-white and 35-millimeter color photographs of the Jason Miller family, formerly of Rio: the murdered family of the

Shell Oil executive. There were also grainy photographs of an American couple who had disappeared in Jamaica, pictures of a Unilever accountant from Colombia, a man named Jordan who had disappeared last spring.

Carroll continued softly. "My name's Arch Carroll. Born right here in New York City. Local boy makes good. . . . Son of a cop who was the son of a cop. Not a lot of imagination at work in our family, I'll admit."

Carroll paused briefly. He lit up a leftover cigarette stub, Crusader Rabbit style.

"My job is to locate terrorists who threaten the security of the United States. Then, if they're not too strongly politically connected, *protected,* I try my best to put a stop to them . . .

"Put it another way, you *could* say I'm a terrorist for the United States. I play by the same rules you do. . . . *No rules.* So stop talking about Park Avenue lawyers. Lawyers are for nice, civilized people who play by the rules. Not for us."

Carroll slowly untied the string bow on the manila envelope. Then he slid out the handful of photographs inside.

He casually passed them to Isabella Marqueza.

"Jason Miller's body. Miller was an engineer for Shell Oil. He was also a financial investigator for the State Department, as you and your people in São Paulo know. A fairly nice man, I understand. . . . Information-gatherer for State, I'll admit. Basically harmless, though."

Carroll made soft clicking noises with his tongue. His eyes briefly met those of Isabella Marqueza.

She was quiet suddenly. His putting-green voice was throwing her off slightly. She obviously hadn't expected to encounter the deck of photographs.

"Miller's wife Judy here. Alive in this photo. Kind of a nice Midwestern smile. . . . Two little girls. Their bodies, that is. I have two little girls myself. Two girls, two boys."

Carroll smiled again. He cleared his throat. He needed a beer—a beer and a stiff shot of Irish would go real good right now. He studied Isabella Marqueza a moment.

"In July of last year, you participated in the premeditated murders, the political assassination of all four Millers."

Isabella Marqueza shot up from her seat in the interrogation room. She began to yell at Carroll again.

"I did nothing! You prove what you say! No! I did not kill anybody. Never. I don't kill children!"

"Bullshit. That's the end of our friendly discussion. Who the hell do you think you're kidding?"

With that Carroll slapped the wrinkled manila portfolio shut, he jammed it back in his lopsided desk drawer. He looked up at Isabella Marqueza again.

"*Nobody* knows you're here! Nobody's going to know what happened to you after today. That's the truth. Just like the Miller family in Brazil."

"You're full of shit, Carroll—"

"Yeah? Try me. Push me a little and find out for sure."

"My lawyer, I want to see my lawyer—"

"Never heard of him—"

"I told you his name, Curzon—"

"Did you? I don't remember—"

Isabella Marqueza stared at Carroll in silence. She folded her arms, then sat down again. She crossed her long legs and lit a cigarette.

"Why are you doing this to me? You're crazy."

This was a little better, Carroll thought.

"Tell me about Jack Jordan down in Colombia. American business accountant. Machine-gunned to death in his driveway. His wife got to watch."

"I never heard of him."

Carroll clucked his tongue and slowly shook his head back and forth. He seemed genuinely disappointed. Sitting behind the bare, bleak office desk, he looked like someone whose best friend had just inexplicably lied to him.

"Isabella. Isabella." He gave an exaggerated sigh. "I don't think you get the total picture. I don't think you really understand." He stood up, stretched his arms, fought back a yawn. "You see, *you no longer exist.* You *died* suddenly this morning. Taxi accident on East Seventieth Street. Nobody bothered to tell you?"

Carroll was feeling dangerously overloaded now. He didn't want to finish this interrogation.

An hour passed. Two hours. He desperately needed a drink.

"You *were* François Monserrat's mistress here in New York. Come on. *We already know about that.* Two summers ago. Right here in Nueva York."

Isabella Marqueza sat with her head hanging. She wouldn't look up at Carroll for long stretches of time. Her right leg kept nervously tapping the floor, but she didn't seem aware of it. She looked physically ill.

"Who the *hell* is Monserrat?" Carroll kept up his attack. "How does Monserrat get his information? How does he get information that no one outside the U.S. government could possibly get? *Who is he?*"

Carroll could hear his own loud voice as if it were a foreign sound in an echo chamber. "Listen. . . . Listen to me very carefully. . . . If you talk to me right now, if you tell me about François Monserrat—*just his part in the bombings on Wall Street.* . . . If you do that much, I can let you leave here, I promise you. No one will know you were here. Just tell me about the Wall Street bombings. Nothing more than that. Nothing else. . . . What does François Monserrat know about the fire bombings? . . ."

It took thirty minutes more of cajoling, threatening, screaming at Marqueza, thirty grueling minutes in which Carroll's voice turned hoarse and his face red, thirty minutes during which his shirt stuck to his sweaty body, before Isabella Marqueza finally stood and shouted at him.

"Monserrat had nothing to do with it! He doesn't understand it either. . . . Nobody understands what the bombings are all about. He's looking for Green Band too! *Monserrat is looking for them too!"*

"How do you *know* that, Isabella? How do you *know* what Monserrat is doing? You must have seen him!"

The woman clapped the palm of one hand across her hollow, darkened eyes. "I *haven't* seen him. I *don't* see him. Not ever."

"Then how do you know?"

"There are messages. There are whispers in private places. *Nobody* sees Monserrat."

"Where is he, Isabella? Is he here in New York? Where the hell is he?"

The woman stubbornly shook her head. "I don't know that either."

"What does Monserrat look like these days?"

"How should I know? He changes. Monserrat is always changing. Sometimes dark hair, a moustache. Sometimes gray hair. Dark glasses. Sometimes a beard." She paused. "Monserrat doesn't have a face."

Now, conscious of having said too much, Isabella Marqueza had begun to sob. Carroll sat back and finally let his head rest against the grimy office wall. She didn't know anything more; he was almost certain he'd gone as far into her as he could possibly go.

Nobody knew anything about Green Band.

Only that wasn't possible.

Somebody had to know what the hell Green Band wanted.

Who, though?

Chapter 28

FADED, YELLOWING NEWSPAPERS, at least a dozen different ones dated October 25, 1929, were haphazardly spread across a heavy oak library-style work table. The thirty- and forty-point headlines seemed as jarring now as they must have been fifty-odd years before.

WORST STOCK CRASH EVER; 12,894,650-SHARE DAY SWAMPS MARKET; LEADERS CONFER, FIND CONDITIONS SOUND.

WALL STREET PANIC! RECORD SELLING OF STOCKS! HEAVY FALL IN PRICES!

STOCK PRICES SLUMP $14,000,000,000 IN NATION-WIDE STAMPEDE TO UNLOAD; BANKERS TO SUPPORT MARKET TODAY.

PRICES OF STOCKS CRASH IN HEAVY LIQUIDATION, TOTAL DROP OF BILLIONS.

TWO MILLION SIX HUNDRED THOUSAND SHARES SOLD IN THE FINAL HOUR IN RECORD DECLINE!

MANY INDIVIDUAL ACCOUNTS WIPED OUT COMPLETELY!

WHEAT SMASHED! CHICAGO PIT IN TURMOIL.

HOOVER PROMISES BUSINESS OF THE COUNTRY IS STILL SOUND AND PROSPEROUS!

Caitlin Dillon finally stood up from the work table and its musty newspaper clippings. She stretched her arms high over her head and sighed. She was on the fifth floor of No. 13 Wall, with Anton Birnbaum from the New York Stock Exchange Steering Committee.

Birnbaum was one of America's financial geniuses. If anyone understood that precarious castle of cards called Wall Street, it was Birnbaum. He had started, Caitlin knew, as an office boy at the age of eleven. Then he'd worked his way up through the market hierarchy to control his own investment house. Even at eighty-three his mind remained as sharp as a blade; a mischievous light still burned in his eyes.

Caitlin had met Anton Birnbaum years before while she was still at Wharton. Her thesis adviser had invited the Financier for a guest lecture during her final year. After one of his iconoclastic talks, Birnbaum had consented to private sessions with a few of the business school's students. One of them turned out to be Caitlin, about whom Birnbaum told her adviser: "She is extremely intense. Her only flaw is that she is beautiful. I mean that quite seriously. It will be a problem for her on Wall Street. It will be a serious handicap."

When Caitlin graduated from Wharton, Anton Birnbaum hired her as an assistant at his firm. Within a year, Caitlin was one of his assistants. Unlike many of the people he hired, Caitlin would disagree with the great Financier when she felt he was off base.

During that period Caitlin also began to make the Wall Street and Washington connections she needed for the future. Her first job with Birnbaum provided an education she couldn't have paid to receive. Caitlin found the

Financier impossible to work for, but somehow she worked for him, which proved to Birnbaum that she was as outstanding as he had initially thought she was.

"Anton, *who* would *benefit* from a Stock Market crash right now? Let's make ourselves a list, a physical list, as some kind of starting place."

"All right, let's explore that avenue. People who would *benefit* from a Market crash?" Birnbaum took a legal pad and pencil in hand. "A multinational that has a huge discrepancy to hide?"

"That's one. Or the Soviets. They'd benefit—in terms of world prestige, anyway . . ."

"Then perhaps one of the Third World madmen? I believe Qadaffi is capable of something like this. Perhaps capable of getting the necessary financing, as well."

Caitlin looked at her watch, a functional, ten-year-old Bulova, a gift from her father one Christmas back home in Ohio. "I don't know *what* to try next. What are they waiting for? What happens when the Market opens on Monday?"

Anton Birnbaum took off his horn-rimmed eyeglasses. He rubbed the bridge of his nose, which was reddened and deeply indented. "Will the Market even open, Caitlin? The French want it to. They're insisting *they* will open in Paris. Perhaps it's one of their typical bluffs."

"Which means the Arabs want *their* French Banks open. Some toady in Paris either wants to take advantage of this situation—or they hope to get some of their money out, *before* there's a complete panic."

Birnbaum replaced his glasses. He gazed at Caitlin for a moment. Then he gave one of his characteristic shrugs, a huffy gesture of the shoulders that was barely perceptible.

"President Kearney is talking with the French. They've never appreciated him tremendously, though. We haven't been able to placate them since Kissinger."

"What about London? What about Geneva? How about right here in New York, Anton?"

"They're all watching France. France is threatening to open their market, business as usual on Monday. The French, my dear, are being carefully, carefully orchestrated. But by whom? And for what possible reason? What is coming next?"

Both Caitlin and the old man were quiet for several moments. Over the years they had become comfortable with long periods of silent thought when they were examining a problem together.

"I'll tell you something, my dear. In all my years on the Street, I have never felt this apprehensive. Not even in October of 1929."

Chapter 29

BERGDORF'S ON 57TH had been open all day Sunday for the usual neurotic rush of Christmas shopping.

François Monserrat entered the department store at a little past 6:30 that evening. Another snowstorm was threatening outside.

Monserrat was wearing thick wire-rimmed glasses and an unmemorable gray tweed overcoat. He also wore a matching hat and black gloves, which created a monochromatic impression. The wire-rimmed glasses magnified his eyes for observers, but didn't distort his view of the world. He'd had them made by a lens grinder on the Rue des Postes in Bizerte, a city north of Tunis.

Monserrat quietly marveled as he got off a crowded elevator onto one of the upper floors.

There was nowhere else, no city he knew of, in which one consistently saw quite so many provocative and stunning women. Even the store's perfume demonstrators were dreamily sensual and exotic.

A stylishly anorexic black girl approached and asked if he'd like to experience the *new* Opium.

"I've already experienced it. In Thailand, my dear," Monserrat answered with a smile and an effete wave of the hand.

A thick gallery of shoppers hugging glittering shopping bags from other department stores moved slowly before Monserrat's wandering eyes. "Winter Wonderland" played from a hidden stereo system.

It was taxing and exceedingly difficult to move forward in certain directions, more like visiting a New York disco than a store at Christmas time.

As he strolled through the store, Monserrat reflected on his reputation with a measure of pride. What did it matter if he'd been responsible for this act or that one—when his only real goal, his sole driving force, was the total disruption and eventual fall of the West? A dead Egyptian President. A wounded Pope. A few Irish bombs. These amounted to nothing more than grains of sand on a beach. What Monserrat was interested in changing was the direction of the tide itself . . .

The crowd inside Bergdorf's ebbed and flowed.

He finally saw the woman he'd followed. She was sifting through a long rack of cocktail dresses, always thinking of her appearance, always defining her existence through her reflection.

Monserrat concealed himself behind a display case of sweaters, and continued to watch. He felt a certain coldness in the center of his head, as if his brain had become a solid fist of ice. It was a feeling he knew in certain situations. Where other men would experience the uncontrollable rush of adrenaline, Monserrat experienced what he thought of as the Chill.

Every man who passed checked out Isabella Marqueza carefully. So did several of the chic, well-dressed women shoppers.

Her fur jacket was left casually open. As she turned, swiveled left or right, a tantalizing glimpse of her breasts floated deliciously into the breach. Of all the women in the department store, Isabella was the most desirable, the most visually dramatic by Monserrat's personal standards.

Now he observed Isabella slink off toward a changing room. He put his hands in the pockets of his overcoat, caught a reflection of himself in a mirror as he moved, then he paused outside the changing room door.

He walked past the closed door, studied the throngs around him pursuing Christmas gifts with forced gaiety, and then he darted back the way he had come.

Pretending to examine a silk shirt, like a wealthy East Side husband picking out a stocking-stuffer, he listened outside the changing room.

Coming closer, he could hear the whisper of clothing as it peeled away from Isabella's skin.

In one swift move, he stepped inside the tiny room and Isabella swung around in astonishment.

Why did she always look so beautiful? Warmth flowed within him. He took his hands from his coat.

She was wearing only panties, tight and sheer and black. The cocktail dress she intended to try on hung limply in one hand.

"François! What are you doing here?"

"I had to see you," he whispered. "I heard you had a little trouble."

Isabella frowned. "They let me go. What were they going to hold me for, anyhow? They had nothing but a stupid bluff, François."

She smiled, but the expression couldn't conceal a look of worry.

He pressed one gloved hand lightly against her breasts. He could smell Bal à Versailles. Her favorite perfume. His as well.

"Are you being followed, Isabella?"

"I don't think so. No, of course not."

"Good. Good," he whispered.

Isabella's mouth fell open and she suddenly stepped back against the wall. There was really no place to go in the tiny dressing room. "François, don't you believe me? I told them nothing. Absolutely nothing."

"Then why did they let you go, my love? I need an explanation."

"François, don't you know me any better than that? Don't you?"

I know you only too well, Monserrat thought and stepped forward.

The tiny handgun made an inconsequential, guttural spit. Isabella Marqueza moaned, then she seemed to faint, collapsing toward the black-and-white checkered tiles.

Monserrat was already out of the changing room and walking, inconspicuously, toward the nearest exit.

She'd talked. She had admitted knowing him, and that was enough.

She'd been broken during the interrogation, skillfully, in a way she might not even have recognized. Monserrat had

heard the news not ten minutes after Carroll finished with
her.

He burst into the cold wind raking West 57th Street. He
turned a corner, to all intents and purposes a drab ordinary
man, losing himself in the crowds that hunted the spirit of
Christmas with red-faced eagerness.

Chapter 30

"I WANT YOU to have lunch with me, Mr. Carroll," Caitlin Dillon had said over the telephone. "Is twelve-fifteen today, okay? It's important."

It was a call that took Carroll by surprise. He'd been going through his back files—sifting through terrorist organizations in his search for some clue to Green Band—when the call came.

"I want you to meet somebody," Caitlin had told him.

"Who?"

"A man called Freddie Hotchkiss. He's kind of important on Wall Street."

She had a nice telephone voice. Music in a tuneless world, Carroll thought. He'd put his feet up on the desk and tilted his head back against the wall. With his eyes shut, he tried to bring Caitlin Dillon's face into his mind. *Untouchable,* he remembered.

"Freddie Hotchkiss is connected with a man called Michel Chevron," Caitlin said.

"The name rings a bell," Carroll said and tried to place it.

"The information I have is that Chevron's a wheel in the stolen securities market and—this is what should *really* interest you, Mr. Carroll—there are rumors of a link with François Monserrat."

Carroll loosened his crimson and blue school tie before he took the first inviting sip of John Smith's Pale Ale in the dining room of Christ Cella on East 46th Street. He found ties uncomfortable, which was one reason he rarely wore them. Actually, he thought neckties pretty much without purpose, unless you impulsively wanted to hang yourself, or get inside some overpriced New York steakhouse.

Christ Cella required a jacket and tie. Otherwise, it was comfortable enough. Actually, it felt good to be sitting here with Caitlin Dillon.

Christ Cella's steaks were sixteen ounces at a minimum, choice prime, and aged properly. The lobsters started at two pounds. The waiters were immaculate and subservient, city cool to a fault. For the moment, Carroll was enjoying himself. For this moment only, Green Band had receded from his mind.

"One of the first things I learned in New York is that you *have* to make 'the steak house' a ritual if you're going to survive on Wall Street." Caitlin smiled across the white linen of the tablecloth. She'd already told Carroll that she was originally from Lima, Ohio, and he could almost believe it, listening to her perspective on New York City living.

"Even to survive in the SEC, you have to know the conventions. Especially if you're a young 'gal,' as a particular brokerage house CEO once called me. 'I'd like you to meet the new young gal from SEC.'"

Caitlin said the phrase with such casual, twinkling malice, it almost sounded nice.

Carroll started to laugh. Then they both laughed.

Heads turned at other tables, staid faces looked around. *Was somebody daring to have fun here? Who?*

Carroll and Caitlin were waiting for the arrival of Duncan "Freddie" Hotchkiss, who was fashionably late, despite the fact that Caitlin had asked him to be on time. ·

A shrimp cocktail eventually found its way to Carroll's place. The fish was perfect and overpriced by at least three hundred percent.

Carroll asked Caitlin about Wall Street—what it was like from her vantage point at the SEC? Caitlin began regaling him with a few of her favorite horror stories about the Street. She happened to have a treasury of true, mind-bending stories which circulated in the inner sanctums, but were usually not shared with outsiders.

"Embezzlement has never been easier on Wall Street," Caitlin said. Her brown eyes sparkled with humor.

"One economist we prosecuted worked at the Federal Reserve Bank of New York. At twenty-seven, he went off and bought a summer house in the Hamptons, then a new Mercedes convertible *and* a Porsche, then a sable coat for his dear mom. Along the way, he managed to get in debt close to three quarters of a million dollars."

"He's still working for the government?" Carroll finished the second shrimp. "In your story, I mean?"

"He *quits* Treasury right about this time—for a much better paying job. Only he takes with him *the security access codes,* which allow him to find out enough to buy or sell on the credit and stock markets. A very, very profitable bit of knowledge. He's got the ultimate on insider's trading information. . . . You know how it fell through? His mother called the SEC. She was worried that he was spending all this money without any job she could see. His mother turned him in because he gave her a sable fur.

"There was an outfit called OPM Financial Services—that stood for other people's money, I swear to God. Michael Weiss and Anthony Caputo opened their company over a Manhattan candy store in the seventies. Along their merry way, Michael and Anthony managed to defraud Manufacturers Hanover Leasing, Crocker National Bank, and Lehman Brothers for about a hundred and eighty million. Don't ever feel bad if you lose a little money on the market."

"I'm real lucky in that respect—I don't have any money to lose. Why is it allowed to happen? What about the SEC?"

Carroll was beginning to feel slightly incensed, though he'd never personally lost a dime on Wall Street.

"It's fairly simple, really. As I said in the beginning, these kinds of stories are rarely told outside of Wall Street."

"I'm honored."

"You should be. . . . The Wall Street banks, the brokerage houses, investment bankers, even the computer companies—they know that the success of their marketplace depends on confidence and trust. If they prosecuted all the embezzlers, if they ever admitted how easy it was, how many stock certificates are actually stolen each year, they'd *all* be out of business. The point is, Wall Street is more afraid of bad publicity than of the actual thefts."

Suddenly, Caitlin was silent.

"Caitlin, will you forgive me? I'm so very sorry."

Freddie Hotchkiss had finally arrived. It was one o'clock. He was forty-five minutes late for their lunch.

Carroll looked up and saw a sparsely blond-haired man with a ridiculously innocent grin on his face. He had the palest, watery-blue eyes, bleached of almost all color, and a face as round and expressionless as a pie tin.

What did they do down on Wall Street? Carroll wondered. Were there genetic laboratories dedicated to the preservation of the pure-blooded, uncontaminated WASP strain? All of them turning out plump little Freddie Hotchkisses?

Caitlin had told Carroll that Hotchkiss was becoming legendary. He was a hot partner at his firm, a frequent emissary to both the West Coast and Europe—where he had extensive dealings with European bankers.

"Truly sorry about the time." Hotchkiss looked anything *but* sorry. "I completely lost track. Roughing it out of the pied-à-terre on Park since the trouble on Friday. Kim and the kids are staying down in Boca Raton, her mom and dad's place. Ah, what exquisite timing you have, sir."

A waiter had spotted Hotchkiss arriving and had scurried to the table for the all-important drink order. Carroll stared at Hotchkiss. This was a type he wasn't comfortable with and didn't particularly like. Poor bastard had to rough it on Park Avenue.

"I'd like a Kir. Anyone for seconds?" Hotchkiss asked.

"I'll have another John Smith." Carroll was *trying* to be good: no hard liquor, no neat shots of Irish. He was also trying not to say something impulsive, something that might lose him the advantage of surprise with Freddie Hotchkiss.

"No, thank you, nothing for me," Caitlin said. "Freddie, this is Arch Carroll. Mr. Carroll is the head of the United States Antiterrorist Division. Out of the DIA."

Hotchkiss beamed enthusiastically. "Oh, yes, I've read about you specialized police folks. The sooner someone can bring a little order to this whole unfortunate affair, the better. I heard yesterday, or maybe I read it somewhere, that there is a Libyan hit team right here in New York. Actually *residing* in Manhattan."

"I doubt it's the Libyans we're looking for," Carroll remarked.

He leaned forward, softly nudging a finger into Freddie's pale blue shirt, seeing a faint expression of surprise float across the man's puffy face. It amazed Carroll that such a face was capable of expression.

"I'd like to cut out the chitchat, okay? You're an hour late, and we're pressed. I have absolutely no personal interest in you, Freddie, you understand that? I don't think I like you, but that doesn't matter. I'm only interested in a man named Michel Chevron."

"He's not one for small talk, Freddie." Caitlin smiled and nursed her drink.

Freddie Hotchkiss, meanwhile, seemed to have stopped breathing. He looked down at Carroll's finger sticking in the center of his chest. "I'm not sure . . . I don't think I understand. I mean, I've heard of Michel Chevron, of course."

"Of course you have," Carroll said.

"Tall, austere-looking French gentleman," Caitlin intervened. "Plush Louis Quatorze offices on rue du Faubourg in Paris. Very affluent digs in the heart of Beverly Hills."

Caitlin flipped open a leatherbound notebook on the dining table.

"Let me see if I can jog your memory. Mm, oh yes . . . on February nineteenth of last year, you visited Michel Chevron's Beverly Hills office. You stayed for approximately two hours. On March third, you visited the L.A. offices again. Also on July ninth, July eleventh, July twelfth. In October, you visited Chevron's Paris Office. You had dinner with Chevron that night at Lasserre. Remember? Can you place him yet?"

Freddie Hotchkiss had begun slowly clasping and unclasping his plump, hairless hands.

"We've known for over two years that Chevron is the largest stolen securities and bond dealer in Europe and the Middle East. We also know he has a personal relationship with François Monserrat," Caitlin continued.

"We know a great deal about your own security trading abilities, as well. Right now, we need to know exactly *who* else Chevron deals with, and we need a rough idea of the nature of these deals, a general feel for the Euro-Asian black market. That's why I thought we all should have lunch." She smiled.

Right then Freddie Hotchkiss found the strength inside himself to frown derisively. He began to snap back, to rally.

"*Really.* You don't expect me to talk about private *and* absolutely legal business dealings here in this restaurant? You had better have *all* your subpoenas and your Justice

Department lawyers ready, if you believe that will happen. I can assure you, it won't be *done* over lunch. . . . Good afternoon, Caitlin, Mr., uh, Carroll."

Carroll suddenly sat up very straight at the dining table. He leaned all the way forward and did the oddest, most unexpected thing.

Carroll placed his forefinger behind his thumb and then flicked it three times very hard against Freddie Hotchkiss's starched white shirt collar.

Thwack.

Thwack.

Thwack.

"Just sit tight now. Just put your nice soft ass back down on the chair. Try to relax. Okay?"

Hotchkiss was so astonished, he obeyed.

In a soft voice, which to Carroll's ears sounded mildly seductive, Caitlin said, "February twenty-first—you deposited one hundred and twenty-six thousand dollars in Geneva, Switzerland. February twenty-sixth—you deposited another one hundred and fourteen thousand. April seventeenth—you deposited . . . is this a typo? . . . four hundred and sixty-two thousand? April twenty-fourth— another thirty-one thousand. . . . Small potatoes, that one . . ."

"What Caitlin has been politely trying to point out to you, Freddie, is that you are a second-rate thief!" Carroll leaned back and smiled at Hotchkiss, who now sat as expressionless as a ventriloquist's dummy.

Carroll raised his voice above the restaurant's usual buzz. "Poor Kim, the kiddos wintering down in Boca Raton. They have no idea, I'll bet. Tennis pals at the club. The boys at the yacht club. They don't know either. . . .

You ought to be in jail. You shouldn't be allowed to eat here, you're such a sad piece of shit."

Other diners in the expensive Midtown restaurant were beginning to place their knives and forks on their plates. In a state that resembled a communal hypnotic trance, they stared across the upstairs room.

Carroll finally lowered his voice. He pointed toward a corner table where two men in dull gray suits were seated.

"Those two guys? See them? They can't even afford to eat the nibbles here. See, they're sharing a three-dollar ginger ale. That's the FBI for you. . . . Anyway, they're either going to arrest you, right here and now . . . *or,* Fred, you're going to tell us a long, very convincing story about Michel Chevron. It's absolutely your move. And yes, it's going to happen *right here* in the restaurant.

"*Then,* in that second case I mentioned, you get to go home absolutely scot free to the pied-à-terre on Park Avenue. No problems, 'cause then you're my main man, see."

Arch Carroll dramatically crossed his two fingers. "We're tight, like that. Except, of course, you're the finger on the bottom."

Freddie Hotchkiss slumped forward at the restaurant table. He hesitated, then he slowly began to tell yet another Wall Street horror story.

This one was about Monsieur Michel Chevron. It was a fascinating story of the most exclusive rat pack of thieves in the world. All of them respected bankers, high-priced lawyers, successful stockbrokers. Every single one of them was in a position of absolute trust.

Was this Green Band? Carroll couldn't help wondering. *Was Green Band a powerful cartel of the richest invest-*

*ment bankers and businessmen in the world? What would
be their motivation?*

Carroll finally signaled to the two FBI guys waiting at
the corner table.

"You can arrest this guy now. . . . Oh, and Freddie? I
told a white lie about letting you go free. . . . Have your
lawyer call my lawyer in the morning. *Ciao.*"

Mike Caruso was outside the restaurant when Carroll finally appeared. Carroll's lieutenant was wearing a garish
beach shirt beneath his overcoat, a devoté of summer who
never embraced the winter season.

He gestured Carroll to step aside from Caitlin. Both policemen huddled together at the far edge of the sidewalk.

"I just got a report on our friend Isabella Marqueza,"
Caruso said. "Somebody murdered her. She was shot four
times."

Carroll glanced at Caitlin, who was standing several feet
away, waiting for him. A lovely vision in a dull gray, wintry city. He tried to imagine Isabella Marqueza dead.

"Shot at point-blank range," Caruso said in the offhand
manner of someone immunized against murders. "It
freaked out all the Christmas shoppers."

"Yeah, I'm sure it would." Carroll was silent a second.
"Somebody thought she talked too much. Somebody was
keeping close tabs on her."

Caruso nodded. "Somebody who knew her movements,
Arch. Or *yours.*"

A ragged wind blew down East 46th Street, dragging
around discarded newspapers. Carroll plunged his hands
inside the pockets of his coat and stared at the cold grim

city surrounding him. He liked this investigation less and less.

He finally pointed back at the doorway of Christ Cella. "Nice place to eat, Mickey. Next time you want to blow a couple hundred on lunch."

Caruso nodded. He tucked in a flap of his flowered shirt. "I already had a Sabrett's."

Chapter 31

THE FOLLOWING MORNING, Anton Birnbaum, appearing on a special edition of the PBS show "Wall Street Week," explained why the destruction of Manhattan's financial district did not exactly signal the end of the civilized world.

"The *major* American market was indeed knocked out this past Friday. *More* markets exist out there, however—*believe it or not*—and they may just possibly become the beneficiaries of this disaster. . . . These markets are the Midwestern, the Pacific, and the Philadelphia exchanges. They handle local issues as well as certain board listings. If Joe Investor has to sell fifty shares of AT and T to meet the balloon payment on his mortgage, his local broker may well be able to make a deal for him outside of New York. Of course, he may not find a buyer at a price even close to what he's asking.

"Obviously," Birnbaum went on, "Chicago is where the significant action is this week. Between the Midwest Exchange, and the two premier commodity exchanges, there are still plenty of opportunities for everyone to lose a lot of money."

Even as he gave this purposely calming and reassuring

speech, Anton Birnbaum knew that the existing situation was more tragic than he dared admit. Like almost everyone intimately connected with the Market, Birnbaum expected a crash.

In a way, somewhere deep in the inner recesses of his mind, he almost welcomed the purification rite, so very long overdue. As of Tuesday morning, the venerable Financier had no idea how large a part he would play in Green Band himself.

Chapter 32

PARIS. ... A MAN named Michel Chevron ... Green Band. ...

The idea of the city filled Carroll with something akin to dread. Even as he sat inside a dark blue State Department limousine, sailing like a proud ship across Boulevard Haussman, Carroll didn't want to look out at the streets. He didn't want to acknowledge that he was back in the French capital.

The street sounds he heard pressing against the limousine were like the rattling of old bones. For Carroll, Paris was a city of sharply painful memories. Paris was Nora and himself in another age and time. Paris was a fading decal on which was imprinted the spectral shapes of two young, carefree honeymooners, who wandered all the boulevards holding hands, who stopped to kiss every so often, who couldn't keep from constantly touching each other.

Carroll stared at the two American flags that flapped on either fender of the luxury car.

Make believe you're someplace else, he told himself.

Christ, though, the memories kept coming back like a tide.

Nora sipping café au lait on the crowded Boulevard St. Germain.

Nora smiling and laughing as they made all the tourist stops—the Eiffel Tower, Montparnasse, the banks of the Seine, le Quartier Etudiant.

Carroll felt something grab tight around his heart. It was a sense of the injustice that had ended Nora's life, and it uncomfortably crowded him now.

Near the Opéra Garnier, a crouching man with a reptilian face made as if to hurl a spoiled grapefruit at the smooth, cruising symbol of American wealth and power.

Seated in the gray velvet rear seat of the car, Carroll flinched at the sight of the man. But when the prospect of the grapefruit assault had passed, he relaxed a little and tried to shake his head free of the fog of overseas jet lag and confused time zones.

He opened his bulky Green Band file and looked over scribbled notes because he knew work would be a salvation from the memories of this town. If he dug into his material on Green Band, he could make himself a foxhole safe from the scenes that passed outside the windows of the car.

How could Green Band have isolated itself so well from the terrorist underground? How could there be no rumor, no concrete leads anywhere out on the street? And what was the ultimate reason for the New York financial district bombings?

Something else occurred to Carroll now: *What if he was still looking in all the wrong places?*

"Société Générale Bank, monsieur. *Vous êtes ici.* You have arrived safely, comfortably I hope. . . . This is *le Quartier de la Bourse.*"

Arch Carroll climbed out of the official American limousine and slowly walked inside Société Générale.

The bank building itself, the cavernous lobby, the hand-operated elevators, were all carved stone and exquisitely gilded. Everything was regal and impressive, the kind of background against which American tourists would take pictures of their European tours to later paste in scrapbooks.

The prestigious French financial institution reminded Carroll of another era. Compared with Wall Street, it was visually softer and more civilized. It was as if money were not the major game being played here. The aim was something less vulgar, something even spiritual, perhaps.

In actuality *le Quartier de la Bourse* occupied the former site of a Dominican convent. On this same site another God had achieved divinity. No matter the history of the place, no matter the artistic appeal, it was the same religion you found on Wall Street. Gentility and manners, these were only illusions. It was the same old God.

Michel Chevron, Carroll thought, remembering why he was there. Chevron and the secretive European black market.

The question was whether Chevron really fit into the frustrating Green Band puzzle, and whether there was a bridge, even a frail one, linking Chevron with Monserrat.

The French bank executive's personal assistant was a thin man of perhaps twenty-eight. He had white-blond hair, closely cropped, almost suggestive of punk in style.

He sat behind an antique desk, which in New York would have seemed inappropriate for anyone except a chief executive. He wore a double-breasted pin-striped suit, a funereal, mauve four-in-hand tie.

Carroll tried to imagine applying for a loan from this chilly character, something for home repair, maybe, a room extension, an underground sprinkler system. He could see the bank assistant sniffling over the application papers with an expression of mild disgust.

"My name is Archer Carroll. I'm here from New York to see Monsieur Chevron. I spoke to someone yesterday on the telephone."

"Yes, to me." The bank assistant addressed him as a country gentleman would address a stablehand on the subject of a gelding's health. "Director Chevron has provided fifteen minutes . . . *at eleven forty-five.*"

Observing the bank assistant's manner and tone, Carroll had the impression that only a very few words could have been substituted for *"Director Chevron"* in the opening sentence—words like de Gaulle, or Napoleon. Maybe even the Lord God Almighty.

"Director has an important lunch at twelve. You will please wait. The sofa for waiting is there, Monsieur Carroll."

Arch Carroll nodded his head very slowly. Reluctantly, he wandered over to a tight nest of Art Deco couches.

He sat down and clenched his hands together. He was trying to fight back anger now. On the telephone, he and the bank assistant had set up a meeting firmly for eleven o'clock. He was right on time, and he'd traveled several thousand miles to be here.

Michel Chevron was right behind those heavy oak doors, Carroll kept thinking.

Chevron was probably laughing up his well-tailored sleeve at the ugly American outside in reception . . .

He steadily drummed his fingers on his knee. His right loafer tapped against the elegant marble floor.

At fifteen minutes to twelve, the bank assistant finally set down his slender silver fountain pen. He looked up from a thick sheaf of paperwork. He smacked his purplish lips before he spoke.

"You may see Director Chevron now."

Chapter 33

A MOMENT LATER, Michel Chevron, an unexpectedly small man with an equine face and shock of ink-black hair that stood up on his head like a fuzzy yarmulke, said, "Mr. Carroll, so good of you to come to Paris," almost as if this transatlantic journey was something Carroll did every other day of the week.

Carroll was led into an intimidating, Old World chief executive's office. Tall, glass-enclosed bookcases filled with antiquarian books crowded one paneled wall. Along the other, there were crimson-draped casement windows looking out onto a narrow gray stone terrace.

Michel Chevron remained standing behind his desk. He was obviously impressed with himself, his position and all the trappings that surrounded him. A regal Fragonard hung directly behind the bank executive.

The Frenchman began to speak rapid, excellent English as soon as his assistant left the room. His tone remained cool and superior.

"There is a problem, Monsieur Carroll. A regrettable circumstance, beyond anyone's control. I'm very sorry, but I have an important engagement at Taillevent. The restaurant, monsieur? The rest of my afternoon is equally bad . . . I can spare these few moments with you only."

Arch Carroll could suddenly feel *a very cold place* in his stomach. He knew the sensation and he tried to ignore it, but a fuse was burning. When the spark reached close to his private emotional arsenal, there was very little he could do to stop the explosion.

"All right, then just shut the hell up now," Carroll suddenly raised his hand, palm out. "I don't have time to be civil anymore. You kept me waiting through my polite and **civil** period."

The bank executive broke into a disdainful smile.

"Monsieur, you don't seem to understand whose country you're in now. This is not America, I'm afraid. You have no authority whatsoever here. I consented to see you, in the spirit of cooperation only."

Carroll reached into his sports coat pocket and sent a light tan envelope spinning across Chevron's desk.

"Here's your spirit of cooperation. It's a signed police warrant. A *French* police warrant for your arrest. It was signed by Commissionnaire Blanche of the Sûreté. The charges include extortion, bribery of public officials, fraud. I'm honored to be the one to deliver the news to you."

Michel Chevron sat down heavily in his chair. His aquiline features appeared to have imploded so that the face seemed squat, crinkled like a concertina that has had air thrust out of it.

"All right, Mr. Carroll. You've made your point. Why exactly have you come here? What information is it that you wish to extract from me?"

Carroll eased himself down into a chair across from Chevron.

"For starters, I'd like to know about the European and Middle Eastern black markets. I need names, places, specific dates. *How* the black market is structured, the principals involved."

Chevron cleared his throat. "You have no idea what you're saying, what you're asking of me. We are speaking of billions of dollars. We are speaking of participants of a less than savory nature."

Chevron sat back in his chair and Carroll could see tiny stars of perspiration glistening on his forehead. The impressive black hair seemed to have lost its color. Carroll felt relaxed and confident for the first time since he'd arrived in Paris.

"I'm listening," he said. "Keep going."

Just then the oak doors into the executive suite splintered and crashed suddenly.

For one incomprehensible moment Carroll imagined that what had happened on Wall Street was repeating itself in Paris.

Three armed men had appeared from the direction of the bank director's reception area. Each had a machine gun pistol. In the narrow corridor behind them stood Michel Chevron's blond assistant.

Carroll didn't hesitate. He was already diving across the floor. Glass and wood was suddenly splintering, shattering everywhere around him. Automatic machine gun explosions slashed through the previously secure and elegant office suite. Carroll's heart felt like it had been caught by a wire garotte.

Out of the corner of his eye, Carroll watched Michel Chevron.

The banker suddenly twisted and turned eerily in the air.

He was nailed against the wooden wall by a terrifying machine gun volley.

His body arched spastically, then spun away toward the floor. His blue suit was blood soaked.

The assailants switched their attention to Carroll. Hollow-head slugs thudded like hammer blows into the oak-paneled walls around him.

His heart pounding, Carroll lunged forward beyond the heavy drapes, which fanned the air as bullets ripped through the fabric. He smacked himself against the glass door to the terrace and was surrounded all at once by splinters of glass, by snapped pieces of the wooden frame that twisted out of the glass like limbs awkwardly broken . . .

Sharp needles pierced his neck, his hands. Violent, numbing cold clawed at his face.

He scrambled to his feet, the glass slivers slicing deeper with every movement.

The outside terrace was a long, narrow stone catwalk, sixteen stories above the Paris street. The walkway seemed to stretch around the length of the floor.

Feet pounding the ancient stone, Carroll ran toward the nearest corner of the building.

He could hear deafening gunshots, followed by screams of incredulous terror and agony inside the French bank offices. Machine gun pistols coughed and fired repeatedly, insanely.

French terrorists? The Brigade? François Monserrat?

What was happening now?

Who had known he was going to be here?

Bullets suddenly whistled past Carroll's face, nicking the brooding stone body of a crouching gargoyle.

Behind him and to the left, Carroll registered the direction of the gunfire and quickly glanced back over his shoulder.

Two of the assassins were closing fast. Their leather trenchcoats flapping, they were the kind of European thugs he thought only existed in movies. Furiously, Carroll raised his own gun. He fired, hearing the muted spit of the silencer.

The man in front grabbed his upper chest, then stumbled and fell over the stone wall. He continued down, somersaulting to the street.

"Oh, goddamnit!" Carroll suddenly clutched his shoulder. Blood spread where he'd been shot.

The thick cords of his neck bulged with the concentrated fear of the last few seconds, possibly the final seconds of his life. He felt as sick as he had ever felt. He temporarily lost his breath as he stumbled around the next carved stone corner of the French bank building.

He moved now, no longer fully aware of himself. He wasn't connected with events taking place. It was all a dream, a very bad nightmare.

Then he started to sprint down another clear stretch of stone terrace. The walkway ended abruptly at a gray brick wall topped by severe iron fencing.

He could taste warm, metallic blood in his mouth. Piercing chest pains came with each breath. The wounded arm ached with a deep, searing pain he'd never felt before.

To die here in Paris suddenly seemed ironic.

To die here surrounded by memories of Nora.

He watched the sky slip away. The wintry sun was a hard uncaring disc.

Carroll used his good arm on the restraining wall and

vaulted over the side. He saw a spinning flash of cars sixteen floors below. And cold concrete, gray as an undertaker's face . . .

As he safely landed on the terrace six feet below, he struck the wounded shoulder hard against a slab of granite. The pain that exploded into his brain was a savage, biting agony. Blinded by it, he forced himself to reel forward toward a casement door which opened as he leaned into it.

He was bleeding badly. He stopped running. A package-crowded stockroom lay before him.

Carroll crouched on trembling legs, and waited inside. Emery Airborne mail was stacked all around. There was no place to hide if they came through. If they found him now.

His thoughts were shattered. His mind was blurred, almost useless. Nothing was left inside his chest but rage. Splinters of glass still ached in his forehead, his cheeks, the back of his neck. He felt dizzy and sick.

Gunshot explosions and screams continued to echo through the Société Générale office building. Then warbling French police sirens shrieked and throbbed outside. They filled the air with the sudden news of disaster. Carroll finally took off his shirt and wrapped it around his bleeding arm.

Michel Chevron would be telling nothing about the powerful black market in Europe and the Middle East now. Nothing about what Green Band might be.

Who was behind this horrifying massacre? What could the banker Michel Chevron have known?

Carroll could no longer stand.

He slumped against a plaster wall, his head drawn between his knees.

What could Chevron have known?

What could be worth this massacre?

What could justify this?

Chapter 34

IT WAS A MAGICAL MOMENT, and one that Sergeant Harry Stemkowsky knew he would never be able to forget. It was like a movie scene he'd been dreaming about for as long as he could remember.

As dawn edged through soiled, slate gray skies, Stemkowsky rolled his wheelchair down the concrete ramp he'd built to get in and out of his house in Jackson Heights, Queens. His wife, Mary, a former nurse, who was ten years older than Harry, sauntered close beside him.

"This is it, sweetheart," she said in a whisper.

"This is definitely it," Harry said brightly.

Mary Stemkowsky carefully set Harry's two new Dunhill travel bags down. She glanced at her husband. She couldn't believe how impressive and businesslike he looked in his dark pin-striped suit.

His hair was neatly trimmed and shaped. He held a soft leather attaché case that looked like it cost big money.

"Excited, Harry? I'll bet you are." Mary Stemkowsky couldn't control a shy, softly blossoming grin as she spoke. She believed that Harry was a saint. You could ask any of his friends at the Vets Cab Company, any of the physical therapists who worked with him at the VA, where she and Harry had originally met.

Mary Stemkowsky didn't know how he'd done it, but Harry seemed to accept what had happened to him more than a decade before in Viet Nam. He never complained about the wounds or the pain.

"Tell the truth, I'm a li-li-little scared. Nuh-nuh-nice scared." Harry tried to smile, but he looked pale around the gills, she thought.

Mary bent and kissed him on both cheeks. It was strange the way she loved him so much. What with his infirmities, his physical limitations. But she did.

"Sa-sorry *you* can't go, Muh-Mary."

"Oh, I'll go next time, I guess. Sure, sure. You better believe I will." Mary suddenly laughed and her broad horsey smile was close to radiant. "You look like the president of a bank or something. President of Chase Manhattan Bank. You do, Harry. I'm so proud of you."

She stooped and kissed him again. She didn't want him to ruin one minute, not a single heartbeat of his European trip because she couldn't go with him this time.

"Oh, here he comes! Here Mitchell comes now." She suddenly pointed up along the row of dull, virtually faceless tract houses.

A yellow cab had turned onto their street. Mary could make out Mitchell Cohen at the wheel, wearing his usual, flap-eared Russian fur hat.

She knew that Mitchell and Harry had been working on their business scheme for almost two years. All they would tell her and Neva Cohen was that it had to do with arbitrage—which Mary loosely understood as trading currencies from country to country, making money on discrepancies in the exchange rates—and that this arbitrage scheme was their ticket out of hacking cabs for the rest of their lives.

"He takes two Dilantins before bedtime," Mary said as she and Mitchell Cohen helped load Harry into the Vets cab.

Harry cracked up at that remark. He loved the way Mary continually worried about him, worried about dumb things, like the Dilantin which he took regularly every night and three times during the day.

"You have a wonderful trip over to Europe, Harry. Don't work *too* hard. Miss me a little."

"Awhh cah-cah-mon. I muh-muh-miss you already," Harry Stemkowsky muttered, and he meant it.

He'd never really been able to understand why Mary had decided to live with a cripple in the first place. He was just happy that she had. Now he was going to do something for her, something that both of them deserved. Harry Stemkowsky was going to become an instant winner in life.

While Stemkowsky and Cohen drove to Kennedy Airport, another of the couriers, Vets 7, was already on board Pan Am flight 311, winging its way toward Japan.

Jimmy Holm was entertaining a first-class stewardess, skillfully recounting the stories of how he had survived three years in a North Vietnamese prison; then two more years in a Bakersville, California, VA hospital. Bakersville, he said, had been much, much worse.

"And now, here I am. This high and mighty clipper class life-style. Europe, the Far East." Holm smiled and drained his glass of Moët & Chandon. "God bless America. With all the ugly warts we hear so much about, God bless our country."

At approximately the same hour, Vets 15, Pauly Melindez, and Vets 9, Steve Glickman, were enjoying first-class treatment on another flight scheduled for Bangkok's Don Muang Airport. Both Melindez and Glickman had most recently worked as private rent-a-cops in Orlando, Florida. Today, December 9, they were personally in control of something over *sixteen million dollars . . .*

"Samples."

Vets 5, Harold Freedman, had already arrived in London. Vets 12, Jimmy Cassio, was in Zurich. Vets 8, Gary Barr, was settled in Rome—where he was sitting on a beautiful stone terrazzo which overlooked the Tiber.

Barr had most recently been a comedy nightclub bouncer for over four years on Sunset Boulevard in L.A. Now he was thinking that this had to be a dream.

Vets 8 finally closed his eyes. He blinked them open again . . . *and Rome along the Tiber was still there.*

So was the twenty-two million for his negotiations.

More "samples."

Chapter 35

IN THE WEST VILLAGE section of New York, Vets 3 wasn't flying, or even living very first class. Nick Tricosas had no four-hundred-dollar Brooks Brothers suit. He had no leather Dunhill wallet full of credit cards. Vets 3 was wearing a cut-off USMC T-shirt, a greaser's head bandana, and faded khaki-drab fatigue trousers.

Tricosas stared around the cramped radio room and felt a rush of claustrophobia tighten his chest. The broom closet was tucked up on the third floor of the Vets garage. The only furniture was a gray metal card table and matching folding chair, the PRC transmitter-receiver, a *First Blood* movie poster taped to the wall.

"Contact. This is Vets Three." Tricosas's index finger finally clicked on the PRC again.

"All right all you brave veterans of foreign wars. You purple heart and medal of honor winners. . . . Who can handle a pickup at Park Ave and Thirty-ninth Street? . . . A Ms. Austin and her day nurse Nazreen . . . Ms. Austin is a very sweet lady with a fold-it-up wheelchair. Fits very nice-like in the trunk of a Checker. She'll be going to Lenox Hill Hospital for her weekly chemotherapy. Over."

"Over. This is Vets Twenty-two. I'm at Mad Ave and five-two. I'll pick up and take Ms. Austin. I know the old chick. Be there in approximately five minutes. Over."

"Thank you kindly, Vets Twenty-two. . . . Okay, here's another hot one. I have a corporate account at Twenty-five Central Park West. Account T-21. Mr. Sidney Solovey is headed for the Yale Club at fifty Vanderbilt. Mr. Solovey used to work for Salomon Brothers. Before somebody blew the living shit out of Wall Street, that is. Over."

"Over. Vets Nineteen. I'm CPS and Sixth. I'll take Mr. Solovey to Yale."

Nick Tricosas stood up. He stretched another three inches into his body, and rubbed the small of his back. He needed a break from the taxi dispatcher radio clatter, the constant radioman duty since five that morning.

Tricosas lit up a cigar, gently rolling it between his thumb and index finger.

Then he wandered down the winding back stairs of the Vets building, trailing clouds of expensive smoke. He climbed down another twisting flight of stairs to the main garage itself.

The basement floor was thick with collected filth and debris. It was a typically rat-infested New York cellar. There was a second dispatcher's office flanked by cabbie waiting benches. Off to the left were rusted candy and soda machines, and an unpainted gray metal door.

Tricosas squinted and started down the serpentine, dungeon-like hallway. He sighed out loud. Colonel Hudson had said nobody was to go inside the locked basement room *under any circumstances*.

Tricosas produced a key anyway. He turned it into the

stout Chubb mortise lock, and heard the releasing click-click-click. He pushed forward the creaking door.

Then he finally peeked inside Colonel Hudson's forbidden holy of holies . . .

Nick Tricosas couldn't help smiling, almost laughing out loud. His breath got completely sucked away. His deep brown eyes might have doubled in size. His head tensed and felt like it might actually explode, blow off his shoulders. Right back up three flights of stairs to the claustrophobic radio dispatcher room.

Nick Tricosas had never actually seen four and a half billion dollars before! What he was looking at, staring at with what he knew must be a dumbfounded expression, just didn't *seem possible.*

Four and a half billion. That was correct, Nicko. *Billion!*

Chapter 36

COLONEL DAVID HUDSON did a highly unusual thing: he hesitated for once before acting. He reconsidered one final time as he waited in the phone booth at the southeast corner of 54th Street and Sixth Avenue and stared at the condensation on the glass panes. He understood that he was taking an unnecessary chance, asking for the same girl again.

He tapped a quarter against the black metal box, then finally let it drop.

Ding. Ding. Connection made.

Yes, he wanted to see Billie again.

He wanted to see her very much.

Less than an hour later, she glided into the buzzing, and crowded O'Neal's on West 57th and Sixth. Hudson watched her from a stool at the bar.

Yes, he wanted to see her again.

Billie. . . . Just Billie.

She had on a long, speckled-charcoal coat, and black leather boots to her thighs. A soft, pearl gray beret was carefully placed on the side of her flowing blond hair. She stood out in the tide of young and middle-aged businesswomen crowding into the popular bistro.

She smiled when she finally saw him and smoothly moved his way.

"They set an hour for your appointment. Should we go some place? An hour isn't that long," she said.

"I'd like to have a drink here with you. We have time. One drink."

Hudson signaled for the bartender, who came immediately in his crisp white shirt and black bow tie, like a man answering a very urgent summons. Hudson seemed to have a way of getting whatever he wanted, Billie had already noticed.

She ordered the house white, finally smiling, shaking her head at Hudson—as if he was a little hopeless, bewildering certainly.

A hundred and fifty dollars an hour, plus the O'Neal's bar tab, seemed steep for the honor of tipping a drink with an attractive girl.

"You don't have to pay. I'll say you didn't show." She said it, then was instantly flustered and embarrassed.

Hudson was certain she hadn't been doing this kind of work very long. Sometimes it happened to young actresses, to up-and-coming New York models.

"I like you. I don't think I understand you, but I like you," she said.

They looked into one another's eyes, and it was as if they were all alone in the hectic, buzzing barroom. Hudson could feel a desire for her growing again.

He leaned forward and kissed her cheek—he kissed her as gently as he had ever kissed anyone. He had the desire to get close, to try and open up a little with her.

"Tell me something about yourself. Just *one* small thing. . . . It doesn't have to be anything important."

She smiled again, actually seeming to be enjoying herself.

"All right. Sometimes I'm too impulsive. I shouldn't be offering you what's commonly called a freebie. I could be fired. Now tell me something about yourself."

"I don't even have enough money to pay this bar tab," Hudson said and laughed.

Billie Bogan started to laugh. "You really don't?"

"Really. Now tell me one *true* fact. Anything, just something true."

She hesitated, then shrugged. "I have two older sisters back in Birmingham. Back in England."

"They're both married. Successfully married. And your mother won't let you forget it," Hudson said with a smile.

"No. They're both married all right. Right on the button there. That's what you do if you're a sensible girl in Birmingham. But neither marriage is successful. And, yes, my mother won't let me forget I'm still single."

Hudson continued to smile. He sipped his beer, cautiously watching her brown eyes, her lips slightly wet with wine. He found himself wondering what was going on inside *her* head.

She laughed out loud, but nicely. "I'm completely losing it! I *don't believe* what I'm doing. I really don't believe this."

"Having a drink of white wine? At midday? Not that unusual in New York."

"I think I have to go. I really should go. I have to call and tell them you didn't keep your appointment."

"That's a problem. If you did that, they wouldn't let me see you again. I'd get a reputation as somebody completely unreliable. And we wouldn't want that, would we?"

"No, I guess we wouldn't. But I *really* have to go."

"Well, that's not acceptable to me. No. Just hold on a minute."

Hudson reached inside his weatherbeaten overcoat. He placed three fifty-dollar bills on the bar.

"Billie what? Tell me your last name at least."

"You can't afford this. Please. It really isn't a good idea."

"Billie what?"

She looked as if she'd been slapped, as if someone in her lower-middle-class English family had caught her at this escort work in New York. She hesitated, then finally spoke up again.

"It's Billie Bogan. Like the poet, Louise Bogan . . . 'Now that I have your face by heart, I look' . . ."

"You *look* extremely beautiful to me."

David Hudson hadn't felt this way in fifteen years. It was inconvenient and the timing was terrible—but there it was.

Feeling—where there had been none for so many years. *Intense* feeling. And warning signals that were going off everywhere, all at once.

Chapter 37

THE MORNING OF December 9 was a gloomy day in Washington. Even the stark, bare trees seemed to be gasping for light and life.

A second emergency meeting was held at the White House for members of the National Security Council and other officials associated with the Green Band inquiries.

As he waited patiently for the President to arrive, Carroll was thinking about pain.

It was hard for him not to. His right arm, which was cradled in bandages and a temporary sling, would flare up every now and again. He'd flinch and curse before he had time to remind himself he was lucky just to be alive. Despite the codeine number 4 he'd swallowed since Paris, his nerve endings felt as if they were being gnawed on.

Lucky to be alive, Carroll thought again. There were four less orphans in the world that way.

A morbid little syllogism clicked in his head.

A cat has nine lives.

I am not a cat.

Therefore I don't have nine lives.

So how many lives do I have? How many more chances if I keep playing the game this hard?

President Kearney finally entered the room and everyone stood.

The President of the United States was dressed casually. He had chosen a navy Lacoste shirt and slightly wrinkled, knock-around khakis. He looked like a kind of regular guy, Carroll thought to himself. You could imagine him, in better times and another season, pottering around the backyard barbecue, poking the center of a sirloin for readiness. Carroll remembered that Kearney had two young boys: maybe he played ball with them. But there wouldn't be much leisure for that these days. Kearney had taken the brunt of press criticism over Wall Street, a case of the press creating a convenient scapegoat for the public. Suddenly, in the space of a mere couple of days, his political moon had severely waned, shedding its former brightness.

The participants inside the White House conference room avoided formal handshakes this time. They'd all brought bulging leather briefcases and portfolios for the early morning meeting: the artifacts, the physical proof of the past four days of relentless investigations were there to be reviewed and acted upon.

Judging from the impressive *look* of the paperwork, someone had to have discovered something about Green Band, Carroll thought as the meeting began.

He looked across the room at Caitlin Dillon, who smiled back at him. She too had an overstuffed briefcase. Today, she looked businesslike and efficient in a tailored navy blue suit, plus an unadorned white shirt. She wore a navy necktie in the form of a large bow.

"Good morning to all of you—although I don't know

what might be good about it. To be blunt, I'm even more
concerned than I was on Friday night."

President Kearney certainly did nothing to relieve the
strain as he delivered his opening remarks. He remained
standing stiffly at the head of the long wooden table.

"Every reliable projection we have says that a Stock
Market panic, a full-scale crash, may soon be on us. . . .
Some of the more manipulative bastards around the world
have actually figured how to make this tragedy work to
their advantage . . .

"I will tell all of you this in strict confidence—the Western economy cannot survive a major crash at this time.
Even a minor Market crash would be catastrophic."

The President had raised his voice and there was the
palest flash of his old campaign style, the inspirational
voice, the characteristic firmness of the jaw—but then, as
suddenly as the echo had come, it vanished.

The President again solicited information, new data
around the table. Each adviser gave a succinct report on
any findings relating to Green Band.

When his turn arrived, Carroll inched his chair closer to
the conference table. He tried to make everything very still
inside his head. He was hazy after Paris. His body was still
numb and cold following the shooting. And his arm was
throbbing again.

"My news isn't good either," Carroll began. "We have
some facts, some statistics, but not a lot that's worthwhile.
The raw information about the bombings is complete, anyway. Five packages of plastique were required per building. They could have leveled lower Manhattan if they'd
wanted to. *They didn't want to . . .*

"They wanted to do exactly what they did. New York

was a controlled, a tightly disciplined *demonstration*. My team has spent forty-eight hours going through every terrorist contact that exists. There are *no connections* to this group.

"There *was* a somewhat unclear, but promising connection with the European black market," Carroll continued, flipping a page on his notepad. Maybe it would have been more promising if Michel Chevron had survived, if some ID had been found on the man he'd shot in Paris. There were too many ifs and maybes; twice as many as the usual police case. One thing was certain, you couldn't build an arrest around conditionals.

"Unfortunately, so many Wall Street computers and brokerage house records were destroyed, we have no way to determine the true Stock Market picture. We don't know if securities were taken, or if there's been a computer scam."

The Vice-president, Thomas More Elliot, broke in on Carroll. Of all the people seated in the room, the stern New Englander seemed the sharpest, the most in control of himself. That morning the Vice-president looked more like the group's leader than the President.

"You're saying we still have *no idea* who it is we're dealing with?"

Carroll frowned and shook his head. "There haven't been any further demands. No bargaining. No contact whatsoever. They seem to have invented a completely new and terrifying game. It's a game where *we don't even get to know what game we're playing!* They move—then we have to try to react."

"Comments?" Elliot asked, his tone clearly acerbic.

The blank faces staring at Carroll certainly weren't encouraging or supportive. The heads of the enforcement agencies were especially cool and distant. The Cabinet members were mostly business-management types who didn't understand the problems of police work in the field. They were indifferent to the trials and demands of a start-from-scratch street investigation.

The Senate majority leader finally spoke. Marshall Turner's familiar voice was Southern and boomed like an echo in a West Virginia cavern. "Mr. President, I'm afraid this simply will not do. All of what I'm hearing is unsatisfactory. Late last week, we came *that* close to a full economic collapse in this country."

"That's what we're told, Marshall."

"Now you tell us we're still in serious danger, maybe even worse danger. A second Black Friday is being discussed. I feel it's our responsibility to make certain we have our best investigative apparatus in place. Now, as I understand it, the Federal Bureau and the CIA are both being underutilized in the current manhunt for terrorists."

The tone in the Senator's voice was offensive to Carroll. He stared at the political leader, who had the kind of swollen pink face you might encounter in the sawdust-filled back room of a country store.

Phil Berger, the Director of the CIA, stepped into the silence. He was a small, lean man whose head, starkly bald and shining under the lights in the room, came to a domed point. He reminded Carroll of a hard-boiled egg sitting in an eggcup.

Berger spoke, "The FBI and the CIA are working

twenty-four-hour shifts. There's no question of underutilization."

"All right. Let's not fight among ourselves." The President abruptly rose at the conference table.

Justin Kearney looked at Carroll and said, "I made a hard decision late yesterday. I would have called you, but you weren't in New York."

"I was in Paris getting shot at."

The President ignored Carroll's remark. "Effective immediately, I'm ordering the following changes. I want you to continue to run the part of the operation that deals directly with known terrorist groups. But I want Phil Berger to supervise *the overall investigation of Green Band,* including the investigation of terrorists inside the U.S. You're also to give the CIA a complete record of your personal contacts, all your files."

Carroll stared incredulously at Kearney. He was almost certain it wasn't legal for him to give his record files to the CIA. He also had the feeling he'd just been floated down the Potomac on a leaky raft. Thanks for all your past help, but your team's working methods leave something to be desired.

He turned away from the President who seemed to have reached this decision single-handedly. That troubled and perplexed Carroll. But there was something else, one thing that disturbed him even more.

It was the boardroom coldness, the sterile, Big Business atmosphere that was growing up everywhere in the government. It was all this super-secrecy, the super-deceit—usually under misleading cover of "security," and "need to know."

They made the command decision, and they no longer felt they had to explain themselves to anybody.

"I guess I understand, Mr. President, and I'm afraid I have to quit under those circumstances. With all respect, I resign, sir. I'm out of this."

Carroll got up and walked out of the conference room, then out of the White House. It was over for him.

Chapter 38

APPROXIMATELY AN HOUR LATER, Carroll sat inside an Eastern shuttle jet destined for New York. Outside, an electrical storm whipped the sky.

From his window he could see dramatic black clouds rushing by. He stared at the gathering storm and felt overwhelmed by a curious loneliness.

It was at times like these when he missed Nora most. Nobody he'd met before or since was as good at making him feel whole; nobody else seemed able to make him laugh at himself. And that was the real trick, being able to laugh when you needed to—and right now, Carroll needed to laugh at something.

He felt Caitlin Dillon's hand on his arm. Turning, he gave her a weary half smile. She was trying to be sympathetic, to be kind. But she wasn't Nora.

"You must *know* it isn't your fault. Everybody's frustrated, Arch. Green Band didn't just do a number on Wall Street, it created an atmosphere of panic. Our President, who is turning out to be even less decisive than I imagined he'd be, made a panicky decision. That's all."

She patted his arm and he felt like a kid with a scraped,

bloody knee. The warm, almost maternal streak in Caitlin surprised him.

"It isn't your fault. Washington is loaded with scared men making inadequate decisions." She paused before asking, "What will you do? Go into legal practice? Draw up wills? Deeds of trust? Maybe something like corporate law?"

Carroll drifted back from somewhere distant inside his mind. Her light sarcasm didn't escape him. He even welcomed it. *Law,* he thought. The reason he'd never used his degree was because he couldn't stomach the idea of law tomes, of hunting down precedents in the dust of unreadable books, and having to fraternize with other lawyers.

He was quiet for a time. Then he said, "Can you honestly imagine me reporting to Phil Berger?"

Caitlin shook her head. "He's an *egghead* in more than one sense of the word. The man must have been hatched."

Carroll suddenly laughed. The storm rocked the plane a moment. "When I was a kid, my mother used to give us hard-boiled eggs for breakfast. Some tradition from the old country. All of us kids would beat the tops open with our spoons. That's what I should have had back there in the White House. A big spoon to beat on Phil Berger's head."

Carroll turned toward Caitlin Dillon. She was laughing now. It was a musical kind of laugh, like some quirky tune you couldn't forget, one that ran through your mind in a tantalizing way but you couldn't put a name to it.

Carroll finally shook with laughter. "You surprise me. You really surprise me."

"Why is that?"

"You look so damn straight and businesslike, but you've got this weird sense of humor."

"Weird for a Wall Street business type, I guess. For a dyed-in-the-wool Midwesterner. A Presbyterian."

Carroll laughed some more, and it felt pretty good. Tension knots in his neck were finally loosening up. "Yeah. Of course. For a country hick from Ohio."

"My father taught me that you need a good sense of humor to survive Wall Street. He survived it, though just barely."

Caitlin gazed at Carroll, saying nothing more. She had stopped laughing and her expression was serious; her eyes searched his face. She looked as if maybe a small important gear had just shifted inside her mind.

Carroll watched her, conscious of something happening in his own body. For a moment, he had the uncomfortable feeling that he was betraying Nora, betraying a memory—

Christ, it had been a long time since he had reacted like this; he was aware of how deprived he was, how hungry he'd become. He raised one hand, his fingers trembling slightly, and he placed the palm against the side of Caitlin's face.

Tenderly, he kissed her.

And then the moment was over as suddenly as if it had never happened.

Caitlin Dillon was looking from the window at the theatrical cloud display and talking about how soon they'd be back in New York—and what Carroll wondered was whether he'd really kissed her?

When Carroll arrived back at No. 13 Wall, all that remained was for him to clear out his desk and leave the world of pointless stakeouts and twenty-hour work days. It was easy and mostly painless, he thought. Something he probably should have done a long time ago.

He was interrupted by a knock on his door. When he turned, Walter Trentkamp was standing there. The FBI man walked slowly across the room. He leaned against the cluttered desk and sighed loudly.

"I'd quit too if I had an office like this." Trentkamp frowned. He stared around the room. "I mean, I've seen bleak before."

"What can I do for you, Walter?"

"You can reconsider the decision you made in Washington."

"Did somebody send you up here? Did they tell you to go talk some sense into Carroll?"

Trentkamp pursed his lips. He shook his head. "What'll you do now, anyhow?"

"Law," Carroll lied.

"You're too old already. Law's a young man's game."

Carroll sighed. Quit, Walter. *Quit it right now.*

Trentkamp continued to frown. "Nobody knows terrorists the way you do. If you leave, lives will be lost. And *you know it.* So what if your pride is a little wounded right now?"

Carroll sat down hard behind his desk. He hated Walter Trentkamp just then. He hated the idea that another person could see through him so easily. Walter was so goddamn smart. There was an impressive superiority that peeked through his policeman's facade every now and then. "You're a manipulative sonofabitch."

"Do you think I got where I am without some small understanding of human foibles?" Trentkamp asked. He held his hand out to be shaken. "You're a cop. Every day you remind me a little more of your father. He was a stubborn bastard, too."

Carroll hesitated. With his own hand in midair, halfway toward Walter Trentkamp, he hesitated. It was one of those moments when his private world seemed to spin on its own axis. He could choose—right now he had a choice.

He shrugged and shook Trentkamp's hand.

"Welcome back on board, Archer."

On board what? Carroll wondered. "One thing I want you to know. When Green Band is settled, I quit."

"Sure," Trentkamp said. "That's understood. Just keep in touch until Green Band *is* settled."

"I want to be a free man, Walter."

"Don't we all?" Walter Trentkamp asked, and finally smiled. "You're so fucking cute when you pout."

Chapter 39

ON THE SECOND FLOOR of No. 13 Wall, Caitlin Dillon sat in dark silhouette on a high wooden stool. Most of the overhead lights in the Crisis Room had been dimmed. She listened to the soothing electronic whirr of half a dozen IBM and Hewlett-Packard computers.

It had been Caitlin's idea to collect and evaluate all the available newspaper information and police intelligence flowing in over the word processor consoles. The news arrived in sudden, urgent bursts, streams of tiny green letters that came from both the financial sectors and police agencies all around the world.

As she sat there, her eyes hurting from the glare of the screens, she pondered two things.

One was the scary and real possibility of a total financial collapse around the world.

The other was the intricate, the almost hopeless puzzle of her own private life.

Many years before, Caitlin's father, who was a principled and intelligent investment banker in the Midwest, had tried to stand up to the Wall Street clique of firms. He had lost his battle, lost an unfair fight, and been thrown into bankruptcy. Year after year, Caitlin had listened as he bitterly lectured against the injustice, the unfairness, and sometimes the stupidity built into the American financial system. In the same way that some children grow up wanting to be crusading lawyers, Caitlin had decided that she wanted to help reform the financial system.

She had come East as a kind of avenging angel. She was both fascinated and repelled by the self-contained world of Big Business, and by Wall Street in particular. In her heart of hearts, Caitlin wanted the financial system to work properly, and she was fierce, almost obsessed with the application of her position as the SEC Enforcer . . .

It was likewise the independent, nontraditional part of Caitlin that enjoyed other mild eccentricities—like wandering the streets of New York in tight-fitting Italian jeans, crumpled oversized T-shirts, leather boots that came almost to her butt.

She might happily devote a Sunday afternoon to some exotic Italian recipe from Marcella Hazan—but she could go weeks abhorring the idea of doing any cooking at all, avoiding all housework in her East Side apartment. She was proud of earning six figures a year at the SEC, but sometimes she wanted to throw it all over and have a baby. Sometimes, she was physically afraid she might never have a child. She *ached* with the idea, the way one aches from a real loss. And she had no idea, absolutely none, whether these opposing impulses could ever peacefully coexist.

She had been thinking along these insane lines ever since *that kiss* on the Washington-to-New York airplane.

It had been quick, and yet she had the instinctive feeling she wanted to go beyond the first kiss with Carroll.

What was she thinking, anyhow?

She hardly knew Carroll. His kiss had been the kiss of a stranger. She wasn't even sure if it had meant anything to him, or whether it had been something thrown up by the peculiar circumstances of the flight, his way of relieving tension, and disappointment, and more than a little justified anger.

I don't really know the first thing about him, she thought.

A shuffling noise made her turn and she saw Carroll in the computer room doorway. She was embarrassed, as if she suspected he'd been standing there, reading her thoughts.

He had his arm in a fresh white sling and he looked pale. She smiled. She'd already heard about the success of Walter Trentkamp's personal appeal and she was relieved—decisions made under duress were almost always the wrong ones, she knew. Carroll's impetuousness was part of his charm: but one day, she thought, one day he might run into the kind of serious trouble he couldn't extricate himself from.

"I had Michel Chevron ready to talk about the European black market," he said.

"Don't keep blaming yourself."

"Somebody knows all our moves. Christ, who knows what Michel Chevron could have told me?" Carroll shifted his weight from one foot to the other. She was reminded of a restless prizefighter warming up.

"How's the arm?" she asked. "Hurt?"

"Only when I think about Paris."

"Then don't think." She slid down from the wooden stool. She wanted to go across the room and somehow ease his discomfort, his embarrassment. She didn't. "I'm glad . . ." she said instead.

"Glad?"

She stared at him. Carroll had a vulnerable quality that inspired her to strange sympathies and concerns, but also anxieties she couldn't quite articulate. He had a lost boy quality, maybe that was it.

"Glad you didn't get yourself killed," she said and finally smiled.

There was a breathless silence in the room.

She finally turned back to one of the computer screens, studying the mass of crawling green letters. The spell between them was broken again.

"Another Baader-Meinhof member was shot and killed in Munich." Caitlin looked up from the display screen message. She watched him, wondering again what the kiss on the airplane had meant.

Carroll merely nodded. "The West Germans are using Green Band as an excuse to solve their local terrorism problems. The BND is pragmatic. They're probably the toughest police force in Western Europe."

Caitlin perched herself atop the high wooden stool again. She loosely hugged both her legs at the knees.

Another message started to blip over the nearest computer. Caitlin turned and watched the computer screen closely.

Her mind had suddenly frozen.

"Look at this, Arch."

Chapter 40

MOSCOW. THE KGB HAS INTERCEPTED PYOTR ANDRONOV. IMPORTANT UNDERWORLD BLACK MARKET SPECIALIST. ANDRONOV HOLDING U.S. SECURITIES, PRESUMED STOLEN. ANDRONOV LINKS STOLEN BONDS TO GREEN BAND. AMOUNT: ONE MILLION, TWO HUNDRED FIFTY THOUSAND DOLLARS. REFERRED TO AS "<u>SAMPLES.</u>"

Moments later, another equally curious item began to appear on the computer display screen.

The second entry was from the Swiss in Geneva.

INTERPOL. RELIABLE LOCAL INFORMER HAS REPORTED "FLOODING" OF GENEVA MARKET WITH STOLEN BOND OFFERS. SELLER LOOKING FOR "SERIOUS BUYER." AMOUNT SUGGESTED AS HIGH AS FIVE TO TEN MILLION AMERICAN DOLLARS. SOURCE <u>VERY</u> RELIABLE.

"I think this could be the moment of truth." Carroll stared and gnawed at his bottom lip.

"*Something's* happening. But why is it happening all at once like this?"

For the next hour and a half, during which the various screens virtually exploded with new information, as many as a dozen U.S. Army and police officials rushed down to look at the messages inside the Crisis Room. News was being transmitted from all over the world now, all at once.

As bad as it seemed, there was relief that *something* was happening. Was Green Band finally moving?

ZURICH. PREVALENT RUMORS HERE TONIGHT OF STOLEN U.S. SECURITIES AVAILABLE. VERY LARGE AMOUNTS. HIGH SEVEN-FIGURE THEFT INDICATED BY SOURCES.

LONDON, SCOTLAND YARD. DURING ROUTINE SEARCH IN KENSINGTON, AMERICAN STOCK CERTIFICATES FOUND. SE-RIAL NUMBERS TO FOLLOW. SUSPECT NOT IN FLAT WITH CACHE. SUSPECT IS JOHN HALL-FRAZIER, A KNOWN FENCE IN EUROPE BOND MARKET. SUSPECT KNOWN TO MICHEL CHEVRON.

BEIRUT. AHMED JARREL ARRESTED THIS EVENING HERE. TRADED THE FOLLOWING INFORMATION . . . JARREL HAD BEEN ATTEMPTING TO SELL U.S. SECURITIES IN BEIRUT. ASKING PRICE THIRTY FIVE CENTS ON A DOLLAR VALUE. VERY HIGH QUALITY BONDS. SOME BLANK CHEQUES ALSO. JARREL CLAIMS AMOUNT AVAILABLE UP TO ONE HUNDRED MILLION AMERICAN!

Half an hour later, using an ordinary hand calculator, Caitlin added up the amounts indicated on the display screens so far. She gasped as she arrived at the final sum.

It came to just under a hundred million U.S. dollars. "Samples."

Next, she made a quick printout of the Fortune 500, America's largest individual corporations, to check against the stolen securities reported thus far.

Nearly all the thefts were in the top 100 companies. Those reported to date created an unusual, elite universe. Was there a clue or potential lead in that?

Rank in Fortune 500	Company	Stockholder Equity
1	Exxon (New York)	$29,443,095,000
2	General Motors (Detroit)	20,766,600,000
3	Mobil (New York)	13,952,000,000
5	International Business Machines (Armonk, N.Y.)	23,219,000,000
6	Texaco (Harrison, N.Y.)	14,726,000,000
8	Standard Oil (Indiana) (Chicago)	12,440,000,000
9	Standard Oil of California (San Francisco)	14,106,000,000
10	General Electric (Fairfield, Conn.)	11,270,000,000
15	U.S. Steel (Pittsburgh)	11,270,000,000
17	Sun (Radnor, Pa.)	5,355,000,000
20	ITT (New York)	6,106,084,000
26	AT&T Technologies (New York)	4,621,300,000
28	Dow Chemical (Midland, Mich.)	5,047,000,000
34	Westinghouse Electric (Pittsburgh)	3,410,300,000
39	Amerada Hess (New York)	2,525,663,000
42	McDonnell-Douglas (St. Louis)	2,067,900,000

43	Rockwell International (Pittsburgh)	2,367,300,000
45	Ashland Oil (Russell, Ky.)	1,084,824,000
50	Lockheed (Burbank, Calif.)	826,200,000
52	Monsanto (St. Louis)	3,667,000,000
55	Anheuser-Busch (St. Louis)	1,766,500,000
67	Gulf & Western Industries (New York)	1,893,924,000
69	Bethlehem Steel (Bethlehem, Pa.)	1,313,100,000
77	Texas Instruments (Dallas)	1,202,700,000
84	Digital Equipment (Maynard, Mass.)	3,541,282,000
89	Diamond Shamrock (Dallas)	2,743,327,000
92	Deere (Moline, Ill.)	2,275,967,000
97	North American Philips (New York)	883,874,000

By 9:15, the Crisis Room at No. 13 Wall was filled with officials from the White House and the Pentagon who scrutinized the computer screens like gamblers nervously watching the outcome of their bets. The Secretary of the Treasury and the Vice-president were both present. Phil Berger of the CIA had been flown in by special Air Force helicopter from Washington.

At eleven o'clock, urgent reports were still chattering in over the computer terminals. The President had been kept informed; another National Security conference had already been called for late that night.

This time, however, neither Arch Carroll nor Caitlin Dillon was invited to travel down to Washington.

"What did *I* do?" Caitlin angrily complained to Carroll when she found out.

"You've got the wrong friends," Carroll said. "You're traveling in bad company."

"You?" she asked.

"Yeah. Me."

Chapter 41

AT 4:30 THAT MORNING, three sets of headlights lanced a dense gray wall of fog. The lights stopped suddenly, making circles on a twelve-foot-high electrified gate dripping snow and ice.

The oppressive gate was meant to help protect the Russian version of Camp David, a heavily fortified hunting lodge called Zavidavo.

"Prajol!" Two militiamen from the Internal Security Division waddled out into the bracing cold. They were carrying machine guns, dressed in bulky coats. It was their job to check the identification of all visitors.

In a matter of seconds, a Cheka and two hand-tooled Zil limousines were cleared to proceed up the icy lanes winding to the main hunting lodge.

The automobiles, side-blinds drawn, carried *six* of the most important decision makers in Soviet Russia. The military guards hurried back into their gatehouse and immediately called for emergency security for the resort compound.

Inside the main dacha, Major General Radomir Raskov of the GRU Secret Police was feeling apprehensive as well; but he was also heady with excitement. Raskov had commissioned an elegant country breakfast to be served in a sun parlor, which was heated by a blazing log fire.

Right after breakfast, General Raskov would drop his private bombshell on the six visiting leaders.

At a little past 5:00 A.M., the Politburo steering group sat down to steaming platters heaped with duck eggs, country sausage and freshly caught fish.

The breakfast table group included Yori Ilich Belov, the Russian Premier; a Cossack, Red Army General named Yuri Sergeivitch Iranov; the First Secretary of the Communist Party; General Vasily Kalin; the heads of both the KGB and GRU.

General Radomir Raskov spoke informally over the clacking noise of forks and knives. His smile, which was usually a small tight fist of teeth, was surprisingly warm. "In addition to the main business of our meeting, I am delighted to report the wood pheasant are back on the north ridge."

Premier Yori Belov clapped his huge hands. A stiffly formal man wearing thick bifocals, he raised his dark, fuzzy eyebrows and smiled for the first time since he'd arrived. Premier Belov was an obsessive hunter and fisherman.

General Raskov continued in a more serious tone. "On December sixth, as you all know, I spoke with our friend François Monserrat about the dangerous and now potentially uncontrollable economic situation developing in the United States . . .

"At that time, he informed me he had been contacted by persons claiming responsibility for the Wall Street attack. . . . During the past two days, Monserrat's representatives have met with representatives from the so-called Green Band faction. In London . . ."

Premier Belov turned sharply to Yuri Demurin, director of the KGB. "Comrade Director, has *your* department been successful in discovering anything further about the *provocateur* group? How, for example, were they able to originally contact Monserrat?"

"We have been working very closely with General Raskov of course," General Demurin lied with unctuous sincerity. "Unfortunately, at this time, we have been able to come up with nothing definitive."

General Raskov clapped his hands harshly for a servant.

Demurin was his only rival in the Russian police world. Demurin was also a capital shit, a petty bureaucrat without a single redeeming characteristic. Whenever he was in a staff meeting with Demurin, General Raskov's blood boiled.

A blond maid appeared, hovering nervously. The maid's name was Margarita Kupchuck, and she had served at Zavidavo since the early 1970s. Margarita Kupchuck's quiet humor had made her a personal favorite with the important Soviets.

"We're ready for more coffee and tea, my dear Margarita. Some preserves or fruit would be nice, as well. Would anyone prefer a stronger libation?"

Premier Belov smiled once again. He had placed a blue packet of Austrian cigarettes in front of himself. "Yes, Margarita, please bring us a bottle of spirits. Some Georgian white lightning would be appropriate."

Belov laughed now and his chins shook, giving everyone the impression that his face was about to slip through layers of his neck and vanish into his body.

General Raskov smiled. It was always politic to smile, at least, whenever Premier Belov took it upon himself to laugh. "We now believe we know the reason for the bombings in America," he said, *finally dropping his bombshell on the group.*

General Raskov silently gazed around the breakfast parlor. The men sitting at the table had stopped lighting cigars, stopped taking sips of Russian coffee.

"This Green Band group has made a frightening proposal to us. Through François Monserrat's terrorist cell, actually. The offer was made last evening. . . . *This* is why I've called all of you here so early in the morning."

General Raskov lightly drummed his fingers on the dining table as he spoke the next words. "Comrades, the Green Band group has requested a payment. A total of *one hundred twenty million dollars in gold bullion.* This sum is in exchange for securities and bonds *stolen* during the December fourth bombings on Wall Street.

"The securities were apparently removed during the seven-hour evacuation itself. . . . Comrades, the *net* worth of the stolen goods offered to us . . . is in excess of two billion dollars!"

The men, the elite who ruled Soviet Russia, were silent; they were reeling at the massive numbers they had just heard.

There was no way anyone could have been prepared for such an announcement.

At first, no word at all from Green Band. And now *this.* Two billion dollars to be ransomed.

"They plan to sell to buyers other than ourselves as well. The total amount would be enough to cripple the Western economic system." General Raskov went on. "This could mean a *cataclysmic panic* for the American Stock Market."

Less than ten miles away from Zavidavo, a delivery truck marked *flour* fishtailed, then regained control. It was barreling down a narrow country road which seemed little more than an ice-slicked toboggan track.

The truck finally plowed to a stop in front of a cottage in the country village of Staritsa. The driver leaped out and ran crunching through bright new snow up to his knees.

The cottage door opened, and a woman's arm, in a drab gray bathrobe, took an envelope.

The driver then high-stepped back to his truck, and hurriedly drove away into the snow.

From the village of Staritsa, the contents of the envelope were relayed in telephone code to a young woman working at the GUM Department Store in Moscow.

The GUM clerk used a special telephone, and another complex code, to make an urgent transatlantic call to the United States, specifically to the city of Langley, Virginia.

The original message had been sent by Margarita Kupchuck, the housekeeper at Zavidavo. For eleven years Margarita had been one of the most important operatives of the Central Intelligence Agency working inside Russia.

The message provided the American team with their first break in the Green Band investigation.

It consisted of just fifteen words:

Ritz Hotel, London. Thursday morning. Two billion dollars. Stolen securities to be exchanged . . . Green Band.

Chapter 42

IT WAS PROBABLY A DREAM, and a very bad one.

He was standing in an unfamiliar room whose walls met the ceiling at angles that would have been impossible in anything other than dream geometry. There was a door halfway open and a pale light, the color of pearl, created a slat of dull color.

A shadow moved into the pearl-colored light and stood there just beyond the door. He knew, without even having to look, that the figure was Nora.

He wanted to move forward, to step out of the room, he wanted to see Nora and hold her but something held him in place, something kept him rooted to the floor.

He cried her name aloud.

And then—

A bell was ringing. And he imagined it rang in Nora's hand.

Disturbed, sweating, Carroll sat upright.

He rubbed his eyes, swung his legs over the side of the rumpled covers on his bed.

And then he realized that the bell was real. Someone

was ringing the doorbell and this was the sound his dream had absorbed.

He wandered from the bedroom. He squinted into the spyhole of the Manhattan apartment he'd once shared with Nora.

"Who is it?"

He could see nothing except swirling blackness where the hallway had definitely been last night.

Years before, he'd lucked into the West Side apartment, a sprawling three bedroom with river views. The apartment was still rent-controlled at four hundred and seventy-nine dollars a month, an impossible bargain. After Nora died, Carroll had decided to hold on to the place and use it nights when he worked late in the city.

"Who is it? Who's out there?" *Doorbell goddamn ring itself or was he still dreaming?*

Whoever was out in the apartment house hallway didn't seem to want to answer.

Carroll reached back for his Magnum.

Arch Carroll finally unlocked the Segal, but he left the heavy linkchain secure.

He swung the front door open about four inches and the chain snapped against the sturdy wooden jamb.

Caitlin Dillon was peering in at him through the doorway crack. She looked frightened. Her eyes were hollow and dark.

Chapter 43

"I COULDN'T SLEEP."

"What time is it?"

"I'm embarrassed to say it's before five. It's about twenty to five. Okay?"

"In the morning?"

"Please laugh at this or something. Oh, God. I'm going."
She suddenly turned away.

"Hold it. Wait. Hey, *stop walking*."

She half turned at the elevator. Her hair was windblown and her cheeks were flushed, like she'd been riding horses in Central Park.

"Come on in. . . . Please come in and talk. Please?"

Inside his apartment, Carroll whisked clean the kitchen table, and he made coffee. Caitlin sat down and twisted her long fingers together nervously. She opened a box of cigarettes and lit one. When she spoke her voice was husky, slightly unfamiliar.

"I've been smoking for hours, which is uncharacteristic of me. I couldn't sleep, I couldn't stop pacing around. All that information about the stolen securities kept spinning through my head, Arch . . ."

Carroll shook the last remnants of the bad dream from his mind, jerking himself into the present. "Green Band's moving. Only we can't figure out the direction they're taking."

"That's one thing that bothers me," Caitlin said. "And then I start to wonder how much has been stolen and how far this whole incredible thing goes. I calculated an amount in the region of a couple hundred million, but God knows how much more has actually disappeared."

She sighed, crushing her cigarette impatiently. "Also, I'm still really ticked off at not being invited to that meeting in Washington. Do they honestly think I've got nothing to contribute?"

Carroll had never seen her in this frame of mind. It was like watching her from a whole new set of angles—she was angry, she was worried, and she seemed temporarily confused. Her usual business-world professionalism couldn't help her now; she was reduced to asking questions which neither of them could answer. Suddenly, Caitlin Dillon wasn't quite so untouchable.

Around five-fifteen they made Sara Lee danishes, the only moderately edible items in Carroll's kitchen.

"When I was thirteen or so I actually won a bakeoff. This was at an Ohio county fair," Caitlin admitted as she pulled the danishes out of the oven.

They moved out to a windowed nook which overlooked the river and the New Jersey Palisades. One whole wall of the room was covered with thirty-five millimeter pictures of the kids. A single, fading picture was of Carroll as an Army sergeant in Viet Nam. He'd taken down the last pictures of Nora only a few months before.

"Mmmfff. Tremendous." He licked sticky crumbs off his index and middle fingers.

Caitlin's eyes rolled back into her forehead. "I'm not impressed with your kitchen supplies, Arch. Your cupboard's stocked with four bottles of beer, a half jar of Skippy peanut butter. Haven't you heard—the contemporary man in New York is a gourmet cook."

Maybe *her* boyfriends were, Carroll thought to himself. None of the "contemporary men" Carroll knew could cook anything much more complicated than tomato soup.

"What can I tell you, I'm basically an ascetic. Skippy peanut butter happens to be cholesterol free."

A different kind of look crossed Caitlin's face right about then. A private joke smile? Carroll wasn't sure he'd read it correctly. Was she laughing at him now?

Then a quick reassuring smile came that was warm and even more comfortable.

"I think we're going to need at least an hour," she said mysteriously. "Uninterrupted time. Phone-off-the-hook seclusion and quiet. You didn't have any big plans for the morning I hope?"

"Just sleep."

"Boring. Also not very ascetic."

Carroll shrugged his broad shoulders; his eyes burned with curiosity. "I'm a boring person. Daddy, sometimes *mom* of four; straight job with the government; occasional terrorist contact."

There was a dense silence as he and Caitlin walked out of the windowed den. They cleared their throats almost at the same moment.

Caitlin reached for him, and then they were lightly, just barely holding hands.

Carroll was suddenly very aware of her perfume, the *shh-shh* of her jeans, the silhouette of her profile . . .

"This is one of the more impressive New York apartments I've been in. I really didn't expect this. All the hominess, the charm."

"What did you expect: hunting rifles on the wall? . . . Actually, I sew. I can knit. I do iron-on patches for four little kids."

Caitlin had to smile at Carroll again.

It was the first time he'd seen this particular smile. Irony, but also nice warmth were glowing in her eyes at the same time. He felt like they'd crossed some barrier, made some slightly more solid connection. He wasn't sure what it was, though.

They started to kiss and touch each other lightly in the narrow hallway. They kissed gently at first. Then the kiss became harder, with urgency and strength on Caitlin's part.

They kissed all the way to the front bedroom where morning light was flooding the room. Huge, curtainless windows faced onto the Hudson, which was a flat, slate-blue lake that morning.

"Caitlin? . . . Is this wise?"

"It *is* really wise. It doesn't mean the end of the world, you know. It's just one morning. I promise not to get hurt. If *you* do."

She put a finger to Carroll's lips. Soften the blow of her last statement. She then lightly kissed the back of her own finger.

"I have one small favor. Don't think about anything for ten minutes or so. No Ohio jokes either. Okay?"

Carroll nodded. She was smart about this kind of thing, too. A little scary smart. She'd been here before . . . *I won't get hurt; don't you get hurt.*

"All right. Whatever you say can be the official rules."

For a moment, they sat together, hugging on the low-slung, quilt-covered double bed. Then they very slowly began to undress. A shivery draft slithered in from the casement windows; the cold air seemed to blow right through the tall black-framed window panes.

Carroll was completely, physically and spiritually entranced. Also frightened. *He hadn't been with anybody for over three years. There hadn't been anything like this for so very long.* He felt a little guilty, automatically comparing Caitlin with Nora, though he didn't want to.

Caitlin's hands had the lightest imaginable touch. Extraordinary control and gentleness as she tugged off his trousers. He felt everything beginning to relax inside.

Her fingers were like elegant feathers over his upper back. Tickling. Dusting his neck.

Then Caitlin's palms. Rotating in easy circles. Into his temple. Gently pulling on the curls of his dark hair.

Carroll remembered that he was ticklish down both sides of his stomach. He had been since he was a little kid.

More feathery fingers. Teasing Carroll up and down the insides of his legs . . .

On to the balls of his feet, his toes, his soles . . .

Then everything was moving slightly faster; up another notch in tempo.

His body suddenly, involuntarily spasmed. *Jesus Christ.* Caitlin was doing some unexpected things to him.

She blew softly on the insides of her hands. She cupped warm fingers over his eyelids, then over his ears.

She spoke in a voice that was nearly as gentle and sensual as her touch. "This is called a thrill massage. Believe it or not, it was the fad at little Oberlin College."

"Yeah? You're good at it."

"Awh, gee blush. . . . Wild youth in long forgotten Midwestern corn fields."

He was beginning to like her.

Maybe an awful lot.

He didn't know if he should, if this truly *was* wise.

She lightly brushed his legs again. . . . His upper back again. . . . Neck, scrotum.

Only much faster, even lighter now. Turning him into jelly, no container.

There was no real impression of fingers, he was noticing.

Quite amazing.

More like the softest combs of air.

How had she gotten this good? . . . A little unbelievable in a way . . . being who she was. . . . Who was she, really?

Her face came down very close then. "Smile for the camera, Arch." Faint smiling whisper from Caitlin. "My heart is pure, but my mind is occasionally kinky."

At some time, somewhere in all of the light touching, brushing, tickling, Caitlin had taken her jeans and blouse off. She still wore pink underpants, wool knee socks. Her breasts had the loveliest, delicate, shell-pink nipples. They were hard now; totally aroused.

She touched one erect nipple, then the other to the head of Carroll's penis.

She was a masterpiece, Carroll couldn't help thinking, completely filling his eyes.

Carroll remembered what she'd said before in the breakfast nook. It made him smile a little now, almost laugh out loud. *We're going to need at least an hour.*

There was no longer such a thing as time; no Green Band urgencies existed right now. Carroll had the comfortable, wonderful idea that he trusted Caitlin Dillon. . . . He almost completely trusted her. How could he so easily trust Caitlin already? . . .

"Tell me all about yourself. Whatever comes out. No editing, okay, Carroll?"

To the continuing rhythm of her fingers; to the slight crooning of bed springs; to dancing morning sunbeams, Carroll spoke the truth, as he knew it:

"Whole life story. About thirty seconds. . . . As a little kid I always wanted to play for the Yankees, maybe, *maybe* for the football Giants. Son of a cop. Honest, *poor* cop. Irish-Catholic family from the West Bronx. That's my youth. Notre Dame. . . . Law School at Michigan State. Then drafted.

"Four absolutely terrific kids. Kind of a perfect marriage until Nora passed away. That's middle-American for *she died* . . . I'm a very different person when I'm with my kids. Childlike and free. Maybe a little retarded . . . um . . . boy . . . that's very nice. Yes, right there. Ohio, huh?"

"What else? You were telling me your life story. *Reader's Digest* condensed version."

"Oh, yeah . . . I have this recurring problem. *Big* problem . . . with *Them*."

"Who's them?"

Arch Carroll suddenly felt a sharp twist of tension. *Not now. He made it go away.*

"Just *them*. . . . Ones who make all the most important decisions. . . . Ones who rob people, without caring one way or the other. On Wall Street, down in Washington. Ones who trade terrorist murderers—for innocent, kidnapped business people. The ones who kill people of brain cancer. The bad guys. As opposed to . . . *us.*"

Caitlin gently kissed Carroll's curly brown hair; she kissed his cauliflower ear. She finally found his mouth, which tasted very nice, she thought. Fresh and clean and sweet.

"I don't like *them* either. I think I like you. I think I like *us*. Please like me a little."

"All I can do is try, Caitlin. You're beautiful. You're witty. You seem to be nice as hell. I'll *try* to like you."

"Now me. Your turn to . . ." Caitlin whispered.

"This an' that, the next thing."

"Really soft, Arch . . . with you that name's more like the verb. To arch. Anybody ever call you Archie?"

"Not more than once."

"Tough guy," she purred.

"Grrr. I'm a street cop."

Carroll slowly rose onto his hands, then his knees. He was very hard, almost painfully hard.

At his first touch, Caitlin tightened her stomach. Then she slowly let herself relax. She tightened the abdominal muscles in her stomach then let herself relax again.

Her breathing was controlled, holding for several seconds. Her pulse was slow, a runner's . . .

Where did she learn all this stuff? Not in Ohio; not at Oberlin College.

Her eyes closed. Such smiling eyes. She was easy to be with.

Carroll's pulse was thumping so damn hard. He'd never in his life held off orgasm this long, never felt excited in quite this way. His head grew light.

"Please wait. Okay?" Caitlin whispered to him. Her body spasmed lightly.

"Trying . . ."

"Just . . . wait . . . Arch?"

Carroll's brain was burning up. His body was a million raw exposed nerves—as he floated down, floated down, floated down. Finally—he went inside Caitlin.

Her eyes slowly, very slowly, shut.

Her mouth opened. Wider and wider, an unbelievably soft, delicately pink mouth.

Her face was so surprisingly sweet in passion. She seemed to be smiling all the time . . .

Then Caitlin's eyes flipped open—looked at him—and she made him feel so good. Wanted again. Necessary to somebody.

"Hi there, Arch. Nice to have you here."

"Hi yourself. Nice to be had."

They moved faster together. Her dark hair slowly danced backward and forward. Her curls spread across the pillow, brushed, flowed majestically across his face—hid her eyes.

Carroll arched dramatically and nearly fell over backwards. Impossible, acrobatic positions.

He spasmed, shuddered, called out her name so loudly it embarrassed him.

"*Caitlin.*"

Completely new feelings were coming so fast. . . .

Again . . . "Caitlin."

He felt as if she knew him—instantly saw through his defenses, his poses. . . . Finally, somebody . . . Jesus.

When it was over, when it was finally, finally over, neither of them could move. . . . Nothing anywhere in the universe could move. Not ever again.

Chapter 44

THOMAS X. O'NEIL, Chief of U.S. Customs at Shannon Airport, Ireland, walked with most of his body weight ponderously thrown back on his boot heels. As he walked, his toes splayed out as if he were wearing ill-fitting bedroom slippers. His size forty-seven waist protruded obscenely, as did his customary, nine-incher Cuban cigar. Chief O'Neil looked like an unflattering caricature of Churchill and he couldn't have cared less. He had a public image and he enjoyed it. He didn't give a good goddamn what anyone thought.

At twelve noon, O'Neil casually waddled across the frozen gray tarmac toward North Building Three at the Irish airfield located outside of Dublin.

As he walked, O'Neil could smell fresh peat settling in the air. Nothing quite like the blessed aroma, he was thinking.

At the same moment, he looked up and saw a majestic 727 just gliding in through a blowing fog from America. Seven years before, he'd come over from New York himself. He never ever planned to return to that syphilitic rat's asshole, either. He had even tried to alter his accent and speech patterns so that he'd sound Irish: it was a ludicrous attempt and he came off sounding like a ham in some third-rate touring company doing George Bernard Shaw.

Inside Building Three there were hundreds of various-sized wooden crates, marked with the usual, faded corporate logos.

A carrot-haired Irish inspector stood with a red marker and clipboard beside a bare wooden desk, right at the center of the cluttered warehouse room.

"This the lot of it, Liam?" Chief O'Neil asked the inspector. "This Pan Am Three Ten from this morning?"

"Aye, sir. These particular boxes're from the Catholic Charities in New York. Clothes and such for sendin' up north. Givin' us all their old Calvin Kleins, their Jordache jeans, so they are. Look very smart and chic on the Provos, I'll bet."

Chief Inspector O'Neil grinned broadly. He was trailing grand clouds of smoke all around the freight inspection shack. He both chewed and puffed his Cubans, to get his money's worth.

Thomas O'Neil had been born and raised in New York's Yorkville section; he'd worked as an inspector at Kennedy International, nearly nine years before his fortuitous transfer as Head of the U.S. service at Shannon.

Before that, O'Neil had been a master sergeant in general supply in Viet Nam. Over in Nam, he'd managed to look like a junior Patton, instead of Churchill.

He was also Vets 28.

"Looks fine and dandy to me, lad. Let the boys load it up for the trip north. Spiffy new clothes for women and children. A very good cause."

Chief Inspector O'Neil laughed for no apparent reason. He was in a chipper mood that afternoon.

And why not? Had he not just succeeded in getting one billion four worth of freshly stolen stock certificates and securities into Western Europe?

Chapter 45

FOUR A.M.

Why were there suddenly so many 4:00 A.M.'s crowding into his life? Carroll wondered.

For a foggy moment he was disoriented: he felt like a man on a treadmill sent spinning off into space, where time zones collapsed, where clocks had no meaning.

This, he remembered, *was the heart of London.*

But that didn't matter because 4:00 A.M.'s were mostly alike. A bleached-out, dour hour of the day when cities slept and only cops and criminals wandered around, following some curious ancient chronology all their own.

Everything always started as the same intense four-bell-alarm emergency, but nothing ever happened after you broke every imaginable speed and safety law getting to the supposed crime scene. Not right away, anyway . . .

First you waited.

Almost always you waited.

And waited.

You drank drums of bitter black coffee, you smoked countless stale cigarettes; you paid your full dues every single time on a police case.

His fingers gently massaged his warm, throbbing temple. He felt weirdly numb as he watched Caitlin, who catnapped across the room in the stuffy Ritz Hotel.

For the past few hours, Caitlin had been drifting in and out of a restless sleep. Her pale lips parted slightly as she swallowed. The scooped hollow in her throat made her look sweet and vulnerable. Her legs were neatly curled under her like a folding pin inside.

They'd been on emergency alert for twenty straight hours now. They were one of several police/financial teams which had been rushed to London following Margarita Kupchuck's warning transmission from inside Russia.

It was exactly like the unpleasantly tense and chaotic Wall Street deadline on December 4.

Nothing had happened when it was supposed to happen.

No Russians with an extraordinary $120 million payment.

No Green Band with their enormous pilfered hoard of stocks and bonds.

First, you wait.

"How in hell did they manage to make contact with François Monserrat? Monserrat is unknown. Virtually without a face. Damned fellow's an enigma to every intelligence agency I know of in the world."

A chief Inspector from Britain's MI6, the secret intelligence service, sat in a leather club chair positioned opposite Carroll in the hotel suite. Patrick Frazier was a tall man with thinning pale blond hair and a pencil-thin moustache. He wore his clothes in a rumpled manner, and he spoke in a cultivated drawl, every word deliberately shaped. Frazier was one of Britain's resident experts on urban terrorism.

Physical pain was coursing through Carroll's body as he listened.

Yes, you paid your dues every single time with police work.

Too much bitter-tasting coffee and unrelieved tension; not enough sleep. Too much being lost and confused without any recognizable point of reference.

And the arm still ached like hell even though he'd discarded the sling in favor of a bulky bandage.

Hours later, the hotel room telephone rang and Frazier eagerly snatched it up. "Ah, Harris. How are you, old man? Oh, we're holding up. I suppose we are. It's for you, Carroll. Scotland Yard."

Perry Harris on the other end was speaking very loudly as Carroll took over the line. Harris was from the Yard's Serious Crime Squad. Carroll had worked with Harris twice before in Europe and respected the man.

"Listen to what we've just found. You're not going to believe it, I'll wager. *There's been an incredible turn.* The IRA . . . the IRA has just contacted us. . . . They want a meeting set up with *you* in Belfast. *You* specifically. They're in the game now, too."

"In what way? How are the Provos involved, Perry?"

Blood was suddenly pounding in Carroll's forehead. Green Band came at you hard, then they pulled away just as fast. They came at you—then they disappeared again. The second you dropped your guard, *bang*, right between the eyes.

Come to Florida, Mr. Carroll. A clue there? Florida?

Go see Michel Chevron. A key somewhere in Europe? And now the Provos.

"They've come into some securities, U.S. bonds. Over a

billion American dollars' worth according to the boyos. . . . They listed names and serial numbers for us to check in New York. *They check.*"

"Hold on, wait a minute," Carroll was sitting upright in his hotel chair.

"The IRA has taken over the stolen securities?"

"I don't know. They're definitely in possession of *some* stolen goods."

"But how?"

"Who knows. They're telling us as little as possible, of course."

"Son of a *bitch*." They'd come so far; they'd seemed so close to some kind of break in the Green Band puzzle. "All right, all right. We'll be in touch as soon as we sort out things here. We'll be back to you, Perry."

Carroll slammed down the phone receiver. He glared across the London hotel room at Frazier, at Caitlin, whose eyes were suddenly wide open and alert.

"*Somehow* the IRA has made a move into this thing. . . . It seems the Provos want to talk about selling some securities back to us. *Over a billion* American dollars' worth. They know we're in London. How could they know?"

The question stuck in Carroll's brain like a shriek.

And since he couldn't answer it, since he hadn't been able to answer it so far, what was the point in asking it now?

How could they know everything ahead of time?

Chapter 46

THE MAN CALLED François Monserrat, who was wearing a black nylon anorak and a dark beret, and who now walked with a pronounced limp, moved down the Portobello Road in the west of London.

He passed through the open market for which this street was famous; now and then he would pause at this stall or that and examine an antique. There were some very fine pieces to be had here. There were also some obvious fakes.

You need a good eye, a practiced eye, to tell the real article from the false, he thought.

In the palm of his hand he turned over a jade piece in the shape of a small lynx. He curled his fingers around it, squeezing hard. . . . He was not a man who gave way to his emotions easily. In fact, he came at them in a circumspect way, circling as if they were live packets of plastique. At any given moment, an emotion could all too easily explode.

Like right now.

The sensation coursing through Monserrat was one of cold anger. If the jade lynx had been fur and bone, the life would have been squeezed out of it. He was angry because he didn't like clever games, *when they were played by the other side's rules*.

Green Band, for instance, had become a threat.

They created their own rules, their own games.

They said one thing.

They did another.

They suggested important meetings that never took place.

They were like air. They were very much wisps and phantoms. Monserrat's admiration was grudging.

He set the jade lynx down and he closed his eyes. He had a trick to guard against emotion. He would retreat into a dark, cool place in the deepest part of his mind: a monastery of silence. In this sanctuary he almost always had control. Nothing slipped away from him here.

This time, though, his little trick of the mind failed. He opened his eyes and the bustling market assaulted his senses.

Green Band was somewhere close. What did they really want?

Perhaps soon, he would know all about Green Band.

Chapter 47

THEY HAD TO wait one final time.

They had to wait at the tiny, fastidious Regent Hotel in Belfast.

Carroll tried to accept the helpless feeling that they had no control over anything that was happening. The Green Band strategy—whatever it was—seemed to be working flawlessly.

Well-coordinated economic terror.

Massive psychological disorientation, designed to create escalating chaos and even more terror.

Patrick Frazier kept up a cheery pep talk under the unusually trying circumstances. The Special Branch man was tirelessly gung-ho.

"When we do meet with them," Frazier slid off his wire glasses and briskly rubbed his eyes, "you'll be outfitted with an internal transmitter. Absolute state of the art. Designed for the military. Armalite Corporation. You swallow the damn thing."

Carroll shook his head. Ah, police work. Sometimes he wondered what he'd *thought* it was going to be like—long,

long ago when he'd first decided on what he now some-times called the *wrong side of the law*.

"If we ever do meet up with them, Caitlin will verify that the securities are genuine," Frazier said.

"If we ever meet up with them."

Six more hours droned by in the most painfully, slow waltz-time. The only perceptible change was the morning sliding into afternoon outside, the day turning to the steel-blue shades of the Northern Irish cityscape.

A red-haired serving girl, no more than sixteen or sev-enteen, finally brought in steaming tea and hot Irish soda bread. Carroll, Frazier, and Caitlin ate out of boredom more than anything.

Carroll remembered to check in with Trentkamp's office in New York. He left a message for Walter, *"Naught, zero, bupkis, zip, goose egg . . . as in wild goose egg chase."*

Ten hours passed inside the Regent Hotel suite.

It was exactly like what had happened the night of De-cember fourth in New York, when the final deadline for the bombings had gone past, and the clock hands had begun to move with intolerable slowness. Why, though? How were they supposed to investigate a chimera or a mirage?

From the fourth-floor window of the hotel suite, Carroll saw an antiquated bicycle bumping over the cobblestoned street outside. It was ridden by a man of about seventy, whose thin frame didn't look like it could survive the shud-dering motions of the bike.

Carroll leaned closer to the dormer window. His brain felt like something shapeless lying in a basin of tepid water.

The rider parked his bike almost directly below the Re-gent Hotel window.

"Could this be our contact?" Carroll asked in a hoarse voice.

Patrick Frazier moved into the window and studied the old man. "Doesn't look the terrorist type. That's a good sign. They never do in Belfast."

The rider hobbled inside the hotel entrance, then disappeared from Carroll's sight.

"He's inside now."

"Then we wait and see," Frazier said, muttering to himself.

Carroll sighed. The tension buzzing inside him was familiar now. He looked toward Caitlin, who smiled at him. How did she stay so calm? The journey, the tension, the awful waiting.

Less than ninety seconds after he went inside the Regent, the old man came marching out again. He rigidly climbed back on his bike.

Almost immediately there came a solid rap on the hardwood door of the hotel suite.

Caitlin rose and opened the door.

"An old man just delivered this message," a British detective entered and reported. He walked forward to his commander, passing both Caitlin and Carroll without so much as a nod.

Patrick Frazier immediately ripped the envelope open and read it without any discernible expression. Frazier's eyes finally peeked over the wrinkled note page at Carroll.

He read the words of the message aloud for both Carroll and Caitlin:

"There's no salutation or date. . . . It reads as follows: 'You are to send your representative with the proof of transfer of funds. Your representative is to be at Fox Cross Station, six miles northwest outside of Belfast. That's the railroad. Be there at 0545 hours. The precious securities will be safely waiting nearby. . . . The messenger is to be Caitlin Dillon.' "

Chapter 48

AT 5:30, the morning air was misty in Belfast.

It was the kind of day in which objects have no hard definition. The railway platform at Fox Cross was silent.

All the trees were stripped and bare and looked arthritic in the wintry absence of clear light. Up beyond the mist the sky was dark gray, and the cloud cover low.

Caitlin shivered slightly and folded both arms around her rising and falling chest. She could hear the drumming of her own heart.

She wasn't going to let herself be frightened, though. She vowed not to act the way a woman would be expected to act under the circumstances.

Caitlin sucked in a raw, cold breath. She shifted impatiently from one boot to the other.

No one was visible yet, not anywhere up and down the weathered railway platform.

Was it all going to be over after this?

Who was Green Band finally going to turn out to be? . . .

What part did the North Irish play? And what could have happened between the Russians and Green Band in London?

A black leather briefcase hung from her wrist. Inside

were codes to release the sums now on deposit at a Swiss bank, which were to be paid outright this morning.

The ransom of the century was to take place here at little Fox Cross Station. Historic Fox Cross Station outside Belfast, Ireland.

Caitlin imagined she looked like a successful businesswoman with the fine, black leather briefcase. Some regular commuter heading into downtown Belfast. Another day at the bloody office. She thought she was playing the part well—on the outside, at least.

She glanced at her watch and saw it was a few seconds before 5:45. The time they'd indicated for the exchange had come. Caitlin cautioned herself that they were not necessarily punctual.

What would their lack of punctuality mean right now? What would it mean in terms of any emergency police action planned for the Fox Cross railroad platform?

Caitlin's body tensed. Every muscle, every fiber inside her involuntarily tightened.

A faded blue panel truck had appeared, and was approaching the deserted station from a thick row of pine trees to the north.

The slow-moving truck steadily got larger and larger. Caitlin saw that there were three passengers, all of them men.

Then the blue panel truck passed Caitlin by.

A gust of frozen wind swept back her hair, and Caitlin let out what must have been the deepest sigh of her lifetime.

Carroll and the British detectives were close by, a thought she found more than a little comforting. They were less than a mile away. Still, there was nothing they could do if trouble suddenly bloomed—if someone panicked, if someone made a simple, foolish mistake now.

A car, a nondescript sedan approached moments after the panel truck.

Caitlin tried to observe everything about the car as it rolled forward over the parking lot gravel. Very possibly it was just a passenger drop-off for the first scheduled train at 6:04.

It was a late model Ford, grayish-green, with a slightly smashed-in front grill. There was a tiny chip in the windshield. Four passengers inside—two in front, two in the back.

Irish working men? Thick, heavy-set types anyway. Maybe farm workers?

But the second car passed her by, too.

Caitlin was both relieved and disappointed. She was confused, trying to keep her wits and remnants of her concentration.

Then the car stopped suddenly. The tires screeched in reverse.

Two burly men in back jumped out; both were wearing black cloth masks, both carried machine gun pistols.

They ran to Caitlin at full speed, workshoes splatting hard against concrete.

"You're Caitlin Dillon, missus?" One of the masked men asked. He thrust forward his menacing gun muzzle.

"I am." Caitlin's legs had begun to slightly buckle; her knees were suddenly on hinges.

"You were born in Old Lyme, Connecticut?"

"I was born in Lima, Ohio."

"Birth date—January 23, 1950?"

"1953. Thanks a lot."

The masked IRA terrorist laughed at Caitlin's response. He apparently appreciated a modicum of coolness and humor.

"All right then, dearie, we're going to put one of these hangman masks on you. No eyeholes for lookin' out. Nothing to be afraid of, though."

"I'm not afraid of you."

The other man, the silent partner, looped a black hood over her hair, then pulled it down tight over Caitlin's face. He was careful not to bump or touch any other parts of her body. How very Irish Catholic, Caitlin couldn't help thinking. They'd put a bullet into her without blinking, she knew that. But no impure thoughts, no accidental touching of a female.

"We're going to lead you back to the car now. Nice and easy. . . . Easy does it . . .

"All right, step up, step inside. Now down in back. On the car floor here. There we go, all comfy."

Caitlin was feeling numb everywhere; her body seemed no longer to belong to her. She found herself saying, "Thank you. I'm fine right here."

"Your mum's name is Margaret?" Cleverly timed.

"My mother's name is Anna. Her maiden name is Reardon."

"No tracking device anywhere on your person?"

"No."

Caitlin had answered a little too quickly, she thought. Her skin went cold. Suddenly she couldn't breathe at all.

There was no apparent reaction, nothing she could perceive as wrong from the Irish men. They seemed to believe her, not even to question what she'd said about the tracking device.

"I have to check you all the same. Pat you down. All right, here goes."

Clumsy, male hands (Mechanic? Some kind of working man?) groped all over her body. Caitlin stiffly tensed her legs as a man's hand wedged up between. The intruding hand felt very harsh and rude. The worst part so far. Probably not the worst she was going to experience today though.

"If you have a transmitter, we have orders to kill you. . . . *If you don't tell us right now.* Don't lie about this, dearie. Don't lie, missy. I'm quite serious. Do you? Do you have any tracking device? We'll check you thoroughly, as soon as we're out of here. Please tell me the truth."

"I have no tracking device on me." *Inside me. Could they really find that?*

There was no more talking after that. The body search ended abruptly.

Caitlin's ears stayed plugged, as if she were trapped in a vacuum. Her heart lodged very high up in her throat. The car's engine coughed and came alive.

Someone suddenly wiped her face with a dripping-wet hand cloth.

Jesus. The fumes were everywhere. The fumes wouldn't let her breathe.

"No, I—"

Chapter 49

"OH, BUGGER IT. Look at this hopeless mess," Patrick Frazier exclaimed.

Torrents of water jackhammered the Bentley that Carroll and Inspector Patrick Frazier were riding in. Rain blasted the steamy windshields, hitting with the solid force of a firehose.

It had begun to spit rain at five minutes to six. Then suddenly it was coming down heavily, piercing the mist, making it near impossible to see the road ahead.

"They're on the Falls Road now. That's in the rough and tumble part of Belfast," Frazier said. "The Provisional Irish Republican Army *owns* it. . . . It's your basic urban ghetto where they regularly ambush our soldiers. Hit and run snipers in there, mostly. Urban guerrilla warfare at its best."

Both Carroll and Frazier were hunched forward in the front seat of the Bentley. The transmitter-beeper tracking Caitlin was coming over loud and clear. It sounded a little like a sequence of radar blips, all originating somewhere deep in Caitlin's stomach.

Carroll couldn't help thinking of a heart-monitoring

device in an intensive care unit, something that registered one's hold on life. Poor Caitlin. But he couldn't have done anything to stop her from going—he couldn't have offered himself as a substitute messenger, the instructions had been specific and final.

The monitoring *blip blip blip* was becoming louder now, and more stubbornly insistent.

The car with Caitlin inside was apparently slowing down. Maybe it was temporarily stopped at a street light? In heavy traffic? What now?

"Range closing fast, sir," reported the driver.

"Hang it. They're at the home base," Patrick Frazier sharply pronounced. His driver immediately stepped down on the gas. The Bentley leaned forward with a thrusting surge of power.

"Either that, or they're switching transportation," Carroll had another thought.

Carroll's mind cocooned tightly around the thought of Caitlin in serious danger. He was both angry and afraid.

"Let's get in closer to her. Come on! Come on, let's move it now!" Carroll snapped at the British Special Service driver.

Less than two miles away, the black cloth hood was raised up over Caitlin's head; she reeled away as acrid smelling salts were passed under her nose. Her watering eyes rolled backward.

"Unhh?"

Focus. There were dull-edged silhouettes rather than faces clustered all around her. Three of them.

Behind the looming shapes stood excessively bright

lamps. Behind the lamps were still more shadowy, unidentifiable figures. Green Band?

She couldn't see who the others were. . . . Not yet anyway.

"Welcome back among the living. You're a brave one to accept our invitation. Probably a little scared right now. That's natural enough."

Caitlin still couldn't see them very well, even the men standing closest to her.

"You *do* have authority to transfer the agreed-upon sum of money? You have the necessary bank codes, Ms. Dillon?"

Caitlin nodded. Her neck was stiff, her throat dry and itchy.

When she spoke her voice sounded hollow and lifeless to her, her words clumsily formed, as if she were being spoken through by a ventriloquist.

"Would you mind showing me . . . some of the stolen securities. I need some reassurance, as well. I need to see what we're getting in the exchange."

"You'll be able to estimate the true value by yourself, aye? And you can tell counterfeit from the genuine article? You've that finely trained an eye?"

"*Touch* is more important than the eye," Caitlin said, hiding any anger she felt. "I can tell a great deal by touching the securities. Enough to release the money in Geneva. Please? May I examine the goods?"

They finally brought the "sample" stolen stock certificates and bonds to Caitlin. She used most of her will to hold in a tiny gasp of amazement.

The *look* of the securities was certainly authentic. She

read off the top names: IBM, General Motors, AT&T, Digital, Monsanto.

She played with the numbers in her mind. It was several thousand times the amount of the *great* train robbery. And who knew how much of the *total* stolen amount this was? What was coming still?

"You can *touch* the documents all you like, darling. They're real though. We wouldn't bring you all the way here for nothing. Just to chat, and admire your fine all-American boobies."

Chapter 50

THE BENTLEY SEDAN Carroll rode in barely slowed as it squeezed around a crumbling white brick wall in the inner city. The wall was blackened in places from petrol bombs. The car's radial tires screeched above bustling city noises.

Suddenly a flatbed truck was in the same narrow, twisting lane as the Bentley. The truck's engine roared and its horn blared loudly.

A blast of gunfire erupted from the cab of the onrushing truck. Spits of gunfire came from the flat tenement rooftops to the right of the threadneedle roadway.

"Ambush!" Patrick Frazier grunted.

Almost instantly, he slumped back hard against the car's passenger door. A jagged hole appeared at the center of his forehead.

Carroll pushed open the door and followed the driver of the Bentley out. Then he lay pressed tightly against the side of the car. He looked up, staring at Patrick Frazier's wound through the open Bentley doorway.

Carroll angrily swung his gun barrel out in the direction of the flatbed truck. Without any accompanying sound, the weapon opened rapid fire. Gaping bullet holes appeared everywhere on the truck's already mottled surface.

One of the Irish gunsels, astonished because there had been *no gun sound*, blew back away from the faded red hood of the truck. Blood spurted from his black-bearded face and throat. And then the body was rolling and rolling across the road like that of a man trapped in a barrel.

Carroll's machine gun pistol had been developed and perfected by the Israeli Army. It fired automatically, up to two hundred and fifty rounds in six seconds. The bullets were attracted by body heat. *Silent death*, the Israelis and their enemies called it.

A stout, red-headed man's forehead was angrily stitched straight across with bullet holes. The man performed a brief two-step then spun off a house's steep-shingled roof.

Carroll was aware of movement on either side of him.

Crowds, mostly women and children, were streaming out of crumbling, low-slung tenement buildings. They mobbed forward instead of hiding away in the safer shadows. They had deep-red faces—anger coming from the heart.

The two remaining gunmen from the truck dodged back among the women in their plaid bathrobes and tattered men's jackets. They crouched among the dirty faced children, many of whom were still in their pajamas, dragged out of the innocence of sleep and made to confront still another horror in their young, sad lives.

Carroll clicked the machine gun off automatic, so it wouldn't fire into the covering crowds.

"British spies!" The Irish people had suddenly begun to jeer, protecting their revolutionary soldiers, some of whom were immediate family members, some less close relatives and friends.

"Damn British spies! Damn you British!"

"Go home, damn Brits!"

Carroll cautiously ran forward anyway. He threw himself into the fierce, snarling faces, the threatening, murderous shouts. His machine gun jutted out, the ugly black snout just menacing enough to keep them off him for the moment. *Who was the real terrorist here?* his mind rambled.

"Big man with yer gun," someone taunted.

"Fookin' coward with your machine gun. Dirty Brit turd! Filthy Brit bastard!"

Carroll almost didn't hear the angry shouts. He had one thought only—follow the beeper, follow the radar blips. Find Caitlin right now.

Caitlin covered her head with both arms. She was trying to squirm and struggle away from the IRA men. The air in the tenement room was like liquid mold, almost impossible for her to breathe.

"You filthy whore, you! You swine!" The head man screeched at the top of his voice; he screamed inches from Caitlin's face. A contact radio was crackling nearby, blaring the latest street reports into the IRA hideout.

"It's a trap! Infuckingsane. She's carryin' some kind of signal, Dermot! Police cars, Brit soldiers are swarming the street out there. Soldiers're everywhere!"

It was the most helpless moment Caitlin could have imagined. She knew what they were going to do to her. She knew she was going to be shot, murdered. She wondered when that moment of resigned calm would come, that transcendental moment you were supposed to experience when you understood you were facing death.

The IRA group leader continued to scream; his black masked face was up close to her. "You bloody knew!"

"No, I didn't know. Please. I don't understand now."

The terrorist suddenly lunged forward, propelling himself out of the blinding white floodlights. He ripped off his mask. She saw a dirty, reddish-blond beard; black holes for eyes. She saw the close-up, gaping mouth of a Russian SKS assault rifle . . .

Tears flooded Caitlin's eyes. She tried to tell the terrorist not to fire, to stop. Her senses were overwhelmed with horrifying impressions. She wondered if this was the way it was going to be, one burst of crazy clarity and then you're dead: that solitary, heightened moment the last thing you take with you.

There were police sirens and ambulances and gunfire outside; the air was pierced with maddening chaos.

She watched the door of the apartment burst open. Somebody she'd never seen before stood poised with a drawn pistol—

A volley of automatic gunfire flared out of the gun aimed into Caitlin's face. It made a rrrrrurrr sound, like a mundane dentist's drill. *Oh, no! Oh God no . . .*

Caitlin tried to twist and turn away. That one, urgent thought stuck in her mind—*get away now! Get away! Get away!*

Only she couldn't move as fast as the sudden automatic rifle fire. She didn't move an inch off her chair.

Then Caitlin simply fell away from it.

Chapter 51

"GET OUT OF MY WAY! *Out of the way, you bastards!"*

Carroll screamed at three men standing in his path. The Irish hoods were stubbornly posted between him and the tenement house stairway. They were waving Gaelic football bats in the dimly lit hallway.

"Why dontcha make us move? Come on now. Make us move. See if you can?"

The tracking beeper was singing desperately, actually vibrating in his jacket vest pocket. Caitlin had to be upstairs. She was right in this building.

Police sirens, emergency Army sirens were shrieking. Sniper gunfire was still raining down on the Falls Road. *Move! Now! Move!*

Carroll leapt between the three surprised youths. They wisely side-stepped the charging, bull-shouldered American.

Carroll crashed two and three steps at a time up a twisty flight of darkened stairs. *Please God no!*

He was fighting against rage, and an even worse fear building inside him. He kept the machine gun clipped off automatic fire. There were civilians swarming inside the tenement house.

Apartment doors kept opening, then rapidly slamming shut. Carroll felt their wind in his face. There were hostile looks and abusive screams.

As Carroll finally reached the top landing, the fourth floor of the building, he saw the dingy yellow door of an apartment thrown open.

His brain clenched unbelievably tight, filled to exploding with unnatural heat. Suddenly he knew what he was going to find there. Carroll knew it.

He could see inside the doorway already. Then he could see her lying there, still in her overcoat. Her striped muffler was off casually to one side. She lay thrown up against a fallen wooden chair where she had apparently been questioned.

The IRA henchmen were gone, up to the roof, up over other roofs, gone, escaped somewhere.

"Oh God no." Carroll choked back a sob, a desperate, hopeless prayer. He experienced that awful, hollow bitterness of death all over again. He felt terrible hurt, from some infinite store of pain.

Slowly then, Caitlin rolled over. She rolled just a few inches. Then Caitlin struggled to sit up and Carroll ran forward. . . . Her face was a blank, dazed stare. . . . But she was alive.

Carroll held Caitlin. He cradled her like an injured child in his arms.

Then she suddenly drew her face away from him; she stared at something that terrified her across the room.

Carroll followed the line of her eyes to an inert shape that lay on the other side of the barren room. The body seemed to be that of a young man, except you couldn't really tell. Half the head had been blown away. The darkish hair was matted with blood. The figure was shrouded with the dark blue uniform of a Belfast policeman.

"Who is he?" Carroll asked.

Caitlin slowly shook her head. "I don't know. I only know that if it hadn't been for him coming when he did, I'd be dead. He came through that doorway. He started shooting at them."

Carroll couldn't take his eyes away from the murdered policeman. A hero, Carroll thought. A hero with no name or face anymore. *Police work in all its glory.*

Caitlin was sobbing, almost without any sound.

"Shhh, now, shhh," Carroll whispered.

Then Caitlin couldn't help herself anymore. The sobbing became uncontrollable. She cried into Carroll's chest. She held him with her remaining strength.

They were enfolded that way, holding one another, when the teams of British Special Branch men and Irish police arrived.

Once again, Green Band was nowhere to be found.

Chapter 52

BY THE EVENING of December 12, the letters, stuffed inside eight-by-eleven manila envelopes, had finally arrived. Over three thousand bulky letters had been mailed to every region across the United States.

The letters had come to the strangest, the most unlikely places. To Sedona, Arizona; to Dohren, Alabama; Totowa, New Jersey; Buena Vista, California; Iowa City, Iowa; Stowe, Vermont; Cambridge, Massachusetts; Boulder, Colorado; Scarborough, New York.

Kenny Sherwood in Erie, Pennsylvania, was one of *the chosen few*.

Sherwood was home from work that day, because if he went to the mill, he'd just say something dumb and get his ass either chewed out, or fired. For nine years he'd been a machine operator with Hammond Tool and Dye.

He made almost twenty-nine thousand, thirty-five hundred of which went for shrink sessions with a psychologist in Pittsburgh, little goateed fellow who treated him for his recurrent war dreams.

There was a neatly typed cover letter inside the envelope; it looked official, a little scary even.

Dear Mr. Sherwood,

During the years 1968 to 1972, you served your country proudly as a Specialist in the U.S. Army. You were a POW from January 1970 to June of 1972. You received a purple heart in Viet Nam.

Please consider the enclosed, a token of our appreciation for your services, a chance for *your country to serve you.*

Kenny Sherwood cautiously slid a piece of parchment paper out of the envelope.

Now what the hell was this?

There was some kind of chained woman, holding a globe of the world at the top of the parchment paper.

Further down, the certificate said *General Motors common stock.*

The legend went on: "This certifies Kenneth H. Sherwood is the owner of five thousand shares."

Tied around the parchment paper was a shiny green ribbon, a kind of green band.

PART TWO

Black
Market

Chapter 53

DAVID HUDSON WOKE with a headache in his room in the Washington-Jefferson Hotel. It was snowing outside, the satiny whiteness evenly blanketing West 51st Street.

Hudson pinched his wristwatch off the wobbling nightstand. It was just past two.

He sat upright and yielded to an uncharacteristic moment of panic. His throat was dry, his hands clammy. His body felt fevered.

It wasn't Green Band troubling him this time.

Green Band was hurtling along without an apparent hitch. Even at its psychological core, Green Band was moving beautifully, creating uncertainty in all the places where Hudson wanted to create it.

It wasn't the time he'd spent in a North Vietnamese prison camp, either. The memories of the taunting Lizard Man had stayed out of his dreams that night.

None of these things bothered David Hudson right now. It was something else. . . . Something unexpected and unplanned.

It was Billie Bogan . . .
Like the poet, Louise.

He was angry with himself, disappointed that he'd let the woman affect him. It was unlike him; it was undisciplined and out of character for Hudson to permit such a distraction before his mission was complete. Yet somehow he felt he could handle it, that he could keep everything in perspective . . .

Or was he fooling himself? Was she going to be the reason he finally ruined everything? The one serious slip-up, his fatal flaw? Would he allow himself to blow Green Band because of Billie Bogan? This woman he barely knew.

He needed to see her at least once more, he decided. *Tonight*, if he could. The most vivid images of Billie suddenly drifted past his eyes.

Hudson felt himself aroused. He threw on an old mufti shirt and trousers and went down to the lobby. He prowled around nervously, watched by a clerk at the desk. He finally called the Vintage service, not wanting to use the phone in his own room.

"I'd like to see Billie. Tonight if possible. This is David. Number 323."

There was a pause as he was put on hold; three or four minutes, which seemed even longer.

"Billie's not on her beeper. She doesn't seem to be available right now." The answer came back. "You could meet one of our other escorts. They're very beautiful. Former and part-time models and actresses, David."

David Hudson hung up the telephone. He felt disappointed, unsatisfied, empty in a cold, gnawing way. . . . Maybe he *couldn't* handle this right now. Maybe he shouldn't ever try to see Billie again.

The idea of blowing Green Band over some English

whore—almost made him laugh. It would be ludicrously funny—if it all ended like that.

Only David Hudson knew that was impossible. The final Green Band plan was flawless. It was so good, *it could work without him from here on.*

Deception, David Hudson remembered. *The very beginnings of Green Band.*

Deception and illusion that had started as far back as Viet Nam.

Chapter 54

La Hoc Noh Prison: July, 1971

CAPTAIN DAVID HUDSON'S TORTURED, one-hundred-and-fifteen-pound frame slumped forward. The fragile shell of his body threatened to shatter into pieces, to collapse in exhaustion or perhaps death. Hudson's mind silently screamed for him to give up this useless fight.

What remained of his body was wracked by pain, intense suffering that would have been unthinkable before the last eleven months in North Vietnamese prison camps. He was unsuccessfully trying to put his mind somewhere else now. He ached to be outside the seething bamboo hut, somewhere safe and relatively sane in his past, even as far back as his Kansas boyhood.

He'd been trained to resist interrogation and enemy brainwashing. *Sisyphus*, the program was called at Fort Bragg, North Carolina.

He remembered that now. *Sisyphus* had prepared him for enemy interrogation—or so the Army instructors had told him.

You must put your mind in another place altogether.

It had sounded so simple, so coldly, attractively logical as a concept. Now it seemed absurd, infuriating in its stupidity and typical American arrogance. *Sisyphus* had been another fraud invented by the U.S. Army . . . The Lizard Man, the North Vietnamese commandant of La Hoc Noh, mechanically raised a white stone game marker.

He put one of David Hudson's black stones in check.

There was a hard *clack* of the playing piece against the polished teak board.

The North Vietnamese prison guards, all dressed in muddy black pajamas, tipped homemade rice wine from long-necked green bottles. They snorted ridiculing laughter at this obvious mismatch of competitors.

The prison camp commandant was swift, completely sure of his game moves. He was on a different skill level, Hudson understood.

According to the rules of Go, the game should have been played with a sizable handicap called *okigo*. *Should have been*. . . . But strict adherence to rules meant nothing here because this was a place beyond all decency, all logic, all understanding.

"Yow play!" the Lizard Man once again screeched. "Yow play now!"

He seemed to want his victory right now: the cruel bloodletting—the slow death for the loser in the festering jungle swamps just beyond the prison camp.

The guards were physical extensions of their leader's personality. They too became impatient now, grumbling and growling for faster action.

Clack!

David Hudson made an obviously ridiculous, almost an arbitrary move on the Go board. He smiled crookedly at the commandant, as if he'd suddenly turned the game in his favor.

"*You* play!" Hudson snapped. He knew the smile on his face was hopelessly spacey, but he savored the small moment of triumph.

The Lizard Man was momentarily confused.

Then he howled shrill, birdlike laughter.

The Vietnamese soldiers howled laughter as well. They inched closer to the two players as the commandant made a surprisingly conservative move with one of his white stones.

Disappointment etched itself across the soldiers' faces. Here was uncertainty for the first time. Hudson was amazed at the commandant's hesitation.

"*Yow!*" Lizard Man screamed. "Fast play! Yow play riii now!"

"Fuck you, asshole. . . . Watch this one."

A smile, hollow and incomprehensible, slipped across David Hudson's blistered lips.

Once again, he made a bizarre, a seemingly pointless and foolish game move.

"You play!" he said in a barely audible whisper. "You play *fast*, too."

The Lizard Man squinted, and studied the exquisite, highly reflective teak board more closely. He gazed into Captain Hudson's bloodshot eyes, then looked down again at the Go board.

The guards crushed in closer still.

This was getting better, more dramatic, finally. A real game was starting to develop.

The soldiers began to whisper among themselves. They

were like the professional gamblers, the unsavory flotsam always crowded into the fantan parlors of Saigon.

Something interesting and curious was happening in the game of Go now. Even the camp commandant was confused, troubled by his American opponent, by his seemingly unfathomable moves.

For the first time, one of the prison camp guards offered a side bet on the American officer. The commandant threw the soldier the most bitter glance.

Suddenly then, smoothly and so coolly, as if he was performing an ordinary movement such as lighting a cigarette, Captain Hudson removed the revolver from one of the Vietnamese soldiers' dangling holsters.

Hudson swiveled back to the straight ahead position, directly facing the Lizard Man.

Once again, the faint half-crazed smile crossed David Hudson's blistered lips. "Fucker. Miserable shit fucker."

A heartbeat later, the revolver thundered.

It was like an Army field cannon in the tiny bamboo room. White smoke blossomed everywhere around the game table.

Unbelievably, the commandant's head flew straight back. Bone cracked hard against the wooden wall's main support post. The commandant's military hat sailed away saucer style across the smoking hut.

A dark hole gushed like slashed fruit in the Vietnamese officer's forehead. The Lizard Man's mouth dropped open to show broken, ugly yellow teeth. A lathering, pale white tongue flopped out.

David Hudson reflexively fired the service revolver a second time.

He fired a third time.

He felt like a weary, wildly confused child—playing with a toy gun. *Bang, bang, bang.*

He thrust the point of the revolver directly in the frozen eyes of the guard who had provided the weapon. The man's face shattered. Skull, flesh, bone flew apart.

Another Viet Cong guard was shot in the throat.

The two remaining guards had dropped their liquor bottles; they were struggling to get out holstered pistols.

The next three deafening gunshots tore through one man's chest, pierced the other's stomach, then his heart. The foul-smelling, boiling jungle hut was suddenly a bloody abattoir.

Then Hudson was running outside the command hut. He limped badly on legs that felt like they couldn't actually be his.

He stumbled, scrambled forward on the unfamiliar, unsteady supports. His legs were like wooden stilts.

Every object he saw seemed part of a blurred, impossible dream. Everywhere he looked, there was harsh unreality. A late-afternoon sun flared orange and bright red over the wall of jungle green. Screeching monkeys skittered away from the place of so many gunshots. Insects buzzed between the trees.

David Hudson awkwardly weaved back and forth across the exposed exercise yard.

He ducked into the thick jungle that kept threatening to swallow up the prison camp, and served as a natural barrier to escape for all the prisoners. Hudson lunged forward. He tripped ahead anyway.

He had no choice now.

Nowhere to go but into the terrifying jungle.

He was breathless already, clumsily crashing against

trees, against thick, tangled jungle brush. He kept running, faster than he thought possible.

Dizziness grabbed and clawed at him. Whirling bright colors came. Shivering cold flashes.

He kept running, zigzagging forward, vomiting bile like it was exhaust. As the jungle foliage got thicker, the trail became darker than he thought possible—almost complete blackness less than five hundred yards from the Vietnamese camp.

He ran forward anyway. A half mile, a mile—he had no idea of either time or space now.

A paralyzing thought struck at him and suddenly held David Hudson tight as the final grip of death. *They weren't even chasing him. . . . They weren't even giving chase back into the jungle.*

Hudson continued running—falling, picking himself up, falling, picking himself up, falling, picking himself up.

Then it was so dark there was nothing left in the world. Hudson kept running. Falling, picking himself up.

Falling, picking himself up.

Falling, falling, falling . . .

A song from the Doors played in his head. "Horse Latitudes" . . . then nothing at all . . .

Hudson woke with a nightmarish jolt. A silent scream never made it out of his tight, dry larynx.

Long grass was stuck to one side of his face. Sticky, gummy tears had formed in his half-closed eyes.

Fat black flies had attached themselves to his lips and nostrils. Hundreds of black flies were plastered all over his body.

Trying to right himself, he nearly laughed out loud. It was exactly as he'd always believed this putrid affair called life to be: resolutely unfair, pointless in the end, and in the beginning, and in the middle, too. Anyone with any reason could see the absurd eternal pattern. *David Hudson fell away into the unrelenting darkness once again.* "Horse Latitudes" played again. Why that fucking song now?

He woke again. Wildly confused. Unnaturally alert.

He had to concentrate everything, every trace of energy he had now. He wrestled with himself to stay awake, to hold on to a thin, sane lifeline. Tormenting waves, disconnected images and thoughts kept coming. Ghosts just beyond his full comprehension. Raging rivers of shadowy, half-formed images, words, hellish fantasy shapes. Almost a psychedelic experience. As if he'd been smoking the strongest Thai sticks. Shooting skag. . . .

This was so horrible, *too horrible*, too much for anyone to take much longer. What happened to him then? What did it feel like when you cracked wide open? . . . The severe gagging stopped as soon as he wasn't thinking about it.

Hudson began to scream. He was swimming toward some kind of release. Eternity was rushing forward—leaping at him in the form of a sea of leeches, screeching, clawing monkeys, indistinct, shadowy, jungle insects and reptiles. He screamed for hours without end.

Then the prison camp guards came!

So suddenly.

They were there! On him! Everywhere!

Busy hands were scrabbling, poking, reaching all over his body . . .

Hot hands were probing, continually poking him. Blood roared in the funnels of Hudson's ears. The vicious leeches were crawling all over him, too. Sharp little leech stings. Strong hands were lifting him.

Then whispering, almost choral voices. There were no distinct, recognizable words.

"Leave me alone! Leave me alone!" Hudson was pinioned down and helpless. *"Please leave me alone!"*

Something large and jet black, a huge flapping bird grabbed on to his face. It smelled like burning rubber, even worse than that. It began to crawl all over his face.

"Get it off me! Get it off me! Please get it off me!"

A shaft of light suddenly opened. Gleaming, almost beautiful light shone in his deep dark tunnel of terror.

A scream came that seemed very far away. . . . *No!* . . . It was *his own* scream.

Impossible.

Impossible.

This was so impossible.

Army corpsmen were staring down . . .

Army corpsmen were staring down . . .

Army corpsmen were staring down . . .

Ours.

Our corpsmen!

Chapter 55

"BREATHE DEEPLY, CAPTAIN HUDSON. Just breathe now. Just breathe. Breathe. There, that's good. That's very good. . . . That's excellent, Captain Hudson.

"It's pure oxygen, Captain. Oxygen! Don't think right now. Breathe. Breathe. Breathe deeply."

White cloth straps were holding him tightly, painfully so. Blue and red plastic tubes ran in and out of his nose. More tubes were connected to his arms and legs. Colored wires, rubber plugs were attached to his chest, and from there to an icy blue machine.

"Captain Hudson. Captain, can you hear me? Can you understand me?"

"You're in the Womack Hospital at Fort Bragg, Captain. You're going to be all right. Just fine. Captain, can you understand me? You're in the Womack Hospital?"

"Oh please help me."

He was sobbing uncontrollably for the first time since he'd been a little boy. What was happening? Oh please, what was this? What was real and what wasn't?

"Captain, you're in the Fort Bragg Center. You're in the JFK Special Forces Center. Captain Hudson? Captain? . . .

just breathe the oxygen! Captain, that's an order. Breathe in . . . breathe out . . . that's *very* good. Very, very good. *That's excellent."*

Lying on his back, staring silently up at vague forms and swimming shapes, David Hudson thought that maybe he knew this man. How was that?

Familiar voice? Familiar drooping blond walrus moustache. Did he know him? Was the man actually there? Hudson reached forward to touch, but couldn't move because of the cloth straps.

"Captain Hudson, you're in the Fort Bragg Center for Special Forces. This was a stress and tolerance test. Do you remember now?

"Captain Hudson, this has been a drug-induced test. You haven't left this room inside the hospital. You were flashing back to Viet Nam."

Nothing real?

None of this happened? . . .

No—there had been a Viet Cong prison camp!

Hallucinations? . . .

There had been a Lizard Man!

Oh, please, make this all stop now.

"Captain Hudson, you revealed nothing about your mission. You passed your tolerance *test.* Flying colors. You were really great. Congratulations."

Mission?

A test?

Sure thing. Just a little pop quiz. Okay.

"You're beginning to understand illusion, Captain. You refused to be interrogated under drugs. . . . You're learning to be illusion's master. You're learning the fine art of deception, Captain Hudson. The art of our deadliest enemies . . ."

"Horse Latitudes" was playing somewhere in the hospital. . . . *In the Special Forces Center.* Deception.

"Breathe that good air, Captain Hudson. Just breathe in easily. Pure, pure oxygen. You passed, Captain. You're the best so far. You're the best we've tested."

Stress and tolerance tests.

The Womack Hospital at Fort Bragg.

Deception.

He was learning to be illusion's master.

You passed, Captain Hudson. Flying colors.

Of course—I'm the best you have!

I've always been the best—at everything.

That's why I'm here, isn't it?

That's why I was chosen for this training.

Hallucination.

Deception.

Important to understand.

The key!

The solution, the answer to everything was deception!

"Breathe that pure oxygen, Captain Hudson."

Chapter 56

CARROLL WAS BARELY AWAKE, barely functioning.

Familiar home surroundings coalesced . . . Books on the mantel—*The Brethren, Fatal Vision, The Pope of Greenwich Village, The Fate of the Earth.* . . . An oil painting of his father, done by Mary Katherine, hung on one wall.

And there were children.

Lots and lots of children.

They were eyeing him suspiciously, waiting for him to speak, to say something characteristically flip and amazing.

Carroll slowly sipped fresh-brewed coffee from a cracked *Revenge of the Jedi* mug. "Sunrise Semester" flickered on the TV with the sound off. The horizontal line lazily flipped out of synch with the rest of the room.

The Carroll clan was together for a rare family conference. Coffee, cocoa, and Carroll's world-famous pop-up toaster French toast comprised the menu.

"Mmff . . . mmff . . . Lizzie mmff . . . Lizzie was a son of a bitch, Dad. While you were gone away."

Mickey Kevin reported this news as he chewed heavily

syruped wads of toast. His mouth flapped open in a rubbery, half-smiling circle.

"I think I told you about that kind of gutter talk."

"Mmff, mmff. *You* use gutter talk."

"Yeah, maybe *my* dad didn't kick my rear end enough. I won't make that same mistake, okay."

"Besides, I wasn't a son of a bitch. He was." Lizzie suddenly glared up from the soggy remains on her plate.

"Lizard! You're not too big to get an Ivory soap sandwich, either. Big bar, right fresh out of the wrapper."

The most angelic smile lit up Lizzie's face. "An Ivory soap sandwich, *Daddy?* . . . Better than Eggo, *still-a-little-frozen* French toast!" She *leveled* her father with a deadpan, brutal evaluation of his not entirely home-cooked breakfast offerings.

They all began to laugh, then. Clancy and Mary nearly fell off their chairs giggling. Mickey Kevin did topple off, like a drunken carnival kewpie doll.

Carroll finally gave up. He broke into a sleepy smile. He winked over at Mary K., who was letting him run the familiar, four-ring circus this morning.

He had been *trying* to tell them about his almost tragic trip to Europe. He'd been trying to be a reasonably good dad for the four of them. . . . He fuzzily remembered how his own father had done the same sort of thing: telling sanitized stories about the 91st Precinct, right in that very same breakfast nook on Sunday mornings.

Finally, after putting it off at least thirty minutes, Carroll came to the really difficult part of his story; the punchline so to speak; the *core* of his tale of adventure and foreign intrigue in England and Ireland . . .

He was going to try and make this all sound very casual now. . . . No big deal, right? So *begin*.

"Over in Europe, I was working with someone. . . . They had these special teams of police with financial people. Our best people. We worked in London, then in Belfast together. She was nearly killed there, in fact. Over in Ireland. Her name's Caitlin. Her name is Caitlin Dillon."

Silence. The big chill comes to the Carroll house.

Keep going. Don't stop now.

"Sometime, I'd like you guys to meet her. No big deal. She's originally, uh, she's from out in Ohio. She's pretty funny, actually. Very nice. For a girl. Ha ha."

Absolute, stone-cold silence . . .

Finally, a very tiny, muffled reply from Lizzie. "No thank you."

Carroll's eyes slowly, ever so slowly, passed from face to small face.

Mickey, who looked all soft and vulnerable in his Yankee pinstripe pj's with slipper socks, was close to tears.

Clancy, in an oversized robe that made him look like ET in the fantasy movie's beer-drinking scene, was silent and more stoic. His small body was rigid with control.

They were angry, and hurt—*all at the same time*. They knew *exactly* what was happening here.

"Hey, come on, lighten up, okay?" Carroll tried to make it seem a little funny. Bill Murray on "Saturday Night Live," which he did pretty well, despite the lack of any facial resemblance.

"I *talked* to a woman who I *happen* to work with. Just *talked*. Hello, blah, blah, blah, goodbye."

They wouldn't say a word to him. They stared at Carroll as if he had just said he was going to leave them. They made him feel so bad—so hollow and hopeless about everything, literally everything in his or their life.

Come on, it's been three years.

I'm closing up inside. I'm dying.

"Come on, kids." Mary Katherine finally spoke up from her low-key spot at the kitchen table. "Be a little fair, huh. Doesn't your father get to have some friends, too?"

Silence.

No, he doesn't.

Not women friends.

Lizzie finally started to cry. She tried to muffle her sobs, choking back the breathless gasps with both little hands.

Then they were all crying, except Mickey Kevin, who kept staring murderously at his father.

It was Carroll's worst moment with them since the night Nora had actually died on some high and mighty, antiseptic white floor in New York Hospital. His chest was beginning to heave now, too; his heart felt as if it was being cruelly, brutally ripped in half.

They weren't ready for someone else—*maybe he wasn't ready, either.*

For the next several minutes, nothing he could say could make it any better. Nothing could make any of the kids laugh. Nothing could make them loosen up at all.

They all hated Caitlin. They weren't going to give her a chance. Period. End of nondiscussion.

They were fiercely determined to hate anyone who wasn't their dead mother.

Chapter 57

TWO HOURS LATER in Manhattan, Carroll felt that he needed a stiff shot of Irish whiskey. He also felt like going back to the role of Crusader Rabbit, *running away* into the strangely comfortable fantasy of the bagman. For the first time, *maybe*, he thought he was beginning to understand the past three years of his life.

Later that day, he would vaguely remember weaving a mostly aimless path inside No. 13 Wall Street at around nine o'clock. The fluorescent lights were too bright; the glaring overhead lamps were harsh, tearing at his eyes.

It was all wrong, the place *felt* wrong. There was too much gloom and doom, frustration was evident everywhere Carroll walked. The police investigators, the Wall Street researchers bent over mountainous documents or hunched in paralysis in front of computer screens—they were like people who have been trapped indoors too long, men and women who haven't seen the light of day for weeks.

Around 9:30, Arch Carroll set to work again inside his monastic office.

Green Band—why did he have the feeling that there was

something important on the top of his mind, an obvious insight that had evaded him until now? It was infuriating and elusive, like soap that gets away from your hand in the tub. Like a forgotten name.

Was it something to do with Green Band's inside information? A spy at No. 13?

But the half-formed thought, whatever it was, had already vanished.

From a transcript taken in Room 312; No. 13 Wall Street; Monday, December 13.

Present: Arch Carroll; Anthony Ferrano; Michael Caruso.

CARROLL: Hello, Mr. Ferrano, I'm Mr. Carroll, antiterrorist division, State Department. This is my associate, Mr. Caruso. Mr. Ferrano, to get right to the point, not to waste any of your time, or mine, I need some information . . .

FERRANO: Figured that out already.

CARROLL: Uh huh. Well, I read your earlier transcript. I just read over the conversation you had with Sergeant Caruso. I'm a little surprised you haven't heard *anything* about the bombings on Wall Street.

FERRANO: Why's that? Why should I have?

CARROLL: Well, for one thing, you being a heavy gun and explosives dealer, Mr. Ferrano. Doesn't it strike you as odd, uh, peculiar, you wouldn't have heard something? There must be rumors floating around on the street. I'm sorry, would you like a sip of whiskey?

FERRANO: I want whiskey, I've got money in my pocket. Listen, I told you, I told somebody, *him,* I don't deal guns. I don't know what you're talking that shit for. I own Playland Arcade Games, Inc., on Tenth Avenue and 49th Street. You got that straight now?

CARROLL: Okay, that's *bullshit*. Who do you think you're talking to? Some punk off the street? Just some street *punk* here?

FERRANO: Hey, all right, fuck you. I want my lawyer in here now! . . . Hey, you understand English, pal? *Lawyer! Now!* . . . Hey! Hey! . . . Ohhh . . . Oh, *shit!*

(Loud scuffling, fighting sounds. Furniture crashing; man groaning.)

CARROLL (Breathing heavily): Mr. Ferrano, I think . . . I feel it's important you understand something. Listen carefully to what I'm saying. Watch my lips . . . Ferrano, you've just entered the Twilight Zone. You *don't* have the right to remain silent in the Twilight Zone. All your constitutional rights have been temporarily cancelled. You have *no lawyer*. All right? We set to continue our discussion, fuckhead?

FERRANO: Shit, man. My tooth's broken. Gimme a break for . . . awhh, *shit*, man.

CARROLL: I'm trying to give you every break in the world. Don't you understand anything yet? What this is here? What's happening? . . . *Somebody* stole money from *the man*. Some very important people are severely pissed off. Big, big people. Why don't you imagine that this is Viet Nam and you're the Viet Cong? Would that help you?

FERRANO: Wait a minute! I didn't do anything!

CARROLL: No? You sell pump-action shotguns, revolvers to fourteen, fifteen-year-old kids. Black, P.R., Chinese kids in gangs. I'm not gonna say any more than that. . . . Your lawyer is a Mr. Joseph Rao of 24 Park Avenue. Mr. Rao doesn't want any part of this . . . I think you better tell me everything you've heard on the street.

FERRANO: Look. I'll tell you what I know. I can't tell you what I don't know.

CARROLL: That I can buy.

FERRANO: All right, I *heard* there was some heavy artillery available. In the city. This was about, beginning, I guess, maybe middle of November. Yeah, five weeks ago.

CARROLL: How heavy are we talking about?

FERRANO: Like M-60s. Like M-79 rocket launchers. Soviet RPD light machine guns. SKS automatics. That kinda stuff. *Heavy!* I mean what the fuck they gonna do with that kind of munitions? That's basic ground assault equipment. Like in Nam. What you'd use, take over a country. That's all I heard . . . I'm telling the truth, Carroll . . . Hey that's all *anybody* knows on the street. . . . Awhh, c'mon, don'tcha believe me? . . . Hey! Seriously?

CARROLL: Tell me what you know about François Monserrat . . .

FERRANO: He ain't Italian.

CARROLL: Mr. Ferrano, thank you so much for your help. Now get out of my office, please. Mr. Caruso will show you to the nearest rathole out.

From a transcript taken in Room 312; No. 13 Wall Street.
Present: Arch Carroll; Muhammed Saalam.

CARROLL: Hello there, Mr. Saalam. Haven't seen you since you had Percy Ellis killed on 103rd Street. Very nice djellaba. Sip of Irish whiskey?

SAALAM: Liquor is against my religious beliefs.

CARROLL: This is Irish whiskey. It's blessed. Well, we'll get right down to official police business then. . . . Tell me, uh, are you a hunter, Mr. Saalam?

SAALAM (Laughs): No, not really. A hunter? . . . Actually, if you stop to think about it, I'm a *huntee*. Ever since I fought for you whites in Southeast Asia. My name is Sah-*lahm* by the way.

CARROLL: Sah-*lahm*. I'm sorry. . . . No, you see, I thought you must be a hunter. Something like that. You see, we found all of these hunting guns, these *hunting* bombs in your apartment up in Yonkers, M-23 squirrel-hunting guns. Opossum-hunting sniper rifles, the ones with star nightscopes. Chipmunk-hunting fragmentation grenades. B-40 duck-hunting rockets.

SAALAM: You bust into my place?

CARROLL: Had to. What do you know about a Mister François Monserrat?

SAALAM: You had a warrant from a judge?

CARROLL: Well, we couldn't get an official bench warrant. We did talk to a judge off the record. He said, don't get caught. We took it from there.

SAALAM: No search warrant or nothing?

CARROLL: You know, this is really shocking. Didn't *anybody* read the June 16, *Time* magazine? Story on me? Little squared-off red box thing? Doesn't anybody understand who I am? *I'm* a terrorist! Just like you guys . . . I don't play by international Red Cross of Switzerland agreements. Mr. Saalam, you sold some M-23 squirrel-hunting guns, also some quail-hunting sniper rifles to a couple of fellas. About six weeks ago. *Who . . . are . . . they? . . .*

(Long pause) . . . Uh, oh. Uh, oh . . . Mr. Saalam, please let me explain something else to you. Explain this as clearly as I can. . . . *You're* a bright, U.S. college-educated terrorist. You went to Howard University for a year; you did a little time in Attica. You're one of the Mark Rudd-El-dridge Cleaver-Kathy Boudin school. . . . Me, on the other hand, I'm a terrorist of the PLO–Red Brigade—Blow-away-anything-that-moves school. . . . Now then. You sold a full case of stolen M-23s on or about November first. That's a *fact* we both know about. You say—"Yes, I did" or I'll break your right hand. Just say "Yes, I did" . . .

SAALAM: Yeah, I did.

CARROLL: Good. Thank you for your forthrightness. Now, *who* did you sell the M-23s to? Wait. Before you answer. Remember that I'm the PLO. Don't say anything you'd be afraid to say to a PLO investigator in Beirut.

SAALAM: I don't know who they are.

CARROLL: Oh, *Jesus* Christ.

SAALAM: No, wait a minute. *They* knew who I was. They knew everything about me. I never saw nobody, I swear it. I felt like they had set me up.

CARROLL: I love former inmate sincerity. Unfortunately, I happen to believe you. . . . Because that's what your current roommate, Mr. Rashad, said, too. Please get the hell out of here now. . . . Oh, by the way, Mr. Saalam. We had to rent your apartment up in Yonkers. We rented it to a very nice Welfare lady, with these three little kids.

SAALAM: You did what?

CARROLL: We rented the apartment you were selling guns out of. We rented it to a nice lady with a batch of kids. Skoal, brother.

Chapter 58

"IT'S ALL SO incredibly methodical. That's what is mystifying. They keep evading all contact with this huge police dragnet. *How?*"

Caitlin and eighty-three-year-old Anton Birnbaum, both red-eyed and exhausted, sat together on stiff leather Harvard chairs in Birnbaum's lower Wall Street office. Caitlin was six inches taller than the birdlike, deceptively frail Financier. Earlier in her career, when she had worked for Birnbaum, he wouldn't walk anywhere on Wall Street with her for that reason.

Now, Anton Birnbaum rubbed the small of his back as he talked. "*Something* so very methodical, so carefully orchestrated. . . . *Something* absolutely systematic is happening throughout Western Europe right now."

Caitlin watched Birnbaum's face. She waited for more to come. It usually did with Anton, who thought much faster than he could speak.

"There is a book. . . . *The Real War*, it's called. The book's central thesis—that Germany, Japan, have found an eminently reasonable road to further world conquest. Through *commerce*. That's the real war. As a country, we're losing that war spectacularly, don't you think, Caitlin?"

The former chairman of the venerable investment house Birnbaum, Levitt was something of a prig, Caitlin knew. He could be savagely impatient with people he didn't like or respect, but he was also brilliant.

"What do *you* think is happening in Western Europe? We're having an impossible time piecing it together, Anton. Some important data is missing. One essential thread of logic that might explain who they are." Caitlin wandered around the old man's office as she talked.

She stopped with her back to the window, and looked at the photographs on the walls. There was Anton snapped in the company of statesmen, controversial industrialists, people from the entertainment industry . . .

Birnbaum scratched the bridge of his nose as he contemplated his choice of the next few words. He was reminded once again that Caitlin was one of the few people on Wall Street he could talk to. Explanations of his theories and insights were unnecessary when speaking with her.

"The Europeans simply don't trust us," he finally began again, hunching forward in his seat. "Which is precisely why they don't talk to us anymore. They believe we have different attitudes, different priorities."

Anton Birnbaum stared directly into Caitlin's brown eyes. His own eyes were watering hopelessly behind thick lenses. He reminded Caitlin of a character in *Wind in the Willows*, Mr. Mole.

"I sound like an alarmist, no? But I feel the intrinsic truth of what I'm saying. Almost *prima facie*, I feel it.

There will be a crash now. I believe there will be a serious crash, possibly another Black Friday. Very, very soon."

Anton Birnbaum spoke again. "I think we could be in the middle of a war. *The money wars.* The great *Third World War* we have so long feared—it may already be upon us."

Chapter 59

"GODDAMN IT! Look at this!" The speaker was Walter Trentkamp, and his voice was harsh with disbelief. "Gentlemen, it's happening everywhere!"

Philip Berger, Director of the CIA, Trentkamp, and General Frederick House were gathered around the computer terminals when Caitlin and Carroll arrived. Several display screens were working simultaneously, flashing words as well as graphics.

Berger glanced up as Caitlin Dillon and Carroll hurried across the Crisis Room floor. He frowned.

"Emergency reports have been coming in for about fifteen, twenty minutes," he said to the others. "Since three-thirty our time. They've got something hopping. Something's happening *all over the world* this time."

At one o'clock Paris time, La Compagnie des Agents was suddenly closed by official order of the President of France.

All stock trading was immediately halted on the Bourse.

Bourse officials reluctantly admitted that the Market's CAC index had fallen *over 3 percent in a single morning*.

The afternoon newspapers in Paris carried the most shocking headline in four decades:

MARKET CLOSE TO PANIC!
BOURSE CRASH!
PARIS MARKET IN SHAMBLES.
FINANCIAL DISASTER!

For once, the tabloids were being written with some understatement, however.

The Frankfurt Stock Exchange was in chaos, but still managed to stay open for the entire session.

The Commerzbank Index had fallen under a thousand for the first time since back in 1982.

The largest losers for the day included Westdeutsche Landesbank, Bayer, Volkswagen, and Philip Holzmann.

As yet, none of the economists in West Germany understood *why* prices were dropping; or how far they might plummet in the near future.

The Toronto Stock Exchange was one of the worst hit anywhere.

The exchange's composite index of 300 stocks *fell 155 points to under 2000.*

Trading volumes set new records, until the major Canadian Exchange was officially closed at 1:00 P.M.

In Tokyo, the Nikkei-Dow Jones index was shaky all day, finally closing at 9200. This was a full 2½ percent decline in a single day.

Hardest hit were all companies trading heavily with the

Middle East. These included Mitsui Petrochemical, Sumitomo Chemical, Oki Electric.

Heavy European and American deposits made the Johannesburg Stock Exchange the only apparent *winner* anywhere around the world. Bullion was suddenly trading at $1,000 an ounce. The rand instantly appreciated to $1.50.

Hundreds of millions of dollars were made in South Africa. Suspicions rose, but still no satisfactory answers came.

London dramatically shut down at 12:00 noon, three and a half hours shy of regular closing.

The *Financial Times* Index of 750 companies had fallen nearly 90 points; it was down almost 200 since the initial Green Band bombings in New York.

The scene on Threadneedle, near the Bank of London, was nearly as bleak and without hope as bombed-out Wall Street in New York.

With its forty-button, telephone-computer consoles, the Crisis Room at No. 13 Wall was beginning to resemble the *Starship Enterprise* more than the traditional Chippendale feel and look of the Street. Nonetheless, the thirty or so police, Army, and financial experts in the room had absolutely no idea what they were supposed to accomplish next.

The Western economic system seemed to be crashing to a disastrous halt. Not one of them had a reasonable clue why.

And still there was only maddening silence from Green Band.

Chapter 60

CARROLL AND CAITLIN DILLON sat on an old floral couch in his Manhattan apartment. A Beethoven concerto played on the tape deck.

Once again, they were waiting for Green Band. There was nothing to do but wait.

"I think I have to turn in," Caitlin finally said in a half-asleep whisper. She hunched forward and kissed Carroll's forehead. "Get a few hours, anyway."

Carroll raised his wristwatch to his face. "What a party pooper. No sense of adventure. It's only two-thirty."

"People from Ohio go to bed at nine-thirty, ten o'clock. The Lima Holiday Inn restaurant is filled at five-thirty. Closed down by eight."

"Yeah, but you're a sophisticated New Yorker now. We party until two or three on weekdays here."

Caitlin kissed Carroll again and the idle talk stopped. He was amazed at how comfortable he was with her. Watching someone you cared about almost being killed seemed to accelerate the courting process.

"Is anything the matter? You look sad? Tell me . . ." Her

eyes were digging for more, more to understand who Carroll really was.

"I'm not quite ready for bed yet. I'm overtired I guess. I'll be in soon. You go ahead."

Caitlin leaned in closer and kissed Carroll again. She smelled so wholesome and nice. She had the softest lips he could imagine.

"Do you want me to stay with you?" She whispered one more time.

Carroll shook his head.

Caitlin left the living room, sleepily huddled in the cocoon of a blanket.

Carroll stood up from the couch. He started to pace back and forth past the darkly reflective parlor windows. His body was feeling all wrong: *wired, incandescent.*

He looked inside an old antique blanket chest he'd bought years back in central Pennsylvania. His mind was wandering into odd places, weird time zones . . .

He wondered if Caitlin liked kids much . . .

Jesus, he was so incredibly wired. So uptight tonight.

Finally, he did it though. The worst thing under the circumstances—the absolute worst.

On the anniversary.

Nora's death three years before.

December 14.

First, Carroll gathered together old photographs. He found most of the photos in a cluttered, bottom shelf inside a glass-enclosed book cabinet.

Next, he pulled a wicker chair up close beside one of the tall windows facing onto the lights of Riverside Drive and the river.

Carroll stared down at the West Side Highway, the peacefully quiet Boat Basin.

He was letting the present go all fuzzy and blurred.

He stood up again.

He dealt three tapes off the stacks on either side of the stereo. One was *52nd Street*, Billy Joel self-consciously holding a trumpet on the cover. The second was mainstream country and western, *I Believe In Love* by somebody called Don Williams. The third was Barbra Streisand and Barry Gibbs' *Guilty*.

Carroll switched on the stereo and the speakers immediately hummed. He felt the power surge through the soles of his bare feet. He turned the volume way down.

He'd never been a big Barbra Streisand fan, but there were two songs he wanted to hear on this album: "Woman in Love," and "Promises." Out in the world, a moving van rumbled along Riverside Drive.

He kept an old framed picture of Nora, hidden away face down in the bottom of the bookcase.

He slid it out now. He propped the photo on the arm of the couch.

For a long, pensive moment, he stared at Nora sitting there in a hospital-issue wheelchair. Anniversary of her death. Pain still sharp and fresh as yesterday.

He could remember *exactly* when the snapshot had been taken. After they'd operated. After the surgeons had failed to remove her malignant tumor.

In the wheelchair photo, Nora was wearing a simple yellow-flowered sundress, a knitted blue cardigan sweater. She had on a pair of crazy high-topped sneakers which became her trademark as an invalid.

Nora was smiling radiantly in the picture. Not once to

his knowledge had she completely broken down during the illness, not once had she felt sorry for herself. She'd been thirty-one years old when they'd found the tumor. She'd had to watch her blond hair fall out from the chemotherapy treatments; then she'd had to adapt to life in the iron clutches of her wheelchair. Nora had *somehow* accepted that she wasn't going to see her children grow up, or anything else the two of them had laughed and dreamed about, and always taken for granted.

Why couldn't he finally accept her death?

Why couldn't he ever accept the way life was apparently supposed to be?

Arch Carroll stopped and listened closely to Barbra Streisand singing.

The song "Promises" made him remember the stretch when he'd visited Nora every night, night after night at New York Hospital. After the hospital visits, Carroll would eat at Galahanty's Bar up the hill on First Avenue. A burger, soggy home fries, draft beer that tasted the way swamp gas smells. The beginning of his drinking problems.

The two Streisand songs had been favorites on Galahanty's jukebox.

They always made him think of Nora—all alone back at that scary, skyscraper hospital.

Sitting in the bar, he always wanted to go back—at ten, eleven o'clock—to talk with her just a little bit more; to sleep with her; to hold Nora tight against the gathering night inside her New York hospital room. To squeeze every possible moment out of the time they had left together . . .

The worst, the very truest line for him in "Promises" finally came. . . .

Tears slowly rolled down his cheeks. The pain inside was like a rock solid column that extended from the center of his chest all the way into his forehead. The sadness, the inconsolable grief was for Nora, though, not for himself: the *unfairness* of what had happened to her.

Carroll began to hold himself fiercely tight, squeezing hard with both arms.

When would this feeling please stop? The past three years had been unbearable. When would it please fucking stop?

He always had the insane urge—*to break glass.*

Just to punch out glass.

Caitlin, meanwhile, stood immobile, perfectly silent in the darkened apartment hallway.

She couldn't catch hold of her breath, couldn't even swallow right then. She had wandered back from the bedroom when she'd heard noises. Faint strains of music . . .

She'd found Carroll like this. So sad to watch.

She walked back to the bedroom. She huddled deep down into the body-warm covers and sheets.

Lying there alone, Caitlin bit down hard on her lower lip. She understood and felt so much more about Carroll—clearly, in an instant. Maybe she understood more than she wanted to.

She wanted to hold him right now, only she was afraid to go and ask. Caitlin was afraid to intrude.

She didn't know how long she'd been alone in the big silent bedroom overlooking the river.

The phone on the bedstand began to ring.

It was 3:30.

He didn't pick up outside. Where was Carroll now?

She waited, four, five rings, and he still didn't pick up.

Caitlin finally grabbed for the receiver.

A very excited voice was on the phone line. A man was talking, before she had a chance to say a word.

"Arch, sorry to wake you. This is Walter Trentkamp. I'm down at No. 13 right now. The Stock Exchange in Sydney just opened. There's a massive panic! You'd better come now. *It's all going to crash!*"

Chapter 61

"WHAT'S HAPPENING, ARCH, *I think*, is a disorderly, almost a riotous Market condition. Everybody desperately wants to sell. Except there's a corresponding lack of buyers," Caitlin said.

"What *exactly* does that mean?" Carroll asked.

"It means the bottom line price of stocks and bonds *has* to plummet dramatically. . . . The crash that's apparently coming could last a few hours, days, or drag on for years."

"Years?"

"Back in sixty-three, on the day Kennedy was assassinated, the Market collapsed and was shut down early. The next day it recovered. But it wasn't until after World War Two that the Market recovered from the crash of 1929!"

Carroll and Caitlin Dillon were hurrying across the immense marble lobby of the World Trade Center.

It was here, on the ground floor and mezzanine, that the fiduciary nerve center of the banks and trust companies had been established after the bombings on Wall Street.

The escalator stairs to the mezzanine were frozen to a stop. An impromptu sign over a red arrow said FINANCIAL SECTION, and pointed straight up.

Carroll and Caitlin started to jog up the oddly motion-less metal stairs. It was just past 4:00 A.M.

"This looks a little more organized than Number thir-teen. Not much though," Carroll observed.

Red and blue intercom wires were strung up every-where, hung like Christmas decorations over the escalators and fire exit stairways. Open radio channels connecting uptown offices with the Financial Center squawked and chattered endlessly.

Even at that time in the morning, the hum and buzz of electronic noise was unrelenting.

Out a row of high, vaulted windows, Carroll and Caitlin could see a black Bell Army helicopter landing. Limos and other official cars were discharging somber-looking men carrying business briefcases.

A crash coming this morning?

Another Black Friday?

"What happened? What's causing the worldwide panic?" Carroll wanted to know as he and Caitlin entered a cavernous marble hallway with no visible way out.

Caitlin rubbed her arms warm as she walked. The glass doors to the outside were constantly opening, and the building was cold as a meat freezer.

"None of the usual safeguards in the systems are work-ing. Not enough fail-safe devices were ever built in for a situation like this. Academic economists have been warn-ing the New York Stock Exchange for years. Every MBA candidate in the country knows that something like this could happen."

Carroll finally pushed open heavy pine doors into a huge, disturbingly frantic business conference room: a miniature Stock Exchange almost. Brokers on complex

NYTECH telephone consoles, analysts with IBM desktop computers, were talking all at once.

The room was absolutely jammed with frenetic, shadowy figures, many of whom were shouting into phone receivers which they managed to cradle, in a practiced defiance of gravity, between jaw and shoulder.

Carroll had the impression of madness, a bedlam: what this place reminded him of, give or take some modern accouterments, was a print he'd once seen of a Massachusetts insane asylum in the late 1800s.

Unconditional orders were being issued to *sell*, at the very best price possible. Jobs and business relationships were being routinely threatened over the long distance telephones.

Jay Fairchild, tall, jowly, bald as an infant, lumbered forward out of a clique of gray suits to meet Caitlin and Carroll. Fairchild was an Undersecretary of the Treasury, a man who'd come to rely regularly on Caitlin's judgments, her usually astute, almost uncanny hunches about the market.

"Jay, what the hell has happened tonight? Who started it? *Where* did it start?" It was Caitlin's turn to appear confused for a change.

The Undersecretary of the Treasury's eyes had the animation of glass beads.

"Just about *every* nightmare scenario you or I have ever imagined has come true tonight," Fairchild finally said.

"At the end of the day yesterday, out in Chicago, metal skyrocketed way up. A ton of futures, coffee, sugar, flopped badly. Bank of America and First National began calling in their loans."

Caitlin couldn't hold back her anger at that news.

"Those unbelievable shits! Morons. The commodity people out of Chicago won't listen to anybody, Arch. There have been all sorts of speculative excesses on the options market long before this."

"None of that is the *real* problem right now, though," Jay Fairchild said. "The crash is being precipitated by the goddamn banks! ... The banks are almost completely responsible. Let's wander back to the lobby. You'll see what I mean. It's worse than it looks up here. It's quite sad, really."

Chapter 62

FBI AGENTS AND hardnosed-looking New York City police officers were screening the credentials of everyone trying to get into the conference room on the ground floor level.

Carroll knew the FBI guys, so they walked right in.

Once inside, the thundering noise and activity was double what Carroll and Caitlin had witnessed and heard upstairs.

It was still only 4:30 A.M., but a nightmarish fear had taken firm hold—you could see it on every face inside the overcrowded room.

"There's another factor contributing to the current disaster," Jay Fairchild said. "The real possibility of a *worldwide crash*, rather than an isolated one in the U.S. This time, the whole bloody world could go up."

Everyone they passed in the conference room appeared hopelessly grave. The scene was something like a general alarm on a Navy warship.

Caitlin said, "Seven days of brokerage transactions are now unresolved. The bankers are competing, they're actually competing to see who can take the most clear-cut, absolutely amoral advantage of the chaos!"

Carroll didn't understand some of what was being said, but he grasped enough. When you misappropriate people's money, *a lot of small investors' money given to you on trust*, he figured you were a criminal.

Call him naive and old-fashioned, but that was how he felt.

"It sounds to me like *nobody's* protecting the ordinary investor right now."

Jay Fairchild nodded. *"Nobody is.* The big banks are all busy maneuvering for the oil billions. They could give a damn about the poor bastard out there with a hundred shares of Polaroid or AT and T."

"Arch, Arab oil money is the name of the game. Arab money is almost always conservatively managed. Since last Friday they've been trying to move out of the U.S. Treasury Bills. Into gold. Into other precious metals. The banks are shamelessly scrambling for the huge Arab fees. They're like rats on a ship, bailing out of the dollar—rushing into sterling, the yen, the Swiss franc, all the more stable currencies . . . Chase, Manufacturers, Bank of America, they're *making* small fortunes right now." Caitlin's lips were tight and her jaw clenched as she spoke.

The three of them stood by helplessly watching the Stock Market crash gain a momentum of its own.

Reports from London, Paris, Bonn, and Geneva came rushing in.

Men in white shirtsleeves and loosened neckties took turns calling out the more substantial Telex quotes for the benefit of beleaguered clerks who reported them into a massive central computer.

Phibro Solomon	bought at	12½	Down 22.
General Electric	bought at	35	Down 31.
IBM	bought at	80½	Down *40*.

By 11:30 on the morning of December 14, most U.S. banks, including every savings and loan, had been closed.

The Chicago, Philadelphia, Boston, Pacific and Midwest exchanges had all been officially shut down.

Chapter 63

AT NOON, AN elderly man made his way toward the hub of action at the front of the World Trade Center Crisis Room.

Many of the young brokers and bankers didn't recognize Anton Birnbaum. Those who did regarded him with sharp, uneasy glances.

Birnbaum looked more like an ancient New York City pawnbroker than one of the world's acknowledged financial geniuses, a man with a reputation that had been unblemished over all his years in business.

President Justin Kearney had arrived by helicopter from Washington less than thirty minutes before. The President warmly greeted the Financier, speaking with deference and respect.

"It's awfully good to see you again, Anton. Especially now." The President spoke formally, as he might to a visiting foreign dignitary.

Kearney and Anton Birnbaum disappeared inside a small private office, the door of which was guarded by the Secret Service.

"It's good to be *seen* out in the world, Mr. President. I

don't get out so much anymore. Mr. President, if I might be allowed to speak first, I have an idea you might wish to consider . . .

"I have just gotten off the phone with two gentlemen you've possibly never heard of. It's worth repeating both conversations. One man is from Milwaukee, a Mr. Clyde Miller. The other man resides in Nashville, Tennessee— Mr. Louis Lavine."

Anton Birnbaum said all this in a slow, deliberate style which made each word seem vitally important.

"Mr. Miller is the CEO for a large brewing company. Mr. Lavine is Treasurer for the State of Tennessee. . . . I have just convinced Mr. Miller to buy five hundred thousand shares of General Motors stock, which is right now at forty-seven. He will buy the General Motors stock, and keep buying it until the price goes back to sixty-seven. He is prepared to invest up to two hundred million dollars.

"I've asked Mr. Louis Lavine in Tennessee to buy NCR stock which is now at nineteen, and continue to buy it until the price moves up to thirty. He's prepared to commit up to seventy-five million dollars for the purchase."

Birnbaum then went on to explain to the President why the plan he'd conceived could work.

"I only hope that the courage of these two gentlemen will actually turn the direction of this catastrophe. I pray it will restore some necessary *optimism*. Mr. President, I have a belief that it will . . .

"Once the market sniffs a demand for these two bell-wether issues, smart money will start moving. The risk arbitragers, who can spot an uptrend in an avalanche and who command billions in ready cash, will begin testing the waters.

"I have advised a select few of my associates, who have responsibility for mutual and pension funds around the country, that a dramatic break in the crisis situation is imminent. I have suggested that they look for opportunities to begin bargain hunting, before they lose out on a very fast and favorable profit spiral. A spiral back close to where the market began this morning."

The news of Birnbaum's recovery plan traveled with appropriate dispatch through the main Trade Center conference room. Emotional arguments over whether the daring strategy was right, or disastrous, raged immediately.

"Clyde Miller has just bankrupted his own corporation." One of the detractors laughed with derision at the news.

Two other middle-aged bankers argued their way into a fist fight. Creaking haymakers were thrown. A loop of bankers and stock analysts surrounded the breathless, wheezing pugilists and a couple of side bets were laid. The fight ended with both bankers leaning against each other in fatigue, as if they were each trying to shore up the other's dignity.

As the winter morning passed into steely gray afternoon, however, it was obvious that the Birnbaum plan was either too late or too little.

The largest single-day losses ever had already been recorded on the world's stock markets.

On October 29, 1929, losses had been fourteen billion.

On December 14, the single day's recorded losses around the world exceeded two hundred billion.

Chapter 64

LATE THAT NIGHT, Caitlin swallowed warm sips of diet soda and sat entranced before a forty-inch television screen just off the main crisis room.

The monitor's reception was crisp, the antennas for the major national networks all being up on the Trade Center roof.

"This is it," she whispered to Carroll. "The exchange in Hong Kong will be the first important one to open around the world. Sydney and Tokyo are both staying closed until noon. Yesterday, the Hang Seng Index fell 80 points. This will tell the story."

Caitlin and Carroll were sitting within a tightly clustered nest of Wall Street bankers, frayed men and women who were like spectators burned out by watching some unlikely sport event that stretched day after day. A closed-circuit TV broadcast was being beamed by satellite transmission from Asia to New York.

On the flickering screen, they watched cameramen and news reporters—live—recording history from behind Hong Kong police lines.

Farther down the crowded, rowdy street, tens of thousands

of Hong Kong residents were loudly chanting, waving hand-printed political placards. Meanwhile, single lines of dark-suited stockbrokers were beginning to solemnly march into the exchange itself.

"The brokers look like pallbearers," Carroll whispered to Caitlin.

"It isn't a cheery sight, is it? It *does* look like a state funeral."

A correspondent for one of the American networks stepped up to a TV camera planted on the mobbed Hong Kong street. The newsman wore a rumpled seersucker suit and spoke with a clipped British accent.

"Never before have we seen such a graphic demonstration of the polarization between Third World and Western hopes and dreams. Here in Hong Kong I believe we are seeing a mini-drama of the imminent future of the world. It is now the day after stock prices have tumbled precipitously everywhere. . . . The bond market is in shambles; the French and Arabs are liquidating their holdings at literally the rate of billions a day. . . . And in Hong Kong this morning, many people are deeply concerned, even sad faced. . . . But *the majority*, surprisingly large numbers, mostly university and street gang youths, but also the unemployed—are shouting anti-U.S. slogans, even praying for a shattering Stock Market crash. The people are rooting for a full-scale world economic crash. They're expecting the worst, and they're gleeful about the disastrous outcome. . . . *The long awaited fall of the West.*"

with their loud whoops, their echoing hand clapping. The gray-suited Chairman of the Federal Reserve danced briefly with the cantankerous Chairman of the Joint Chiefs.

"I don't believe I've ever seen bankers so joyous before," Caitlin said.

"They still dance like bankers though." Carroll smiled at the odd but affecting scene of relief.

He couldn't help feeling elation in the midst of this crazy, almost riotous room, though. It wasn't as if they'd actually found Green Band, but it was something, a sliver of merriment at the heart of the recent grimness, the frustration trailing back for days.

Caitlin nuzzled the side of his face with her mouth. "I'm already getting worried again. I only hope . . ."

"What do you hope?" Carroll gently held Caitlin's arm. He felt unbelievably close to her. They had already shared more charged moments than some people do in a lifetime.

"I hope that it continues like this, and doesn't come crashing down."

Carroll was silent, studying the oddly uplifting scene in front of him. Somebody had found a tape player and the sound of Scottish bagpipers could be heard over the general din. Somebody was dragging in a couple of cases of champagne. There was something just a little forced in the celebration—but what the hell? These were people who'd been about to fall off the edge of their world and, slippery though it might be, they'd found temporary footing.

Still . . .

Still . . .

Even as Carroll sipped champagne, something inside

kept him from getting too hopeful. *This is all premature,* he was thinking as the party heightened in intensity.

Where is Green Band? Is Green Band watching right now?

What are they thinking? Where are they taking us next? What kind of party are they having today?

Chapter 66

CARROLL HAD DECIDED to start at the beginning. Square one again. He thoroughly checked and rechecked every early lead, every hunch he'd ever had about Green Band. The task would take countless hours, he knew. It would require an intense search through the computers, even allowing for the fact that he had high-speed data at his disposal.

Ah, police work.

He asked for clearance from both the CIA and the FBI to make a search of their computer files. Neither organization gave him trouble, although Phil Berger imposed limitations on Carroll's access.

Nearly eleven hours later, Carroll stood before a dozen or so computer screens inside the Emergency Room at No. 13 Wall. Carroll stared at the screens and his eyes ached from the dull green glow.

He glanced at Caitlin, who sat with her fingers raised over a computer keyboard, ready to type out a password for further access to the FBI's files.

When the display screen answered, she typed again, this time requesting a readout of active and nonactive Viet Nam veterans who, for whatever reason, had been under police surveillance during the past two years—a time frame she and Carroll had agreed on.

She added the subcategory: *Explosive experts. New York and vicinity. Possible subversive leanings.*

There was a long pause, a spooky electronic pause, then the machine began its requested readout of American soldiers.

Carroll had been down this particular route of investigation, only not with the Crisis Room equipment and Caitlin's help. American terrorist-related groups were out there, but none were considered powerful or well-organized. Phil Berger of the CIA had been investigating paramilitary groups himself. He had waved Carroll off that trail.

"Can you print out a list of the hard cases?" Carroll asked Caitlin.

"This is a computer. It can do anything if you ask nicely."

The printer obligingly kicked back into life. Paper slid through it as the dot matrix clacked back and forward. A total count showed no more than ninety names of current soldiers and veterans with extensive explosives experience in Viet Nam; men who the FBI considered important enough to keep track of. Carroll ripped the scroll of paper from the printer and took it to a desk, spreading the thing out.

Adamski, Stanley. Corporal. Three years VA Hospital, Prescott, Arizona. Member of left-wing oriented veterans group called the Rams, ostensibly a biker's club.

Carroll wondered how much of this was standard FBI paranoia?

The list was filled with dizzying cross-references, he soon discovered. One name was connected to another, creating a mazelike effect. You could spend months working on all the permutations.

Keresty, John. Sergeant. Munitions expert. Discharged VA Hospital, Scranton, Pa., 1974. Occupation: custodian, plastics corp. Member of the American Socialist Party. Ridgewood, New Jersey. SEE: Rhinehart, Jay T.; Jones, James; Winston files.

The lists went on and on for pages.

Carroll massaged his eyelids. He went for two coffees, returned to the work desk and even more sprawling computer sheets.

He said, "Any one of these men, or two or three of them, working in tandem, *could* have helped blow up the financial district."

Caitlin gazed over his shoulder at the printout list. "So where do we start?"

Carroll shook his head. He was filled with doubts again. They would have to investigate, maybe even visit every name on the lists. They didn't have time.

Scully, Richard P. Sergeant. Plastique expert. Hospitalized Manhattan 1974 for alcoholism. Extreme right-wing sympathizer. Occupation: cabdriver. New York City.

Downey, Marc. Military assassin. Hospitalized 1971–73: Occupation: bartender. Worcester, Mass.

Carroll gazed at the burgeoning list again. He had another idea. An Army *officer,* maybe? A disaffected officer with a grudge, or a cause? Somebody exceptionally smart, nursing a grievance, year after year.

Carroll laid his hands on the warm computer console. He wished he could coax all the secrets out of it, all the electronic links of which it was capable. He stared at the already lengthy printout again. "An officer," Carroll said. "Try that."

Caitlin went back to the keyboard to request more information. He watched her fingers move expertly over the keys. She was requesting information on *known or suspected subversives, who had been officers in Viet Nam.* Under the general rubric of "subversive" were included all kinds of people.

The screen began to issue more names. Colonels. Captains. Majors. Some were listed in these official records as schizophrenics. Others were supposedly burnt out on drugs. Others still had become evangelists, panhandlers, small-time bank and liquor store robbers. Carroll received a printout of these names as well. There were twenty-nine of the hard-core category in and around New York City.

The screen flickered again.

Names of the various officers on the FBI list now shimmered forth. Carroll once again ran his eye over them.

Bradshaw, Michael. Captain. Discharged VA Hospital Dallas, Texas, 1971. Occupation: Real estate salesman, Hempstead, Long Island. Post Traumatic Stress Disorder victim.

Babbershill, Terrance. Major. Discharged dishonorably 1969. Known Viet Cong sympathizer. Occupation: English-language tutor for various Vietnamese families. Brooklyn, New York.

Carroll blinked and tried to focus. His eyes were beginning to water. He needed to feel the fresh cold night air on his face. He didn't move: he continued to run his eyes up and down the screen.

Rydeholm, Ralph. Colonel.

O'Donnell, Joseph. Colonel.
Schweitzer, Peter. Lieutenant Colonel.
Shaw, Robert. Captain.
Norsworthy, Robert. Colonel.
Boudreau, Dan. Captain.
Kaplan, Lin. Captain.
Weinshanker, Greg. Captain.
Dwyer, James. Colonel.
Beauregard, Bo. Captain.
Arnold, Tim. Captain.
Morrissey, Jack. Colonel.

Too many names, Carroll thought.

Too many casualties in a war of total waste.

"Can you get me cross-references, Caitlin? Associations and connections between any of these men? The officers. The real hard asses out of Viet Nam?"

"I'll try." Caitlin tapped a few keys. Nothing happened this time.

She stared at the screen thoughtfully, then tapped another brief message.

Nothing happened.

She tapped out another message.

Nothing happened.

"Is something wrong?" Carroll asked.

"This is the best I can get, Arch. Damn it."

The message that shone in front of them read:

Further data: see files

"See files?" he asked. "These *are* the files."

"They apparently have more information in FBI files that *aren't* on the computer, Arch. They're down in Washington. *Only in Washington.* Why the hell is that?"

Chapter 67

AT TEN O'CLOCK ON the evening of December 15, Sergeant Harry Stemkowsky was thinking that he was actually solvent. He was financially comfortable, probably for the first time in his life.

He'd just bought a new Ford Bronco, also a luxurious beaver coat for Mary. Life was suddenly getting decent for them, for the first time in their four married years together.

But Stemkowsky couldn't bring himself to comfortably believe in any of it. This was all like Santa Claus, and trips to Disneyworld—that kind of transient shit.

Who could identify with the sudden net worth of $1,152,000?

Harry Stemkowsky felt a little like one of those loonie-tunes who won the New York State Lottery, then nervously kept their little jobs as janitors or U.S. postal employees. It was a matter of too much, too fast.

At twenty past ten that evening, Stemkowsky nosed his Vets cab out of the street noise and blazing yellow lights of Midtown Manhattan in the East 60s. He'd finished his regular ten-hour shift, all according to the Vets' master plan, Colonel Hudson's prescribed step-by-step plan for their ultimate success.

The Checker cab bumped and rattled onto the 59th Street entrance to the bridge.

A few minutes later, the Checker cab turned onto a busy avenue in Jackson Heights, then edged onto 85th Street, where Harry Stemkowsky lived with his wife, Mary.

He absently licked his lips as he drove down 85th. He could just about taste the French stew Mary had said she was fixing when he'd left in the morning.

The sudden expectation of beef, shallots, those little, light puffed potatoes she usually made, was exhilarating. Maybe he and Mary should retire to the south of France after this was over, he began to think. They'd be filthy rich enough for sure. They could eat four-star French food until they got absolutely sick of it. Maybe move on to Italy. Maybe Greece after that. Greece was supposed to be cheap. Hey. Who cared if it was cheap or not?

Harry Stemkowsky began to accelerate down the last flat stretch toward home.

"*Jesus Christ, buddy!*" Stemkowsky suddenly shouted out loud and pounded his brakes.

A tall, balding guy, with an incredibly pained look, had run out in front of the cab. The guy was frantically waving both arms over his head; he was screaming something Stemkowsky couldn't make out with the windows up.

Harry Stemkowsky recognized the look from Viet Nam though, from dreaded clean-up patrols into villages after devastating Phantom air strafes. Something horrible and unexpected had happened here—something awful had happened in Stemkowsky's neighborhood.

The terrified man was up against the cab window. Still

screaming at the top of his voice. "Help me, please! Help! Please help!"

Stemkowsky finally got the window rolled down. He had his radio mike in hand, ready to call for whatever kind of emergency help was needed.

"What the hell happened? What happened, mister?"

Suddenly, a small black Beretta was shoved hard, crunching like a nightstick against Stemkowsky's temple. "*This* is the matter! Don't move. Put back that mike."

A second man appeared now, emerging out of the smoky side street darkness. He yanked open the creaking passenger side door.

"Just turn the cab right around, Stemkowsky. We're not going home quite yet."

An indefinite time later—Hours? Maybe it was days? There was no way to accurately gauge because all time had collapsed under him—Stemkowsky felt hands angrily ripping under his armpits, lifting him rudely.

The hands propped him hard onto a badly creaking wooden chair again.

A man's face, a blur of soft pink, seemed to float down and stop close to Stemkowsky's face. The man was uncomfortably close.

Then his mind went into complete shock! Sergeant Harry Stemkowsky's watery eyes began to blink rapidly; he tried to look away from this *particular closeup face* . . .

Harry Stemkowsky couldn't believe who this was.

His eyes kept trying to lock into focus.

This face, he'd seen it before, recently, always distilled by a network TV screen or a newspaper—

No, he was confused: the injected drug had fucked his brain over—

What was going on here? This person couldn't be—

The face smiled horribly and said, "Yes, I'm François Monserrat. You know me under another name. This is an extraordinary shock, I know."

Harry Stemkowsky shut his eyes a moment. *This was all a bad dream; make it go away.*

Stemkowsky opened his eyes: he shook his head.

Suddenly, Harry Stemkowsky's head ached unbelievably. His eyeballs felt indescribably heavy, as if they were hanging on elastic bands. He simply could not believe it. So incredibly near the top. The ultimate traitor . . .

When Stemkowsky finally spoke, he was close to being incoherent; incomprehensible words squirmed through his gummy, swollen lips. His tongue seemed at least twice its normal size.

"Ga fuh-fuh-fuck yrrself. Fuh-fuck yrrself."

"Oh, please. Your time for being morally indignant is long past. . . . All right, then . . . look at what we have here. Look at this."

Concentrate, Stemkowsky fiercely reminded himself. *Focus. Concentrate.*

Monserrat's hands were holding out a brown paper shopping bag. Up close to Stemkowsky's face.

Monserrat was taking something out. "A blue cooking pot. Familiar?" Once again, that horrible smile.

Harry Stemkowsky screamed! He fought insanely against his bonds, forcing them to rip into his skin.

Up close to Stemkowsky's eyes, a fork dipped slowly into the depths of the pot. The fork speared a dripping chunk of beef bourguignon that oozed brown gravy.

Stemkowsky screamed once again. He screamed and screamed.

"It seems you guessed my secret. You should also know by now how deadly serious this interrogation is. How important this is to me." Monserrat turned to his lieutenants.

"Bring in the unfortunate cook."

Harry Stemkowsky recognized his wife Mary, but only slightly. She was a pitiful caricature of her former self. Her face was bruised, purplish and raw in extended areas. Her mouth opened crookedly as she saw Harry. Some of her front teeth were missing; her gums were pulpy and bloody.

"Puh-puh-pleez?" Stemkowsky struggled; he lifted the chair legs right off the floor with his tremendous arm strength. "*She doe kno.*"

"I know that. Mary doesn't know how you came to possess stolen Stock Market bonds in Beirut, then in Tel Aviv. *You* know, though."

"Pleez. Doh-doh-don hur' her . . ."

"I don't want to hurt her. So you tell me what you know, Sergeant. Everything that you know. You tell me right now. How did you get the stolen Stock Market bonds?"

Once again, that horrible smile from Monserrat.

It took another cruel and gruesome fifteen minutes to get the information, to find out *some,* not all, of what Sergeant Harry Stemkowsky knew . . .

Information about the stolen bonds and Wall Street securities; about the bombings on December 4. Not where Colonel Hudson was right now. Not even precisely who the Vets leader was. But a start, a beginning at least. And a beginning was better than what Monserrat had been accustomed to recently.

François Monserrat stared down at crippled Harry Stemkowsky and his wife. From Stemkowsky's perspective the terrorist leader seemed to be looking right through them, as though they were both insubstantial.

"You see now? None of your pain, none of poor Mary's suffering was necessary. It could have been five minutes of talking together at most. Now, how's this for just rewards?"

A compact black Beretta appeared, paused so that the Stemkowskys could see what was coming, then fired twice.

The very last thing U.S. Army Sergeant Harry Stemkowsky ever thought . . . he and Mary never got to enjoy their money. Over a million dollars, which they'd earned. It wasn't fair. Life wasn't ever fair, was it? That same question always left hanging, always unanswered in the end.

Chapter 68

THAT NIGHT, CARROLL traveled home to the Bronx. As he slumped up from the garage, the ground around him seemed to be spinning.

He climbed creaky front porch steps. Twinges of guilt struck hard. He'd been neglecting the kids for too long this time.

The nightlight was on, but nothing much else downstairs. There was the electric buzz of kitchen appliances. Carroll took off his shoes, and tiptoed quietly upstairs.

He stopped and peeked inside the front bedroom where Elizabeth, a.k.a. Lizzie, bunked with Mickey Kevin. Their tiny baby figures were delicately sprawled across twin beds.

He remembered buying the beds years before, at Klein's on 14th Street. *Just look at the little creepolas. Not a problem, not a care in the world. Life as it ought to be.*

An ancient Buster Brown clock from Carroll's own childhood glowed and clicked softly on the far wall. It was next to posters of Def Leppard and the Police. Strange world to grow up in for a little kid.

Strange world for the big kids, too.

"Hi, you guys." He whispered, too low to be heard. "Your dad's home from the salt mines."

"Everybody's just fine, Archer," Mary K. spoke. She'd snuck up from behind, and scared the living shit out of him.

"They understand the problems you're having. We've been watching the news."

Mary K. gave her brother a hug. She'd been nineteen when their parents had died in Florida. Carroll had looked after her after that. He and Nora had always been around to talk to her about her boyfriends—about Mary Katherine wanting to be a serious painter, even if she couldn't make any decent money at it. They'd been there when she needed them, and now it was the other way around.

"Maybe they understand okay about my work. How about the other thing? Caitlin?" Carroll's head turned slowly toward his sister.

Mary K. took his arm and draped it over her housecoat and shoulder. She was such a softie, such a sweet, gentle and good lady. It was time she found someone as terrific as she was, Carroll often thought. Probably she wasn't helping her cause, living with him and the kids, either.

"They trust your parental judgment. Within reasonable bounds, of course."

"That's news."

"Oh, you're the Word and the Light to them, and you know it. If you say they'll like Caitlin, they instinctively believe it—because you said it, Arch."

"Well, they didn't show it the other morning. I *think* they'll like her. She's a terrific person."

"I'm sure she is. You have good instincts about people. You always knew which of my beaus was worth a second look. You're a sucker for people who are full of life, full of love for other people. That's what Caitlin's like, isn't she?"

Arch Carroll looked down at his sister, and gently shook his head. Finally he grinned. Mary K. was so smart. She had an artist's sensibility, but she was so practical. A curious combination, and irresistible in his opinion.

Carroll stretched his arms. The wound, that souvenir of a morning in France, still ached. "One day soon, I'm going to take a week off. I swear it. I've got to get back in touch with the kids."

"What about your friend, Caitlin? Could *she* take a week off too?"

Carroll said nothing. He wasn't sure if that was such a good idea.

He went off to bed, where he lay exhausted, but unable to fall over the edge into sleep. The No. 13 Wall computer screens were still running through his mind, perplexing images. If there was any one avenue he could follow on the trail of Green Band, it would lead inevitably to Washington, and deeper into the restricted files of the FBI.

Arch Carroll snored quietly, slept dreamlessly, and when his bedside alarm went off it was just before dawn and dark still.

Chapter 69

WASHINGTON, D.C., CARROLL had always thought, was the ultimate Hitchcock movie location: so elegant, so quietly lovely and distinguished, yet with paranoia.

At 9:00 A.M. he squirmed from a blue Metro cab with a dented fender. His face was slapped with raw cold and drizzle on Washington's 10th Street. Carroll hiked his jacket collar up. He squinted through a thick, soupy, morning haze, which obscured the concrete box that was the J. Edgar Hoover Building.

Once inside the Hoover memorial, he found the procedure at the escort desk mechanical and unnecessarily slow. It irritated Carroll in the worst bureaucratic way. The Bureau's famous procedures, the inefficiency they created, played like a skit appropriate for "Saturday Night Live."

After several minutes of phone checks, he was granted a coded blue tag with the FBI's official insignia. He slid the plastic card into a metal entry gate, and passed inside the hallowed halls.

An attractive woman agent, a researcher for FBI Data Analysis, was waiting outside the elevator on the fifth floor. She wore a man-tailored suit; her chestnut hair was wound back in a tight, formal chignon.

"Hello, I'm Arch Carroll."

"I'm Samantha Hawes. People *don't* call me Sam. Nice to meet you. Why don't you come this way, please."

She started to walk away, pleasant but efficient. "I've already collected as much material as I can for you to look at. When you told me what you were fishing for, I put in some hours of overtime. My material comes from the Pentagon and from our own classified files. Everything I could collect this quickly on your lists of names. It wasn't easy, I must say. Some of it I transcribed from material already on computer file. The rest—as you can smell—is contained in some really musty documents."

Samantha Hawes finally delivered Carroll to a library-style carrel beside a silent row of gray metal copiers. The desk was completely covered with thick stacks of reports.

Carroll's heart nearly stalled as he gazed at the mountainous stacks. Each report looked like any other. How was he supposed to find something unusual in this great, yawning heap of history?

He walked around the table, sizing up his task. Hidden among all these folders were connections between men— the tracks, the spoor they laid down; the events they lived through during and after Viet Nam. Somewhere, surely, tracks would crisscross, correspondences would have been made, relationships established.

"I have more. Do you want to see them now? Or is this enough to hold you for a while?" Samantha Hawes asked.

"Oh, I think this will do me pretty well. I didn't know we collected *this much* dirt on everybody down here."

Agent Hawes grinned. "You should see your file."

"Did you?"

"I'll be back over there, working in the stacks. You just holler if you need any more light reading, Mr. Carroll."

The FBI agent started to turn away, then she suddenly turned back. Samantha Hawes *seemed* to be a very contemporary Southern woman, pretty, very confident, genteel and proper Southern from her looks, anyway. In days of old, Carroll couldn't help thinking, she would already have been a young mother of two or three tucked away in Alexandria. She would have been a Sam, too.

"There *is* something else." Her face was suddenly quite serious and concerned. "I don't know exactly what this all means. Maybe it's just me. But when I went through these files yesterday evening . . . I had the distinct feeling that some of them had been tampered with . . ."

A very unpleasant warning rang in Carroll's head. "Who would tamper with them?"

Samantha Hawes shook her head. "Any number of people have access to them. I don't know the answer."

"What do you mean when you say they've been tampered with, Samantha?"

The agent looked straight at Carroll. "I mean, that I think documents are *missing* from certain files."

Carroll reached out and lightly grasped her wrist. He was excited by this information because it meant that certain files, in some ways, were already different from the rest. They stood out.

Someone else had looked at them.

Someone had possibly pilfered documents from them.

Why? Which files?

He saw a strange look crossing her face, as if she were asking herself about the precise nature of this unorthodox man who'd been admitted into FBI headquarters.

"Can you remember *which* files?"

"Of course I can." She moved toward the work table and began sifting. She picked out five thick files, dropping them in front of Carroll, saying, "This one . . . and this . . . this . . . this one . . . this one."

He gazed quickly at the names on the files.

Barreiro, Joseph.

Doud, Michael.

Freedman, Harold Lee.

Melindez, Pauly.

Hudson, David.

"Why these five?" he asked.

"They served together in Viet Nam, according to their documents. That's one good reason."

Carroll sat down. He still expected to come away from Washington empty-handed. He expected that the faint sense of anticipation he felt now would turn out to be nothing more than a false alarm. Five men on the FBI computer list of "subversives"—a term he knew was next to meaningless, at least the way the FBI used it.

He checked his own printouts, and his heart suddenly clutched.

Barreiro and Doud had been explosives experts.

And David Hudson had been a colonel, who, according to the brief note on the printout, had been active in the organization of veterans groups and veterans rights after Viet Nam.

Five men who had served together in the war.

Five men who were on both his list, and the FBI's.

He slipped off his jacket, then the tie he'd worn especially for his big trip to Washington.

He began to read about Colonel Hudson.

Chapter 70

WHEN HE HAD finished reading, Carroll tilted his creaking chair back. He shook his head.

The ledger on U.S. Army Colonel David Hudson lay flopped open before him. Hudson's thick 211 file, his entire life in the U.S. military, was spread out on the desk.

Suddenly, the Green Band investigation was more hopelessly complex and confusing than it had ever been.

Colonel David Hudson was the final enigma.

David Hudson's military career had begun with high promise at West Point, where he was an honor graduate in 1966. He'd been a four-year member, and finally captain, of the tennis team. He was also a popular cadet according to all the available reports.

It got even better, or worse, from there. Hudson had subsequently *volunteered* for Special Forces "Q" courses, followed by a special Ranger training. On a first impression at least, the Army couldn't have asked for a more diligent or professional young soldier.

Colonel David Hudson: All-American Boy.

Every succeeding report Carroll read was highlighted and underscored with phrases like "one of our very best";

"the kind of young officer who should make us all proud"; "a model soldier in every way. Unbridled, absolutely infectious enthusiasm"; "definitely one of our future leaders"; "the kind of material we can build the modern Army around."

In Viet Nam, Captain Hudson had been awarded the Medal of Honor and the Distinguished Service Cross during his first tour. He had been captured and transported into North Viet Nam for interrogation. He'd spent seven months as a POW.

Hudson had almost died in the prison camp. . . . He had then *volunteered for a second tour,* and performed with "conspicuous gallantry and intrepidity" on several occasions.

Then, three months before the evacuation of Saigon, he'd been savagely wounded by a Viet Cong grenade blast and subsequently lost his left arm. Hudson reacted with characteristic bravura.

A hospital report read: "David Hudson has been a godsend, helping other patients, never seeming to feel sorry for himself. . . . In every way, a thoroughly idealistic young man."

Following Viet Nam though, quite suddenly after his return to the United States, Colonel Hudson's career, his entire life, seemed to become disturbingly unhinged. According to the files, the change was bewildering to his friends and family.

"It was almost as if a different man had returned from the war." His father was interviewed and quoted several times. "The fire, that wonderful, contagious enthusiasm was burned out of David's eyes. His eyes were those of a very old man."

Colonel David Hudson: enigma, almost phantom after coming home from the Viet Nam War.

First at Fort Sam Houston in Texas, then at Fort Sill in Oklahoma; at Fort Polk, Hudson was quietly disciplined for "activities detrimental to the Army." . . .

Another report indicated that he was transferred twice within three months, for what seemed on the surface to be petty insubordinations. . . .

His marriage to Betsy Hinson, his hometown sweetheart, ended abruptly in 1973. Betsy Hinson said, "I don't even know David anymore. I don't know this man who I'm supposed to be married to. David's become a stranger to everyone he knows."

Hudson, in the postwar years, had become almost obsessive about his participation in a handful of Viet Nam veterans' organizations. As an organizer and spokesman at rallies around the country, Hudson had met and been photographed with liberal motion picture stars, with sympathetic big business leaders, with recognizable national politicians.

At one point during the morning, Carroll meticulously laid out Xerox copies of every available photo of David Hudson.

He rearranged the pictures until he liked the pattern of his collage. One photo was stained with coffee or cola. *The stain looked recent. Samantha Hawes? Someone else? Or was he just getting squirrely?*

In the photographs, at least, Colonel Hudson looked like the classic, idealized military man of past decades. With his Jimmy Stewart wholesomeness, he looked the way American soldiers had been pictured in the years *before* Viet Nam. He had short blond hair in almost all the war photographs, a tightly set somewhat heroic jaw, a pinched, slightly uncomfortable smile, that was disarming, anyway. Colonel Hudson was clearly very sure of himself and what he was doing. He was obviously proud, fiercely proud, to be an American soldier.

Carroll got up from the mess of official papers and wandered around the research library room.

Okay—what did he have here?

A leader, a natural soldier, who somewhere along the way had fucked up royally.

Or maybe Hudson had been royally fucked?

There were probably hundreds, maybe even thousands of men like David Hudson across the country. Some of them went berserk and had to be removed to the "screaming floors" in VA hospitals. Others sat quietly in dingy, lonely rooms and ticked slowly, like time bombs.

Colonel David Hudson? . . . Was he Green Band?

Samantha Hawes reappeared with a pot of coffee, deli sandwiches and assorted salads on a tray.

"Getting into it, I see."

"Yes, it's something, all right. Odd, and absolutely mesmerizing. Hard to figure though."

Carroll rubbed the palms of his hands in circles over his red-rimmed eyes. "Thanks for the food, especially the coffee. The whole file is extraordinary. Colonel Hudson especially. He's a very complex, very strange man. He was so perfect. The perfect soldier. Then what? What happened to him after he returned to the States?"

Samantha Hawes sat down at the FBI researcher's desk beside Carroll. She took a healthy bite of an overstuffed sandwich.

"As I said, there are some really peculiar gaps in his military records. In all of their records. Believe me, I look at enough of them to know."

"What sort of peculiar gaps? What *should* be in there that isn't?"

"Well. There were no written reports on his special training at Fort Bragg, for example. There was nothing on his 'Q,' or his Ranger training. There was almost nothing on his time as a POW. Those should all be in there. Marked highly confidential if need be, but definitely there in the file."

"What *else* is missing? Would there be photostated copies or originals anywhere else?"

"There should be more psychological profiles. More reports after he lost his arm in Viet Nam. There's very little on that. He was tortured by the Viet Cong. He apparently still has flashbacks. All the backup data on his POW experience is conveniently missing. I've never seen a 211 file without a complete psych workup, either."

Carroll selected a second, thick roast beef sandwich half. "Maybe Hudson took them out himself?"

"I don't know how he could get in here, but it makes as much sense as anything else I read yesterday."

"Like? Please keep going, Samantha."

"Like the way they made him a cipher right after Viet Nam. He had *very* high level intelligence clearance in Southeast Asia. He was a *heavy* commander in Viet Nam. Why would they give him such a nothing post back in the States? The arm? Then why not write it up that way?"

"Maybe that's why he quit the service," Carroll suggested. "The second-rate assignments once he got back home."

"Maybe. Probably, I guess. But why did they do it to

him in the first place? . . . They were *grooming* David Hudson before he came home. Believe me, they had serious plans for him. You can see tracks to glory all over those files. In the early years, anyway. Hudson was a real star."

Carroll jotted down a few notes to himself. "What would a more predictable assignment have been? Once he was back in the States? If he was still on the fast track?"

"At the very least, he should have gotten the Pentagon. According to his records, he was on an *extremely* fast track. Until the disciplinary problems, anyway. He got all these bush-league assignments *before* he did anything to deserve them."

"It doesn't make sense. Not yet, anyway. Maybe they'll know something at the Pentagon. That's my next stop."

Samantha Hawes put out her hand to shake. "My sincere condolences. The Pentagon makes this admittedly austere place seem like a hippie commune."

"I've heard they're a party group." Carroll smiled back at Agent Hawes.

"Listen," she said. "There is something else you should know. One other person went through the 211 files. At least one other person in the past two weeks. On *December fifth*, actually."

Carroll stopped packing up and stared at Samantha Hawes. "Who?" he asked.

"On the fifth of December, certain 211 files were ordered over to the White House. *Vice-president Elliot wanted to see them. He kept the files for over six hours.*"

Chapter 71

THE YOUNG CARROLL BOY had his marching orders, really strict orders, too.

Six-year-old Mickey Kevin Carroll had been allowed to walk the three blocks home from CYO basketball practice since the second month of the school year.

He had very precise orders for the walk, which his Aunt Mary K. actually made him *write out* inside his salt-and-pepper composition note pad. *Mickey's orders were:*

Look both ways at Churchill Avenue.

Look both ways at Grand Street.

Don't talk to strangers for any reason at all.

Don't stop at the Fieldstone store before supper.

If you do, it's instant death by torture.

Mickey Kevin was pondering the confusing mechanics of the basketball layup as he covered the long double block between Riverdale Avenue and Churchill Street. Brother Alexander Joseph had made it *look* kind of easy—the layup. Except when Mickey tried it himself, there were just too many things to remember to do, all practically at the same time. Somehow your leg, and your same arm, had to come up; then you had to throw the ball perfectly into the high, high hoop. All at the same time.

As he rehearsed the confusing sport's primary action, Mickey Kevin gradually became aware of footsteps growing loudly behind him.

He finally turned and saw a man. The man was walking his way. Walking pretty fast.

Mickey Kevin's body tightened. TV movies and stuff like that made you scared when you were alone by yourself. Somebody was always out to get the little kid, or the baby-sitter all alone at home. It was a pretty creepy world. Some of the people out there were unbelievably creepy.

The man walking behind him looked pretty normal, Mickey guessed, but he decided to hurry it up a little, anyway.

Without looking too obvious, he started to take longer steps, faster steps. He walked the way he always did when he was trying to keep up with his dad.

There weren't any cars or anything at the corner of Grand Street. Mickey stopped according to his rules anyway. He looked both ways.

He looked back then—and the man was really close. Really, really close.

Mickey Kevin *ran* across Grand Street, and Aunt Mary K. would have killed him on the spot. His heart was pounding a little now. Really thumping out loud. Right down into his shoes, he could feel his heartbeat.

Then Mickey Kevin did the really, really dumb thing.

He knew it the second he did it. The instant!

He suddenly cut through the empty lot at the Riverdale Day School.

There were all these tricky bushes and stuff back there.

Everybody left empty beer cans and broken wine and liquor bottles. Mary K. had forgotten to put that on the list: *don't cut through the Riverdale Day School lot.* It was too obvious for words.

Mickey pushed the prickly bushes out of his way, and he *thought* he heard the man coming through the lot behind him. *Crashing* through the lot.

He wasn't completely sure. He'd have to stop walking, to listen close enough to tell. He decided to just keep running, to run like hell.

Full speed ahead running now. As fast as he could run with all the dark, thorny bushes, the hidden rocks and roots trying to trip him up.

Mickey Kevin stumbled forward, his feet seeming to catch in dirt holes. He glided over slippery leaves.

He nicked a rock and almost went over, head first. He was panting now, his breath was too loud in his own ears, his footsteps were echoing like gunshots.

The back of his house suddenly appeared: the glowing, amber porch lights, the familiar gray outline against the much darker blackness of the night.

He had never been so glad to see home.

Fingers touched the side of his cheek and Mickey loudly yelled out. "Hey!"

A stupid tree branch!

He almost had a heart attack. Mickey then ran like a midget halfback bound for seven across the last icy patch of back lawn.

Halfway there, his metal lunchbox popped open. It just about exploded as an orange, rolled-up papers, a thermos tumbled out.

Mickey Kevin dropped the lunchbox.

He crashed up the back steps and got his hand on the cold metal stormdoor.

And then . . .

Then Mickey Kevin turned. He *had* to look back.

His chest was pounding nonstop now. Ka-chunk, ka-chunk, like a huge machine was inside there. Making ice or something equally noisy to hear. He *had* to look back.

Nobody was there!

Nobody was following him at all.

Oh brother! Oh boy, oh boy.

Nobody was behind him.

Nobody!

It was completely quiet in the backyard. Nothing moved. His lunchbox lay overturned in the middle of the snow. It glowed a little in the dark.

Mickey squinted real hard.

He was feeling pretty stupid now. He'd made it all up; he was almost sure of it. . . . Except he still wasn't going to go back and pick up his fallen lunchbox. Maybe in the morning. Maybe in the spring some time.

What a little baby! Afraid of the dark! He finally disappeared inside the house.

Mary K. was dicing vegetables with a big knife on the butcher block in the kitchen. The TV was turned on to Mary Tyler Moore.

"How was practice, Mickey Mouse? You look beat up. Wash, huh. Dinner's almost ready. I *said*—how was your basketball practice, fella?"

"Oh, uh . . . I don't know how to do a stupid layup. It was okay."

Then Mickey Kevin smoothly disappeared, slid like a shadow into the downstairs bathroom.

He didn't wash his hands and face inside, though. He left the overhead light switched off.

Mickey Kevin very slowly lifted a handful of lace bathroom curtain. He stared out into the dark, very creepola backyard, squinting his eyes tightly again.

He still couldn't see anybody.

The stupid cat, their stupid cat Mortimer, was playing with his lunchbox. There was nobody else. Nobody had really chased him, he was suddenly sure. He couldn't see anybody . . .

He couldn't see the real-life bogeyman watching the Carroll house from the darkened back lot.

Chapter 72

IT WAS JUST AFTER FIVE O'CLOCK when an Army colonel named Duriel Williamson emphatically strode into a windowless office hidden away inside the thirty-four-acre Pentagon complex.

Carroll was already waiting in the Spartan, bureaucratic green room.

So was a Captain Pete Hawkins, who had formally escorted Carroll from the visitor's pickup desk, back through the dizzying grid of tightly interlocking Pentagon corridors.

Colonel Williamson was outfitted in the full dress uniform of the U.S. Special Forces—including a blood-red beret, cocked jauntily. Colonel Williamson's hair was short and bristling, a salt-and-pepper crew which looked appropriately stern. His voice was starched as well, but showed heavy hints of irony.

Everything about Duriel Williamson said: *no bullshit permitted here. State your business, mister.*

Captain Hawkins made the introductions in a polite if strictly formal military fashion. Hawkins was clearly a career bureaucrat, a survivor.

"Mr. Carroll from the Defense Intelligence Agency, on special assignment by order of the President . . . Colonel Duriel Williamson from Special Forces. Colonel Williamson is stationed at Fort Bragg, North Carolina. Colonel Williamson was David Hudson's immediate superior during both phases of his Special Forces training. Colonel, Mr. Carroll is here to ask you some questions."

The Special Forces officer put out his hand to Arch Carroll. He smiled amicably, and most of the preliminary nervousness and formalities dissolved. "Glad to meet you, Mr. Carroll. May I sit down?"

"Please, Colonel," Carroll said. Both men sat, followed by Captain Hawkins, who would remain in the room for the interview, a matter of protocol.

"What is it you need to know about David?"

Carroll's eyes widened and rose from a short, written list of questions he'd prepared for the interview. "The two of you were on a first-name basis?" he asked Colonel Williamson.

"Yes, I knew David Hudson fairly well. I should amend that, to be as accurate as possible. I spent some time with David Hudson. Not at or because of the Special Forces school. This was after the war. I bumped into him a few times. At different veterans' affairs, mostly. We were both active. We had a couple of beers together, a couple of times."

"Tell me about it Colonel Williamson. What was Hudson like? What was he like to have a beer with?"

Carroll controlled his eagerness to ask more probing questions. His mind was still clouded from the long morning at the FBI, but he knew better than to pressure a Special Forces Colonel.

"David Hudson was stiff at first. Though he tried like the devil not to be. Then he was just fine. He knew a lot about a lot of things. He was a thoughtful man, extremely bright."

"Colonel Hudson's Army career seemed to disintegrate after Viet Nam. Do you have any guess why?"

Duriel Williamson shrugged his shoulders. He appeared mildly puzzled over the question. "That's something that's always troubled me. All I can say is that David Hudson was a *very* outspoken man."

"Meaning, Colonel?" Carroll continued to probe carefully.

"Meaning he was capable of making important enemies inside the Army. . . . He was also extremely disappointed. *Bitter,* I guess is the better word."

Bitter, Carroll thought. Exactly how bitter? Carroll studied the Army colonel in silence.

"The treatment our men got after Viet Nam made David Hudson a very angry person. I think it disillusioned him more than most of us. He considered it a national disgrace. He blamed President Nixon at first. He wrote personal letters to the President, also to the Chief of Staff."

"Just letters? Was that the extent of his protests for the veterans?" I need somebody, Carroll thought, with the kind of bitterness that would go well beyond letters. Hell, anybody could sit down and write a crank letter—

"Actually, no. He was involved in several of the more vocal protests."

"Colonel, any answers you can elaborate on would be helpful. I've got all night to listen."

"He called attention to Washington's long string of broken promises to our veterans. All the betrayals. *'The disposable GI*' was a phrase he liked to use. . . . Let me tell you, Mr. Carroll, *that* kind of high-profile activity can earn you a fast assignment to Timbuktu or to some Podunk reserve unit someplace. That would put him in the Pentagon computers too. Hudson was very active with radical veterans."

"What about his training at the Special Forces school? At Fort Bragg?" Carroll then asked. "Colonel, these answers of yours, as I said, *please* try to be thorough."

"Some of this was quite a while ago. It didn't seem so important at the time. I'll try."

For almost an hour, Colonel Williamson was painstakingly thorough. He elaborately described a brilliant young Army officer, with seemingly boundless energy, with small-town American enthusiasm and talent—a model soldier. Many of the epithets Carroll had read earlier in the 211 files, he heard again from Colonel Williamson.

"What I remember most, though," Williamson said, "what stands out to this day about Hudson is the time at Fort Bragg. We were instructed to push and drive him. Push him to his physical and emotional limits. We redlined David Hudson at Bragg."

"More than other officers who were assigned to the Bragg program?"

"Oh, absolutely. Without any doubt we pushed him more. No punches were pulled. His POW experience was *used* to pump up his hatred for 'our enemies.' Hudson was programmed to seek revenge, *to hate.*"

"Who instructed you to do that, Colonel? Who told you to push Captain Hudson? Somebody obviously must have singled him out for special attention."

Colonel Williamson paused in his answers. His dark

eyes didn't leave Carroll's eyes, but there was a perceptible change in his broad, severe face. Carroll couldn't quite
read the change at first.

"I suppose you're right. At this point, uh, after all these
years. . . . I'm not sure I can tell you *who* though. . . . I remember we were unusually tough on him. Also that Hudson was pretty much up to it. He definitely had character
to spare."

"But his training wasn't typical, not the regular course?
His was different somehow?"

"Yes. David Hudson's training at Fort Bragg was beyond the established norm, which was demanding in itself."

"Give me *some* idea, Colonel. *Put me* at the training
camp. Can you make it come alive for me? What was the
actual training like?"

"All right, I don't think you can imagine it, unless you
actually went through it. . . . Up at two-thirty in the morning. Physical abuse. Drug-induced nightmares. Interrogation by the best in the Army. Pushed like a dirt farm tractor
until you dropped at eight. Up again at two-thirty—I mean
pushed, *drained.* Each day was one hundred percent harder
than the last. Physically and emotionally, psycho-
logically. . . . The men chosen to go to Bragg were all considered top rank. Hudson had West Point *and* extensive
combat behind him. He'd been a successful commander in
Nam. . . . Uh, Captain Hudson was also a military assassin
in Viet Nam. He was very heavy. With a good rep."

Carroll, hearing the word "assassin," felt that he had
taken still another step into the endless Green Band maze.
The further he moved, the more confused and lost he became. The All-American soldier had an even darker side:

assassin. He brought Hudson's clean-cut photographs back to mind: the sunshine face of determination, the bristling crewcut hair, the honesty in those eyes.

"Meaning what, Colonel? What does a good rep mean in that context? As a military assassin."

"It means he wasn't a thrill killer—which some of the top hitters were. . . . A real problem is what to do with some of *those* guys, once they *leave* the Army. If the generals had decided to take out Ho Chi Minh, something very big, very delicate, Hudson most likely would have been considered."

"You seem a little awed by Hudson yourself."

Williamson smiled; he chuckled softly into his chest full of medals.

"I don't know about awe. Awe isn't the right word. Definitely respect, though."

"Why, Colonel?"

"He was one of the best soldiers I've ever trained. He had physical endurance and all the technical skills. He had strength and tremendous smarts. He also had something else, dignity."

"So what went wrong? What happened to Hudson after the war? Why did he finally leave the service in 1976?"

Colonel Williamson rubbed his clean-shaven jaw. "As I said, the one problem was his attitude. He could be extremely judgmental. . . . He also thought he had answers to some controversial Army problems. Some career officers might not have appreciated Hudson's judgment of them and their actions. The other thing was the loss of his arm. David Hudson had big, big plans for himself. How many one-armed generals are you aware of?"

Carroll paused and thought before he spoke again. For

all the apparent cooperation, he had a sneaking feeling that Colonel Williamson was still holding something back. It was the Army way, he remembered from extensive past dealings with the Pentagon. Everything had to be a huge "need to know" secret, shared only inside the sacred fraternity of Army blood brothers, shared with the other *warriors* only.

"Colonel Williamson, I've got to ask the next few questions with the authority of the Commander-in-Chief. That means I need complete answers."

"That's what you've been getting."

"Colonel Williamson, did you know the *official purpose* of David Hudson's Special Forces training at Fort Bragg? Why was he at the JFK school? If that information was in any of your orders, if you heard it anywhere on the base, *I need to know it, Colonel.*"

Colonel Duriel Williamson stared back hard at Carroll, then at Captain Hawkins.

When he spoke, his voice was softer but seemed an octave deeper than it had been.

"Nothing was ever *written down* in any of the orders. . . . As I said, I don't remember who actually issued our daily orders. I do know *why* he was supposed to be there though . . ."

"Go on. Please, Colonel."

"It was something we were told at the very first briefing on David Hudson. *Verbally* told. This first briefing sounded like CIA bullshit by the way. Until we actually *met* Hudson. . . . You see . . .

"They told us Hudson had been specially chosen to be our version of the Third World superterrorist. David

Hudson had been selected, and he was being *trained to be our version of the terrorist Juan Carlos.*"

Carroll's stomach had suddenly dropped; his forehead felt flushed. He leaned forward in his chair.

"That's why he was at the Bragg school? Why he was pushed ahead, beyond all the others?"

"That's what we helped teach him to be. . . . And Mr. Carroll, Captain Hudson was good at it. He *is* still good, I'm sure. From planning a terrorist raid—even a murder if it was necessary, *David Hudson was on a level with Carlos.* . . . The Army trained Hudson to be the best . . . and in my opinion, he was. Maybe *that's* why they couldn't keep him content in the peacetime Army."

Carroll didn't speak—because at that moment, he couldn't. The realization that the Army had secretly trained its own Carlos, and that he had possibly *turned*—it was unbelievable.

"Colonel, in your opinion, could Hudson have been involved with Green Band? Could he have technically masterminded an operation like that?"

"I don't doubt it, Mr. Carroll. He has all the technical skills."

Williamson paused, sighed. "One more fact about Hudson, though. When I knew him, at least, and I think I knew the man fairly well, he loved the United States very much. He loved America. Make no mistake, David Hudson was a patriot."

Chapter 73

THAT EVENING, VERY LATE in Washington, President Kearney was feeling completely debilitated and old, decades older than his forty-two years. The sheen of sweat covering his neck was cold and made him feel ill.

It was past 1:30, and the White House was quiet.

As he walked the corridors of power, the President of the United States held a confidential document under his arm. The sheaf of papers was pressed tightly against his right side by his elbow, but seemed to burn through the material of his suit and shirt, to scald his skin.

Nearly every president, as well as a few *chosen* first-time senators and key congressmen, had learned an important U.S. history lesson when they arrived in the capital city of Washington. Kearney had learned his within the first month of his Presidency. The lesson was that within the broadest scope of American power and its immense wealth, the politician was little more than an appendage to the system. A concession to form, a necessary inconvenience in many ways.

The politician—senator, congressperson, judge, even

the President—was grudgingly tolerated, but each was expendable.

The presidents before Justin Kearney—Reagan, Nixon, Ford, Carter, Kennedy, Johnson—had all learned the lesson in one way or another.

Even the seemingly powerful and secure Secretary of State Kissinger had eventually learned his lesson . . .

There was a higher order working inside, working above and beyond the United States government. There had been a higher order for decades. It made all the sense in the world, actually; it made sense of almost everything that had happened over the past forty years: the Kennedys, Viet Nam, Watergate, Koreagate, the "Star Wars" plan.

They were waiting for President Kearney in the dramatic and imposing National Security Council briefing room. Twelve of them had been inside there for some time, working through the night.

They appeared to be an ordinary enough committee, all in white shirtsleeves and loosened ties.

They stood en masse as the President of the United States entered. They rose out of respect for the office, for the lofty traditions, for what *they themselves* had rigorously maintained about the office.

The forty-first President of the United States then took his accustomed seat at the head of the highly polished oak wood table. Pens and lined yellow writing pads had been set neatly at his place.

"Did you read the position papers through, Mr. President?" One of the twelve committeemen quietly asked Kearney.

"Yes, I read it in my office just now," the President

solemnly answered. His strongly handsome face was pale, drained of its natural color.

The President then laid the substantial packet of confidential papers he'd been carrying on the table. The booklet was approximately 160 typewritten pages. It had never been copied, and never would be. It looked somewhat like an investment offering book or perhaps a condominium plan.

On the dark blue cover something had been printed in regal-looking gold letters.

Green Band. Extremely Confidential and Classified.

The title page was dated May 16.

Seven months before the actual bombing attack on Wall Street.

PART THREE

Arch
Carroll

Chapter 74

FRIDAY IN WASHINGTON dawned with rain clouds rolling across a nearly colorless horizon. A spitting wind blew wintry gusts in from Maryland. The temperature was dropping hourly. From 7:00 A.M. on, Carroll waited impatiently in the front seat of a rented sedan parked in the Washington suburb of McLean.

The dark car blended with a wall of even darker fir trees overhanging Fort Myers Road.

Detective work, Carroll thought as he stared off into nothingness. *First you wait. Always the waiting.*

Carroll passed the early time eating breakfast out of a warm cardboard box from Dunkin' Donuts. The doughnuts weren't as hot as the box itself. They also had no taste. The coffee he sipped was room temperature, a little less satisfying than the doughnuts.

Carroll read some Tracy Kidder, *The Soul of a New Machine,* and that was good, at least. Several times he found himself thinking about Colonel Hudson.

The All-American Boy? West Point honor student . . .

Then Viet Nam assassin? America's jackal? America's François Monserrat?

He wanted to meet Hudson. He wanted to encounter him one-on-one, face-to-face. Maybe inside the interrogation room at No. 13 Wall, Carroll's own turf. *Tell me, Colonel Hudson, what do you know about the Green Band fire-bombings? What about the stolen Wall Street securities? Tell me why you left the Army, Colonel?*

He wondered how far he'd get with somebody like Colonel Hudson, a U.S. saboteur trained to resist interrogation.

About 7:30, a second-floor light finally blinked on inside the white colonial across the roadway. A second light followed moments later. Bedroom and bathroom, probably.

Moments later, a light went on downstairs. Kitchen? The porch light blinked out.

Just past 8:00, which Carroll thought a respectable hour, he trudged up the flagstone front walk and rang a bell which made a chimey sound like old department store bells.

A tall man of about sixty appeared in the pristine white doorway. He wore plaid trousers, house slippers, a powder blue cardigan sweater. His head, shaped like a torpedo, was topped with white-gray stubble.

General Lucas Thompson, former Commander-in-Chief of the United States Evacuation Forces in Viet Nam, still had a craggy, commanding presence. He still appeared capable of taking on combat duty demands. There was something hard and alert in his eyes, like small electric lightbulbs burning there.

"General Thompson, I'm Arch Carroll with the DIA. Sorry to bother you so early in the morning. I'm here about the Green Band investigation."

General Thompson looked appropriately suspicious: his eyes became slats of loose flesh. "What about it, sir? I'm up, but as you say, it's still quite early in the morning."

"I would have called last night, to say I was coming, General. It was late when I left the Pentagon. I thought that might have been a worse breach of etiquette than just coming out here this morning."

The look of consternation and puzzlement faded on General Thompson's face. It was as if the mention of the word "Pentagon" had reassured him; a look of pleasant recognition spread across his features.

"Of course. Arch Carroll. I've read about you."

"General Thompson, I have just a few questions. It's about your command in Southeast Asia. It shouldn't take more than, say, twenty minutes."

"That means an hour," Lucas Thompson said with a sniffling laugh. He swung open the front door anyway. "That's fine. I have the time. Time is plentiful these days, Mr. Carroll." He spoke in the tone of a retired soldier stricken by writer's block halfway through his memoirs. Vaguely frustrated, a little bored, abandoned not only by his muse but by his sense of purpose.

General Thompson led the way inside, through a formal 1930s dining room, into an even more imposing library chamber. There was a white birch fireplace screened by a brass curtain with heavy brass andirons. Tall oak bookshelves stood erect on every wall; a double bay window looked onto a backyard with a covered pool and yellow-and-lime-striped cabana.

General Thompson sat in a comfortable wing chair.

"Out of sight in Washington, pretty much out of mind. Since my retirement, I've had very few *official* visitors down here. Other than my two granddaughters, who fortunately live up the lane, and who adore their grandmother's baked goods and double fudge."

General Thompson shook his head and smiled. He was easing into the interview more than Carroll had expected or hoped.

In Viet Nam, Carroll had heard that Thompson was an extremely rigid disciplinarian. Now, in his retirement, Lucas Thompson seemed like just another grandfather, patiently waiting for the next Kodak snapshot to be taken.

"I'm searching—groping, is the word I think I want—for some useful information about a Colonel David Hudson. Hudson was on your command team in Saigon, right?"

General Thompson nodded in the manner of a practiced good listener. "Yes, Captain Hudson served on my team for about fifteen months. If my recollection is holding up better than the rest of me."

"Your recollection and my records match exactly," Carroll said. "What can you tell me about Hudson?"

"Well, I'm not sure where you want me to start. It's fairly complex. David Hudson was an extremely disciplined and effective soldier. Also a very charismatic leader, once he got his command over there . . .

"When I first met him, he was ramrodding a, I believe it was a demolition team. He'd also been trained to sanction human targets. He sanctioned trash, Carroll. War profiteers, a couple of high-level infiltrators. Traitors."

"Why was he chosen to be a military assassin?"

"Oh, I think I have the answer for that one. He was chosen because he didn't like to kill. Because he *wasn't* a psycho. I think Hudson's philosophy was that once you undertook to fight in a just war, you *fought*. You balls-out fought with everything you had. I happen to believe that philosophy myself."

During the next thirty minutes, General Lucas Thompson elaborated on his association with David Hudson. It was an overall laudatory review, an A-plus for Hudson—high marks for conduct, combat team leadership, especially high marks for courage and charisma, that latter a nebulous quality the modern Army seemed to take into account the way a Civil War battalion, say, would have given a man a commendation for his musket aim.

Arch Carroll kept getting the very uncomfortable feeling that he was chasing after a goddamned American war hero. Once again, it didn't make complete sense.

Carroll leaned way forward in the red leather easy chair he'd taken in the retired officer's library. General Thompson was beginning to repeat himself slightly. He seemed to be slipping into a genial story-telling mode.

It might have been sad, ordinarily. In a way, it reminded Carroll of his own father, retiring from the New York police force to Sarasota. Dead of heart failure, or maybe it was boredom, within nine months.

Except that Carroll didn't believe General Lucas Thompson's act for a minute right now . . .

Carroll had checked carefully—and General Thompson *had* been receiving official visitors out in McLean; high-ranking VIPs from the Pentagon, even regular visitors from the White House. General Lucas Thompson was *still* an influential adviser to the National Security Council.

"There are a couple of things that still bother me, General."

"Shoot away, then."

"Just for openers . . . why can't anyone tell me where Colonel Hudson is now? . . . *Second* point. Why can't anyone explain the mysterious circumstances under which he left the Army in the mid-70s? *Third* point, General Thompson, why did somebody rifle through his war records at the Pentagon and the FBI before I could see them?"

"Mr. Carroll, judging from the *tone* of your voice, I think maybe you're getting a little out of order," General Thompson said in a voice that remained low, perfectly in control.

"Yeah, well, I do that sometimes. *Fourth* point. The last thing that bothers me. Really frosts me . . . *Why was I followed from the Pentagon last night, General? . . .* Why was I followed out here to McLean, General? On *whose* orders? What *the hell* is going on here in Washington?"

General Lucas Thompson's shiny, clean-shaven cheeks, his crinkle-cut neck blossomed bright red. "Mr. Carroll, I think you'd better leave. I believe that would be the best for all concerned."

"You know, I think you're probably right. I think I'd be wasting my time here. . . . General, I think *you* know a whole lot more about Colonel Hudson, though. That's what I think."

General Thompson smiled, just a faint condescending twist of his upper lip. "That's the unappreciated beauty of our country, Mr. Carroll. It's free. You can think whatever you like. . . . I'll show you to the door."

Chapter 75

ON THE MORNING OF December 17 in New York, David Hudson was feeling more self-conscious about his affliction than he had in years.

Clutching Billie Bogan with his good arm, he steered her in a protective manner through an onrushing tide of people on Fifth Avenue. He didn't want to think about the resumption of Green Band—not for a few more hours anyway.

David Hudson's self-consciousness was particularly unnecessary that morning. The two of them, paired together, were striking. They looked as if they'd been painted with thick, bold strokes—while everyone else had been lightly drawn by pencil or pen.

Billie Bogan watched David from the corner of her eye; so very serious charting their appointed path through the crowd. She felt an odd but growing fascination. That he was obviously taken with her made the attraction she felt much more irresistible. She allowed herself to be pulled forward . . .

Toward whatever was looming up ahead.

Where *were* they headed anyway?

"Are you a Christmas lover?" Billie asked, as they moved ahead through the cold flat knife of the winter day around them.

"Oh, it depends on the Christmas. This Christmas, I have a strange passion for the season . . . I want to drink in the sights: the evergreen trees and the holiday wreaths, the glimmering store windows, Santa Clauses, churches, choral music."

"You do seem to go all the way on things," she lightly teased Hudson.

"Or not at all. Just look at *this* insanity! This wonderful monstrosity!" He suddenly whooped and grinned broadly. It was quite unlike his usual self, at least the part she'd seen.

They'd finally come up close to the glittering, extravagantly overdecorated Rockefeller Center tree. A crowd, lovers mostly, from college aged to quite elderly, was clustered over the top of the skating rink and attached restaurant. A small boys' choir, innocent in cassock and surplice, sang the loveliest carols down below.

Colonel Hudson's brain had finally slowed; he was relaxed and relatively comfortable right now. An exceedingly rare treat. To be savored.

He occasionally felt a stab of guilt about his mission, about losing concentration, but he knew the release of tension could be valuable, too.

"Do you miss your family, your home? Being away from England during the holidays?" he asked.

He and Billie caught one another's eyes, and held on for a long few seconds. As it had been with the two of them from the start, they seemed almost alone now. In spite of the shoving masses crowding the square.

"I miss certain incidents from the past. . . . Some charming things about my sister, my mother. I don't miss home too much, no. Life in the Midlands. Birmingham is one of those places from which all the young people, all the reasonably bright ones, want to get away . . .

"If you remain in Birmingham, you work for British Steel, or perhaps the new exhibition center. Once you marry, you stay home with your brood. Watch the new morning BBC. You get fat, your thinking petrifies. After a few years, no one can imagine that any of the women were ever pretty slips of young girls. Almost no one over forty looks like they were *ever young*."

"So you escaped? London? Paris?"

"I went to London when I turned eighteen. I was crude, unpolished, in the way that I looked, the way I thought about the world. I wanted to be an actress, a fashion model, anything that would keep me from ever going back to Birmingham. *Ever.*"

Billie smiled, and she was so charmingly self-effacing. "I made a few minor misjudgments in London," she said with a mocking laugh.

"And then?"

"After, I guess it was five years there, I decided to either come to New York, or Paris. That's me up to the present. I'm hopeful I can do well as a model. I'm putting together a book for press advertising—that's magazines and newspapers. I know that I'm attractive—physically attractive, at least."

She had delivered most of the autobiographical speech very shyly, with her eyes downcast, glancing anywhere but into David Hudson's eyes. Color had crept up from her neck, finally covering her entire face.

"I've made a few tiny misjudgments myself. Just a few." Hudson laughed then. So many stored-up emotions were being released inside him now. It had been so long since he'd allowed himself this.

Billie began to laugh again. "Oh, to hell with the past," she said, her eyes a little sad however, ironic, slightly pinched at the corners. They both ran out of words at exactly the same time. The moment seemed especially poignant for some reason, confused, with far too many emotional crosscurrents.

Billie finally turned to face Hudson again. She spoke very softly, feathers of her warm breath lightly touching his ear.

"Please kiss me, David. That might not sound like anything so very dramatic. . . . Except that I don't think I've said it to anyone, and meant it, since I was about sixteen or seventeen years old."

Hudson and Billie Bogan, her slender body loose and pliant, his strong, almost at military attention, kissed in the shadows of the grand Christmas tree at Rockefeller Center.

Holiday music sweetly played around them: "Adeste Fidelis," "Silent Night," "Joy to the World."

For that moment, at least, Hudson conveniently forgot his *other* plans for the world.

Not *joy*, exactly. No, something else that was badly needed, though.

Justice for mankind.

Revenge for a special few.

Chapter 76

CAITLIN DILLON HURRIEDLY entered the crowded conference room inside No. 13 Wall.

She passed repairmen plastering over cracks in cement. Three cleaning women hauled buckets at the end of the hallway, clanking as they moved. Caitlin paused at the buzzing entrance to the conference room and raised one hand to her hair.

She was thinking how much she missed Carroll, who was expected back from Washington at any moment. He'd called, but his voice had been strained, almost as if he'd been afraid to tell her anything.

She stepped into the meeting room, passing through a phalanx of policemen and Army personnel.

The word had already spread up and down the hallways—*there had been some sort of break in the Green Band investigation. Finally, a break.*

Walter Trentkamp of the FBI stood in silence before the restless audience. He was obviously tense. Streaks of light sweat highlighted his face and the collar of his shirt was damp.

Trentkamp cleared his throat. The scene reminded

Caitlin of high-level press conferences held in Washington, emergency meetings called on short notice.

"You have no doubt heard the rumor that a significant development has occurred in the Green Band case. . . . It was uncovered through the tireless effort of Captain Francis Nicolo and Sergeant Rizzo in NYPD Ballistics."

Nicolo, Waxy Frank, appeared in the crowd alongside Joe Rizzo. Both men were beaming, taking an imperceptible bow.

"These men have been working tirelessly since the bombings on December fourth. Their labors have paid a big dividend."

There were a couple of appreciative mumbles in the room and a half-hearted attempt at applause. Nicolo and Rizzo shuffled their feet like schoolboys at an honors presentation.

"Sergeant?" Trentkamp said. "Come up here please."

Rizzo awkwardly stepped forward, hoisting a Styrofoam chart up on a metal stand. On the chart a police artist had sketched the major buildings of the financial district in black and white. The structures which had been bombed were colored traffic-signal red. Each of the bombed-out buildings also had a bold violet ring drawn around it. Caitlin noticed that the purple rings were at widely different levels on the fourteen buildings.

Rizzo began, "The buildings marked with red were all hit around six-thirty on December fourth. The bombs were definitely detonated by remote signals. The signal might have been operated from as far away as eight to ten miles."

Rizzo paused, blew his nose unselfconsciously in a big white handkerchief, then went on: "The violet rings on the buildings were drawn to indicate where the explosions actually took place. The plastique packages were actually placed. *Here, here, here,* et cetera.

"As you can see, the plastique was planted on *different* floors in all fourteen buildings. The second floor at Twenty-two Broad. Fifteenth floor at Manufacturers Hanover. And so on. You can see that plainly."

Rizzo looked around at the faces in the room as if he were challenging someone to disagree.

"There's no special pattern to this. At least, that's what we've thought up to now. Last night though, we found a connection we'd missed . . .

"Look here! Each of the circled floors actually contains one of that building's messenger drop-off and pickup rooms. Either a drop-off *or* a package mail station. What threw us off this approach was the fact that messenger drop-off stations and the mail room in these buildings isn't always the same. Not even on the same floor. Some of the Wall Street buildings have drop-off stations on *every* floor. You all see what I'm driving at?"

Sergeant Rizzo paused for effect.

Rizzo said, "Gentlemen, the bombs were all hand-delivered. Probably by a *regular commercial messenger,* who would go unnoticed."

Rizzo once again looked around the quiet room. "There are more than two hundred messenger services in and around Wall Street. Jimmy Split. Speedo. Fireball, Bullet, to name a few. You've seen most of them yourselves. Chances are at least one of them was contacted by our friends Green Band. Perhaps several were used to deliver the plastique on December fourth!"

Rizzo paused again. "What this means is that some goofball messenger is going to help break this thing open!

Tonight we hit the streets and run this thing down to earth!"

Caitlin felt the tremendous energy that coursed through the meeting room as the men began to disperse. They had come alive, after days of pounding on unyielding walls, days of pursuing an investigation that had been going absolutely nowhere. She was almost swept aside as policemen and detectives crushed toward the door.

A Wall Street messenger service.

A shiver suddenly traveled through her.

Messenger service? . . .

Caitlin turned and left the meeting room; she started back in the direction of her own office. She had just remembered something, except she wasn't sure now if her memory was playing tricks on her.

Caitlin started to run down the corridor inside No. 13.

Chapter 77

CARROLL WAS CERTAIN he had been followed back from Washington. A dark car had tracked his Checker taxi-cab from Kennedy Airport all the way into the Financial District.

When he stepped out of the taxi at No. 13 Wall, the tracking car went skirting past.

He couldn't see faces inside, only shapes, two or three men huddled together. *Why were they following him? Who had sent them? Who was tracking the tracker?*

He disappeared inside No. 13 and went straight to Caitlin's office on the second floor. He hurried because he was filled with the strongest need to see her, to talk to somebody he could trust.

She rose from behind her desk, where she'd been studying a printout of the names of U.S. veterans the computer had supplied before. She stepped out to hug him, and Carroll didn't seem to want to let her go. They pressed tightly into one another's bodies.

Caitlin finally disentangled herself. "How was Washington?"

He told her about the FBI's file on David Hudson, about his visit with General Lucas Thompson.

Caitlin brought him up to the moment on developments explained by Sergeant Rizzo. She indicated the computer printout she'd been studying when he had arrived.

"Maybe this is coincidence. Maybe it doesn't mean a thing. But on this FBI list of veterans there's an explosives expert whose occupation is cabdriver and *messenger.* The home address is New York City."

"Which name?" Carroll asked. He was already scanning the lengthy list.

"A man called Michael Doud . . . who just happened to serve under Colonel David Hudson in Viet Nam."

"Does it say which messenger service?" Carroll looked up from the printout.

Caitlin shook her head. "It shouldn't be too difficult to find out. Let's see."

Carroll waited while Caitlin made a quick couple of telephone calls. He slid his investigation notebook out of his coat and impatiently flipped through those familiar pages that had chronicled Green Band's false starts and stops from the beginning.

There were several different organizational headings now: *Interviews. Physical Evidence. Suspects. Miscellaneous.*

David Hudson . . . the mastermind of all this chaos?

West Point. 1966. Special Forces. Rangers.

Golden Boy?

Fort Bragg. JFK Training School. Severe stress testing. Experimentation with drugs. Preparing Hudson for what?

Special terrorist training. By whose orders? Where did that chain of command end?

Carroll finally shut the notebook in frustration.

What do I know, that I don't know I know? Carroll's thoughts went back to Green Band.

What could I know? What have I seen that's crucial? Washington, D.C.? General Lucas Thompson?

He watched Caitlin put the telephone receiver down.

"Vets Cabs and Messengers," she said with a sudden grin. "They have a garage near here in the Village."

Carroll stood up. "Call Philip Berger. Then could you call Trentkamp? Tell them to get their men organized, to meet me at . . ."

Caitlin interrupted, "There's more, Arch."

She paused for just a beat.

"David Hudson works there, too. He's been there for over a year."

Chapter 78

JUST PAST MIDNIGHT on December 18, Colonel Hudson emotionally addressed the assembly of twenty-four Vets gathered inside the Jane Street garage.

"This has been a long and particularly hard mission for you," he said. "I know that. But at each important stage you've done everything that has been asked of you. . . . I feel humble standing here before you."

Hudson paused and looked over the upturned faces that watched him motionlessly. "As we approach the final stages of Green Band, I want to stress one thing. I don't want anyone to take needless risks. Is that understood? Take no chances. Our ultimate goal from here on is zero KIA."

Again, Hudson paused. When he finally spoke, there was an uncharacteristic edge of emotion in his voice.

"This will be our last mission together. Thank you once again. I salute you all."

From that moment, Green Band was designed to be a thoroughly disciplined, Army-style *field maneuver*. Every detail had been scrutinized.

The grease-stained garage doors at VETS CABS AND MESSENGERS rolled open with a heavy metallic roar. Diffuse amber headlights suddenly pierced the darkness.

Vets 5, Harold Freedman, ran outside the Vets building. He looked east and west on Jane Street, then Freedman began to bark orders like the Army drill sergeant he'd once been.

It was just past 12:30 A.M.

If anyone in the West Village neighborhood saw the three Army transport trucks emerge from the garage, they paid little attention, in the tried and true tradition of New Yorkers.

The trucks finally hurtled up Tenth Avenue.

Hudson crouched forward in the passenger seat of the lead troop truck. He was in constant walkie-talkie contact with the two other troop transports. . . . This was a disciplined Army field maneuver in every respect.

They were moving into full combat again. None of them had realized how much they missed it. Even Hudson had forgotten the clarity that came before a major battle. There was nothing like this anywhere in life; nothing to compare.

"Contact. This is Vets One. You are to follow us straight down Tenth Avenue to the Holland Tunnel entrance. We'll be maintaining *strict* military speed limits inside the city. So sit back. Just relax for the ride. Over."

Two hours passed before the lead transport truck pulled to a shuddering stop at a military guardpost less than sixty yards off Route 34 in New Jersey.

Over the wooden sentry box the sign said FORT MONMOUTH, UNITED STATES ARMY POST.

The Army private on duty had been close to falling asleep. His eyes were glazed behind horn-rimmed glasses and his movements wooden as he approached the lead transport truck.

"Identification, sir." The private cleared his throat. He didn't look much more than eighteen years old to Hudson. Shades of Viet Nam, of wars fought by boys.

Hudson silently handed across two plastic ID cards. The cards identified him as Colonel Roger McAfee of the 68th Street Armory, Manhattan. The inspection that followed was pro forma. The regular duty guard speech was given by the sentry.

"You may proceed, sir. Please obey all posted parking and traffic regulations while you are a visitor at Fort Monmouth. Are those transport vehicles behind with you, sir?"

"Yes, we're going on bivouac. We're here to pick up supplies. Small arms and ammunition for our weekend in the country. Two helicopters have been requisitioned. They'll have the details inside. I'm to see Captain Harney."

"You can all proceed then, sir."

The Army base sentry finally stepped aside. He crisply waved the small Army Reserve convoy onward.

"Contact. This is Vets One." As soon as they passed the gate, Colonel Hudson spoke into the PRC transmitter. "We're now less than twelve hours until the termination of the operation code-named Green Band. Everyone is to use extreme, *repeat*, extreme caution. We're almost home, gentlemen."

Chapter 79

INCONSPICUOUS AND DRAB, the Vets garage on Jane Street wasn't the kind of place to draw attention. It sat in the middle of a West Village block, its large metal doors rusted and grease stained and bleak.

At both ends of the block, the desolate street had silently been cordoned off. NYPD patrol cars were positioned everywhere around the garage. Carroll counted seventeen of them.

Beneath the darkened edifice of a Shell gas station, he could see unmarked FBI cars and as many as thirty heavily armed agents.

The police and the FBI agents carried M-16 automatic assault rifles, 12-gauge riot shotguns, .357 Magnums. It was as frightening an attack force and arsenal as Carroll had ever seen.

Carroll leaned against his own car, studying the metal doors, the crooked, bleached sign that read VETS CABS AND MESSENGERS. He tapped his fingers on the car hood.

Something was wrong here. Something was wrong again.

Carroll peered hard in the direction of the Shell station.

The FBI guys stood perfectly still, waiting for the signal that would bring them rushing into action.

At his side was Walter Trentkamp. Carroll had kept Walter informed. Now Trentkamp was inside the maze with him.

Carroll took out his Browning. He turned the weapon over in the palm of his hand and thought it was strange how some voice inside was telling him to be careful. *Careful*, he thought. He hadn't been careful before—so why start now? Carroll thought he *knew* why.

"Archer." Walter nudged him. A limousine was suddenly threading its way down the grim, quiet street.

Police Commissioner Michael Kane solemnly climbed out. The Commissioner, whose street experience was limited, and who was more politician than cop, had a bullhorn in one hand.

"Oh Christ, no . . ." Carroll muttered.

Commissioner Kane's voice echoed down the West Village street. "Attention . . . this is Commissioner of Police Kane. . . . You have one minute to emerge from the Vets garage. You have sixty seconds before we open fire."

Carroll's eyes roamed over the red brick garage. His body was tense, his neck and forehead damp. He slowly raised his pistol to the firing position.

The Vets garage remained quiet.

Something definitely wasn't right about this.

"Twenty-five seconds . . . come out of the garage . . ."

Walter Trentkamp leaned close and forced a whisper. One of the things Carroll appreciated was that Walter was still basically a street cop. He still needed to be in on the action himself. "Suppose this is all bullshit? Suppose we've got the wrong men, the wrong messenger service? Something's not right here, Arch."

Carroll still said nothing. He was watching, and thinking.

"Twenty seconds . . ."

"C'mon Walter . . . come with me."

Carroll suddenly stepped forward. Walter Trentkamp somewhat reluctantly followed him toward the garage doors. The Police Commissioner had stopped counting down.

Then FBI agents and city cops were everywhere, pushing through the jagged edges of the broken doors and into the darkened building itself.

Somebody turned on a light revealing a somewhat ordinary, gloomy and cavernous garage.

Carroll, Browning in hand, froze.

His eyes blinked several times. He could smell oil and grease, all the harsh odors left behind by sick and aging automobiles. Slick puddles of oil covered the concrete floor. There were professional mechanics' tools lying around in disarray.

But nothing else was left in the Vets garage.

There were no vehicles on the basement floor.

There were no people, no Viet Nam veterans. Colonel David Hudson was nowhere to be seen.

Nothing was left of whatever had been here before.

Carroll and Trentkamp wandered around the garage, their guns still clutched in their fists. They entered each small room in a careful police crouch. They finally climbed narrow, twisting stairs to the top floor.

And then they both saw it . . . the message left for them.

It was taped to the grease-stained wall and it mocked

them, mocked them all. It laughed at all the helpless police investigators—a shrill funhouse cackle, the screeching caw of jungle birds.

A green ribbon had been tied in a perfect bow, and it hung on a barren wall like something left over from a Christmas package.

Yeah, Arch Carroll thought.

Have a merry one.

Green Band had disappeared from the garage on Jane Street—as always, one frustrating jump ahead.

One cold, calculating jump . . . *moving toward what?*

Chapter 80

CAITLIN CARRIED A leather portfolio overflowing with her notes as she walked down the darkened hallway of an Upper West Side apartment building. The door to 12B was halfway open.

Anton Birnbaum was there waiting. Caitlin wondered why he had called her so late at night? What did Anton want from her now?

He let her in and they walked together to his library, a room crammed to its high ceiling with old books and periodicals.

"Thank you for coming right away," he said. He seemed incredibly relieved to see Caitlin.

"Coffee? Tea? I've been living on the unhealthy stuff lately." He gestured to a tarnished espresso pot near the glowing fireplace.

Caitlin declined.

His hands were trembling slightly. This whole room, in its papery disarray, indicated that Anton Birnbaum had been burning the midnight oil with a fevered vengeance.

"Let me begin all the way back in Dallas, Caitlin." Birnbaum, his small face looking like a burned-out moon, finally sat down alongside her. "The tragic assassination of

President John Kennedy . . . it's a good place to start, I think. In terms of the fantastic versus the expected reality. The assassination was probably orchestrated, as we all know.

"Next comes Watergate, 1973. I think, I firmly believe that Watergate was *permitted* to escalate. Its flames were fanned . . . in order to remove Richard M. Nixon from office. That, my dear, is history. American history." Birnbaum's cup gently rattled in the saucer. "Both these events were clearly *orchestrated*. Both events were devised by a cabal working both inside and outside the United States government. This elitist group is a remnant, Caitlin, a cell of the old OSS, our own World War Two intelligence network.

"I have heard them called the Wise Men. I've also heard them called the Committee of Twelve. They *exist*. Permit me to continue before you comment.

"In 1945, the men who ran the OSS realized that the cloak of responsibility they had assumed in wartime was coming to an end. They were faced with giving their enormous power back to the same politicians who had almost managed to obliterate the human race a few years before. . . . They had no desire to do so, Caitlin. In many ways, one can almost justify their actions."

Birnbaum sipped his coffee. "A high-ranking clique of these OSS men surrendered only *some* of their wartime powers to President Truman. They remained behind the scenes in Washington. They began to maneuver a series of political puppets. These men, and their protégés, the *current* Committee of Twelve, have gone so far as to select the presidential candidates for political parties. For *both* parties, Caitlin, in the *same* election."

Caitlin stared at the old man. The Wise Men? The Committee of Twelve? A secret cabal with unlimited powers? She already knew a great deal about real and imagined government conspiracies. They had always seemed woven into the tapestry of American history. Unconfirmable rumors; uncomfortable realities. Uncomfortable whispers in high places.

"Who are these men, Anton?"

"My dear, they are not exactly faces familiar from *Newsweek* or *Time* magazine. But that's beside the point right now. What I am trying to tell you is that I have *no doubt* this group is involved in the Green Band incident. Somehow, Caitlin, they encouraged or caused the December fourth attack on Wall Street. They're behind *whatever* is happening right now."

Caitlin didn't have the words to respond to what Birnbaum was saying. With any other person, she might have dismissed this whole thing; with Birnbaum she knew he wouldn't have told her any of this if he wasn't certain himself.

The Financier stared at Caitlin and there was an unusually weary glaze over his eyes.

"This veterans' group—" Birnbaum started again.

"You've heard of them already?" Caitlin was surprised. An alarm sounded inside her brain.

Birnbaum smiled. A slender fissure opened across his small face. "My dear, information has always been the wellspring of my success. Of course I have heard of the veterans group. I have my sources inside Number 13.

"But what I don't know is whether the Committee of Twelve manipulated these misfits, or whether the veterans are paid operatives. . . . I do believe I know why the dangerous mission was undertaken. . . . I think it can be traced to a Soviet-run provocateur called François Monserrat. A mass-murderer. A killing machine that has to be destroyed."

"But what is Monserrat's connection with the Committee of Twelve, Anton? What's going to happen now? Can you tell me that?"

Anton Birnbaum smiled, but the smile was tight. "I believe that I can, my dear."

Chapter 81

EARLY ON SUNDAY MORNING David Hudson patrolled the dimly lit corridors of the sprawling Queens VA Hospital. *The home of the brave,* he thought bitterly.

The Queens VA was situated at Linden Boulevard and 179th Street. It was a dismal, red brick complex that called no attention to itself. Eleven years before, Hudson had been an outpatient there, one of tens of thousands who had been subjected to VA hospitals after the War.

A hollowness, like that at the heart of an empty gymnasium, caused his footsteps to echo as he plunged deeper into the hospital complex.

There were buzzing voices, but no people he could see. Ghosts, he thought. Straining voices from another dimension of reality. Voices of cruel pain and madness.

He turned a corner—and suddenly he encountered a gruesome row of veterans. They were wraiths mostly, but a few were overweight. The odor in the still, dead air was overpowering: part industrial disinfectant, part urine, part feces. A synthetic Christmas tree blinked spastically at the heart of the claustrophobic room.

At least half of the patients seemed to have tiny metal

radios pressed like cold packs to their heads. A black hussar in a torn, pinstriped johnny was discoing around an amputee fitfully sleeping in his wheelchair. Hudson saw broken, gnarled bodies harnessed into steel and leather braces. *"Metals of honor"* the hospital aides used to say when Hudson had been there.

He felt such rage now, such hatred for everything American, everything he'd once loved about his country.

There were still no hospital personnel in sight. There wasn't a single corpsman, not a nurse or nurse's aide in any of the halls.

David Hudson kept walking—faster—almost hearing a soft military drum roll in his head.

He went down a bright *yellow* hallway, a falsely cheery one.

He remembered all of the surroundings with clarity now. Almost uncontrollable rage swept through his body.

In the fall of 1973, he'd been admitted into the VA, ostensibly for psychiatric evaluation and tests. A smug doctor had talked to him twice about his affliction, his unfortunate loss of an arm. The Army doctor was equally interested in Hudson's POW experience. Had he killed a Viet Cong camp commandant while making his escape? Yes, Hudson assured him, in fact the escape was what had first brought him to the attention of Army Intelligence. They had tested him in Viet Nam; then they sent him back to Fort Bragg for further training. . . . The interviews lasted no more than fifty minutes each time. Hudson had then filled out endless Veterans Administration questionnaires and numbered forms. He was assigned a VA caseworker, an obese man with a birthmark on his cheek, whom he never saw again after their first half-hour interview.

At the end of the yellow hallway were glass double doors to the outside. Through the hospital doors, Hudson could see fenced-in back lawns.

The fences were not intended to keep the veterans in, he knew. They'd been built to keep the people outside from seeing what was inside: *the terrifying, awful disgrace of America's veterans.*

David Hudson hit the glass door squarely with his right shoulder. He was instantly plunged outside into sharp winter cold, into the dark clinging dampness.

Directly behind the main hospital building was a steep frost-covered lawn which ended in threadbare scrub pines. Hudson moved across it quickly. Concentrate, he instructed himself. Don't think about anything but the present. Nothing but what's happening right now.

Two men stepped suddenly from behind a row of thickly snow-laden firs.

Chapter 82

ONE MAN HAD the formal appearance of a United Nations diplomat. The other was a common looking street thug with a tough, expressionless face.

"You might have chosen the Oak Bar at the Plaza just as easily. Certainly that would have been more convenient," the impressive-looking man spoke first. "Colonel Hudson, I presume? . . . I am Monserrat."

The distinguished man's English was accented. He might have been French? . . . Swiss? . . . *Monserrat.*

Hudson smiled without any real mirth. He showed slightly parted teeth. Every one of his senses was coming alive now.

"The next time we meet, it can be your turn to choose locations. Under the clock in the Biltmore Hotel? The observation deck of the Empire State Building? Whatever site pleases you," he offered.

"I'll remember that. You have a proposition for me to consider, Colonel? The remainder of the securities from Green Band? *A substantial amount,* I take it."

Hudson's eyes remained hooded, showing almost no emotion, not a hint of the seething rage inside.

"Yes, I would say substantial. *Over four billion dollars.* That's enough to cause an unprecedented international incident. Whatever you wish."

"And what do you want from us, dare I ask? What is your reward out of this, Colonel?"

"Less than you might think. The deposit of one hundred fifty million in a secure, numbered account. Your assurance that the GRU won't pursue my men afterward. The end of Green Band, as far as you're concerned."

"That's all? I can't accept that."

"No, I suppose it isn't all. I have something else in mind. . . . You see, I want you to destroy the pathetic American way of life. I want you to end the American century a little early. We both hate the American system—at least what it's become. We both want to set it on fire, to purify the world. We've been trained to accomplish that."

The terrorist stared into Colonel Hudson's eyes. Hudson's apocalyptic words hung in the chilled air. Finally, Monserrat smiled. He understood Hudson perfectly now.

"You're planning to complete this transaction soon I take it? The exchange?"

Hudson looked at his wristwatch as if to check the time. He knew precisely what time it was. He was only going through the motions. "It's ten-thirty now. In six hours, gentlemen."

Monserrat hesitated, an uncharacteristic flicker of indecision and doubt, but only a second's pause.

"Six hours is acceptable. We will be ready by then. Is that all?"

Hudson seemed to have a sudden insight as he stood huddled with the two men. His head cocked slowly, at an odd angle. A smile finally appeared, full of charm, his old West Point charisma.

"There is another matter. One more serious problem we have to discuss."

"And what might that be, Colonel Hudson?"

"I realize that no one is supposed to know who you are. That's the primary reason I wanted you here. Why I insisted on it, if you were to get the bulk of these bonds. You see me, and I see you. . . . Except for one thing . . ."

"Except what?"

"Next time, I want to see the *real* François Monserrat. If he doesn't come in person, there will be no exchange."

Having said that, David Hudson turned away. Hudson walked briskly back toward the VA hospital and disappeared inside.

His revenge, his fifteen-year odyssey was almost complete now. The final, telling moment was coming.

Deceit! As it had never been seen before. Not since the War, anyway . . .

They had taught him so very, very well to destroy. . . . Whatever he wished to destroy . . .

Chapter 83

IN A FASHIONABLE and expensive part of New York City, Vice-president Elliot was alone and troubled that morning. He walked at a quickening pace along the edge of the East River, directly behind the United Nations complex.

There was the customary parade of bundled-up joggers plodding along the concrete promenade. A spinsterish woman looked like she might be contemplating suicide. A slender young model walked her dog.

There were no bodyguards for the Vice-president of the United States, no crew-cut Secret Service men were anywhere in sight. There was nothing and nobody to protect Thomas Elliot from recognition and possibly from harm.

The walk alone was something the Vice-president did infrequently, but it was something he needed to do now. It was a fundamental human need: simply to be alone. Thomas Elliot needed to be able to think, to be able to see a complex and challenging plan in its entirety.

The Vice-president finally let his mind settle on the real reason why he desperately needed to be off by himself . . .

He paused and stared into the sluggish wintry gray river.
Smoke drifted lazily upward on the other bank. He thought
about his childhood then, as if those comforting recollec-
tions might put everything in perspective. The casual rise
of smoke reminded him of those autumnal bonfires on the
grounds of his family home in Connecticut—how could
that boy, whose face he saw in memory, have come all this
way? All the way to this seminal moment in American history?

Vice-president Elliot placed his gloved hands in the
pockets of his overcoat. Green Band was almost at an end.
Out there, someplace in this vast city, the terrorist François
Monserrat, the New York police, Colonel David Hudson
and his men were rushing toward their rendezvous with
destiny. Meanwhile, other powerful forces were slotting
quietly into place.

He frowned. A barge crawled over the oily surface
of the river. Dirty washing hung on a rope and smoke
rose upward from a blunt funnel. The Vice-president
thought he saw a shapeless figure move aboard the
barge.

Colonel David Hudson had his moment of destiny to
come . . .

As did he, the Vice-president of this country.

In a very short time, when the dust had cleared on the
brief reign of Justin Kearney—a disillusioned man who
hadn't been able to come to terms with the limitations of
his power, a man who would resign his office in the wake
of an economic crisis, who would be exiled to some rustic
estate and live out the remainder of his days writing heavily censored memoirs—when all the dust had cleared,

Thomas More Elliot, like Lyndon Baines Johnson twenty-odd years before, like Gerald Ford a little more than a decade ago, would step up to the presidency of the United States.

Everything depended on the final act of Green Band.

Thomas Alive killed, like Lyndon Baines Johnson to carry
out what better. The Gerald Ford a little more than a
decade ago, would step up to the presidency of the United
States.

Everything depended on the final act of Green Band.

Chapter 84

THE VETS CABS appeared suddenly. They paraded single file out of an abandoned warehouse garage in downtown Manhattan.

The cabs were assimilated into normal traffic flow until they branched onto Division and Catherine streets leading toward the East River and FDR Drive.

Each of the Checker cabs had been equipped with PRC-77 transmitter-receivers, known in Viet Nam as *monsters*. The PRC units automatically scrambled and unscrambled all transmissions. There was no way the New York police could intercept messages traveling between the cabs.

There were six cabs, which could carry fourteen heavily armed Vets: an assault platoon with rifleman-snipers, M-60 gas-operated machine gunners, a thumper man with an M-79 grenade launcher, a communications operator.

The most spectacular touch in the commando raid was that the ground attack force had air support. Two Cobra Assault copters would be backing the Vets if any combat action started on the street.

David Hudson, who scouted and studied the street from the lead cab, was beginning to feel an unexpected sense of release. It was almost over. Finally, dignity. Finally, revenge.

He experienced some of his old combat sensations from Viet Nam, only this time with a difference.

A big, important difference.

This time, they were going to be allowed to win.

A New York police detective, Ernie "Cowboy" Tubbs, who had been dragged unceremoniously out of bed to join the manhunt, saw one of the cabs go past on Division Street.

Then he saw two more Vets cabs.

He turned to his partner, Detective Maury Klein, a short man in a black tent of a raincoat. Tubbs said, "Christ, that's them. That's Green Band. Bingo, Maury."

Detective Klein, who was addicted to Rolaids *and* Pepto-Bismol, peered sorrowfully through the windshield. His stomach was already killing him.

"Jee-sus Christ, Ernie! Half those bastards are supposed to be Special Forces."

Ernie "Cowboy" Tubbs shrugged and swung their late model Dodge out behind the line of yellow cabs. Only a single car separated them from the rearguard Vets cab.

"*We've spotted Green Band!*" Tubbs rasped into the hand-mike on his dashboard.

Maury Klein uneasily cradled an American-180 submachine gun in both arms. The assault gun looked out of place inside the Dodge, middle-class family car. The American-180 fired thirty rounds per second. It was never used in city fighting for that reason.

"This sucks, man. *Sucks!* Bar on 125th Street, I tangled with *one* Green Beret Special Forces dude. That was enough for me, *forever.*" Maury Klein continued to complain. The notion of mixing it up with ex-Special Forces veterans seemed like one of the worst ideas he'd ever had in his police-force life. Maury Klein was a vet, too, class of '53, Korea.

At Henry Street there were only a few working traffic lights. There was almost no other traffic. An eerie, dockside feeling pervaded the steamy gray area of lower Manhattan.

"Looks like they're going to the FDR Drive for sure. . . . Entrance is down here somewhere. Right around Houston."

"North or south?" Ernie Tubbs yelled to his partner and gave a quick glance.

"I think both ways. South for sure. We'll see it here any . . . *there!* That's it."

Just then, Tubbs spotted the dilapidated ramp to the south lanes of the drive himself.

The Vets cabs were approaching fast from both directions. The first cabs were already rattling up the crumbling stone and metal rampways.

Tubbs flicked on his hand mike again. "Contact! All units. They're getting on the FDR! They're heading due south! Over."

Suddenly the rear Vets cab veered sharply. It tried to cut Tubbs' car off.

"Son of a bitch!"

Tubbs swerved left with skillful, near-perfect timing. The unmarked police sedan continued to shoot up the half-blocked entranceway that didn't look wide enough anymore.

"Jesus Christ, Ernie! Watch the walls!"

The Vets cab meanwhile had finished its tailspin. It was

blocking off every police car except one, Tubbs's, which had somehow slipped by.

"Son of a bitch! Son of a bitch!" Detective Tubbs yelled as he fought the unmarked car's steering wheel for control.

"All units, all units! They set a roadblock on the FDR! Repeat. There's a roadblock on the FDR! Over."

Meanwhile, the single police sedan was screeching into teeming traffic filling all three narrow, twisting lanes of the FDR south. A truck slammed to a jolting stop behind. Horns blared from every possible direction.

The police car was hemmed in tight by two of the Vets cabs. The black barrels of M-16s were jammed out both windows of the cab to their left.

Ernie Tubbs couldn't breathe. He was bottled in at fifty-five miles an hour. One of the M-16s fired a round.

The warning shot flared over the police sedan roof like night tracers in a combat battle zone.

A Vet in military khakis and black greasepaint screamed over at Tubbs. His voice was muffled under the traffic whistle, but Tubbs could hear every word.

"Get off at the next stop! Get the fuck off this road! . . . Everybody but the driver hands up! *I said hands up!* Hands up!"

Closing on the next exit, Tubbs spun his wheel hard right toward the guardrail. The unmarked police sedan shot at a seventy-degree angle toward the off ramp.

It bumped hard over loose plates, sending off sparks. The patrol car went up on two wheels. It threatened to turn over. After a moment when gravity seemed an indecisive force, the car finally bounced back onto all four wheels. It shimmied down the off ramp, then stopped dead on the bordering city street.

"*We lost them! Over.*" Tubbs screamed into his radio transmitter. "We lost them on the FDR!"

Detective Maury Klein finally whispered out loud inside the police sedan, "Thank fucking God."

Chapter 85

AS SOON AS he heard the news that Green Band had been spotted, Carroll spun down several steep flights of stairs inside No. 13.

He took the rubber-edged steps two and three at a time. He was racing outside, hoping to find a police helicopter waiting.

Everything was happening at once on the street.

Crashing footsteps of other running men. Police squad car engines starting. Tires screeching up and down Wall Street and Broad and Water.

Carroll was carting an M-16 rifle, which felt weird bouncing against his body. *Flashback time*—he was an Army infantry soldier again. . . .

Except for one thing: this was downtown Manhattan and not Viet Nam.

His sports coat flew open as he ran, revealing the Browning holster as well as a bulletproof vest. His heart was pounding at a volume consistent with the street noise.

A radio squad car he passed relayed the latest information on Green Band's whereabouts.

"They're moving at about thirty-five miles per hour. Six

vehicles. They're all regular Checker cabs. All are heavily armed. They're proceeding *east*." *It's a set-up for something else*, Carroll thought.

What though? What were the Vets going to do now? What was Hudson's plan?

A silver and black Bell helicopter was waiting in a Kinney parking lot. A few weeks earlier, the parking lot would have been filled with the luxury cars of Wall Street workaholics. The police helicopter was whirring like an outsized moth. It was ready to fly.

"M-16 and a Bell chopper." Carroll winced as he swung his body inside the hot, cramped helicopter cockpit. "Christ, this brings back memories. Hi, I'm Carroll," he said to the police pilot seated inside.

"Luther Parrish," the pilot grunted. He was NYPD, a heavyset black man with a leather flak jacket and clear yellow goggle glasses. "You ex-Viet Nam? You look like it. Feel like it." Parrish snapped a thick wad of gum as he talked.

"Class of 1970." Carroll finally smiled. He played it a little combat cool, like you would boarding a copter in Nam. The truth was, he hated choppers. He hated *seeing* the goddamn things. Carroll didn't like the idea of being suspended in air with nothing to rely on but slender blades that furiously slashed the air.

"How 'bout that! Class of '70, too. Well, here we go again, sports fans. I take it you don't much like airplane rides?"

Before Carroll had a chance to answer in the extreme negative, the Bell copter jumped straight up from the parking lot cement. The ascent left Carroll's small intestine somewhere behind. The chopper pierced the smoky city morning, hugging the dusky walls of nearby buildings. The pilot cleverly avoided swift winds sweeping off the river.

Then the copter swung out wide toward the East River. A second helicopter, another Bell, joined in from due south.

"No, I'm not real crazy about helicopters. No offense, Luther."

Adrenaline flowed wildly, it raged like a flooding river through Carroll's body. Down below, he could see traffic streaming on the FDR highway.

The police pilot eventually spoke up over the rotors' noise. "Beautiful morning, man. You can see Long Island, Connecticut, almost see Paris, France."

"Beautiful morning to get shot in the fucking heart."

The black pilot snorted out a laugh. "You been to Viet Nam all right. Let's see, we've got two, three armed patrol helicopters on them right now. Pick up more help once we find out which borough they're goin' to. I think we'll be fine."

"I hope you're right, Luther."

"You see them down there? Little toy taxicabs. See? See right there?"

"Yeah, with little toy M-16s, toy rocket launchers," Carroll said to the pilot.

"You talk *just* like ex-infantry. Ironic-type shit. Makin' me all misty-eyed."

"*Still* infantry from the look of things. Except I'm afraid *we're* fighting the Green Berets today."

The pilot turned to Carroll with a knowing look. "They're *bad* dudes all right. *Definitely* Special Forces." He nodded as if to a secret beat. He almost seemed proud of the Vets' bravado. Their street fighting style had hit a chord.

A thousand feet below, the FDR Drive was a delicate ribbon of silver and shiny jet black. The Vets cabs looked intensely yellow, almost tawdry down there. As the lineup of cabs crossed the Brooklyn Bridge, both Bell helicopters swung high and wide to avoid being seen. The copters actually briefly disappeared into low-flying clouds.

Carroll's shirt was already soaked through. Everything seemed to be happening at a distance. The world was slightly fuzzed and unreal. *They were going to solve Green Band after all.*

On the Brooklyn side of the bridge, he could see that traffic was heavy but moving. The steady whoosh of cars, an occasional bleating horn, traveled all the way up to the helicopter cockpit.

"They're getting off at the Navy Yard exit! This is Carroll to control. The Vets convoy is exiting at the Navy Yard! They're proceeding northeast into Brooklyn!" Carroll screeched into the microphone.

Chapter 86

AT THAT SAME INSTANT, a deafening explosion jarred the underbelly of the police helicopter with a jolt that seemed to rattle right through Carroll's bones.

His head cracked hard against the metal roof and sharp bolts of pain stabbed behind his eyes.

Then a second jarring blast struck the reverberating cockpit.

Splinters of glass flew in all directions. Star fractures cobwebbed across the windshield. Everywhere, metal was ringing with gunshots. Glaring red flashes were angrily ribboning the sky.

"Ohhh, goddamn, I'm hit. I'm hit," the pilot moaned as he slumped forward.

Meanwhile a machine gun loudly chattered off to Carroll's left. Carroll caught a brief glimpse of floating, blinking red lamps *on the right* and the hulking shapes of two choppers he hadn't seen before.

Christ! Two Cobras were attacking them.

Suddenly the sky was filled with bright, jarring yellow orbs of light, with roaring fire and billowing black smoke.

The companion police helicopter had disintegrated before Carroll's disbelieving eyes.

Where the chopper had hovered just seconds before, there was nothing except for leaping gold and orange flames. Nothing was left except this eerie, fading afterimage in the sky.

Carroll could see that Luther Parrish had been hit badly. Puddles of blood were collecting from a wound somewhere on the left side of his head. The electric circuits in the helicopter cockpit seemed to be useless.

Heavy machine gun fire welled up from below. The pilot temporarily revived, moaning, grabbed both his legs. The helicopter had begun to fall, to somersault and plummet helplessly. Parrish didn't notice.

Carroll fired his M-16 at one of the attacking Cobras. The red light winked derisively—then the copter calmly disappeared from sight.

Carroll froze. He was pressed extremely hard into his helicopter seat. Blood was rushing, swirling through his head. The police helicopter had suddenly flipped completely upside down.

Then the helicopter was in a dead fall, sailing and spinning into the gauzy gray nothingness of the Brooklyn Navy Yard below.

A flat black rooftop with a water tower mounted on it suddenly loomed enormously, coming as fast as another airplane at the copter's windshield. The flailing helicopter skimmed over an expanse of shadowy factory buildings a block long, at least. It missed a smoking industrial chimney by inches. The copter's tail was clipped off by a high brick retaining wall.

A deserted grid of avenues and streets appeared through

the windshield as the helicopter cleared the last building. Cars were parked in long, uneven lines up both sides.

Carroll reflexively grabbed at the controls. He knew what everything was, from too many trips in Viet Nam, though not how to really use any of it. His body was trembling. Deep, jolting spasms flew up his spine.

He was beyond any compartment of fear he'd previously known. Beyond anything he'd felt in combat or police action. He was in a new realm of sensation—a clear, hard place where he seemed acutely conscious of everything going on around him.

This was the moment of impending death, he thought without real comprehension.

The helicopter's belly cleanly sheared the rooftops off a half dozen parked cars. Carroll covered his face. He shielded the wounded police pilot as best he could with his body.

The helicopter struck the street on a side angle. It skidded, bounded violently. The copter's belly issued a grinding shriek, and Carroll could feel his blood turn to ice.

Sparks, plumes of intense red flames, flew in every possible direction. Whole sides of parked automobiles, headlights and bumpers were effortlessly cut away. A red fire hydrant popped out of the cement like a bathtub plug.

The police helicopter, skidding on its side, finally slowed. It plowed to a tearing, screaming, crunching halt up against two crushed compact cars.

A man in a factory security uniform was running crazily, zigzagging down the deserted street toward the unbelievable accident.

"Hey, hey! That's my car! That's my *car!*"

Carroll was cradling the badly wounded pilot, "Grab

hold. You just hold me," he whispered, hoping the man wasn't already dead. "Just hold me, Luther."

Then he was limping away from the burning helicopter wreckage. He was half-dragging, half-carrying the hulking NYPD pilot in his arms.

His eyes nervously searched the skies for the attacking Vets' Cobras, but there was nothing there now.

Nothing at all.

The choppers might as well have been the vehicles of some unlikely nightmare. It was like being in the war again. It was exactly like combat duty.

Except that the helicopter crash had happened right here on the streets of Brooklyn.

Chapter 87

THE VETS CABS proceeded northeast, then almost due east across Brooklyn.

They were moving inexorably toward Monserrat. They were headed toward the appointed end of Green Band.

Erect and alert behind the wheel, David Hudson was experiencing a moment of anxiety. It had something to do with being this close to the end. They were less than seven minutes from the rendezvous point with Monserrat.

Hudson tried to concentrate as if he were entering a combat zone. Nothing could distract him from Green Band now.

Nothing could look mildly suspicious either . . .

Monserrat's soldiers could be watching the streets from neighborhood rooftops and darkened apartment windows. If they spotted the attack force, the final exchange of Wall Street securities wouldn't happen. Green Band would fail.

Like an advance scout, Hudson checked and rechecked the squat, cheerless brick buildings as he drove closer to the meeting place. Hudson noted everything. A knot of youths was easing out of Turner's Grill. Their voices carried—low, guttural sounds in syncopated street rhythms.

Hudson drove slowly on. He found a parking spot further down the slope-shouldered Bedford-Stuyvesant side street.

He parked and climbed out of the car. He continued to look around the quiet neighborhood chosen for the meeting. He finally popped open the cab's dented and scarred trunk. The Wall Street securities were there in ordinary looking, gray vinyl suitcases.

Hudson hoisted up the bags, and he began to trudge as rapidly as he could toward a red brick factory at the next street corner.

He was almost certain he was being watched. Monserrat was nearby. All his senses and instincts corroborated that single message.

This was the moment of reckoning, then. All of Hudson's Special Forces training to be matched against Monserrat's experience, his deceit.

Hudson shouldered open the wood front door of a building which housed shabby apartments and a small Italian-American shoe factory, *The Gino Company of Milano.*

He pushed into a dark hallway, where trapped cooking smells immediately assaulted him. The musty scent of old winter clothes hung in the air. The meeting place seemed appropriately isolated.

"Don't turn around, Colonel."

Three men appeared in the dim corridor with Magnums and Berettas drawn.

"Move up against the wall. That's good. Right there. That will be fine, Colonel Hudson."

The leader had a Spanish accent, more than likely Cuban. Monserrat ran the Caribbean, and most of the terrorist activities in South America. At the rate he was going, one day Monserrat was going to run the entire Third World.

"I'm not armed," Hudson said.

"Have to search you anyway."

One of the men positioned himself less than three feet away from Hudson. He pointed his gun at an imaginary spot between Hudson's eyes. It was a popular gunman's trick, one Hudson himself had been taught at Fort Bragg. *At close range, shoot out the eyes.*

The second man patted him down.

The third man searched the gray suitcases, slashing them with a knife, looking for false siding, a bottom that wasn't actually a bottom.

"Upstairs!" The terrorist who held the gun finally commanded Hudson. He spoke like a military officer.

They began to climb a steep and creaking flight of stairs, then another flight. Were they leading him to Monserrat? Finally, the enigmatic Monserrat himself? Or would there be more deception?

"This is your floor, Colonel. That door straight ahead. You can just walk inside. You're most definitely expected."

"Point of information? I have a question for you, for all of you. Curiosity on my part." David Hudson spoke without turning to face his escort group.

An impatient grunt came from behind . . .

The Lizard Man. Past interrogations. Special Army training. Hudson's mind continued to churn at a furious rate.

All to prepare him for this very moment?

"Do they ever tell you what's *really* happening? Has anyone bothered to tell you the *truth* about this operation?

Do you know what this meeting really is? Do you know why?"

David Hudson was introducing some element of doubt into their minds, petty doubts and confusion, paranoid unease he could use later, if he needed to.

Deception.

Always deception.

"Don't bother to knock, Colonel." The man in charge calmly spoke again. "Just go right in; you're expected. Everything you try to do is expected, Colonel."

A slice of dull, yellow light emanated from within as David Hudson peered inside the fourth-floor tenement room.

Hudson paused at the doorway's edge.

He was about to confront the mysterious and dangerous Monserrat. He was about to conclude Green Band's appointed business, to end his mission.

The Viet Cong's Lizard Man had taught Hudson an essential lesson in Viet Nam: *it was to play games in which your opponent wasn't given the rules.* This was the principle behind all successful guerrilla warfare.

Colonel David Hudson versus Monserrat.

Now it began.

Chapter 88

"ALL BLUE AND WHITE UNITS! We've picked them up again. . . . We've got our friends Green Band!"

NYPD cruiser radios echoed brassily above the noise of whining police and hospital emergency sirens at the helicopter crash site near the Brooklyn Navy Yard.

"They're moving into a residential neighborhood. Bedford-Stuyvesant. It's right in the heart of the fucking ghetto. They're traveling on Halsey Street in Bed-Stuy, now. Over."

Carroll sagged heavily against the open front door of one of the half-dozen police cruisers that had arrived after the helicopter accident. Crime-scene technicians were already swarming onto the fire-lit street.

He wasn't sure if he'd heard the radio report right? . . . *Green Band appeared; Green Band disappeared. Which was it?*

Carroll tried to clear the gauze from his head as he listened to the minute by minute updates squawking over nearby police cruiser radios.

He couldn't feel any recognizable emotion. His regular

system of response to stimuli had come to a halt. He was beyond pain as he'd known it before.

The police helicopter pilot had been carried on a litter into a waiting EMS ambulance. KIA, Carroll was almost certain.

"Carroll? You're Arch Carroll, aren't you? Do you want to go with me? I'm heading to Halsey Street. It's about ten minutes from here." A police captain, a plump, white-haired man Carroll knew from a saner niche in his life, came up alongside him.

Carroll knew he appeared dazed and confused. In fact, he felt far worse than that, but he nodded. *Yes, he definitely wanted to witness the end. He had to be there.* Colonel Hudson—Monserrat—Carroll—they all had to be there, didn't they? Why was that? Why had everything led to this point—like veins of glass back toward the impact point in a shatter?

A moment or so later, he was hunched forward in a police patrol car, feeling like he might be sick. Hammers of fear were tripping off inside his head.

The police cruiser lurched into motion. The flashing light began to revolve, cherry red. The siren of the speeding car warbled above the rooftops of Brooklyn.

Chapter 89

THIS WAS THE MASTER, *Monserrat.*

Hudson could not believe what his eyes told him was true.

Monserrat? . . . Or was this more misdirection? Another trick? The highest manifestation of deception?

Smoke sifted through his mind, obscuring his vision, scrambling his understanding. And there was renewed tension: an electric tingling in his fingertips, his arm, his legs.

He watched the dark-suited figure come forward toward him. He noted the gunmen who waited in shadows against the far wall.

"Colonel Hudson." The handshake was quick, firm. "I'm François Monserrat. The real one this time." A smile played at the corners of the terrorist's mouth. It was the most confident and assured look David Hudson had ever witnessed.

Monserrat's smile dimmed. "Let's get to business. I believe we can complete our transaction quickly. Look at what he's brought, Marcel. *Rapidement!*"

Another person in a suit stepped inside the room at Monserrat's command. The man was perhaps sixty, and had the pallid complexion, the weak eyesight of someone who spends much of life looking through the lenses of microscopes and magnifying glasses. He bent low to examine the securities Hudson had brought with him.

Hudson watched closely as he rubbed the individual trading bonds carefully, lightly testing their texture between his thumb and forefinger.

He smelled selected bonds, testing for fresh ink, for any unusually pungent odors, anything that would suggest too recent printing. He worked extremely fast.

Each minute nevertheless passed with excruciating slowness.

"For the most part, the bonds are authentic," he finally looked up and spoke to Monserrat.

"Any problems at all?"

"I have a slight question about the Morgan Guaranty, perhaps about the smaller Lehman Brothers lot. I think there are possibly some counterfeit papers in those stacks. As you know, there are *always* some counterfeits," he added. "Everything else is quite in order."

François Monserrat nodded curtly. Even Monserrat seemed uneasy now. The terrorist picked up the plain black telephone on the table. Monserrat dialed a telephone company business office, gave a four-digit number, then spoke to what was clearly an overseas operator. Seconds later, the terrorist was speaking directly to someone obviously known at a bank in Geneva, Switzerland.

"My account is Number 411FA. Make the agreed-upon deposit into the account . . ." Less than four minutes later, Monserrat hung up.

Moments afterward, the phone rang and Hudson received a confirmation that the money had indeed been successfully transferred in Europe. *Over two hundred million dollars* had gone out of the Soviet accounts into special accounts opened by the Vets in London, Paris, Amsterdam, and Madrid. Vets 28, Thomas O'Neil, the Customs Chief of Shannon Airport, had come through again. The Green Band plan *was* perfect.

"Colonel, I believe our business is concluded. You seem to have won each round. This time, anyway." Monserrat executed a deferential bow.

As Hudson stood up from the table, he felt that a terrible weight had finally been lifted. He was free of an obsession he'd carried for almost fifteen years.

At that exact moment, *he was silently counting down to zero.*

Green Band was almost at an end.

Almost, but not quite.

Just one more twist, one final surprise.

Deception at its best.

secretly transferred in Europe. Over two hundred million dollars had gone out of the Soviet's coffers into special accounts opened by the Vets in London, Paris, Amsterdam, and Munich. Vets IX, Thomas O'Neil, the Systems Chief of Shearson Airport, had come through again. The Green Band plan was perfect.

"Colonel Hudson," Monserrat finally called out. "You seem to have wound up nowhere. Perhaps we can help you. Monserrat performed a deferential bow."

As Hudson stood up from the table, he felt that a tremendous weight had finally been lifted. He was free of an obligation.

At that exact moment . . .

Chapter 90

LESS THAN FORTY SECONDS REMAINED. . . . Two pistols drawn in the room . . .

Concentrate.

Hudson eased himself toward a controlled calmness.

Talk to them. Keep talking to Monserrat.

"I have one question before I leave. May I? May I ask one question?"

Monserrat nodded.

"What harm? You may *ask* anything. Then perhaps *I* have a question."

Colonel Hudson watched Monserrat's eyes as he spoke. He saw nothing there—no affect, no emotion. The two of them were close in so many ways.

"How long have you been with the Russians? How long have you been one of their moles?"

"I was *always* with the Russians, Colonel. I *am* a Russian. My parents were stationed in America. They were among hundreds of agents who came here in the late 1940s.

"I was taught to *be* American. There are others like me. They're all over the U.S. *Waiting*, Colonel. We want to destroy the United States financially, and in every other way."

Fourteen seconds. Twelve seconds. Ten seconds.

Hudson kept counting in his head, kept talking in a monotone to François Monserrat.

"Harry Stemkowsky . . . Do you remember a man named Stemkowsky? Poor crippled sergeant? One of my men?"

"One of the casualties of war. Your war, Colonel, not ours. He wouldn't betray you under any circumstances."

As he reached *three* in his countdown, Hudson took two fast, unexpected steps to his left. Both Russian terrorists swung up their pistols to fire. Too late.

Hudson tucked his chin down hard against his chest. He dove head-first through a glass window pane, crashing into the factory section of the building.

At that moment, the entire building shook from the first round from the M-60s, which completely pulverized the tenement's fourth floor.

Flash fires broke out in three separate areas of the factory. Bright orange and crimson flames danced, straining to reach the stained yellow ceiling. Huge panes of glass buckled, then leaped from their casements and crashed to the cement below. Everywhere, the old struts and supports of the building were beginning to sag, warped by the rising heat, the hungry reaches of the lapping flames.

M-16 rifles coughed and rattled everywhere.

The Vets attack was under way.

Hudson waited in a combat crouch behind heavy factory machines. The thick smoke from the fire was an advantage and his enemy at the same time. The billowing smoke and flames made it impossible for Monserrat and his people to locate Hudson, but it also made him vulnerable, exposed to attack from any side.

At that instant, Hudson heard the sound he'd been waiting for. The whirring of the helicopter rotors was loud and clear.

The Cobra had arrived on the rooftop. Exactly as they'd planned it. *Everything was perfect, right to the final escape.*

Colonel Hudson finally allowed himself a trace of a smile.

Just a trace.

Chapter 91

"GET THE FUCK out of my way! Move it! Move it! *Move, move, move!"*

A roaring, unbelievable firefight had erupted. Carroll saw rows of flat rooftops shooting flames as he pushed and elbowed his way through the crowd already gathered on Brooklyn's Halsey Street to watch the action. *Ghouls,* he thought. The worst kind of ambulance chasers.

He winced in pain. His left arm was numb and something was wrong with his spine: when he ran like this the contact of his heels with the pavement sent jarring shudders climbing up his backbone.

None of the neighborhood people—leather-jacketed teen-agers, sullen young women, small, grinning children—seemed to realize that this violent spectacle was for real. They were shrieking with what almost sounded like joy.

"Get back! Dammit, get back!" Carroll yelled as he ran forward. "Get inside with those kids! Get back inside your houses!"

Expectant, wide-eyed faces were crowded into every apartment window. Further down Halsey Street, hundreds of neighborhood people filed outside into the cold, rainy afternoon. They were peering toward the explosions, enthralled by the blazing fire, the sudden jolting volleys of M-16 rifle and pistol shots.

Carroll continued to run in his clumsy battle crouch, moving closer to the exploding, gunshot riddled building.

A police bullhorn boomed out to his left. It thundered over the cacophony of gunblasts and human shouts.

"You there! You, running! Stop right there!"

Carroll ignored the voices. He kept charging forward.

His steps weaved as he struggled with pains that attacked his body from every direction.

As he reached the fiery building, an even more familiar and terrifying sound seized his mind.

The same Army Cobra was hovering over the factory roof. *The same helicopter that had shot him down was back. Green Band was here.*

His body low to the ground, Carroll vaulted up the building's stone steps. He took the stairs three at a time and with each leap thought he could hear the rattle of his own skeleton, loose bones flying under his flesh.

A heavyset man suddenly burst out of the open doorway in front of Carroll. He was holding an 870 riot gun across his chest.

Carroll's gun was set on rapid-repeat. A round of .30-caliber bullets disintegrated the terrorist's face. He reeled back inside the doorway.

The smoke, forcing itself out of the broken first-floor windows, took root in Carroll's lungs. He kept running.

Then Carroll was climbing over the body of the dying gunman sprawled inside the doorway.

Instinctively, Carroll hugged the hallway wall. Cheek tight against cold, peeling plaster, he gasped.

His head seemed to be spinning at an unbelievable speed.

An Army Cobra helicopter? How did they manage a Cobra? Getting an Army Cobra wasn't possible. . . . Green Band was waiting upstairs, and that didn't seem possible, either.

BLACK FRIDAY

His head seemed to be splitting at the most invisible seams.

At least COLONEL Hudson's plans had worked . . . except Laski's stamp on things. It was impossible. . . . Green Band was waiting somewhere, and that didn't seem possible either.

Chapter 92

A GRATED IRON DOOR opened slowly onto the tenement rooftop.

Columns of smoke, scattered by the wind, temporarily blurred Hudson's vision. The doorway was less than forty yards from the waiting Cobra helicopter.

Colonel Hudson walked cautiously at first, then he began to trot like a victorious athlete toward the waiting Cobra. He'd done it. They had all done their jobs almost perfectly. The Green Band mission was finally over.

The sudden exhilaration of victory was unbelievable to savor.

Hudson never saw the second figure on the roof until the assailant was on top of him. His heart squeezed into his throat. He'd been careless.

For *once,* just once, he'd forgotten to check, to double-check every possibility.

"You can stop right there, Colonel."

Face and shoulders still obscured in shadow, a figure appeared from behind the water tower. One hand, which held a revolver, preceded the rest of the body. Then a face came into the light.

A face came into the light.

François Monserrat stood fully exposed before Colonel Hudson.

Monserrat smiled—a final smile of triumph.

"My congratulations, Colonel. You *nearly* achieved the perfect crime."

François Monnerat shot fully exposed before Colonel
Hudson . . .

Monnerat smiled, a final smile on your clr. . .

"My commandant, Colonel, I'm sorry you won't be
here . . ."

Chapter 93

CARROLL WAS UNSURE which way to head inside the
burning tenement building.

He choked on a thick gust of smoke, and thought he was
going to be sick. His lungs chafed as if they'd been rubbed
down by sandpaper.

Crackling reports of M-16s, booming incendiary bombs
rang against his eardrums. He could make out the sharp repeating sound of the rotors of the Cobra helicopter that had
*landed on the rooftop. Monserrat and Colonel Hudson
were inside the building. . . .*

Carroll coughed and gasped as he climbed sets of steep
winding stairs. All around him, flames curled at shadows,
throwing off violently flickering light and heat. The shooting pain in his legs was unbearable. Something felt wrong,
cracked at the base of his spine.

At the head of the stairs, there was a heavy metal door
blocking his way. It stuck at first—then Carroll put his
shoulder into it hard. He shouldered the stubborn door a
second time.

The metal door finally swung open with a loud shriek.

The rooftop was revealed. Carroll's eyes widened.

The crimson taillights of a U.S. military helicopter shone and sparkled in the haze of smoke.

The Army Cobra was being readied for takeoff. The rotors were spinning out thunder and sparks.

Somewhere in the smoke shrouding the rooftop, Carroll heard voices. The voices were strident and angry.

They originated from off to his left, beyond a high brick retaining wall. Fear raised the hammers of Carroll's heart. Fear because he was finally beginning to understand.

"You see, you *must see* that governments of the past are no longer viable. The elected governments are mere illusions. They are ghosts of a sentimentalized reality. You must understand *that* at least. There *are* no more democracies." The voice was filled with the tension of the moment.

The second voice was harsh, erupting like another gunshot in the air.

The wind muffled the exact words. Whatever the second person had to say was whipped away by the roar of the chopper and the wind that was shuffling the clouds.

Carroll pressed his body closer to the brick wall. He edged toward the voices.

The conversation became clearer now. Each word pierced the noise and swirling smoke. His heart ached from the relentless pressure.

"I love this country," one of the two shouted above the wind. "I hate what it did to the veterans after the war. I hate what some of the leaders did. But *I love this country.*"

At that moment, Carroll saw them both. Just as he thought he was beginning to understand, he realized that he understood nothing.

Colonel David Hudson. The same man pictured in all the FBI library and Pentagon photographs . . . tall, strikingly blond . . . "the consummate military commander," according to his classified records.

And the other . . .

Dear God, the other.

Carroll felt something vital subside deep inside him. It wasn't really a physical thing. It wasn't a bone, or a pain in the heart, a collapse of muscle. It was worse than that. Suddenly, he remembered the first time he'd experienced the horror of death—his father's death in Florida. He remembered his exact feeling on the night Nora had died.

His mouth was dry and his head a cave of sad, hopeless chaos. His emotions were wilder than the guerrilla war raging everywhere around him. He was without speech and numb. All he could do was stare straight ahead.

Nothing could have prepared him for this awful moment. All his years as a policeman hadn't prepared him.

The man Colonel David Hudson had addressed as Monserrat was Walter Trentkamp. . . . Except the clenched, shadowy face Carroll saw on this man was almost a stranger's. The face was ruthless and uncaring.

Carroll's world wheeled violently and turned on its side. Whatever sense of reality he had left, shattered. He closed his eyes. He raked one hand over his smoke-blackened face.

His mind's eye seemed to flood with exploding light. *Uncle fucking Walter.* It was the worst hurt, the worst betrayal of his life.

He thought about everything Trentkamp had been privy to in the past. He reviewed his own investigation of Green Band, how Trentkamp knew every detail he'd learned at each maddening turn.

Had Trentkamp dispatched him on the early wild goose

chases? *Why?* Well, he knew the answer to that. So he could watch, and control Carroll. So he could control the DIA's terrorist group. *Talk to me on this one, Archer. Let me know what you find out. Will you promise me that?*

Talk to me, Archer . . .

Promise me, Archer!

Walter Trentkamp had sat in on the highest level meetings inside the White House, always observing and studying. What incredible self-confidence and gall. How many years had this been going on? How many years? . . . François Monserrat! The most ruthless of the world's terrorists was none other than Trentkamp. It was impossible for him to conceive of. Yet it was true.

The rage inside Carroll seemed to clutch and rip at the back of his throat, tearing at his flesh. He'd been used. Just like the Vets, he'd been used. He'd been violated one more time. Contradictions attacked his mind from every angle.

Carroll moved forward toward Trentkamp and Hudson. The rage inside him heightened. He was fighting against the blind, overwhelming urge to wildly fire his Browning. He wanted to pull the trigger. Right now, he ached to *fire* on these two men. He couldn't; he couldn't shoot. Somehow, he was more than a trained killer. *And what are you, please tell me, mister?* Somehow he was more than these other two bastards.

Carroll finally stepped out from behind the shadowy retaining wall. He spoke in a whisper that carried with the wind.

"Hello, Walter. I wanted to keep my promise. I did promise to talk to you about everything I found out."

Trentkamp's face registered surprise, then the terrorist

seemed almost indifferent to Carroll's presence. He was Monserrat now.

"It was never anything personal," he spoke, then shrugged at Carroll. "You were my *listok.* That's a Russian word. You were my *solution* to a problem."

Carroll raised his Browning to eye level. Colonel Hudson . . . François Monserrat . . . himself. It seemed that none of them could win. Carroll wasn't even sure what "win" meant now. *And what are you, please tell me, mister?*

"How do you live a life made of nothing but lies?" He edged closer to Hudson and Trentkamp. "Nothing but deceit and lies."

"I don't believe in the same truths as you. It follows that I don't believe in the same lies. Don't you realize that *you're* living with lies, too. Your own people have deceived you again and again. . . . Everyone has lied to you, Archer. Your government is the greatest lie of all."

Chapter 94

NOTHING BUT HIS INSTINCTS counted from here on.

Colonel Hudson rigidly held that thought.

Nothing but his reflexes counted.

Hudson had a flashing image of the camp in North Viet Nam. Lessons he had learned there.

Deception, Hudson remembered. Sometimes you even had to deceive yourself . . .

Monserrat was like the Lizard Man, he thought. *Monserrat was the same as the Lizard Man.*

Instincts.

Reflexes.

Monserrat seemed to be concentrating on Carroll . . . *"Everyone has lied to you, Archer. Your government is the greatest lie of all."*

A scream rose from Hudson's throat. At that moment, Hudson's arm chopped upward in a short, powerful arc.

The bone in Monserrat's elbow shattered. The Beretta dropped. A harsh growl escaped from his mouth—his teeth were bared like an animal's.

A needle-thin knife seemed to appear from nowhere in

Hudson's hand. A pocket in his trousers flopped open in the wind.

Assassin.

Monserrat took a fast, agile step away from Hudson and the knife. Monserrat was better than the Lizard Man had been.

David Hudson followed as if he were Monserrat's shadow. The sleek stiletto lanced forward, an extension of his arm. Everything was *instincts, reflexes for survival.*

François Monserrat's hands rose and shielded his face, shielded his upper body. His arm was slashed. It seemed nothing to him.

He was moving into a martial arts crouch, almost dancing.

Hudson screamed as he feinted one move, a second move, *then* he struck. . . .

Seemed to strike? . . .

Feinted? . . .

The knife blade shivered forward with accuracy and fierceness . . .

The surgical knife blade drove several inches into its target area. The long, piercing needle disappeared into the flesh and bone of Monserrat's rib cage. Monserrat kept coming.

The knife blade was twisted, then pulled away, unplugged it seemed.

The stiletto was thrust forward again. This time it split the center of Monserrat's throat. Blood gushed everywhere.

The terrorist's legs suddenly went limp. He began to convulse. His face no longer seemed smug—no longer confident and in control. Monserrat was surprised, in shock as he fell forward.

Carroll hadn't known whom to shoot. He'd watched, waiting for the victor. He trained his Browning on Colonel Hudson now. His finger tightened, turned to stone around the trigger.

Suddenly he heard the distinct *click* of yet another automatic weapon!

The disturbing sound came from directly behind him in the thickening smoke.

Carroll started to whirl around.

His mind was suspended by pain and the moment's chaos. He needed all of the madness to stop for a moment.

He saw men he thought he recognized. Four men in tattered khaki green were closing around him on the Brooklyn rooftop. Their M-21s were pointed at him.

They looked like soldiers Carroll had fought with years before. *They were Vets,* he realized. *This was Green Band.*

Here was everything he'd wanted to know—only now Carroll didn't want to know it.

The outrage continued.

The outrage.

Walter Trentkamp's throat had been slashed. His coat had spread open like an umbrella in the wind. His chest was bloodied, redness seeping down into his trousers. His eyes were already glazed and sightless. *Christ! Christ!*

Carroll tried to grab hold of something. He began to shout at the top of his voice. "Who are you, Hudson? *What the hell do you want?* Who sent you to Wall Street?"

Outrage!

Something hard crashed, the most brutal force exploded against the top of Carroll's head.

His skull was crushed so easily.

He staggered, he almost fell, but he stayed upright. The insane streetfighter inside him wouldn't go down.

Goddamn! Them!

Carroll saw streaks of blood merging. He felt as if he must be going blind. The pain and chaos, the sudden light show was unbearable inside his skull.

"Who are you, Hudson?" One final, maddening question formed on his lips. He had no idea whether he spoke the words or not.

He took another step toward Hudson, toward the fallen body of Monserrat—of Walter Trentkamp.

The metal base of the revolver fell on his skull again. It struck the same tender spot, harder than the first time.

A terrible, *mashing* noise echoed inside Carroll's brain. Fire lit on the left side of his chest.

He was falling then, collapsing against his will. Carroll heard himself moaning. He had the thought that he was choking on his own blood. So sad, so wrong.

The revolver crashed down another time.

He spun around and saw Hudson rigidly standing there. Carroll tried to speak. Shit, he couldn't. He had so many questions. He fought the onrushing unconsciousness with the strength he had left. *Not much. Not enough!*

Chapter 95

WITH A SHAKING HAND, Anton Birnbaum poured Sandeman port for himself and for Caitlin.

He felt at least a thousand years old.

He had a piercing headache from his recent sleeplessness and hyperactive mental activity. Now, in the thin daylight that streaked his apartment, he went to the window and peered into the streets of his beloved New York.

Caitlin Dillon, whose head also reeled from the hours of intense concentration without sleep, took a cigarette from her purse and started to light it. She changed her mind. Her throat was raw and there was a heavy pressure behind her eyes. What she needed, she knew, was a long sleep. Both she and Birnbaum were waiting for final news of Green Band, news from Carroll. Caitlin now understood what it was like to be a policeman's wife.

"We know *some* of what we need to know," Birnbaum said. "Two years ago, in Tripoli, Monserrat met with important leaders from the Third World. In particular, he met leaders from the Middle Eastern, oil-producing countries. The heads of these nations' military forces were in attendance there as well." Anton Birnbaum walked away from the apartment window.

"I'm convinced that they planned a cunning way to disrupt the economic system of the West. Their plan called for the cartel to ultimately gain control of *the entire American Stock Market.*"

"They already had enough economic leverage to influence the Market," Caitlin said. Her head pounded mercilessly. Some small sadist with a jackhammer was working way back in the recesses of her skull, digging for God only knew what. She thought about Carroll, who was out there in pursuit of Green Band. Why hadn't they heard anything?

"That spring, our newly elected President learned of the Tripoli plot. More important, the Committee of Twelve must have heard. Only they moved much faster than President Kearney could in Washington."

The old man's eyes became as cold as fire going suddenly out. "Caitlin, I believe they created Green Band to counter the plot. Effectively, the Committee of Twelve has *stolen* the Arabs' billions away. Green Band is the very finest of *trompe l'oeil,* the best.

"Now, they're selling them back their own funds. This has been *an economic world war.* The first of its kind—unless we include the 1970s oil embargo."

Caitlin thought that if it had been anyone other than Birnbaum making these accusations, outlining these hypotheses. . . . But *it was* Birnbaum. And he was serious about everything he was proposing. . . .

"How does Hudson fit in? What's his part in this, Anton?" Caitlin asked.

"Ah, the enigmatic Mr. Hudson." Birnbaum allowed a

smile to cross his face. "I've given great thought to Colonel Hudson. Either he's in the pay of the Committee of Twelve . . . or they're ruthlessly *using* Hudson and his veterans group. It wouldn't be the first time, would it? It wouldn't be the first time these men were used by those who wield power in this country. Either way, we'll know in a few hours. We'll know the truth soon, won't we?"

Chapter 96

AS HE ARRIVED at the designated address, Hudson felt exactly the way he'd always known he would—*if they had won in Viet Nam.* The adrenaline, the excitement of victory, was pumping, rushing furiously through his body.

This would certainly be the most unusual safe house he'd ever used, Hudson thought as he reached York Avenue on Manhattan's fashionable East Side. He entered an elegant glass-and-grillwork doorway just beyond the corner at 90th Street.

Billie Bogan's apartment was located on the river side of the modern building, a building which apparently had paper-thin ceilings and walls, because Hudson could hear a piano playing as he approached the doorway on the fifteenth floor.

The lovely music surprised him. He hadn't known that Billie played.

Hudson hesitated before pushing the doorbell. *Warning alarms,* his usual alert signals were going off again. It was all perfectly natural. One didn't stop being a military terrorist and saboteur overnight.

Billie answered the door seconds after the first ring. She

was wearing a pink T-shirt that said *winter* across her chest. She had on tight black French jeans, no shoes or socks.

"David."

Her brilliant blue eyes passed from the slightest puzzlement to undisguised pleasure as she saw who it was at the door.

She reached out and pulled Hudson toward her. She held him in the doorway.

"Was that you playing the piano?" he asked.

Billie pecked at his cheek and gave him an extra hug. "Of course it was me. . . . You know, I think the piano is the reason I ultimately escaped from Birmingham. As I found out about Mozart, Brahms, Beethoven, I was convinced there had to be more than the dreary dullness I was used to. Come inside. I'm so happy to see you. It's so *good* to see you." She kissed him again.

Hudson smiled more willingly than he had in a long time. "I'm happy to see you. I feel like I'm home at last," he said.

Once inside, they talked. They held one another. They stared into one another's eyes for a long time. Hudson told Billie about his past, talking with the speed of a man who has observed vows of silence for too many years. It all came tumbling out—West Point, the horrors of Viet Nam, his early career in the Army.

Hudson told her everything, except about the past year, which he was tempted to do as well. How his revenge had become sweet victory. A material reward—millions of dollars for himself and the other Vets. He wished he could share it with her, share everything right now.

Under the tent of a brightly striped wool blanket, with

the windows thrown half open, they made love. Hudson was still learning to feel, and the lovemaking helped enormously. She brought him closer and closer to climax . . . right to the edge. He just couldn't make it over. Then the most debilitating wave of exhaustion swept over Hudson.

He felt shaky. Then he was sliding headlong toward a tranquil dream state. The warning alarms still hadn't completely stopped. The warning alarms almost seemed a natural part of him, now.

One moment he was softly stroking Billie's blond hair, touching the elegant oval of her face. The next, he was falling into sleep.

Billie lay awake in the large brass bed, watching the ember glow on a filtered cigarette. She sighed quietly, blowing smoke between lightly touching teeth.

Sometimes she surprised even herself with her ability to create a lie, *in perfect context,* consistent with a whole world of other lies. . . .

Deception.

Her being able to play Chopin, and fitting that so naturally into the Birmingham, England, framework, was an inspiration. But then again, wasn't that precisely why she was here with Hudson?

She rose from the double bed, tossing off rumpled designer sheets. She was certain it would be a miracle to wake Hudson with a cannon.

She returned to the bedroom with something close to that: a gun with a blunt-nosed silencer attached.

She knew better than to hesitate for even a second. She swung both arms up stiffly. She moved to fire the revolver into his temple, just below the hairline.

Then, she hesitated.

The sleeping body went rigid and jumped forward. Hudson's eyes blinked open and he fired through the bedsheets. He fired again and again and again.

Warning signals were shrieking in his head. Sirens of terrible pain screamed out at David Hudson.

Deception—*forever,* deception.

Horrifying deception everywhere he turned. Even *here.*

The Committee of Twelve, the American Wise Men—there was no way they could have let him live once Green Band ended. They had recruited him after the disappointments of Viet Nam, the disappointment in knowing his early promise in the Army could never be realized. He'd been their *agent provocateur* for crises around the world. They had been so attractively intelligent, every bit as smart, as precise as he was. They'd sent the girl, of course, his *escort.* They'd known about all his habits. They'd *used* him so well.

Finally, Hudson understood Green Band himself.

Chapter 97

CARROLL SLOWLY OPENED his eyes and pushed himself into a sitting position. All around him were startling crashing sounds, police and U.S. Army personnel, blinding bright lights, flashing, running shapes. There was more chaos and confusion than before on the rooftop.

Faces peered down at him. New York cops, a physician? There were others he couldn't place right now. The images registered sporadically.

"What happened?" Carroll asked. "How long have. . . . *What happened to the body that was up here?* A body was over there!"

The body of Walter Trentkamp had been near the water tower—except there wasn't any body there now . . .

A uniformed New York cop knelt down alongside him. Carroll had never seen the man before. "What other body are you talking about?"

Carroll rotated his head so he could see all the way around the rooftop. "There was a body there, over near the Cobra. Walter Trentkamp of the FBI was killed right there."

The policeman shook his head. "I was one of the first up

here on the roof. There wasn't any other body. You know, you've got a small watermelon growing up on top of your head. You *sure* you're all right?"

Carroll pushed himself to his feet, then he nearly fell back to the suddenly spinning cement. "Oh, yeah, I'm fine. Tip-top shape."

Carroll's eyes were watering badly. His body wasn't his own. Using bricks in the wall for handholds, he started down the metal stairs winding away from the roof.

Somebody had taken Walter Trentkamp's body away.

The cop called after him, "Hey, buddy, you ought to get yourself treated! Have somebody look at your head. There wasn't any body up here."

Carroll hardly heard the policeman's last words.

Suddenly he had a different priority in mind: *he wanted to go home.* He needed to go home right away.

Carroll thought about his kids and about Caitlin.

He thought about Caitlin's meeting with Anton Birnbaum and wondered what might have transpired there. He was worried about the people he loved. . . . *There wasn't any body up here on the roof. . . . Sure thing—this was all a dream, a horrible nightmare.*

He had no clue how he managed the first wild minutes of the drive to Riverdale. Maybe it was practice—all those half-drunken nights of his recent past. Maybe God *did* look after babies and drunks. But there was a time coming when God might abdicate his responsibilities, all his watchfulness . . .

And what then?

Chapter 98

THE FAMILIAR LIGHTS of the old house in Riverdale were glittering brightly.

As he drove up his street, Carroll remembered a time when his father and mother would have been there, a time when everything had seemed so much saner ... when Trentkamp was Uncle Walter.

Walter Trentkamp had been his father's friend for all those years. Had his father begun to guess anything? We had all been so naive about foreign governments back then. About our own government as it was turning out. Americans thought of democracy as the world's one superior political system. We thought we understood the parameters of our government's power.

Trentkamp and the KGB had been brilliant at fooling everyone. Walter Trentkamp had been so confident, he hadn't hesitated at using Carroll. What better conduit for information? Walter's hubris was startling, but his modus was consistent at least. As Carroll thought back now, he remembered that Walter had spent time in Europe after World War II. He recalled "fact-finding" trips to South America, to Mexico, to Southeast Asia. It was no wonder they had never been able to identify Monserrat. *They hadn't been looking in the right places.*

No one had thought to look right there in New York or Washington. No one had begun to suspect Trentkamp. And Trentkamp had obviously *known* that they wouldn't. His confidence was galling. He had no fear or respect for American Intelligence, and he had been right not to. His ruse, the misdirection had been perfect—the life-work of a master spy, this decade's Donald McLean or Kim Philby.

Suddenly, Carroll's eyes were watering again—only now it was because he was so glad to see his kids. They jumped up and ran to him as he stumbled inside the house. Then the Carroll family was hugging and kissing. They were squeezing their father as tightly as they could.

"We have to get out of here," Carroll whispered to Mary Katherine as the two of them got to hold one another. "We have to move out of the house now. . . . Help me dress them. Try to explain as little as you can. I have to call Caitlin."

Mary Katherine nodded. She didn't even seem that surprised at the news. "You go call Caitlin now. I'll outfit the troops."

Two hours later, the Carrolls, the family of six plus Caitlin Dillon, quietly checked into the Durham Hotel on West 87th Street in Manhattan.

Carroll's plan was to stay there for a night, maybe a few nights, until they could decide how to work with Anton Birnbaum, how to work with the New York police, whoever they could trust. Life was suddenly full of treacherous false bottoms. Carroll didn't want another one to suddenly fall out.

Once they were together in the West Side hotel, Caitlin

and Carroll fell into an embrace. They shared a long kiss which neither of them wanted to end. Caitlin pushed against Carroll with a fierce need. There was no more reason to hide anything, to hold back her feelings.

"I love you." She locked her eyes into Carroll's gaze.

"I love you, Caitlin. I was afraid today. I thought . . . that I might never see you again."

They made love in the hotel room, and it was all passion, definitely not Lima, Ohio. When they did it a second time, Caitlin and Carroll held hands—almost as if they might never do this beautiful thing again.

"I hated it when you were out there after them," Caitlin finally whispered as she lay beside Carroll. Her breath was like feathers on his cheekbone. "I've never felt so alone and afraid. I don't want to feel that way again."

Carroll brushed strands of hair away from her face. She was so precious to him. "I told Walter Trentkamp that I planned to quit once Green Band was over. I haven't changed my mind."

Caitlin stared into his eyes. "There's a catch, though."

"Yes, there's one catch. Green Band isn't over."

There was so much evidence to be considered and studied. There were classified files from the FBI and Pentagon; there were taped statements from Birnbaum's contacts in Washington and Europe . . .

. . . *They just had to get to the right people with what they knew, with the truth.*

Who were the right people, though? Whom could they trust now?

The New York Times?

The Washington Post?

"Sixty Minutes"?

The New York police?

The CIA?

The Committee of Twelve seemed to be everywhere. Were they connected with the police, the CIA? Did they control the newspapers and TV?

Whom could they go to with the truth?

During the first hours in the hotel, Carroll and Caitlin read every newspaper report. Twice that afternoon, Carroll took cabs to the large out-of-town newspaper stand in Times Square. He and Caitlin read and reread everything written about Green Band.

They searched for a faint shadow of what they knew to be the truth.

There was none that they could find. *Nothing* had been reported about secret intragovernment groups. *Nothing* had been reported about the whereabouts of Walter Trentkamp. Had the body been spirited away by the Twelve? . . . Nothing was said about Colonel David Hudson's Special Forces training at Fort Bragg. In the news, Colonel Hudson was described as a "Jackal-like *provocateur*," the renegade mastermind of Green Band. Hudson was depicted as an obsessed man looking for justice, some personal meaning, years after Viet Nam . . .

It all sounded plausible and right, if you didn't know any better.

Chapter 99

THE MORNING OF December 21, Caitlin and Carroll had visitors at the hotel.

The visitors were Anton Birnbaum and Samantha Hawes, the FBI researcher who had helped Carroll in Washington. They met in another room on the same floor as the Carroll suite.

The best and the worst part of the Green Band investigation had begun. The tension and pressure were even more relentless than before. Carroll's stomach had been doing an uncomfortable dance of panic for the past twenty-four hours.

A working picture of Green Band was emerging. If not a complete portrait, it was at least an outline, a foreshadowing of the truth. The story was different from anything reported in the newspapers or on TV.

"The Twelve, the American Wise Men, are descended from our own OSS, America's intelligence team during World War Two," Birnbaum said in a voice that seemed to grow weaker each day. "The route is serpentine, but it can be followed. . . . The existence of the Twelve goes back to the elder Dulles, his reluctance to surrender his wartime intelligence machine over to the politicians in 1940s Washington. When the OSS was transformed into the CIA, the Twelve began to meet *outside* official circles. They were still the most powerful men in Washington. At first they gave counsel, then they took things into their own able hands. . . . The original OSS was the best American intelligence unit ever.

"*The Twelve still smugly believe they are the elite.* They're *convinced* they are doing the country a grand service, guiding us through the Cuban Missile threat, the time of the assassinations, Watergate, now Green Band. Every year, each decade, they become more and more powerful."

Samantha Hawes spoke after Birnbaum. She had information about Hudson. She'd managed to retrieve some of the missing Vets files during the past few days.

"David Hudson was approached by at least one Committee member when he was still in the Army, while he was at Fort Bragg after Viet Nam," she told the others. "General Lucas Thompson, his old commander, approached Hudson first. Thompson knew everything about Hudson's POW experiences. He knew about Hudson's training at Fort Bragg, too. Army Intelligence had prepared Hudson to be their Juan Carlos. They backed off when Hudson lost his arm. Well, *the Committee* had plenty of uses for Hudson and his skills.

". . . Another interesting note—Philip Berger of the CIA ran Hudson's original commando training at Fort Bragg. Several Committee members have spoken at veteran affairs over the past few years. The connections are there, the manipulation is feasible."

Carroll had read the missing FBI and Pentagon files which Hawes had brought with her. "Hudson was given a lot of help with Green Band. The help came in the form of Wall Street information, and tips about what we were doing inside Number 13. That's why he was able to play so many cat-and-mouse games. He also had Pentagon files on all the candidates for Vets. Hudson chose men who'd served with him in Viet Nam. The Committee promised him millions as a reward."

"Yes, only half the Vets are dead now," Birnbaum spoke. "The rest are missing. Hudson is missing. Where is David Hudson now, I wonder?"

Caitlin had been quiet for most of the session. She had retrieved the necessary financial backup information. She was still angry. She felt *used* by this *Committee* which believed it was above the government, above laws.

"We're beginning to make progress," Caitlin finally spoke in a quiet manner. "But we're still faced with an overwhelming problem. Whom do we trust beyond the people here in this room? Do we take our information to the newspapers? Do we go to the FBI, Samantha? Whom can we tell this story to?"

There was silence in the room. They were all beginning to understand the power that was in the grasp of a select few. They were beginning to understand the real political system.

The question remaining was so simple, yet so impossibly complex—*whom could they trust with the truth?*

Chapter 100

FOR ANOTHER TWENTY-FOUR HOURS on December 22, the Carrolls lived in cramped quarters in the West Side hotel. They had no other choice to consider. *Whom could they trust?*

Late at night, Carroll and Caitlin stayed in the smaller of the two bedrooms. They lay in each other's arms, passing the long, eerie hours. They were realistic enough to know that something nightmarish might still happen—that they might never be together like this again.

"Hudson said something on the rooftop in Brooklyn," Carroll whispered as he stroked Caitlin's hair. "He said that he loved his country. You know, I still feel that way. I almost feel closer to Hudson than to the others."

Caitlin nodded.

Her eyes were stinging when she finally whispered to Carroll, "I feel so *angry* at whoever was deceiving all of us, at the ones who've lied and misled us *all these years.*"

When Caitlin and Carroll made love, it was more tender than it had ever been. They fell asleep holding each other, like children allowed to sleep together during a storm.

At six o'clock, Caitlin found that she couldn't sleep anymore. She pushed herself up in bed.

When she switched on a tiny portable radio, Caitlin heard the last thing she wanted to hear in all the world. Caitlin heard the news that finally broke her heart.

"*. . . adviser to several U.S. Presidents, Anton Birnbaum, was killed on Riverside Drive near his home in Manhattan early today. The elderly statesman was struck in late-night traffic by an unidentified hit-and-run driver . . . Birnbaum was eighty-three years old at the time of his death.*"

Caitlin shook Carroll until he mumbled and finally blinked awake. In a voice that was racked by sobs, she began to tell him what had happened.

"Oh, Arch, they killed him. They killed Anton this morning. *They killed him as if he was nothing.* What's happening now? What's going to happen?"

Carroll shivered as he got up from bed. He dressed, then hurried down to Broadway, where he bought the *Daily News, The New York Times,* the *Wall Street Journal.*

All the front-page stories about Anton Birnbaum contained respectful eulogies. They also contained lies. At best, the newspapers revealed a small fragment of the truth.

At the newsstand, Carroll read the articles with trembling fingers. It was as if nothing real had ever happened. There was no high-placed traitor in the FBI. There was no Monserrat, no mention of the whereabouts of Colonel Hudson.

That same morning, trudging back to the hotel from Broadway, Carroll saw the two men following him.

There was no way anyone connected with Green Band could live.

Chapter 101

ESCAPE. It was the only possibility left.

On the night of December 23, Carroll, Caitlin, the four children, and Mary Katherine tightly locked hands. They walked down Columbus Avenue. There had to be a way for three adults and four small children to escape a surveillance team. So far, Carroll had found none. But the New York crowds would provide temporary safety.

Columbus Avenue was still buzzing with holiday music and a festive bustle at night. The energetic crowd—every other person holding a bright Christmas bundle, a tree, a Lincoln Center program—parted reluctantly for the family.

It wasn't like any Christmas that Carroll had ever known before—it was as if a terrible, unfathomable darkness lurked in the shadows between the bright lights and the fir trees. Caitlin, Mary K., the kids—how could he shield them when he felt that some unknown gunmen lingered in every doorway?

"Can we please stop running, Daddy? Please?"

A tiny voice trailed after Carroll, echoing thinly inside the symphony of the New York City street noise. The bizarre cacophony of Christmas sounds wouldn't stop, wouldn't let up for a moment of relief. Why did he think it would?

Four-year-old Lizzie was dragging herself along on the hem of his sports coat. "Please, Daddy. Just for a minute? Please?" Up ahead of them, Caitlin and Mary Katherine had the three other children in tow. They were bravely hurrying the children forward.

Carroll finally stopped and stooped to wrap his arms around his little girl. He whispered soothingly against Lizzie's chilled, red-rimmed ear. "Please, baby, please be good. Just a little longer, sweetheart."

Carroll immediately straightened again. It was so sad—what he was almost certain was going to happen next. It was so unfair. He had reached the most hollow place of his existence, a terrible numbness hung around his heart.

He gazed north, then down the bright lights of Columbus Avenue. His weary eyes brushed over colorful signs that said Sedutto's, Dianne's, Pershings, La Cantina.

Columbus Avenue had changed dramatically since he'd last been above 72nd Street. The area had once been crowded with Spanish food stores as well as transient hotels, and oriental rug dealers. Now it was a trendy, self-conscious version of Greenwich Village.

Carroll glanced over his shoulder again. The same pair of men was still following. Now, though, there were more than two. There were as many as five men following the Carroll family.

And they were closer—no more than half a city block away.

Where in the name of God do we go? Somebody help us, he thought to himself.

The back of Carroll's neck was soaking wet, even in the

chill air. His skin, his brown hair, was plastered against his shirt collar.

He was hopelessly tired. He felt he could lay down on a parked car, sleep right there in the middle of Columbus Avenue.

The passersby looked so preoccupied, so self-interested and city cool. Would any of them help?

Carroll's mind was silently screaming, pleading for some form of reason to finally prevail.

This is happening, he thought. Whether I choose to believe it or not, this is happening.

Escape was the only reality.

He had one idea, a kind of prayer, which he didn't think could work. His mind was close to bursting. There was nothing left but rage, the constant, maddening stab of fear. He could see the same emotion pressed onto Caitlin's face. As for Mary Katherine, her face looked blank. All its usual ruddy color was gone.

He reached out suddenly for Caitlin. He held her narrow shoulders. "Listen to me. Listen closely." He whispered something *hopeful,* something so innocent it started tears in her soft brown eyes. "I love you so much, Caitlin. Everything *has* to be all right."

"Oh, Arch, why now? Why now?"

Then Carroll pushed her away. He sent Caitlin and his sister and the tangle of children in the opposite direction.

Up 72nd Street. Away, far away from him.

"I'm going down Columbus! Take them! Take them away, please! Caitlin! Take them now!"

"Daaa-ddy! . . . Daa-ddy!"

The final thing Carroll heard was his babies' cries as he raced away.

As he put his head down, chin into his heaving chest.

As he started to run as fast as he could along the clogged sidewalk.

Suddenly, powerful arms grabbed him, wrenched him to a spinning stop. A hand clamped down hard, twisting into his face. Searing pain ripped through Carroll's eyes.

His mind was racing: *they were attacking him in the middle of New York City, in one of the most crowded, residential areas of the city. They had come for him in full view of a hundred witnesses . . .*

They didn't even care about the witnesses anymore.

"Get the hell off me! Get off me, you pieces of shit!" Carroll's shouts rose like fighting kites above the honking horns, above the city's deafening street rumble. "Somebody, please help!"

They were giving him a needle! Some kind of long, terrifying needle pierced through his trousers into his leg.

They were giving it to him right out here in the open.

Right on West 70th Street in New York City.

"Somebody help! Somebody fucking help!"

There were obviously no secrets anymore. There was no bullshit pretense that this was a police bust, that they were New York detectives.

"Get off! . . . *no needle . . . nooooo!*"

Carroll roared his last words savagely. He screamed and he fought back. He clawed at them with his remaining strength. He broke a jaw with a short, powerful punch. His elbow smashed hard into a forehead. A bone snapped loudly. His?

Everything was unreal. Everything was impossible to comprehend, or slow down even a fraction.

Carroll was being dragged into a dark blue sedan. *He was being held upside down!*

He looked back as they pulled him off Columbus Avenue, out of the crowds.

As he was hanging *upside down,* he saw the second car arrive!

He saw Caitlin and his sister and the kids being snatched away.

"Not the kids! You goddamned bastards! Not my kids, not my kids! . . . No, *please,* not my kids!"

Chapter 102

THOMAS MORE ELLIOT'S palms were dry and cold. He suppressed a nervous tic which was starting to pulse in his throat.

He finally stepped out of the dark blue stretch limousine and into the chill Virginia winter air. Dead trees hung against the gray skyline and in the distance there were the gunshots of bird hunters.

He turned and walked up the fieldstone steps that led to the large double doors of an imposing, thirty-room country house. He paused at the top of the steps and sucked air deeply into his lungs.

Inside, the cavernous front hall was badly overheated. He felt a trickle of sweat run along his collar with the stealth of an insect.

His footsteps echoed on marble as he crossed to a great curving flight of stairs that led upward to the floors above. It was not a house that Elliot enjoyed. Its very size, but more, its history made him uncomfortable.

When he reached the landing he came to a door ornately carved out of walnut. It shone so deeply from years of meticulous care that he could see his own indistinct reflection in the wood.

He opened the door and entered the room beyond.

A group of men sat around a long, polished oak table.

They were dressed mostly in dark business suits. Some of them, including General Lucas Thompson, were retired military and naval commanders. Some ran large multinational corporations. Others were influential bankers, landowners, proprietors of TV stations and newspapers.

The man at the top of the table, a retired admiral whose bald head shone in the room like a bone, waved one hand at the Vice-president. "Sit down, Thomas. Sit. Please."

The Vice-president sat.

The Admiral smiled and it wasn't an expression of mirth. There was an immediate silence in the room.

"A year ago," the Admiral said, "we met in this very room. Our mood that day was one of some agitation . . ."

There was a polite ripple of laughter. Self-satisfied laughter spread around the formal library table.

"We debated, I'm sure we all remember, the complex problem posed by the so-called Red Tuesday plan, the plan hatched—if that's the word—by the oil-producing nations in Tripoli. . . . There were rather heated arguments that day."

The Admiral smiled. Elliot thought he resembled a smug school principal on award day at a private academy.

"On that day we reached a decision—unanimous—to create what we called Green Band. I believe the name was something I suggested myself, a name with both financial and military connotations."

A bird appeared against the casement window of the

room, a bleak little sparrow that briefly looked in, then hopped off into the late afternoon light.

The Admiral continued in sanctimonious tones, "We are here today to confirm that the paramilitary operation called Green Band was a success. We created *temporary* panic in the economic system. A panic we were able to control.

"We usurped the terrorist plan known as Red Tuesday. The world will find Jimmy Hoffa before they locate the body of François Monserrat. . . . And with the destruction of Green Band, the inevitable death of our volatile associate, Colonel Hudson, the file should be closed on this unfortunate episode in our history. . . . We are making *every* effort to make certain that it is."

Elliot shifted his body in his chair. The atmosphere in the large room was changing subtly. The men were beginning to loosen up, to move toward as celebratory an atmosphere as they might ever aspire to—which meant muted, quiet and, most of all, tasteful.

The Admiral said, "In approximately two weeks, Justin Kearney will dramatically resign his presidency. . . . He will be remembered chiefly as a scapegoat for the economic near-tragedy. . . . More importantly, though—" and here all eyes in the room turned toward Thomas More Elliot—"Thomas Elliot will ascend to that office . . ."

There was an outbreak of applause. Elliot looked around at the eleven men in the room. His own presence brought the number to an even dozen.

"Later," said the Admiral, "there will be champagne and cigars. For the moment, Thomas, our congratulations to you. . . . And I think to everyone in this room . . ."

The Admiral looked reflective for a moment.

"In a few weeks, for the first time, *one of us* will occupy the highest office in the land. And that means our control is tighter, more sure than ever before . . ." The Admiral looked down at the white hair on the back of his hands. "Which means we will no longer need to contend with a President who doesn't think the way we do . . . someone who imagines his power is independent of what we bestow."

Thomas More Elliot stared off into the gray light that lay against the window. He blinked his pale eyes twice.

He licked his lips, which had become dry. He opened his mouth and his throat felt parched.

He realized that he was about to say something that would not contribute to the general mood of contentment within the room. But that couldn't be helped. He didn't like the prospect, but somebody had to deliver the news.

He said, "I have heard from our people in New York City."

Eleven heads swiveled toward him.

"A man called Archer Carroll is in police custody there."

A silent pause came to the room with all the suddenness of a stilled pulse.

"It is my information that he is talking. . . . That he's telling his story to anyone who will listen. . . . And that media representatives are paying close attention."

The silence was a long, unhappy thing.

Thomas More Elliot sipped his tepid water.

"What does he know?" the Admiral asked eventually.

"Everything," the Vice-president said.

Chapter 103

NEW YORK POLICE Sergeant Joe Macchio and Patrolman Jeanne McGuiness were rolling out of the wooded 72nd Street transverse through Central Park when they spotted a scene they wished they hadn't spotted, especially not so close to the end of their four to twelve o'clock night shift.

"This is Car One-three-eight. Please give me *immediate assistance* at Seventy-second Street and Central Park West!" Patrolman McGuiness, a tall skinny woman with an impassive face, was already speaking into the patrol car radio. The red police bubble on top of their cruiser had begun to revolve.

Up ahead on 72nd Street, traveling at maybe fifty or fifty-five miles per hour, was a dark blue Lincoln. That *wasn't* the problem.

The problem was some suicidal or homicidal maniac trying to wiggle out of the shattered back-seat window of the Lincoln.

He had his torso halfway out. The only thing holding him inside were two other men. They looked as if they were trying to land an ocean-sized fish in the speeding vehicle.

"Look! Look there! The second car behind!" McGuiness pointed straight ahead. Inside the second car, children, a host of screaming kids, seemed to be fighting and struggling *to get out*.

"Godfuckingdamnit!" Joe Macchio growled even louder. He had been dreaming of Christmas Day and something of the peaceful spirit had created a glow inside him. Now all that was gone.

Sergeant Macchio and Patrolman McGuiness left their police cruiser with revolvers drawn. They cautiously approached the two sedans, now stopped against the southwest corner of 72nd. Other police blue and whites, sirens screaming, were already racing up 72nd from the direction of Broadway.

"We're Federal agents." A man in a dark suit burst out of the lead sedan. He was holding out a portfolio wallet and an official-looking badge.

"I don't care if you're the Commander-in-Chief of the United States Army," Sergeant Macchio croaked in his most convincing street-cop voice. "What the hell's going on here? Who the hell's this guy? Why are all these kids screaming like somebody's being murdered?"

A second dark-suited man stepped out of the trailing sedan. "I'm Victor Kenyon of the CIA, officer." He said it calmly, but authoritatively. "I think I can explain this whole thing."

Carroll was still half in, half out of the back window of the lead sedan. He was groggy, almost out on his feet. He hollered at the two police officers. "Hey! *Please!*" His speech was slurred. "My kids. . . . They're in danger . . . I'm a Federal officer . . ."

Sergeant Macchio couldn't help himself—he started to laugh. "Not that I think this is funny, pal. *You're* a Federal officer?"

Ten minutes later, the situation wasn't any closer to being solved. Several more police blue and whites had arrived. So had cars from the New York FBI, and more from the CIA. There was a cluster of police officials on 72nd Street.

Two EMS ambulances had pulled up, but Caitlin and Mary Katherine wouldn't let them take Carroll to Roosevelt Hospital, *or any place else without them.*

Caitlin was yelling at the policeman, telling them that she and Carroll were part of the Green Band investigation team. She had proof in her pocketbook.

The CIA agents had lots of impressive proof that they were who they said they were. The arguing continued on the corner of 72nd Street, getting more heated with every passing moment. It began to draw a New York sidewalk crowd.

Mickey Kevin Carroll finally sidled up to Sergeant Macchio, who had walked off to try to think the whole crazy thing out.

"Can I see your hat?" Mickey Kevin asked. "My dad's a policeman. He doesn't get to wear a hat."

Joe Macchio looked down at the small boy, and offered a tired smile. "And which one *is* your dad?" he asked. "Is your dad here now?"

"*That's* my dad." Mickey Kevin pointed at the man slumped, seemingly sleeping on an EMS litter-cot, looking like Crusader Rabbit one final time.

"He's a policeman, son?"

"Yes, sir."

Well, that settled it for Sergeant Macchio—because the alleged CIA agents were claiming that the other man *definitely wasn't* a police officer. "That's what I needed to know, son. That's what I needed to know for *starters,* anyway."

NYPD Sergeant Macchio stooped down and handed Mickey Kevin his hat. Then he walked in the direction of the disturbance that had closed down 72nd Street, not to mention the downtown lanes of Central Park West, and the park transverse.

"Tell you what we're gonna do, eh!" Sergeant Macchio clapped his hands for a little old-fashioned order and attention. "We're gonna sort this all out *down at the station house!*"

At that news, the entire Carroll family started to do a very odd thing, at least Sergeant Macchio and the rest of the New York cops thought it was peculiar. The kids started to balls-out cheer and clap for the NYPD.

The New York cops weren't used to that. A couple of the older patrolmen started to blush. They'd almost never been treated like the arriving cavalry before, like the good guys in the white hats.

"All right, *all right* now! Everybody pile into the wagons. Let's get this show on the road. See who's been naughty and nice, eh?"

Photographs of the scene were snapped by somebody from *The New York Times,* also by a free-lance photo-journalist who lived across 72nd Street in the Dakota. A shot of Mickey Kevin wearing Sergeant Macchio's hat was featured in *Newsweek* magazine.

Eventually, the *Newsweek* shot of Mickey Kevin appeared framed on the Carroll's Riverdale house mantel. . . . Lizzie, Mary III, and Clancy all loudly complained about favoritism. Arch told them to shut their yaps. So much had happened to them in a relatively short time. Not the least of it was that Arch had fallen in love with Caitlin, and slowly, but surely, so had the kids. They were all family now, weren't they?

They truly were family.

EPILOGUE

Hudson

Chapter 104

A LINE TO the President of the United States signaled through at 6:00 on the morning of March 7.

Clustered inside the Oval Office were most of the members of the National Security Council. Not one of the officials could believe what was happening.

A prerecorded message came over the telephone.

"The White House is scheduled to be firebombed this morning. In a matter of a few minutes. . . .

"This decision is irrevocable.

"This decision is nonnegotiable.

"You are to evacuate the White House immediately."

Inside a telephone booth less than a mile from the White House, David Hudson pushed down the recording machine's stop button. He stuffed the compact recorder into the pocket of his fatigue jacket.

Hudson was actually smiling. For the briefest moment, Hudson laughed out loud.

All of Washington *waited*, but the White House was never struck that morning.

Instead, the home of General Lucas Thompson was firebombed. So was the home of Vice-president Elliot. The homes of Admiral Thomas Penny, of Philip Berger, of Lawrence Guthrie . . . twelve homes in all.

David Hudson finally climbed into a light green touring van. He drove west out of the strikingly lovely capital city. For a moment, at least, no nightmare voices screeched inside his head. His arm had stopped aching—the arm that was no longer there.

He had done the right thing, he believed, especially for his men, the other Vets. They had scattered like leaves after a fierce storm; he hoped they would prosper, or at least be at peace. Finally, they had justice.

Finally, there was an end to deception.

Note
from the Publisher

Please turn the page
for a
bonus excerpt
from

CRADLE & ALL

a Little, Brown Hardcover
available wherever
books are sold.

Chapter 3

GIVEN EVERYTHING THAT HAS HAPPENED, it isn't too much of a stretch to say that this is one of the most incredible stories ever, and the strangest I've ever encountered. The weirdest thing of all is that I am part of it. A big part.

I remember how my involvement began, remember every detail as if it happened just moments ago.

I was in my small, hopelessly cluttered, but comfortable office in the Back Bay section of Boston. I was staring off in the general direction of the Hancock and Prudential towers.

The door opened without so much as a tap, and an elderly man stepped inside. He was wearing a gray pinstriped suit, a white-on-white shirt, and a dark blue silk tie. He looked like a successful Beacon Hill lawyer or a businessman.

I knew that he was neither; he was Cardinal John Rooney of the Archdiocese of Boston, one of the most important religious leaders in the world, and a friend of mine.

"Hello, Annie," he said, "nice to see you, even under the circumstances."

"Nice to be seen, Eminence," I said, and I smiled as I rose from my seat. "You didn't have to get all duded up to see me, though. *What* circumstances?"

"Oh, but I did," Rooney said. "I'm traveling incognito, you see. Because of the *circumstances.*"

"I see. Nice threads. Very high WASP, which all us Catholics aspire to. Be careful, some chippie might try to pick you up. Come in. Please sit. It's nearly six. Can I offer you something to drink, Eminence?"

"'John' will do for tonight, Anne. Scotch if you have it. An old man's drink for an old man. Getting older in a hurry."

I fixed the cardinal a scotch, then got a Samuel Adams out of the minifridge for myself.

"'I'm honored. I think," I added as I gave him his glass. "Here's to—the circumstances of your visit," I said and raised my beer.

"The perfect toast," Rooney said and took a sip of his drink.

I have a rather complicated history with the Archdiocese of Boston, but most recently, I've worked several times with certain members as a private investigator. One case involved a teacher in Andover. She had been raped by a priest who taught at the same high school. Another case was about a fifteen-year-old who'd shot another boy in their church. None of the cases were happy experiences for either the cardinal or for me.

"Do you believe in God, Anne?" Rooney asked as he sat back in one of my comfy, slightly tattered armchairs.

I thought it an odd question, almost impertinent. "Yes, I do. In my own, very unusual way."

"Do you believe in God the Father, Jesus, the Blessed Mother?" the cardinal went on. He was making this very strange meeting even stranger.

I blinked a few times. "Yes. In my way."

Cardinal Rooney then asked, "As a private investigator, are you licensed to carry a gun?"

I opened my desk drawer and showed him one of Smith & Wesson's finest. I didn't feel obliged to tell him that I had never fired it.

"You're hired," he said and knocked back the rest of his drink. "Can you leave for Los Angeles tonight? There's something there I think you should see, Anne."

I laughed a grim laugh. Jesus, Simon, in your name, I be—
Fco. I anyways," Dashun said.

"Do you believe in God the Father, Jesus, the Blessed Mother?" The sudden shift on the way making his very sanity seeming even stranger.

I turned a few times," he, being very...

Charlie? Jerry then asked, "As a private investigator, do you happen to say yes now?"

I couldn't, low truth drawer..." and around him one or half of it was at a finish. I didn't feel obliged to tell him chances... never find it.

"You're blind," he said and knocked back the rest of the scotch. "Can you leave for Los Angeles tonight? There's something there I think you should see, Aaron."

Chapter 4

I WILL NEVER FORGET LOS ANGELES and what I found there, what I felt there.

I had first seen the graphic pictures of the terrible disease on CNN, and then on every other TV network. I had watched, cringed in horror, as the children of Los Angeles burst upon Cedars-Sinai Medical Center by the carload, all with aching joints and fever, with symptoms that could kill within days.

When I arrived at Cedars, the scene was more intense than what I had seen on TV. It was so very different to be there in the midst of the suffering and horror. I wanted to turn away from it all, and maybe I should have. Maybe I should have run into the Hollywood Hills and never come out.

The sound of chaos and fear was well over a hundred decibels inside the fabled hospital, which had been turned into a confused mess. The shouting of the emergency-room nurses and doctors, and the wailing of their young patients, ricocheted sharply off beige tile walls.

It was so sad, so ominous. A portent of the future?

A curly-haired boy of four or so in yellow pjs, was waiting to be intubated. I winked at him, and the boy managed to wink back. On another table, an adolescent girl was curled up in a fetal position around her stuffed sandy-haired bear. She was crying deep, heartrending sobs as doctors tried to straighten her contorted limbs. Other children were banked in a holding pattern along the perimeter of the room. Policemen, their radios squawking loudly, manned the doorways as best they could. They restrained desperate parents from their babies. The long linoleum hallway was packed wall to wall with feverish children tossing and turning on blankets laid across the bare floor.

Each room off the corridor had been turned into a dormitory of tragically sick kids. Their families seemed eerily related by the flimsy, blue paper gowns and the masks they all wore. Each new image was indelibly stamped into my mind, and then into my soul.

The doctor walking beside me was named Lewis Lavine, and he was the hospital's director of pediatrics. He was tall and somewhat gawky, and his black pompadour made him look even taller, but I found him heroic in his own way. Dr. Lavine had the presence of a rock in a sea of chaos. He was giving me the grand tour when clearly he had no time for it.

The same deeply mysterious plague had just broken out in Boston. Before I left for L.A., I saw the devastation at St. Catherine's, a very large hospital run by the Church. The archdiocese had sent me to L.A. on a fact-finding mission. I was their investigator.

6

"You know what it is, don't you?" I asked Lavine as we walked hurriedly down the hall.

"Yes, of course," he told me, but seemed reluctant to go further, to actually give a name to the horror. Then he spoke gravely. "It's basically poliomyelitis, only this time the virus is faster, even deadlier, and it seems to have appeared out of nowhere."

I nodded. "It's the same in Boston. I talked for over an hour with Dr. Albert Sassoon at St. Catherine's. He's a terrific doctor, but he's baffled, too. It's polio—the second coming of the dreaded disease."

Polio had once been a killer plague that attacked more than six hundred fifty thousand people, mostly children. It killed some twenty percent of the infected, receding from the rest like a lethal tide, leaving behind deformed limbs and crippled spines, bodies that would never heal. Dr. Salk's and the Sabin vaccines had eradicated polio, ostensibly for good. There had been only a handful of cases in this country since 1957. But this present, mysterious epidemic had a much higher fatality rate than the polio of old.

"All of these children were vaccinated?" I asked.

Lavine sighed. "Most of them. It doesn't seem to matter. We're looking at the Son of Polio," he said. "The old menace with a new, more potent kick. It rushed past the old vaccine without blinking. Some of the World Health people think a broken sewer line contaminated a water source, and that's how it spread. But in Los Angeles we don't know how the hell it originated. Here. In Boston. Or wherever it breaks out next. And we certainly don't know how to stop it."

As if to emphasize his point, he looked around at the sick children—the dying children. Many of them wouldn't be going home, and that was so sad, so incomprehensible.

"No, Doctor, neither do the doctors in Boston. They don't know how this could have happened. But it did. What the hell is going on?"

To read more, look for *Cradle & All* by James Patterson